A Court of Mythics and Magic

Rose Gravestone

Copyright © 2024 by Rose Gravestone

ISBN-13: 979-8-9905058-3-4

All rights reserved.
No part of this book may be reproduced, distributed, or transmitted in any form or by
any means, including photocopying, recording, information storage and retrieval systems, or
other electronic or mechanical methods, without the prior written permission of the author,
except for the use of brief quotations in a book review.
This book is a work of fiction. The story, all names, characters, and incidents portrayed in this
production are fictitious. Any resemblance to actual persons, living or dead, places, buildings,
events or incidents is entirely coincidental.
Book Cover by: Marina Lexa on Fiverr

To all those who love a book-long redemption arc with a groveling king, a bantering coven of witches and warlocks, so much magic you'll see spells in your dreams, and a difficult path to a hard-earned happy ending.

Author's Note

Hello lovely readers and welcome to A Court of Mythics and Magic, the conclusion to the duet that began with A Court of Wolves and Witches, and Book Two in the Court of Mythics series.

I'd like to warn you in advance that this book includes horrible war that breeds tragedy for many characters, including our lovely heroine. Sierra gets her heart broken repeatedly and the path to mending it is paved with sorrow. You will see children orphaned by war, battles that make my stomach churn, and blood staining cobblestone streets, but it's tempered with family, care, and unity. The path to the happy ending is rife with difficulty, which makes the ending all the more exhilarating.

I hope you enjoy watching Cam and Sierra come back together and be all the stronger for their trials.

Contents

Chapter One

Camden Kent

She's gone.

Sierra's gone.

The bond between us is in tatters.

I'm bordering on a war I cannot win without my mate, and I drove her away.

Wyatt lets out a blistering string of curses and paces the room. I run my hands through my hair with a vicious tug, trying to collect my thoughts so I can take action, but my thoughts are too invasive. All I can think is that my mate is gone and that I am the reason for that—nothing else quite registers.

I hear Wyatt talking to me and feel his hand on my shoulder, but the words don't get through to me. In the front of my mind is the image of Sierra, her face pale, fingers clawing at the hand I had wrapped around her throat. I nearly killed her; of course she left. I can't honestly say I blame her for that, because it's impossible to. If the roles were reversed, odds are I'd have done the exact same thing. I proved to be the monster she feared, so of course, she picked up and took herself and her sister away from here.

While I understand her reasoning, and my own monumental mistake, I can't simply let her stay gone. I need her, my people need her, the whole world needs her for the upcoming war. Beyond her usefulness in battle, however, I need her for my own sanity. I hadn't realized how integral she'd become to me until this moment when I can no longer seek her out.

I need to find her.

I push off the couch, shove my brother out of the way, and storm out of my chambers. The guards scurry to follow and Wyatt catches up to me, asking, "Where the hell do you think you're going?"

I don't respond to him; I don't have the mental capacity to fight with him right now. I snap at one of the guards, "Find Claude, bring him to Sierra's chambers. If there was witchcraft involved in Sierra and Leisel's escape, he could be useful."

The guard bows his head, then turns and jogs down the hall, presumably towards wherever Claude's currently holed up. I quicken my pace until I'm also nearly jogging through the hallways. I only slow when I enter the East Wing of the castle, where both Sierra and Leisel are—*were*—staying.

On the floor leading up to her room are drops of blood, which I assume were spilled after I nearly crushed her windpipe and Wyatt had to carry her back to her room. A deep shame squeezes my chest and makes my wolf growl and whine and just about lose his mind at the idea that we've permanently driven Sierra away.

I swallow, then step into Sierra's room. The scent of her blood permeates the air, making my wolf growl yet again. I walk straight to her bathroom, barely taking note of the unkempt state of her room and the half-empty bookshelf in the corner, absent of all books of witchcraft.

On the mirror in her bathroom is a strange symbol drawn in blood, which is now dried into a dark rusty color. I can feel the magic coming from the symbol; it radiates a low hum of power that fills the entire bathroom and even spills over to the bedroom. I approach the mirror carefully, just in time for Claude to appear in the doorway.

"I heard you might be in need of magical assistance," he says, his tone calmer than I would've expected since the Queen and Princess are both absent.

"What is the sigil on the mirror?" I ask him, the words filled with agitation.

Claude slowly walks up to the counter and presses a hand to the mirror beside the sigil. He pulls his hand away as if it's on fire, then lets out a stuttering breath. "That's a portal key," Claude says. "Portals are simple enough to open if you have magic and know the proper sigils; this one's coded to take the creator to a very specific location. My best guess is that Sierra's now across the continent, with the Nightshade Coven in the northernmost parts of Acuria."

Fuck. I suspected as much, but hearing his confirmation is disheartening. If Sierra's with the witches on the very far end of Acuria, thousands of miles away from Kinrith and me, I have no way of getting to her unless they allow me to come to her, which I very much doubt they will. Witches are loyal to and protective of their own; they aren't known for leaving fellow witches behind.

On one hand, I believe Sierra will be safe under their protection because magic *is* the best protection. On the other hand, I know nobody would ever protect her as fiercely as I will, however, neither Sierra nor the witches have any reason to believe that. I'm sure she'll tell them what prompted her escape—me going into a rage and fucking up in a spectacular fashion—which means they won't let me near her.

A violent, longing ache starts up in my chest, feeling like a deep hole that only she can fill. Without her, there's nothing but pain, loneliness, despair, and heartache.

"Can you re-open it?" I ask Claude. "Open the portal again so we can get through?"

Claude appears contemplative. "I can re-*activate* the portal, but we won't be able to get through unless whoever's on the other side allows us through. With the portal activated, we'll at least get a glimpse of where Sierra went and perhaps talk to someone on the other side."

"Do it," I command.

A hidden, silly part of me hopes that when Claude activates the portal, I'll see Sierra on the other side. I'll be able to apologize, perhaps talk to her, make her understand that what happened was a freak accident brought on by a rage, something that will never happen again.

Unfortunately, it isn't Sierra who's revealed when Claude reactivates the portal by re-tracing the sigil with his own blood. The mirror ripples as if it's made of water, warping our reflections. Then our reflections disappear entirely, as does the reflection of the bathroom. It's replaced with a much different room—made of dark wood, showcasing a glimpse of a large shelf filled with jars of strange-looking herbs and substances—along with the high priestess of the Nightshade Coven, Odelia. She's seated in a wooden chair, her attention on the pages of a book she holds. That attention shifts to me, Wyatt, and Claude, as she looks up at each one of us, her grey eyes filled with barely-leashed anger.

"I was wondering how long it'd take your witch doctor to figure out the portal," Odelia says, her tone perfectly calm and placid. "He works faster than I'd have thought. Sierra warned me he'd likely be your first attempt at reaching out, so I decided to stick around and wait."

"Send Sierra and Leisel back," I demand, rational thought overshadowed by my need to have my mate back with me. I place a palm on the mirror, finding it solid and unsurpassable. "They belong here, with their mates."

Odelia lets out a light, ringing laugh that bounces around the bathroom. The laugh abruptly cuts off, and she glares at me. "They belong where they are safe, protected, and surrounded by their own kind. You had your chance, Alpha. You threw it away because wolves are not fucking trustworthy. Be glad our treaty is bound by magic; otherwise, you'd have turned into my enemy the moment you laid a cruel hand on a witch."

"I am bonded to Sierra, marked and consummated," I growl. "We can't be separated indefinitely. The bond won't allow it."

Odelia's laugh is cruel this time. "I examined the bond when she came to me. It's barely hanging on by a thread; it won't impede her. Funny enough, even mythical mate bonds can't survive attempted murder intact."

"She once attempted to murder me," I point out, thinking back to the first night I had dinner with Sierra in Aesara. She'd tried to use her black flame to kill me when I informed her I'd be taking Leisel to Kinrith. The bond wasn't very strong at that point and her attempt didn't even manage to really hurt me, so it suffered no ill effects. I understand that what I did was drastically different because I almost succeeded in killing her without even attempting to.

"Did she?" Odelia asks, sounding interested. "Clever girl. I can't say I blame her. Now, listen to me, Alpha, and listen well. You will still abide by our treaty, as will I. You will send pack reinforcements to the sorcerer territories I've previously indicated, and I will send some of my witches—not Sierra, so don't waste my time asking—to the capital and other shifter territories to install proper magical warding and protection. In the interim, you will not try to get to Sierra. If you do, I will consider our alliance null and will treat you like the enemy you've done such an excellent job convincing your mate that you are. Are we clear?"

I open my mouth to growl a *fuck no*, but Wyatt slaps his hand over my mouth, bands another around my neck, and forcibly throws me out of the bathroom before saying, "If you don't want me to go back to beating the shit out of you, stay there."

His features are taut with rage, muscles bulging, veins and tendons on his neck straining, and I understand that it isn't just my mate I pushed beyond the point of no return; it's also my brother, because my actions didn't just rob me of my mate, they robbed him of his as well. For once, I don't fight back or steamroll him, because I've already ruined one relationship today and I am not prepared to ruin another. That is, if I haven't already.

So, I stay in place and watch from the doorway as Wyatt walks back to the sink, addressing Odelia, who now appears one part intrigued, one part amused.

"Well, now. I'm glad to see at least someone in your monstrosity of a palace has some sense," she says.

"We'll arrange for several units of witch-friendly warriors to make their way up north to you," Wyatt says. "Please inform your outlying villages so they don't presume the wolves are there to harm and kill them on sight. We will be waiting gratefully for you to send your own reinforcements to help us ward our territories. Camden will not make any attempts to get to Sierra. I will see to that myself."

Odelia looks surprised by Wyatt, and when she speaks again, I notice a new tone of respect in her voice. "So, the Prince Beta is more sensible than the King Alpha. Interesting. Thank you for your confirmation, Wyatt. Is there anything else before I go tend to the newest members of my coven?"

Her words drive an invisible knife through my chest, twisting deep, making my soul feel like it's tearing apart.

"You have no reason to help me or trust me, but I'll ask that you allow me to communicate with Leisel," Wyatt, says. "Even if it's just through letters, I need contact with her. I won't harm her or pressure her to return, I just need to know that she's safe and content."

Odelia's silent for several moments, contemplating. She stares at Wyatt, looking him over, probably trying to gauge his sincerity against her responsibility as the leader of all witches in Acuria. Should she allow Wyatt to have contact with his mate or should she keep him at bay like she intends to with me?

Finally, she says, "I will speak to Sierra and Leisel. That decision is theirs to make. If they agree, I will set up a similar halfway portal that'll allow you to see and speak with Leisel. If they don't allow it, however, I will not push them. They've been pushed around enough recently, haven't they?" Her gaze flicks to me, her latter words clearly directed towards me.

My wolf whines again, sulking deeply, not impressed with me and my destructive actions in the least.

"Thank you," Wyatt says. "Can we contact you again this way if anything comes up?"

Odelia waves a hand. "If need be, fine. Now go, before I change my mind and decide vengeance is in order."

Chapter Two

Sierra West

I thought I'd discovered the depths of true sorrow when my parents died. After my father's death, I fell into a deep depression and was only pulled out of it when my mother found out she was pregnant. I felt responsible for making sure she didn't overwork herself on the farm, but then my mother died, and my depression was so deep I wanted to die until I held Leisel for the first time and saw my purpose for living.

All of that sadness, all of the sorrow I'd experienced in my youth, couldn't compare to what I feel now. My true calling in this life is being a mother; I discovered that through raising Leisel. It's why I didn't want to rid myself of my pregnancy even when I understood that I only got pregnant because of the lies and deceit of my mate.

That choice was taken out of my hands. Rogues cut my child right out of me and then Camden nearly killed me, leaving me shrouded by a deep darkness and sadness that refuses to let me out of its grip.

Escaping Kinrith was easier than I thought it would be; the portal worked seamlessly, and it let out right into Odelia's office, where she was already waiting to receive my sister and me. I remember little of our conversation when I first arrived, just as I remember little of the last days I've spent holed up in the room Odelia took me to, which is meant to be my room for the duration of my stay with the coven.

The only person I can bring myself to speak to is my sister, and only because I don't have the heart to ignore her; my instincts would never allow me to leave her feeling alone and abandoned. Even still, I have no interest in leaving my room and exploring, no interest in *anything*, really.

Leisel stays in the room right beside mine, though she's been spending her nights in my bed. I hold her while she and Chip doze peacefully unable to fall asleep myself. We've only been here a scant collection of days, and in that time, Odelia's visited us both repeatedly, inviting us out to meet the coven.

I've told her each time that I don't have the strength to meet anyone new right now, to speak to people, to function. I can't crawl out of the darkness that's slowly consuming me, and the chasm that remains open and gaping within my chest only makes matters worse.

"Sierra?" Leisel's tentative voice pulls me from my thoughts.

I look over to the doorway where she stands, Chip perched on her shoulder as usual, wringing her hands in front of her.

Odelia took her out earlier to explore the beautiful territory surrounding us. The Nightshade witches live in the center of a stunning mountain range, in a cavern system carved right into the mountain itself. I've barely had the energy to admire the formation of my room—polished cavern walls and stone floors—let alone leave it to wander about.

"What is it, sweet girl?" I ask her tiredly, my voice coming out faint and dejected.

Leisel steps into my room and closes the stone door behind her, walking up to me. I'm seated on the cushioned chair in front of the fireplace, staring into the flames, as I've found myself doing every moment since our arrival.

I pat my knee, inviting Leisel to join me. She does, climbing onto my lap and cuddling close to me, wrapping her small arms around me. I wrap my arms around her too and rest my chin on her head, feeling a brief flicker of warmth pass through me at the contact with my sister. That warmth only lasts a few moments before once again being overshadowed by the abysmal coldness that's plagued me since I escaped Kinrith.

"Why are you so sad?" Leisel asks me, her voice wobbly. "Why won't you come out of your room? It's so pretty here, I promise you'll love it."

A long sigh escapes me as I kiss her forehead. I haven't told Leisel about my miscarriage; she's too young and too sweet for me to burden her with such a heavy truth. All I've told her is that Camden betrayed me, betrayed *us*, and that's been enough for her until now.

"I miss you," Leisel goes on quietly.

"You don't have to miss me, my love, I'm right here," I respond, but even I can tell how hollowed out my voice is.

It strikes me that, in grieving my unborn child, I've neglected the other child under my protection. Not intentionally—I'd *never* knowingly do anything to hurt Leisel. Nevertheless, she's suffering because of me, which isn't something I can allow to continue. I'm better than that, and more, I love Leisel with every fiber of my being. I've already let down someone under my protection recently, even though the child inside of me was barely formed. I can't let down the living witchling in my arms; I never have before, and I certainly won't start now.

"You're here, but you're not," Leisel says, sounding miserable. That misery tugs at my heart and makes me crave doing whatever it takes to alleviate it.

I can't stay in my room forever. I might want to, but that's not a viable option. I have to emerge eventually. Technically, I am still a queen—though I've turned my back on my king and kingdom—and my recent behavior is not the behavior of a queen or powerful witch, it's the behavior of someone pathetic who's given up.

Depressed or not, I can't give up. Not when I have Leisel relying on me. Not when I have a coven of witches to integrate with. I might have very little wind left in me for politics and diplomacy, but I'll always have energy when it comes to my sister. I just need to draw on it; draw on the core of my being, which is that of a mother. It has been for nearly a decade.

I give my head a firm shake, shore up my strength, and draw on the emotional reserves I learned I had when I first held Leisel when she was just an infant. I was grieving my mother's death and wishing to meet my own end, and then decided to live for my sister. "You're right, sweet girl. I'm sorry I haven't been here." I gently lift her and set her on the ground, before standing up myself.

It feels like I weigh a million pounds, even the simple act of standing is exhausting, and I understand that's not just because of turmoil, it's because I haven't eaten since arriving. I haven't had an appetite thanks to the emotional maelstrom that's been taking place within me, but I can't continue like that. I have to be strong for my sister.

Leisel's eyes, glimmering with a jaded hope, meet mine. She takes my hand in hers and, just like that, I feel some of the strength return to me. I realize that's because, in many ways, Leisel is my strength. She always has been, even when I hadn't known.

"Dinner's being served soon," she says quietly. "Will you come? Everyone's been asking about you."

That feels like a physical blow to my chest. I have enough trust in Odelia, just based on the fact that she put herself at risk to take us under her protection, to allow her to take Leisel around and to meals. I should've been doing that myself, especially when there are members of the coven actively seeking to meet me.

"Of course, I'll come," I tell her, as if that's a given when we both know it hasn't been. It will be now though. My turmoil has had plenty of time to chain me down; it's time for me to figure out a way to stand back up again.

Leisel's eyes light up, as does her face, and a brilliant smile spreads on her lips. She bounces on her toes, hand tightening over mine, and says, "Let's go! I'll show you around the cavern system; Odelia told me it's ancient and easy to get lost in, but I'll guide you."

I chuckle, brushing a kiss over her head. Then, realizing it's probably best for me to freshen up before going to meet everyone, I tell Leisel, "Wait out here while I bathe and change, my love. I'll be out in ten minutes, then we'll go together, okay?"

She nods, eagerly, climbing back onto the chair in front of the fireplace. I turn, take a change of clothes from the wardrobe standing along one of the walls—clothes that Odelia had the witches put here in anticipation of my potential arrival—and make my way into the bathroom, which is through a small cavern opening on the right side of my room. The bathroom has running water and electricity, as does my room and I'd assume all others, which is impressive—whether courtesy of magic or brilliant engineering. I make quick work of bathing myself in the glass shower, scrubbing my body and hair clean, before changing and emerging back into my bedroom.

Leisel's seated exactly where I left her, telling Chip about how she wants to try to climb a cliff with the witches tomorrow.

"Unless there's some guarantee of safety, no climbing cliffs for you, Leisel. It's dangerous," I say loudly.

She pouts, turning towards me. "But it sounds fun."

Dying from a long fall to a rocky bottom doesn't sound very fun, and I can't bear the thought of something happening to her after my recent loss.

"We'll see after I've talked to Odelia about it. Now, weren't you saying something about dinner?"

Leisel leaps to her feet, deposits Chip back onto her shoulder, then runs up to me and takes my hand. She leads me out of my room and into a long cavern hallway. The walls are rougher out here, I notice, with jagged edges and even stalactites hanging from the ceiling. Each stalactite holds an orb of light almost like a lamp, illuminating the space. The stone floor is flat and polished, and the echoing sounds of my footsteps and Leisel's bounce around us.

"Odelia does meals out on a balcony this way," Leisel explains to me when we come to a junction in the hall, taking me down the left side. As we walk, the sounds of voices and laughter grow louder, along with a few odd-out swearwords that I think are said by Reyna. I haven't seen her or Claire since arriving; I only spoke with Odelia long enough to get formal asylum and be led to my room, and I haven't been taking visitors.

At the end of this hall is another junction; one entrance leads to the left, which opens up into a room filled with couches and comfortable chairs. The walls are lined with bookshelves. The other path leads to the balcony Leisel was telling me about. I let out a soft gasp as she pulls me onto the balcony where a large stone table is set with at least a dozen witches milling about it. My attention doesn't go to the witches though; it's entirely taken up by the *gorgeous* view.

The edge of the natural stone balcony has a railing, and it overlooks a stunning mountain range. I can see the snowy peaks of five separate mountains as I stand and observe, with many more mountains farther out and behind them, and the sight is *breathtaking*. The beauty of nature surrounds us from every side, and the sight of that alone feels like it gives me even more strength. I know that nature is the very source of my magic—it's why I've always enjoyed the outdoors—but the sheer power in this mountain range specifically is so concentrated I can feel it in the air, seeping into me.

"Sierra." Odelia sounds pleasantly surprised to see me as she emerges from the crowd of witches milling around and approaches me. Her long, raven-black wavy hair is up in a high ponytail today, and her golden skin almost looks like it glows in the light of the setting sun.

All of the witches go silent in unison, and I find myself on the receiving end of over a dozen scrutinous gazes. I spot Claire and Reyna standing together at the edge of the table and tip them a nod. I clear my throat and smile at Odelia as she stops in front of me.

"Please forgive my manners these last days. I haven't been in the best state." I run my eyes over every witch gathered as I say the words, trying to show contriteness because I know my actions have been remarkably selfish and rude, two things I can't afford to be.

Reyna waves an impatient hand. "At least you're done sulking now. Great timing, too, as we're planning which human village we should visit first to aid."

Chapter Three

"Aesara!" Leisel says as she turns to Odelia, walking up to her and taking the priestess' hand in a gesture of familiarity that tells me my sister is very comfortable around the high priestess, despite her station and the staggering amount of power she gives off. "Can we go to Aesara, please?"

Odelia smiles down at her fondly, stroking her free hand through Leisel's hair. "I have no problems with it, but we'll need to convince your sister to come with us since you two know the village best."

Leisel turns pleading, puppy-dog eyes on me, and I feel myself cave. Coming out of my room today feels like a monumental achievement, but I know it's not enough. I need to be present and involved. I'm a member of this coven—a guest since I'm still technically affiliated with the Rockwell Pack and all the shifters it rules over—but a witch who's been taken in nonetheless, which means I need to help the coven.

"I'd be happy to visit home," I tell Leisel warmly. "I'm sure Marike-ta, Parker, and Wesley will be glad to see us." I can't say for sure as to the rest of the villagers, since when Leisel and I left there was already a crowd of those who were quite upset that Aesara had played host to witches without anyone's knowledge for decades, but I'm confident our oldest friends will be glad to get a visit from us.

"It's decided, then," Odelia says, tapping Leisel's nose. "Now, why don't you head to the kitchens and see how dinner's coming along? The cooks should be readying to bring out the dishes soon enough."

Leisel beams at Odelia and me before skipping off the balcony, leaving me alone with the witches, most of whom are still staring at me with open interest.

"Alright, ladies," Claire says loudly, she's an earthly witch, not a damn exhibition. Stop making fools of yourselves and go back to your conversations." The witches follow her lead, and I understand that as an elder, she must wield a great deal of power here. Not as much as Odelia but enough. That's somewhat amusing since Claire is the shortest and most docile-looking person of everyone gathered here; standing at somewhere around five feet tall, she has long red hair a few shades darker than my own, sharp green eyes, and delicate features reminiscent of a pixie in old fairytales. She steps away from Reyna and walks up to me, surprising me when she takes both my hands in hers and stares into my eyes with her forest-green orbs.

"I am so, *so* sorry for your loss," she tells me earnestly, green eyes glittering with empathy. Then, quietly so only Odelia and I can hear, she says, "I, too, have lost a child before I could even meet them. Few pains in this world can match such a tragedy. If you need anything or anyone to talk to, please come to me."

She squeezes my hands, then wanders back to Reyna, leaving me a little stunned. When the witches first informed me I was pregnant during our meeting at Camden's castle, something no wolf around me had the courtesy to do, they offered me a way out; an elixir that would cleanse my womb. Claire seemed on board with that idea, so I certainly didn't expect empathy from her, which is why it's so surprising.

Odelia smiles at me. "We've all experienced our own heartache, but Claire most of all. She lost everyone she loved before we found her and then lost even more afterward. She's a good confidant. I hope you seek her out if you need to."

"Why are you being so kind to me?" I ask before thinking my question through.

Odelia may have given me asylum, but asylum doesn't encompass the kindness and leeway she's showing me right now. She'd have every right to be offended by the fact that I haven't taken a step out of my room since arriving; instead, she's offering her support.

Odelia's smile falls. "Because I've also lost people I cared for. Tragedies land with a different impact on witches than they do on all other mythics and humans. Emotions, negative emotions, are both our Achilles heel and greatest fuel. Heartache handicaps us and anger exponentially intensifies our power. I've been where you are—not precisely, not like Claire—but close enough to understand. I won't fault you for your grief."

I do recall Claude mentioning something about witches being most susceptible to the effects of harsh emotions, but I hadn't given too much credence to his words. I assumed my depression the last days was only what any expecting mother who'd lost her child would feel, even though I only had an hour to connect with my child before it was taken from me.

"Thank you," I say, "but it's time to push past it. It's started affecting Leisel, which is a horrible mistake on my part. That girl deserves to be surrounded by happiness and vibrance, not pain and sorrow."

Odelia nods firmly. "You've come out of your slump faster than most—when Claire miscarried, we didn't see her for a month."

"I'm not out of my slump," I tell her frankly. "There are just more important things in life than my grief, such as the witchling who may as well be my daughter."

Odelia blinks slowly. "You have great strength of soul. More than most. That is very respectable and very good. We're about to enter war, Sierra, and war means tragedy for everyone. At least you know you have the capacity to survive it."

She squeezes my shoulder, then links her arm with mine and walks me to the table. Once again, everyone falls silent, and all eyes are back to me. "Alright, ladies, the moment you've been pestering me for. This is Sierra, wielder of the black flame, Queen of all shifters, and one of the very few earthly witches in existence."

I raise an awkward hand in a half-wave. "Hello. Thank you for having me, and for looking after Leisel these last days. She's enjoyed spending time with you very much."

A witch with long, curly brown hair and warm grey eyes approaches me and sticks out her hand. "Hi, Sierra. I'm Madeline, but everyone calls me Maddy or Mad. The latter nickname came when I toppled a mountain on some dark faye a few years ago. It's a pleasure to meet you, and I'd like to say that Leisel is an absolute delight. We've loved having her."

As if summoned by her name, the small person in question skips back onto the balcony as I'm shaking Maddy's hand and beams at us. "Dinner's ready!"

As she speaks, four witches walk out of the hall behind her and onto the balcony, each carrying a tray full of dishes. I don't sense any great deal of magic emanating from them, which may explain their positions in the kitchen. They each tip me a brief, not altogether interested look, before setting up platters of many different foods on the table.

The sight of such an abundant bounty reminds me of the times I dined with Camden, which makes the chasm in my chest pulse with something that might be...*longing*. I shove that feeling away because I refuse to long for a man who betrayed my trust, then topped it off by crushing my throat and very nearly killing me. I might not be entirely sane, but I'm not *that* crazy.

"Let's eat," Odelia says as the witches who brought the food retreat back into the cavern halls.

The table only has chairs at the head and the tail, with benches along each side of the length of it. Odelia leads me over to the bench on the side of the table facing out so I still have the gorgeous view in front of me and seats me at the very edge of it before taking her place at the head of the table. As soon as she does, every witch falls on the contents as if starved. I hear Reyna throwing threats at someone that they better back off her chicken salad before she decides they don't need a hand that's used for thievery. All of the witches talk and banter as they fill their plates and eat. The atmosphere is so warm, familial, and inviting that I feel myself relax. Leisel takes a seat on the bench right next to me, and Claire sits on the other side of her, giving Leisel's long hair a playful tug.

"Hey, trouble. You gotten up to anything naughty since the last time I saw you?" When Leisel shakes her head, Claire tsks. "Well, we'll need to fix that after dinner."

Leisel giggles, and my heart warms at the sound. I find I enjoy spending time with the witches much more than I thought I would, and being out of my room makes me feel lighter. For a little while, I forget about my sorrows and just enjoy getting to know members of my kind. They're all extremely talkative, but none more so than Maddy, who sits across from me at the table and fires question after question at me.

Odelia tells me a bit more about the Nightshade Coven's territory, which is apparently surrounded by many other coven territories that all look to the Nightshade witches for guidance and instructions. She tells me that the other side of the cavern system is meant for the Nightshade warlocks, who she no longer allows to dine with them outside of special occasions because they're too damn rowdy and prone to starting fights over the food.

At the end of dinner, I find myself feeling at least slightly refreshed and rejuvenated, as if dinner with the witches is just what I needed. Claire and Leisel disappear somewhere with my blessing—to kick up some mischief, I suspect—while I stay at the table with Odelia and Reyna long after the other witches have retired back inside. The air turns biting and cool, so Odelia creates a fire that hovers mid-air, radiating warmth for her, me, and Reyna.

"It's good to see you pulled your head out of your ass and showed up," Reyna tells me. "It's been long enough."

"What Reyna means to say is how glad she is that you're feeling well enough to join us," Odelia says with a sigh, giving Reyna an unimpressed look. Then back to me, "We'll make for Aesara first thing in the morning after breakfast. I've teleported witches there before; we'll teleport directly to the fountain in the town square. We'll be taking a good number of things with us: steel for weapons, medical supplies to help restock the clinic, along with other items that'll come with our aid package."

"That sounds great," I say warmly. I've missed my home village desperately since leaving it and I'm looking forward to checking on Mariketa, Parker, and Wesley. I'm sure Leisel is equally excited to see them—they were very much like grandparents to her, and she's told me a couple of times that she misses them and their son.

Odelia nods. "There's one order of business for us to discuss. I hadn't brought it up before because you weren't in a fit state for discussion, but now that you've emerged, I'd like to. It has to do with the Rockwell Pack's Prince Beta."

I feel myself stiffen at her words. I haven't given much thought to Wyatt; I haven't really done much productive thinking the last few days. I've just been grieving. I'm still angry at him for keeping the news of my pregnancy from me, but now that I've had time, I find my anger doesn't run quite as hot as it did at first.

Wyatt told me that Camden threatened to lock him away from Leisel if he spoke to me about the truth. I can't fault him for keeping quiet; his instincts and loyalty towards Leisel would have forced his silence. I'm not *happy* with him by any means, but I also understand he was in a very difficult position and tried to do his best by his mate and my sister, even if that meant keeping me in the dark. I don't think he would've kept his mouth shut if he had another option.

"What about him?" I ask Odelia.

She reaches forward to pluck a strawberry from a fruit platter that was brought out after dinner. "After you and Leisel came, when you told me your worries that the witch doctor might try to re-open the portal, I stayed behind. Nobody can open a *portal* from outside—it has to be expected and allowed by someone here—but the witch doctor managed to reactivate the sigil and open a communication with me through the mirror. I spoke with your mate for only a few moments before his brother quite literally tossed him out of the room, then asked me for a single favor; to permit and facilitate his communication with Leisel. I told him the decision would lie with you and your sister. The Beta seemed very contrite and truly sorrowful, so I don't have any problems with him maintaining contact with Leisel remotely as long as you don't. It would be quite simple to set up a mirror spell that connects a mirror in her room to a mirror somewhere in Kinrith's castle, allowing Wyatt and Leisel to speak."

The mere mention of Camden is enough to make that chasm in my chest pulse with pain, reminding me that the bond connecting us has suffered right along with me. Goosebumps raise along my arms and legs and I feel my body stiffen with tension but force it to relax and switch my thoughts over to Wyatt.

Objectively, I see no reason to stop him from speaking with Leisel via mirror spell. To do so would be deliberately cruel. While I can't profess to be the kindest or most open-minded person in this world, I am not a cruel person either. Besides, I suspect Leisel misses him, though I don't think she'd tell me if she did because she wouldn't want me to worry.

"I'm fine with it," I say. "I'll talk it over with Leisel before bed. Assuming she's fine with it, the mirror can be set up tomorrow, after we've returned from Aesara."

Odelia inclines her head. "Then it will be done. Goodnight, Sierra, rest well. I'll see you in the morning."

Chapter Four

Later that evening, I ask Leisel before bed if she'd like to have an open communication with Wyatt. She thinks for a long time before finally asking me if her speaking with Wyatt would upset me. Feeling like I've failed in my role as her guardian, I tell her that of course it wouldn't upset me and that even if it did she should still be honest with me. She tells me that she does want to talk to him and even confides that she misses sharing a castle with him.

It makes my heart clench to know that the distance is weighing on her, even if only a little. Since Leisel's so young, the bond connecting her to Wyatt is currently subdued and much weaker than the bond between me and Camden, even in my bond's current tattered state. For now, her connection with Wyatt is currently more sibling-like or even paternal from his side to her, and the witches assured me that the distance would be manageable for her more so than it would be for me, so I didn't think she'd be so eager to speak with Wyatt.

Seeing the hopeful glint in her eyes as we speak about the mirror portal, I'm not altogether surprised when she runs off to find Odelia to set up the portal now rather than wait until tomorrow. I join Odelia and Leisel in Leisel's room and watch as Odelia performs a ritual on Leisel's vanity mirror right beside her armoire that'll connect it directly to one in Wyatt's room. How she manages to pinpoint the location of Wyatt's mirror, I'm not sure and I don't bother to ask—perhaps she paid more attention during the castle tour than I'd previously assumed.

Since I don't want Odelia to draw Leisel's blood to create the portal key—a sigil drawn in blood—I offer up mine. Since we're of the same bloodline, the effects are equally as potent, and a moment after I've finished drawing the sigil on the surface of the mirror per Odelia's instructions, I watch the reflective surface warp and shimmer in a familiar way before turning into a window of sorts that shows a view of a large bedroom, one I presume belongs to Wyatt.

I spot Wyatt lounging on a sofa in front of a fireplace on the left side of his room, not far from the bed, and immediately step away from the mirror before he sees me. Odelia leaves the room, giving us privacy, while I hover by the doorway, out of sight but within viewing distance of the mirror and earshot to make sure Wyatt doesn't pressure my sister into returning or giving away our location.

Leisel perches on the wooden stool in front of her vanity, her eyes wide and filled with wonder and hope. She calls out softly, "Wyatt?"

He stiffens on the couch, and his head turns towards Leisel very slowly. Then his entire face lights up as he leaps to his feet, sprints across the room until he's directly in front of his mirror, and blinks several times as he stares at my sister. "Leisel?" he says, hesitantly. "Am I dreaming?"

A pang of pain goes through my chest because I have dreamed about Camden every night since leaving, no matter how much I try not to. I have to wonder if he dreams about me too and if he's plagued with thoughts of me the same way I'm plagued with thoughts of him.

Leisel gives a soft giggle. "No, some witches helped me do a spell that connects my mirror with yours so we can talk."

Wyatt presses his palm flat against his mirror, and a soft smile spreads on his lips as he stares at my sister, affection filling his gaze. The affection isn't romantic, which is why I don't tense. Instead, it's a brotherly sort of fondness.

"I've missed you, Leisel," he says.

Leisel's eyes flicker over to me for a brief moment before she focuses back on Wyatt and says, "I've missed you too. I miss the castle library even more though."

Wyatt gives her a faux-hurt expression, pouting. "You like books more than you like me? Ouch, Leisel, that hurts."

Leisel giggles again. "Books are awesome, and you're pretty great too."

"Well, what have you been reading?" Wyatt asks.

Satisfied that their conversation won't go in a harmful direction and trusting Wyatt not to take advantage of the chance he's been given, I leave the room, blowing Leisel a kiss before closing the door. Hearing Wyatt's voice and seeing his face somehow stirred up a longing within me to see another male, a longing that disgusts me.

I shouldn't miss Camden; I shouldn't be secretly wishing that I had a mirror to speak to him through as well. I know that it's most likely the bond driving me to want to seek him out, even though the bond isn't at its best, which just speaks to the strength of the mythical connection. Even greatly damaged and on its last legs, the bond still makes me crave Camden, which just makes me angry.

Most of me despises him. The argument we had before I left, where he had the godsdamned *audacity* to try to blame my miscarriage on me, didn't just infuriate me—it also broke a great deal of hope I was starting to have for our relationship. It proved to me that Camden would not be able to keep a level head and be who I needed during crises. Considering that every living being on this planet is about to experience a crisis with the start of the war, I can't afford to rely on someone so hot-headed let alone someone prone to rages that can drive him to nearly kill me. It simply isn't safe.

On the other hand...there's a teeny-tiny part of me that misses Camden. A brief image flickers through my mind as I take a seat on my bed; the memory of the time I held Camden on the couch in his living quarters, the night after he learned of his father's passing. I felt so connected to him in that moment, as if we were finally on the same page of our book after spending so much time fighting. It's moments like that that I miss, but as for everything else, most of my time in the castle was spent living in fear and uncertainty.

I can't ignore the fact that the change of scenery hasn't made that fear and uncertainty go away. To be fair, before today, I was so deep in my sorrow that I couldn't even function, but now that I'm at least somewhat back to myself, I don't find myself any less afraid of the future. Now I'm even more afraid of it because my horrible conflict with Camden made a difficult situation even worse. We're still on the verge of war, only now, we're more divided than ever. I don't know how the witches and shifters will come together for battle. Previously, the idea was that my presence in the capital of shifters would make the witches more amenable to teaming up with them; now that I'm no longer there, the witches have no draw to shifters left. They share a common enemy, of course, which will bring them together, but I don't know if a common enemy will be enough to make two wildly different species fight cohesively, even with the treaty they're both bound to.

I'm drawn from my thoughts when Leisel creaks open the door to my room and peeks inside.

I give her a smile. "How was your talk with Wyatt?"

She smiles. "It was good. He, um, wants to talk to you. Says it's important—something about Aesara. He wouldn't tell me no matter how many times I asked, so I think it's bad."

That's quite literally the one thing that could get me in front of Wyatt right now. I stand from my bed, walk over to Leisel, and say, "Well, we can't have anything bad happening to our home village, can we?"

Leisel shakes her head. "No. I miss Mari, Parker, and Wesley. I hope they're okay."

I brush a kiss over her forehead. "I'm sure they are, sweet girl. I'll hear whatever it is Wyatt has to say and then tomorrow we'll see for ourselves. Stay here while I talk to him, yeah?"

If Wyatt didn't want to tell my sister the problem, that means the problem is probably of a graphic nature that shouldn't be spoken of around a nine-year-old. Fear curdles in my gut at the idea that some ill fate might have befallen Aesara, making my stride quickly into Leisel's room, close the door, then take a seat at the vanity, and look into the mirror.

Wyatt's still visible, as the portal is still active—to deactivate it, the blood sigil needs to be wiped off and then redrawn to reactivate it once again.

Wyatt gives me a small smile. He has dark circles under his eyes and a drawn, almost gaunt expression on his face that tells me the last few days have been no easier for him than they have for me.

"Hey, Sierra," he says, somewhat quietly. As if he's afraid I'll snap at him merely due to seeing him.

I clear my throat. "Wyatt. Leisel said something about Aesara—what is it?"

He nods. "Right. Camden received reports a few days ago of great amounts of smoke coming from Aesara's territory—a scout from a nearby pack noticed it and wanted to pass the information on since it's common knowledge that the Queen and Princess originate from that village."

I feel my brows furrow at his use of titles for me and my sister, though I don't bother refuting them. Instead, I say, "If it's just reports of smoke, that could be some villagers burning farmland. We have to do that on occasion, when the land's overwrought with weeds or pests, to prepare for the next planting season."

Wyatt nods. "Let's hope it's just that. The reports spoke of a lot of smoke, Sierra. They're unconfirmed as of now, but I thought you might like to know."

I appreciate him reaching out, though this sounds like a routine burning of land to revitalize it. There's a small niggle within me that hints there could be something more to it, but whatever the case is, I'll see for myself tomorrow.

I look Wyatt up and down again, guilt settling over me at seeing just how bad it seems he's been faring.

"You look like shit," I tell him.

He snorts. "You should see Cam. He hasn't slept since you left."

Irritation flares to life in my stomach at the mention of Camden's name. Mostly because my instinctive reaction is to ask more about him. Wyatt's words breathe life into the part of me I thought Camden killed when he nearly killed me—a part that inherently worries about his wellbeing.

"Well, then, turnabouts fair play," I say flatly. "I didn't sleep for several nights after meeting him, which culminated in me passing out."

Wyatt smiles a little, though the smile is sad. "All's fair in love and war."

"Is that all?" I ask a little snappily. I came here to hear what he had to say about Aesara, not to be told that my mate is faring poorly in my absence. I shouldn't care; I don't *want* to care, and yet, some part of me does.

"Are you okay, Sierra?" Wyatt asks.

The question makes me fall silent. I'm not okay; I'm far fucking from it. A few days ago I experienced dissection via rogue shifter claw, which literally cut my pregnancy right out of me. When I woke up after that, feeling raw and groggy and heavy with loss, I then had to deal with an absolutely psychotic Camden who nearly finished what the rogues started. That prompted me to quite literally flee for my life, which brings us to here and now.

Thousands of miles apart, and yet I still can't get away from my mate.

Since Wyatt doesn't *really* deserve my ire, I don't take out my building anger on him. Instead, I reply bluntly, "No, but I will be."

Wyatt gives me a sad, somewhat withdrawn smile. "Of course you will. I think you should know, I got revenge on Camden on your behalf. Crushed his windpipe since he nearly crushed yours—he was spitting blood for a little bit too."

Instead of bringing me satisfaction as it should, that thought brings another wave of pain to my chest. I wish I wanted to hurt Camden, but I don't.

Nevertheless, I tell Wyatt, "Thank you."

He nods. "If you need anything, you know where to reach me. The witches refused to portal the warriors we sent as reinforcement, so they're still making their way to you, but they should be there within a few days. We received the witches Odelia sent yesterday, and they've already warded the entire capitol and are now moving to surrounding outlying pack territories. Please thank her."

"I will," I tell him. "It's been good speaking with you, Wyatt. I hope you take care of yourself and Camden."

With that, I reach forward and rub my thumb across the sigil painted on the edge of the mirror, smudging it. Instantly, the mirror ripples again before returning to its normal reflective state, showing Leisel's room.

With a long sigh, I stand from my chair and collect Leisel from my room. I ask her if she wants to share my bed again tonight. She tells me since I'm here now, she doesn't need to, which makes me understand that she's been sleeping beside me for my sake more than her own. A heartwarming idea, but also one that makes me feel guilty because I'm supposed to be the one that takes care of Leisel, not the other way around.

I tuck her into her bed and then read to her from the book of fairytales she took with her from the castle until she falls asleep with Chip snoozing beside her on her pillow. I turn off the light, return to my room, and resolve to be better in the morning. Be a better caretaker to my sister, be a better coven member to the Nightshade witches, and try to return to some semblance of normalcy.

* * *

Breakfast is held in the same place as dinner—the balcony overlooking the mountain range. The only difference is that we're joined by a few warlocks for the meal, who offer to lend their services in our upcoming trip to Aesara. Odelia thanks them politely and informs them that the witches should be fine on their own, instead instructing them to head to the next village over with aid of their own.

I tell her about my brief conversation with Wyatt and of what he informed me. She agrees that we'll see what's going on once we're in Aesara and can choose how to proceed from there.

Maddy's the designated coven teleporter—in addition to having some power over a person's mind, she also has the unique ability to transport not only herself but groups of other people across the world in the blink of an eye. She's been to Aesara before, so after breakfast, once a few witches have gathered the supplies we intend to bring with us to mark the beginning of the humanitarian program written into the treaty, she tells about a dozen witches to join hands with each other around her.

Since it's both Leisel's and my first time teleporting, she tells me, "You'll probably throw up when we get there—don't be bothered by the nausea or dizziness, it's totally normal. My best recommendation is to sit on the ground and breathe deeply until your senses have returned to you." Arching an eyebrow, she asks, "You ready?"

"After that warning? Who wouldn't be?" I respond dryly, before adding, "Yes, let's go."

My stomach drops as the balcony and mountain range disappear, turning into a senseless blur. It feels like great pressure encases me from all sides, like I'm suddenly buried in stone. Simultaneously, there's the sense that my body's getting ripped in a hundred different directions, and after a moment, I start to fear that my limbs might actually tear off. Then, as suddenly as the process begins, it ends. I find myself tumbling face-first onto cobblestone ground, rolling to my back just in time to catch Leisel as she falls.

Maddy wasn't exaggerating; I really do feel like I'm going to throw up. I heave as my stomach flips again and again. Remembering her advice, I breathe deeply, clutching Leisel and shutting my eyes tight until the worst of the dizziness has receded and I no longer feel like I'm going to spew the contents of my breakfast onto the ground beside me.

I become aware of an eerie sort of silence, one that has never accompanied life in Aesara. Even on the farm, there was always the noise of birds chirping, bugs buzzing, and wildlife skittering about, and the village was always loud with voices of people trading and selling and speaking animatedly to each other.

I open my eyes, only to startle when I see that the bricks that were once a dark grey have now been stained with a deep red, rusty-looking color. My eyes wander forward, and my heart feels like it stops when I take in the sight around me. I scramble to my feet, holding Leisel close, suddenly feeling very close to vomiting again.

Ice fills my veins as I look around the town square that was once loud, lively, and teeming with activity. It's been destroyed.

Chapter Five

Vendor carts are either overturned or burned, with a collection of textiles and products having fallen onto the street. There are also bodies everywhere. I see the man who I bought art supplies from slumped against the side of his cart, his throat gouged open, staring lifelessly into the distance. The woman who I sold the produce I grew on my farm is laid out in the center of the street, naked, with horrible gashes covering her back and bruises that indicate she was assaulted before being killed.

My heart clenches as I grab a hold of Leisel's arm and pull her face-first to me, hiding her from the gruesome, horrible scene. She's already glimpsed some of it though; her cries are so loud they echo through the square as she grieves for the fallen and mourns the destruction.

As much as I want to stay here and comfort her, I can't. I need to take a good look around, catalogue the damage, and search for any survivors, though the scene around me makes me doubt there are any.

I tell Claire, "Watch Leisel. Make sure she doesn't see anything, console her. I need to go check our farm."

"Do you want someone to come with you?" Odelia asks.

I shake my head. "No." I need to be alone when I check my cabin.

"I can come with you for protection," Reyna offers.

I shake my head. "Thank you, but I'm quite sure whoever did this is long gone. This massacre didn't happen today or even yesterday."

Reyna nods, accepting that.

The baker and butcher shops are both burned down and smoking, but some niggle is telling me that I won't find my closest friends and the people who functioned as grandparents to Leisel there. No, I'll find them on the land I gifted them, in the cabin where I raised Leisel.

I know that the odds of them having survived are very slim, that they're probably dead along with their son, but I have to know for sure. I transfer Leisel from my arms to Claire's, shielding her view from the gruesome destruction surrounding us, then take off in a run, blowing through streets stained with blood and littered with human bodies, feeling tears prickle my eyes.

This feels intentional. The destruction of my home village feels like a personal sleight to me. It's not unfathomable that the vampire and dark faye targeted this village because I grew up here, and they wanted to strike a personal blow.

Once I reach the outskirts of the village and the dirt road that leads to my farm, I speed up my run to a sprint, desperate to get to my childhood home. I spot my farm in the distance, and my heart clenches when I see the fields around it, ones I spent nearly a decade farming and nurturing, have been burned to a char and defiled by my enemies. I disregard that, continuing towards my cabin. When I reach it after what feels like an eternity, I take the steps of the front porch two at a time. The front door is closed; I open it and rush in, then nearly gag at the stench of death that surrounds me. It's putrid and harsh, filling my nose and lungs with decay.

That stench is nothing compared to the scene that greets me when I walk into the living room, a sight that makes my heart drop into my stomach. The sofa in front of the fireplace has been turned around, facing the entryway of the room, and on it sit Mariketa and Parker. I feel bile rise in my throat as I take them in; their heads are severed from their necks, propped up on their laps. Their limbs have also been severed, with a bouquet of arms and legs on the floor in front of them.

I clap a hand over my mouth and shut my eyes, needing a moment to gather myself before looking again. I understand that this setup was very deliberate. Whoever did this wanted me to find my oldest friends and most trusted villagers this way; most likely, they hoped the sight would break me. It doesn't break me, though I do feel the fissures along my heart crack further and expand; instead, it angers me immensely. This is a grave insult, a horrific crime, and something that fills me with the sort of rage I've never felt before.

I have to avenge them. I *will* avenge them. I will find out who did this and fucking *annihilate* them, the same way they destroyed my village. I will hear their pleas for mercy and cries of pain for a long time before I give in to the begging and finally deal them a slow, miserable death.

I open my eyes again, feeling torn between rage and sorrow. The dark sorrow that I've only just started crawling out of threatens to swallow me whole, so instead, I lean into the fury. I let it energize and enliven me.

I pry my eyes away from Mariketa and Parker, shaking my head, silently vowing to create new forms of torture to practice on whoever did this to them. I need to give them a funeral—I need to give every villager a funeral, with special honors to Mari and Parker—but first, I need to find their son. I suspect he's also set up in some horrendous way in one of the cabin's rooms.

I check my room first, finding it's been redecorated—probably by Mariketa and Parker when they moved in—but other than a few extra knickknacks that weren't there when I left, it's empty. Leisel's room is next, and I immediately understand that Wesley's been living here; it's in the unkempt state that one might expect from a teenage boy, but I don't see the boy anywhere.

Finally, I check my painting room at the back of the cabin. It's the only door that's closed, so I steel myself with a deep breath before stepping in, knowing that what I find on the other side will probably be as horrible as the sight in the living room. I creak open the door slowly, glancing around. The room *looks* empty, but I sense a presence here. I step in and let the door close behind me, only to startle when the curtains by the window rustle, before a *living Wesley* runs from them, holding a meat cleaver and sprinting at me full speed. He lets out a battle cry, his features twisted with rage—I don't think he even takes a moment to check who I am before attacking.

I intercept the arm wielding the cleaver with a hand on his wrist when he reaches me, grip his chin with my free hand, and say very clearly, "Wesley, it's me."

The boy blinks his hazel eyes a few times, the rage clearing from them. He jerks his chin and arm from my grasp, stepping backward, looking me over slowly as if confirming that it is in fact me. He almost looks like he's seeing a ghost.

"Sierra?" he asks, quietly.

I nod, feeling choked up. "Hey, Wes. It's been a while."

I stumble back a step when he drops the cleaver and launches himself at me, wrapping his arms around my waist and holding on tight. He's taller than me and bigger than me, having been working labor since the time he could walk, but right now he seems like such a fragile, broken boy it breaks my heart even more.

I was close enough with Wesley when living in Aesara, both because of my relationship with his parents and because, despite their age difference, he was Leisel's best friend. He'd come around the farm a few times a week to take her out into the forest; more often than not I'd have him stay over for dinner. Then we'd play board games or sometimes he'd even join me for Leisel's bedtime story before returning to his parents in the village.

It breaks something inside of me to know that he's been here for who knows how long, sharing a space with the rotting bodies of his parents, clearly waiting until whoever attacked returned to kill him—otherwise, he wouldn't have been hiding with a cleaver.

"I thought you were dead," he says. "The wolves took you without even letting you or Leisel say goodbye. Mom and Dad tried to tell me you were both fine, you'd visit soon, but I didn't believe them."

I stroke a hand through his hair, letting out a long sigh. "I'm here, Wes. You're safe now. Nobody will hurt you while you have me. You have no idea how happy I am to see you."

"What about Leisel?" Wes asks, stepping back and looking around.

I scratch behind my ear. "She's back in the town. A lot's happened since I left here, Wes, but the short version is Leisel and I currently have asylum with a coven of witches who live in the northern territories of Acuria. The coven we're staying with is with her now, shielding her from seeing the sights in the village."

Wes's bottom lip trembles as he looks at me. Feeling a pang go through my chest, I tug him close and wrap an arm around his shoulder, pulling him into another hug. If he's still here, alive, I take that as a sign from fate that I was meant to find him. Which means he'll be coming with me. I owe a great debt to his parents who helped me through many difficult times, and I see this as my chance to repay it.

"How did you survive, Wes?" I ask him letting him go but keeping a hand on his arm. "From what I've seen, everyone who lived here is dead. Even people who were here trading whenever the attack happened are dead. What happened?"

"I was out in the forest hunting when it happened three days ago," Wes says. "I came home to see Mom and Dad...like they are now. I ran to the village to get help, only to find there was nobody left alive to help me. I didn't know where to go. This was the only building that remained standing, so I just came back here."

My heart clenches at that again, and I feel tears sting my eyes. This boy has been here for the last two days, entirely alone, sharing a cabin with the rotting bodies of his parents. Nobody should ever have to go through something like that. I can't even blame him for coming at me with a meat cleaver.

Poor child. He's not a child, technically. Wesley's already fifteen, but that's far too young to see the horrors he's been subjected to in the last week. I feel personally responsible for his well-being, which is why I say, "Don't look when we go out into the living room. Keep your eyes closed, I'll lead you out."

Wesley lets out a scoff, his chest puffing out. "I'm not afraid. I can handle it."

"I know you're not, Wes, and I know you can handle it," I tell him sincerely. "*I'm* afraid of you experiencing more pain than you already have. Do me a favor and turn away. I'll coordinate a burial with the witches before we leave, but for now, I can't have it on my conscience that I've subjected you to more horror. Okay?"

Wesley contemplates my words for several moments before finally nodding. "Fine. Okay."

I sling an arm around his shoulder and walk with him out into the hallway. He closes his eyes as we pass through the living room, while my eyes stray to the horrendous sight once more. I make Mariketa and Parker two silent vows as I leave; first, I will avenge them, and second, I will care for their legacy—Wesley—as if he's my own. It's the very least I can do for them and him.

Once we're outside and I've closed the door, Wes opens his eyes again. He says quietly, "Whoever came even killed the horse we bought when we sold our house in the village to move here."

I squeeze his shoulder. "We'll get you another. For now, let's go find Leisel. I'm sure she's missed you like crazy."

Once we get onto the dirt road that leads to the town, I release Wesley so we can step around ditches and loose stones on the ground.

"You left with wolves, and now you return with witches," Wesley says, confusion lacing his words. "What happened?"

I don't really want to talk about my current situation, but I figure if anyone deserves an explanation, it's Wes. This could also be a way to distract him from the reality he's been living in the last few days, which is so awful it's hard to fathom.

"Well, you know the Alpha found me to be his soulmate, just as the Beta found Leisel to be his," I tell Wes. "The wolves came up with some crafty tricks to get us to end up going with them to Kinrith, even though I won my duel. For the first little while, Leisel and I needed time to settle—it was a difficult adjustment, even living in a castle surrounded by astounding wealth."

As we walk, I regale him with tales of my time in the castle and how I ended up manning the helm to open shifters up to the possibility of alliances with different species. I tell him about the brewing war with vampires, the fact that the vamps have magic on their side in the form of dark faye and hybrids and that I thought it was necessary to get some magic on the shifter's side so Leisel and I stood a chance.

By the time I'm done with the story, we've crossed onto the cobblestone path leading into the village. Wes's jaw clenches at the sight of blood in the street and bodies and limbs strewn around everywhere, but he perseveres and continues to walk with me until we've hit the town square. Claire is right where I left her, still holding Leisel against her, with one of her hands shielding Leisel's eyes. Wes visibly perks up at seeing my sister, while all the witches gathered share questioning glances with each other. I take Wes's hand and lead him up to Odelia.

"Wes, this is the high priestess of the Nightshade Coven, Odelia. Odelia, this is Wesley. He's the son of the town baker and butcher, who Leisel and I were close with. He was out on a hunt when the attack occurred and returned once it was done to find...all of this."

Leisel gasps at my words, then breaks away from Claire. Her wide eyes zero in on Wes, thankfully not looking at the death surrounding us, and tears spark in her eyes as they stare at each other. Then Leisel sprints at Wes, leaping into his arms and hugging him tightly. I feel a smile pull on my lips as I watch them embrace—at least Leisel will finally have a friend around.

"Looks like these two are close, as well," Odelia says.

I nod. "They are. Wes, please keep Leisel's line of sight on you and not around us. Leisel, my love, you're doing very well, we'll be out of here soon."

Claire walks over to the fountain and perches on the edge of it, saying, "Things are starting to get interesting."

Ignoring that, I tell Odelia, "I can't leave Wesley here. I know it isn't fair of me to ask, but could we bring him with us?"

Odelia lets out a light laugh that confuses me. I look at her, only to see an expression of shock on her features as she stares at Wesley. "Of course, we're taking him with us," she says. "After all, a warlock belongs with his own, whether his power stems from earth or somewhere else."

"*What?*" I ask.

Chapter Six

Wesley's eyes widen as he stares at Odelia, his jaw falling open. He abruptly shuts his mouth as his eyes shutter, and he says, "I don't know what you're talking about." His arms flex around Leisel, as if holding her tighter will protect him.

"Wes," I say, my voice quiet and subdued. "We're not going to hurt you. *I'm* a witch as is Leisel. Leisel's a healer, while my powers are far more dangerous and destructive. Whatever it is you can do, *if* you have any discernible powers yet, you need to tell us."

Leisel peeks her head up from Wes's chest. She reaches her fingers up towards his cheek, where there's a small cut—probably something he got while surviving on his own these last days. She ghosts her fingers over the cut, and a golden glow sparks from them. When she removes her finger from his cheek again, it reveals smooth, unmarred skin.

Wesley blinks a few times, reaching up to touch his cheek. Then, he looks down at Leisel with an accusing stare. "You never told me you could do that." His eyes flick to me, narrowing. "You didn't say anything, either. I had to find out from my parents, and then you both just *disappeared.*"

"Not by choice," I say, a little sadly. "We left because we had to. Likewise, we hid our abilities and magical heritage from the village because I thought we had to."

"You thought right," Wesley says, tucking Leisel's head back against his chest when her eyes start to wander. "Those who knew you well stuck by your side, Sierra, such as my parents and the vendors you worked with regularly. Many others didn't. The day after your duel, the few villagers who hadn't liked that we'd been sheltering witches—earthly or not—decided to get loud about their displeasure. It's good that you left when you did because they started spreading propaganda. Mom and Dad moved away from the village and to the cabin after the mob threatened to burn our home for supporting you, even though you were gone. Things were a little tense in Aesara for a few weeks."

Claire snorts. "Yeah, humans historically don't do well with people who aren't like them. They're happy to accept our aid, but to accept *us*? Never. They won't even accept witches whose power stems from earth." She takes a few steps away from the fountain, approaching Wes. "You have power too. A power more intricately tied to earth than either of those," she says, nodding towards Leisel and me.

Wesley's eyes flicker as he looks between me, Odelia, and Claire, looking like he's deciding whether or not to trust us. I hope he trusts me for the simple fact that we were close because of his friendship with Leisel. He should know I wouldn't let anything happen to him.

Reyna sighs. "Here's the deal, kid, either tell us what you can do, or I'll have one of my sisters take a walk through your memories and we'll find out either way. Forewarning; getting your memories searched is said to be really, *really* painful."

I cast Reyna a glare before turning back to Wesley. "Nobody's going to hurt you. As far as I'm concerned, the death of your parents makes you my ward, which puts you under my protection. My protection is no small thing, Wes. Besides, if you have magic, the coven can help you grow and hone it."

"Magic is evil," Wesley hisses, and I get the vague sense he's merely repeating what he heard from the mob—words that he probably took as warnings to keep parts of himself locked away from everyone around him.

He second guesses his words before I can force him to—I see it when he looks down at Leisel, blinks, and then an expression of regret overtakes his features.

I arch an eyebrow at him. "Is it? The way I see it, *people* are either evil or they aren't. Regardless of whether they're a mythic, human, or an earth witch or warlock—monstrosity is a decision, not a nature. I, for one, can absolutely be a monster when it comes to protecting those I love. I nearly started a war using my power to protect Leisel from evil, and the only time I will use my powers is to protect those I care for. Then there's the small healer in your arms, who is the very definition of goodness in this world. If you want to talk about evil, think about the mob that villagers in Aesara formed—one that probably would've run Leisel and me out if we hadn't already left." A thought that makes my stomach clench with pain, though I try to ignore it. "Think about the people who destroyed Aesara and killed everyone here. There are many evil things in this world, Wesley, but magic isn't fucking one of them. It's simply a reality—something that you either have or you don't." I close the distance between us, crossing my arms and staring at him. "So, are you going to choose to use your power for evil, or will you train it and use it for good?"

Wesley swallows, then says, "I'll use it for good."

I nod at him. "Good decision. What is it you can do?"

Wesley's eyes stray to Claire for a moment before returning to me. "It started a few weeks after you left when I was on a hunt with Dad. I was clumsy and not my usual self—I felt sort of fuzzy and just...off. After failing to get my third rabbit with my bow and arrow, I got pretty mad. Dad tried to tell me we all have our bad days, but then, the ground started to shake beneath our feet. We thought it was an earthquake at first—I started to get worried, and the more scared I got the harder the ground shook, until trees started falling. I figured if I was going to die in an earthquake, I didn't want to die a coward, so I calmed myself down and waited for the earthquake to either stop or take me. As soon as I calmed, the ground stopped shaking.

"I didn't think anything of it that time; figured the earthquake had just ended. Then, a while later, one of the people who were talking badly about you and Leisel came to Dad's butcher shop while I was working. The idiot started spewing his usual nonsense, even said he'd have hurt you if you'd stayed here. When he mentioned some terrible things about Leisel, I lost it. I was ready to put my cleaver through his back to get him to shut up but before I could, *another* earthquake started up. That time I somehow knew it was me. I calmed myself down and the earthquake stopped. Dad chased the asshole out of the shop, then gave me a look that said he knew too. We moved to your cabin after that, away from the villagers."

I find myself somewhat awe-struck that Aesara's played host to several magical beings whose magic stems from earth and nature. I'm equally as amazed by Wesley's power; having control over the earth as an element, to the extent where his anger makes it shake, is beyond impressive. The fact that he figured out how to calm himself to avoid disaster is even more impressive.

Odelia closes the distance between her and Wesley, and places a hand on Wes's shoulder, causing Wes to tense, though he doesn't move away. Her eyes flutter closed, and I assume she's trying to get a better sense of his magical capabilities. She did the same to me and Leisel when we first came to her coven. After a few moments, her eyes snap wide open, and she takes a quick step back. "You're not just a warlock whose power lies with earth," she says, cautiously. "The elements favor you. I can feel it."

"What does that mean?" I ask her.

Odelia blinks several times before looking to me. "Warlocks and witches whose power stems from the earth aren't just accidents of nature; nothing is an accident when it comes to nature. The energy and elements of earth are living, sentient beings, and on occasion, they'll choose to favor a person and infuse them with magic. That's how magical bloodlines are started in this realm." She looks back to Wesley, blinking. "You...gods, you're the first of a bloodline. You were handpicked in a way no other living being has been in a very, *very* long time."

She shakes her head, taking another step back. "I thought the earth stopped infusing power into humans long ago, simply allowing the existing bloodlines to either continue or die out. Apparently the magic of this realm isn't done with its native residents quite yet. Interesting."

I'm fascinated with the information on how earthly witches, and warlocks, are created, and also a little curious as to what it could mean. I don't know *exactly* how far back my bloodline goes, who was the original witch, but my mother told me her bloodline has been producing witches for centuries. Wesley's blood was entirely human until nature took a liking to him and decided to make him into something more.

"That can only mean one thing," Claire says, speculatively. "This planet, the magic on it, knows we're about to go to war and it's creating soldiers to protect it. You might be the first, Wesley, and possibly the only so far, but I don't think you'll be the last."

"If this planet is gearing up for war as much as the beings on it, then that means whatever's coming is going to be very bad," Reyna mutters grimly. "I expected one hell of a war filled with battles, but if Earth and

Mother Nature herself are intervening, that means the battles will end up threatening the very existence of this planet."

"I'll communicate with my counterpart in Sukarmir," Odelia says. "Let them know to be on the lookout." Noticing my puzzled expression, she explains, "The land that was once Russia has now become an empire to witches called Sukarmir. I'm on good working terms with their covens; they'll appreciate the heads up."

Claire wanders off towards one of the half-burned and overturned vendor carts, eyes narrowed. After a few seconds, she hisses, and says, "The sigil of the dark faye, and the royal vampire seal. They're the ones who did this. Those fucking *imbeciles*—this is their declaration of war, combined with a slaughter to mark the first battle."

I stride up to her, looking at the vendor cart. Like she said, there are two symbols painted on the side of the cart in blood; one that looks somewhat like a scorpion, another that just seems to be a nonsensical conglomeration of scribbles.

"Why here?" I ask. "Why would they start a war in a human village? They're not fighting humans, they'll be fighting witches and shifters."

Claire bends down to pick up a piece of loose paper stuck under the side of the cart, one I hadn't noticed until now. She unfolds it, and her eyes scan the contents before she releases another louder hiss. She hands the page over to me, and I feel my gut churn as I read the scribbled words.

To the Queen of Mutts,

Blood for blood. You take something from us, we take something from you.

Looking forward to our upcoming battles and to ensuring your destruction and the decimation of all you hold dear,

Rhaelar

I swallow several times then crumple the piece of paper in my fist. This was a deliberate provocation directed solely at me, just as I suspected. An entire village of humans died because of *me*. I inhale a deep breath, trying to ward off the guilt that washes over me.

"Who's Rhaelar?" I ask, looking to Odelia.

She pales. "The vampire king."

So, somehow, the vampire royal family learned that I was the one who killed Kyron, and their revenge came in the form of destroying my home village, probably in an attempt to weaken or break me. The thing is, the massacre surrounding me doesn't fill me with in-consolable, insurmountable grief. It fills me with pure, unadulterated rage. I want to destroy the people who did this, and I have every intention of doing so.

Reyna walks up to me and snatches the piece of paper from my grip, giving it a quick once-over. Once she's done, she hands it off to Odelia.

"This won't go unanswered," Reyna tells me. "We'll take revenge on behalf of all lives lost and blood spilled here. There will soon be rivers of vampire and dark faye blood decorating streets, and they will learn the true meaning of fear."

"Yes," I agree. "They most certainly will."

Maddy whistles from where she stands at the edge of the town square, beside the burned-down butcher shop. Everyone looks in her direction; she tips her chin to the side and says, "We've got company. Rockwell wolves."

I tense, my thoughts speeding up until they're racing a mile a minute. Last night, Wyatt told me of reports he heard of disruptions and smoke coming from Aesara; it's not unbelievable that he or Cam-den may have sent out their own unit to follow up on those reports. The terrible nature of the timing, overlapping with our visit here, is simply a bad stroke of luck. I don't want to be anywhere near Rockwell wolves right now—I'm still too raw and too angry to face any of them.

"Let's go, before they see us," I say, my voice coated with urgency.

Maddy winces. "Yeah, too late. They've already scented us; if we leave now it could be seen as cowardice."

"More, it's a good time to convene with the wolves and discuss our next steps," Odelia says, shooting me an apologetic glance. "I know you don't want to, Sierra, but we need them as much as they need us. The shifter population is twice the size of the witch population; we need their manpower."

From a logical perspective, I understand Odelia's stance and her need to use her new alliance with shifters to her advantage. However, my thinking right now is less logical and more enraged. Whether or not the witches need them, *I* don't want to be anywhere near them. I don't want to see any Rockwell wolves, or any shifters at all for that matter. Presently, I can't stand the thought of them. When I think of the Rockwell Pack, I think of the expression of sheer rage on Camden's face when his hand was around my throat and he was choking the life from me, directly after I found out I miscarried. In one of my most painful, vulnerable moments, he brought me more pain and heartache—I can't get over that. I don't know that I'll ever be able to because that one act proved just how right I was to distrust and stay away from him.

I feel stupid for having given him as much of myself as I did; I feel like a silly, naïve child who started giving in to the life of luxury provided for me by my status as the King Alpha's mate—I started believing we could do good work together and make positive changes. In return for my faith, I was nearly killed. I won't be stupid enough to misplace my faith a second time.

Still, Reyna's right; witches can't afford to be seen as cowards right now, especially with the pack to whom our treaty is bound. So, I shore up my strength and pull Leisel from Wesley's arms into mine.

I put my hand on Wesley's shoulders, tucking Leisel's head into my chest. "Don't talk, don't stare at the shifters for too long, and do your best to avoid notice."

Wesley doesn't argue, thank heavens. Instead, he gives me a single nod, then moves several paces away to hover by the fountain, just in time for me to hear the nearby click-clack of horse hooves on cobblestone. I inhale a deep breath, closing my eyes to try to summon enough strength to get through this bullshit, then open them back up in time to see several shifters ride into the town square on horses.

When I see Aspen, a shifter who I dueled with in an attempt to escape mating with Camden my last time in Aesara, I tense. Camden once told me that Aspen is one of the warriors who he takes with him wherever he goes for protection; if she's here, it stands to reason that he's here as well. My grip tightens on Leisel and breathing becomes difficult as my throat constricts, as if in remembrance of what happened the last time I was with Camden.

To my horror, my eyes start to sting with tears, and I have to blink several times to force them away. Along with the memory of nearly dying comes a fresh wave of pain and a sense of failure, because what led up to my disastrous encounter with Camden was a group of rogues deciding that they hated witches so much they couldn't stand the thought of one reproducing.

I train my gaze on the ground in an attempt to avoid losing my shit altogether, because if I look at the shifters right now, there's every chance that things will start burning to ash. I feel my fire rise within me, intense and violent and *so angry*—angrier than I've ever felt it. It's almost as if the black fire that lives within me has turned into its own entity—the rage I feel emanating from it is something I never thought was possible, which worries me as much as it should.

I look at Odelia when she claps her hands together several times, slowly, before saying, "How very like shifters to arrive late to the party. Camden, I'd say it's lovely to see you, but it truly isn't."

I tense even further at the mention of Camden's name, and my fire pushes against my skin so hard I have to release Leisel for fear that it'll come tearing out of me and, gods forbid, harm the small healer in my arms.

Reyna, who's standing a few feet away from me, wordlessly pulls Leisel into her arms, giving me a nod that silently transmits she understands how close I am to losing my shit, and has my back. Leisel stays silent as she has been for the last little while, probably lost in her own thoughts.

"Lovely to see you, too, high priestess." The sound of Camden's voice raises the fine hairs on the back of my neck.

Underneath my current hatred of him is a small bit of longing—the tiniest part of me that misses the illusion I had with him for a little while, the illusion of a better life and better future than what I would've had in Aesara. The lie I bought into, the one that made me believe I had sway and power, when seemingly I was only ever a pawn to give Camden heirs. When I failed in that duty, his response was attempted murder.

"Sierra," Camden says. I don't look in the direction of his voice; I'm pretty sure seeing him will kick my fire into overdrive and bring it out of me, whether I want it to or not. Granted, my fire is incapable of hurting him, but it could very well hurt the people around me.

"Don't presume to speak her name," Odelia says, her voice little more than a threatening hiss. "You speak with me. You lost the right to address your mate when you made a mockery of the sacred bond."

Warmth fills me at hearing just how protective Odelia is of me, though we've only known each other for a short time. It makes sense; witches are notoriously protective of their own, as they've had to be to avoid persecution from other Mythics who fear their power.

I hear the sounds of fabric and saddles shifting, along with footsteps along the cobblestone that inform me the wolves have dismounted their horses. More, I feel Camden moving closer; the chasm in my chest expands, swallowing my rage, replacing it with a forlorn feeling of numbness where there was once a vibrant, steady connection between him and me. Granted, that higher state of the bond only lasted about a week before he all but destroyed it.

I hear Wyatt's voice say testily, "Cam."

Leisel, still wrapped in Reyna's arms, lets out a soft gasp at Wyatt's voice and the approaching footsteps stop just as the witches all gather in front of me, presenting a unified front of solidarity that makes my heart warm. My eyes flick to my sister as she peeks over her shoulder to look at Wyatt, and her eyes brighten with excitement. That excitement dims as she looks over to me, a frown marring her youthful features. I can sense from her nonverbal cues that she wants to go to him, but she doesn't want to offend or hurt me.

Reyna arches a questioning brow at me, silently requesting permission. I incline my head once because I saw last night just how happy Leisel was simply speaking to Wyatt. I don't have it in me to deprive her of happiness simply because I'm wounded and upset.

Reyna clears her throat. "You, Beta, can approach. The rest of you, stay the fuck back."

I look at Wyatt as he rounds the barrier made up of witches and approaches Leisel.

"Just don't let her see the carnage," I say.

I know that at this point Leisel has gotten at least a few glimpses of our surroundings—it's inevitable with how long we've been here—but I want to minimize her exposure to the terrible sights.

Wyatt nods at me, giving me a small smile, before approaching Reyna.

"Hey, trouble," he says fondly. "I've missed you."

Reyna loosens her hold on Leisel, allowing Leisel to spin around and face Wyatt. She blinks several times as she looks at him, and then says, "I've missed you too." With that, she leaps into his arms. He catches her with a small chuckle, and the sight of their embrace is at once heartwarming and heart-wrenching. Heartwarming because I can feel the strength of their connection; there's nothing romantic about it, but I can tell they both have deep regard for each other. Heart-wrenching because right now they're acting as the very symbols of what I've lost, and that hurts.

Judging by the soft noise of pain that escapes Camden, he's thinking along the same lines. I wrap my arms around my waist, feeling terribly cold and empty all of a sudden.

Needing a distraction, I tell the witches, "You guys have fun parlaying, I'm going to go start digging graves for the fallen."

Wes steps forward at that. "I'll come with you."

"So will I," Claire says. "I know a spell that'll expedite things, and another that can get bodies from point A to point B with relative ease."

Deciding that the first graves I'll dig will be for Mariketa and Parker, two people who made my life in Aesara fruitful and bearable, I nod. I don't want to do this task alone; it'll be a painful one, but it's necessary nonetheless. I need to say goodbye, as does Wes. We have to honor our past before looking to the future.

Chapter Seven

The burned land outside my cabin is quickly transformed into a graveyard. Claire performs an incantation to animate a few shovels lying around the toolshed by my cabin making them self-sufficient, digging holes without needing a person to lift and maneuver them. The graves still take time to finish, but within ten minutes, the first of them are dug. Claire performs another spell that transports the bodies and limbs of Mariketa and Parker into the graves without us having to do the gruesome task of moving them.

All the while, Wesley stands beside me, and I feel the depth of his grief. When he looks down at his mom and dad, resting in their graves, a few silent tears roll down his cheeks. I wipe them away and pull him close, letting him know that he isn't alone. Not anymore. He now has the protection of a powerful coven, not to mention the status as my ward. I wasn't kidding when I told him I consider him my ward now; I feel responsible for him.

It's not just a sense of responsibility or duty I feel to him, however. There's a great deal of affection both for him and his late parents that makes having him as a part of my makeshift family an honor, not a hardship, and I tell him as much, which calms the worst of the fear in his eyes, though it doesn't take care of the sorrow.

Once all the graves are dug, Claire returns to the village to start transporting bodies, leaving Wes and me to say goodbye to his parents alone. I start to cry; I've never been good with goodbyes, and yet I've had to say goodbye to almost every person I've ever cared for, except for Leisel.

I had to say goodbye to my parents when I was little more than a child, both of them taken from me before their time because humans didn't have the proper resources to care for them. My father's cancer took him from me, and the hemorrhage my mother experienced on the birthing bed while bringing Leisel into this world took her from me. Then Camden and his pack came along and took my home and only friends from me. Now, I'll never see them again. I'll never get to break bread with Mariketa or Parker, see the shimmer of pride in Parker's eyes when I bring him a particularly good haul after a bountiful hunt, or feel Mariketa's maternal affection as she slips extra cookies or an additional loaf of bread into my weekly order.

"They loved you like you were their own, you know," Wes says quietly. "Talked about you all the time, even after you left. Dad told me that he promised your father to look after you before your dad passed, and he took that as a great honor. Mom adored you and Leisel beyond words. They were crushed when you left, and so grateful that you passed your legacy in Aesara onto our family."

"I loved them, as well," I say, my voice choked up. I didn't even realize how much I loved them until this moment. "They took care of my legacy when I left. Now it's my turn to take care of theirs. You'll be safe with me, Wes, I'll make sure of it."

He takes my hand in his, holding it in a tight grip, his features twisted in pain. "They didn't deserve to die. Not like this, not with such dishonor. Decapitated and dismembered as if they were nothing when they were everything."

"They were," I agree, squeezing his hand. "Your father would've been proud to see you running at me with a meat cleaver earlier—butcher's boy through and through."

A small, sad smile spreads on his lips. "Yeah, that one would've been right up Dad's alley."

"Every time he talked about you it was with such pride," I tell Wes earnestly. "Each week when I'd bring him my haul, he'd have something new to say about you; usually something along the lines of your growth and strength. You were his pride and joy. Your mother's too, though she often worried about how thin you were."

Wes's smile expands. "She worried that a gust of wind would blow you and Leisel away too. Unless you're round as a wheel, my mom would assume you're malnourished and underweight."

"The nature of bakers, I think," I say, fond memories with Mariketa overtaking the worst of my grief. "Your mom taught me how to take care of babies. When Leisel was first born, I was only fourteen. Didn't know how to properly bundle and hold her, let alone feed her, calm her, or put her to sleep. Three days with your mother in the house with Leisel and me, and suddenly I knew everything about babies. Leisel always adored your parents."

"And they adored her," Wes responds. "She's a good kid. Smart, clever, and quick to pick up on things. Never managed to get her to like hunting, though I did my best. Dad did too."

I let out a small, weak laugh. "Yeah, as a natural healer, inflicting harm will never come easy to her. She was put on this earth to fix people and animals, not hurt them."

Wes takes a few steps forward, as do I. We gaze down at his parents together, each of us lost in thought. Tears continue to streak down Wesley's cheek, just as they do mine. Mariketa and Parker left a profound mark on my life, and taught me the value of friendship and family—they largely helped turn me into the person I am today. Saying goodbye to them is no easy task.

"Thank you," I say quietly, "for everything you taught me, for all the ways you helped me. A big chunk of who I am is owed to the both of you. You will not be forgotten, and I vow to bring you the honor in death that I could not in life. You will not go unavenged."

A choked sound escapes Wes, as he gives me a look that's at once filled with pain for his loss and gratitude for my being here with him, and for my words. He turns back to his parents. "Hope there's plenty of game to hunt wherever you are now, Dad. Mom, I'm sure you'll have everyone in the afterlife scrambling for a batch of your cookies." He inhales a deep breath. "Until we meet again."

With that, he releases my hand and grabs one of the shovels that are discarded, lying on the ground, and begins shoveling dirt back into the grave. I pick up another and join him, feeling my heart ache as I cover the bodies of the people who made my life in Aesara bearable with dirt. We could let the bespelled shovels do this job, but there's catharsis in doing the task ourselves.

Once we're done, Wesley looks at me, and this time, there's anger twisting his expression rather than sorrow. "Whoever did this, tell me we'll make them pay."

"We will," I promise him. "In the most painful way possible, we will. But you need to understand, Wes, the people who did this...they're evil, cruel, and more powerful than I know. The war that this massacre commenced will not be an easy one. It will not be a matter of vampires fighting wolves or dark faye fighting witches—the whole world will be pulled into the conflict. I expect each Mythic species will declare for one side or the other, and there will be bloodshed on every continent, but most especially in Acuria. Our enemies will probably come here first. I don't want to pull you into something blind, so I need you to understand the magnitude of what's impending."

"I don't care," Wesley says emphatically. "I'm not afraid."

"I am," I admit. "I'm fucking terrified, Wes. I was terrified when it was just Leisel I had to protect, but now with you…I'm so, *so* afraid I won't be able to keep you safe. If you want to participate in battle, there's no chance for me to guarantee your safety—it would be difficult to guarantee it if you decided to sit the whole thing out. I know you want revenge, and I promise you I'll get it, but if you want to join me in taking it, you need to understand the risks. I'll do everything in my power to protect you, but in war, a great deal is decided by chance, not by intent."

Wesley nods. "I get it," he tells me. "I still want to fight."

I let out a long breath. "We'll see how you do in training."

"My dad taught me how to fight," Wesley says. "He had to declare duelum in his youth to get away from a shifter of his own, claiming he was her mate. He won his duel by a stroke of luck, then spent two hours every day training with swords, every single day for the rest of his life. He started training me with swords when I was eight. I'm not a novice."

"Sword training won't get you very far up against creatures who move with the sort of speed the human eye can't track. A sword won't be able to deflect a spell—"

"Actually, that's not true," Odelia calls out. I turn around to see that she, Claire, and Reyna had made their approach while I was busy with my impassioned rant on the potential dangers of war. Reyna's holding Leisel's hand, and my sister's eyes are finally uncovered. Fine by me, since there's no carnage out here to see, so long as she doesn't go back into the cabin where the stench of death lingers along with bloodstains.

"What do you mean?" Wesley asks Odelia.

She gives him a smile, trekking closer with her entourage of witches. "There are spells that can be done on swords made with certain materials. Spells that make the sword capable of deflecting magic."

"I stand corrected," I admit. "I guess there are spells that can make your sword more powerful, but even still...that's not enough. You need to get trained in the magical arts, Wes."

"As do you," Odelia tells me. "You need to train up your fire to be able to better control it, and start on learning many other forms of magic. Claire specializes in fire; she can help you with that. Reyna will help you with combat magic—that's a specialty of hers. We also have a warlock who specializes in tactile combat magic, Cedrick. You'll learn from him as well. As for me, I'll be teaching you the basics of magic. Magical theory, if you will; spells are only the surface level of magic, it's important to understand how they work and what drives them. Usually young witches and warlocks start by learning the mechanics behind spell work and then work their way up to higher magical arts. Things will be a little backward with you, Sierra, especially since we're now officially in wartime."

As long as I learn how to wield and fully utilize the magical arts, I can't say I particularly care which order I learn them.

"When do we start training?" I ask Odelia.

She smiles. "As soon as we return. I'll introduce both of you to the Nightshade warlocks, and they'll take you on, Wes. We have some phenomenal warlock teachers; you'll be in good hands."

"Will I still be near Leisel and Sierra?" Wes asks.

Odelia nods. "Yes, we'll all reside in the same mountain and cavern system, so they'll never be more than a ten-minute walk away." Then she says to me, "I spoke with Camden and Wyatt about sending extra protection to the remaining human villages, to ensure something like this doesn't happen again. There's a good possibility that the dark faye and vampires don't intend for humanity to survive the upcoming war—"

"That can't be allowed to happen," I say.

Another nod. "I know, and it won't, which is why people will be sent to protect them."

"I don't know that humans will accept the protections of Mythics," Wesley says, scratching his head. "We...*they* aren't exactly on good terms with your species. You know, with the mass slaughter and near-extinction and all."

"Witches have never targeted humans or singled them out," Reyna says. "In fact, we've made a pointed effort to give them aid in these difficult times."

"I'm not sure that matters," I add, agreeing with Wesley. "They see Mythics as Mythics, and to them, all Mythics are monsters."

Growing up in Aesara, I was privy to the human mindset of hating all mythics, regardless of their species or faction. I can't exactly blame humans for their hatred, considering Mythics took the world that was theirs to begin with from them. Granted, there's the fact that humans didn't exactly do a good job taking care of this world to consider, but that doesn't excuse the mass persecution they've had to endure. As the weakest species left on the proverbial food chain, they've functioned as bitches to mythics for centuries now.

"What about you?" Odelia asks me. "What if we sent you with wolves and witches and whatever reinforcements we can spare to protect them? You could explain that our intent right now is to preserve them, not harm them."

I shrug. "I can try, but I don't see what reason they'd have to believe me. I'm technically the Queen of Shifters, and I'm an earthly witch who's mated to a wolf. From what Wes told me, my being an earthly witch was enough to turn a good deal of people in Aesara against me. It stands to reason I'll be regarded with similar distaste in other places as well."

Reyna lets out a sigh. "All we can do is try. Worse comes to worst, we'll protect them from a distance—hover in the background in case danger arrives, ready to intervene."

"Now that that's settled, what method of revenge are we thinking?" Claire asks. When I give her a quizzical look, she shrugs. "The destruction of Aesara was a personal strike at you, Sierra. If we don't take swift revenge, the opposition will assume they can get away with pulling shit like this."

She's right, I realize, and we can't let that happen. If there isn't a quick, deadly response to this, it'll give the dark faye and vampires the impression that they can get away with slaughtering human villages, which I will not stand for.

Odelia lets out a thoughtful hum. "They destroyed a village on our continent, it would only be fair if we return the favor." She tilts her head to the side, contemplating. "If the vampires and dark faye have officially allied, which considering the note we found and the reports I've been getting, they have, then they'll have strongholds as bases—probably more than one. There's a Nightshade warlock who specializes in tracking and locating, I'll ask him to find the locations and numbers of our opposition's strongholds. Once we have that information, we can decide where to hit them."

"Or we can send a message another way, without having to leave our continent," I suggest, an idea formulating in my mind. "It doesn't seem like what the vamps and dark faye did to Aesara will be the last time they target a human village in Acuria. If that's the case, the next time they step foot on this land we cut them off and destroy whatever group we happen upon, sending a very clear message to Rhaelar that trespassing will be met with swift, deadly retribution."

"Even better," Odelia agrees, a smile pulling at her lips. "Defending our territory and causing bloodshed; our coven will certainly be glad with that. I'll see if I can get any information on the future movements of the vamps and dark faye."

"We need to get back," Reyna says, looking up into the sky and at the sun, which has just started to lower on the horizon. "We've been gone nearly all day, and there's no way to know for sure that enemies won't return here." She turns to look at me and tacks on, "Both vampires and dark faye are creatures of the night; they're most powerful when it's dark out. That's when they carry out most of their attacks."

"Excellent way to catch enemies unaware," Claire says, nodding. At Reyna's glare, she shrugs. "What? It's true. I exploded the volcano on that rogue pack after sunset, when they were fighting over dinner instead of paying attention to their surroundings."

Claire's a strategic thinker, with a sort of darkness to her strategy that I have to respect. She's led a very difficult life, the details of which I don't know but am becoming more and more curious about. One of these days, I'll need to get her drunk and get a retelling of her life story.

"Are the witches back in the town square ready to go?" I ask Odelia.

She exchanges a glance with Reyna that makes me nervous before turning back to me and clearing her throat. "Camden's being rather insistent that he speak with you before we disappear. I had the others stay behind to magically bar him from following us. They set up a sigil in the town square to trap him, we'll need to go to them before teleporting out."

It brings the smallest bit of amusement and satisfaction to me, hearing that Camden's trapped in place and unable to get what he wants. There was a time when he'd trapped me where I didn't want to be and prevented me from getting what I wanted back; my freedom and my life in Aesara. I no longer crave those things. I've outgrown them and seen too much of the ugliness of the world to go back to my naivety, but I was once desperate for them and Camden took me away from the life I knew and loved.

On the heels of my satisfaction, however, is a small ache in my chest, coming from the chasm. It's an ache that silently transmits that I shouldn't enjoy the pain and difficulties of my mate, regardless of the pain and difficulties he's brought me. Thankfully, his actions have made it rather easy to ignore that ache.

"Let's finish up with the bodies and graves, then we can go," Claire says.

I'm grateful that she's committed to giving everyone who died, even the people who likely would've tried to kill Leisel and me if we'd stayed in Aesara, a proper burial. I suspect that Claire's actions are primarily for my sake; after all, she has no personal attachment to the villagers.

Leisel walks up to me and takes my hand, looking at the fresh graves that Wes and I just finished filling, the ones that hold Mariketa and Parker. She crouches down, puts her hand on top of the soil, and says, "I'll miss you so much. Thank you for everything, and for bringing us Wesley."

My heart clenches at the pain in her words. I'm not even sure how Leisel can identify that these graves hold Mari and Parker—after all, I kept her away from the cabin and have tried to shield her from seeing the worst of the sights. Most likely, she used deductive reasoning—after all, Wes's parents would get priority out of all the villagers.

Once Leisel stands up, silent tears rolling down her cheeks, her eyes red-rimmed, Wesley pulls her into his arms before I can. My heart warms at the sight, and I silently echo Leisel's gratitude to her honorary grandparents. Wes's survival really does seem like a gift from the gods.

Chapter Eight

Over the next half hour, as the sun sets, the witches work together to magically transport the bodies into their graves, and then fill all of them back up. By the time we're done, darkness has fallen, and the moon has risen along with many glittering stars becoming visible. Then it's time to return to the town square where Camden is still trapped.

I walk behind the pack of witches, because I really, *really* don't want to look at or interact with my so-called mate. I'm still extremely raw from our last encounter where he almost killed me. I don't want to face him. If I had it my way, I might never have to face him again.

I know that's impossible, however. My emotions towards Camden, though primarily negative, have been ambivalent. Last night I found myself missing him for a brief moment, even while I'm so furious with him I want to tear him in half. I realize that a great deal of my anger comes from the fact that what he did ruined us when we were just starting to truly come together. I was beginning to trust him, even rely on him in some ways, and he showed me how utterly wrong I was to do so. I resent him for the fact that I've lost him more than anything else.

As we walk down the dirt road to the village, me holding one of Leisel's hands and Wes holding the other, I can't stop my thoughts from flickering back to the times I had with Camden that were good. The majority of our time together was combative, but there were also a few moments where I felt so connected to him, so in tune with him, it almost felt like I'd found my home. I hadn't realized it at the time, but when his father passed away and I held him close, trying to chase away some of his grief, I felt like we were finally on the same wavelength.

I spent much of my time in the castle resenting my new position and frantically trying to protect Leisel, but I also learned a good deal about Camden. Not just from Camden himself but from his brother and the Rockwell Pack's witch doctor, Claude. Camden and I have a lot more in common than I assumed upon first meeting him. He lost his mother as a child and grew up too fast after that. Likewise, I lost my parents as a child and became a mother the day mine died. I learned the true meaning of responsibility before I even learned how to deal with menstruation.

As furious as I am with Camden, and as *sad* as I am beneath that fury, I can't hate him. I know too much about him to hate him. He's a good ruler to his people, has values he sticks to and lives by that have helped his people prosper. He's insular and hot-headed, sure, but so am I. Before he did what he did, I was starting to understand that fate matched us well together. Then I understood that fate didn't take into account the danger of a wolf in a rage.

When I come upon the town square, I see the faint outline of a shimmering shield surrounding the space—one that I presume prevents the wolves from leaving. Maddy's sitting on the edge of the fountain, looking bored as Aspen rants at her to let them out. She pauses as we approach though, shooting me a scathing glare that I ignore.

Wyatt's leaning against an overturned vendor cart, staring off into space. Camden's standing by his horse, arms folded across his chest, appearing to be lost in thought. His eyes snap up the moment I step through the faintly visible shield and into the town square, and I see so many emotions in the silver-blue orbs of his eyes. Regret, longing, and even the glimmer of affection that I'd become accustomed to. Instead of pissing me off, it just makes me sad. I've had an awful day and some part of me craves being held and comforted right now, but I don't have that luxury. Instead, I'm the one who needs to hold and comfort both Leisel and the newest addition to our family, Wesley.

Wesley's grip tightens on Leisel protectively as we near the wolves, pulling her away from me and into him. Wyatt notices the exchange and his eyebrows furrow before he gives me a questioning look. He might not have any romantic sentiments towards my sister as of yet, and won't for quite some time, but our time in the castle taught me that he's extremely protective of her and cares for her deeply.

I need to parlay with one of the wolves if even for a moment to discuss steps moving forward, so I crook my finger at Wyatt in a gesture inviting him to approach. He looks mildly surprised at that, which makes sense—if today had turned out in any way other than how it did, I would be running far away from the wolves. Unfortunately, I understand their necessity and usefulness in the battles to come.

Camden tries to approach as well, but three witches physically shield him from doing so, one of them being Maddy, which gives me room to focus on Wyatt.

He stops in front of me, casting another frown at Wes, who in turn glares at Wyatt.

"Wyatt, this is Wesley," I introduce tiredly. "He was the son of Mariketa and Parker, my closest friends in the village. Now he's my ward."

Wyatt tilts his head to the side, considering Wesley, before asking me, "Is he even young enough to be your ward?"

"Yes," I respond. "We're heading back to the coven territory soon. There's some concern that the dark faye and vampires will target human villages." I fill him in on our intentions, specifically those involving me joining the witches in an attempt to get humans to accept the aid they'll be offered. I might not be humanity's biggest fan on account of the way they nearly destroyed this planet, but I still see the value in their existence, unlike some mythics.

Once I'm done, Wyatt nods. "Fine. We can arrange for some wolves to travel with you for protection when you venture around the human-populated areas."

I shake my head. "Please don't. Humans might dislike witches on the principle of them being mythics, but they absolutely despise shifters. If they sense a shifter in their midst, they won't let us anywhere near them."

Wyatt clenches his jaw but gives me a single, tense nod. Then, unsurprisingly, he asks, "When can I see Leisel again?"

"In person? No idea. As for through your mirrors, I'll open the connection nightly after dinner," I respond.

Wyatt blinks slowly, looking surprised. "You'd do that for me?"

I laugh. "Not for you, Wyatt. I'm still not feeling the happiest with you. I will open the mirrors for the sake of my sister. You can thank her for that."

Wyatt nods. "Fair enough." After a pause, he says hesitantly, "Camden's not in good shape, Sierra. I know you have no desire to speak with him or be near him, but I'd be remiss if I didn't ask you to at least once. He's been a wreck since you left."

The ache in my chest returns with a vengeance, and the chasm there reminds me exactly why I left; for literal fear of my life. While the logical part of me understands that Camden is a wolf who was in a rage when he hurt me, the fact remains that he did hurt me, almost fatally. If anyone else had done that, I'd have my fire swallow them whole and be done with the matter. As that isn't an option with my mate, I'll settle for staying as far away from him as fucking possible. I know that's not a permanent or even long-term solution—I won't be able to avoid him forever, despite the tattered state of our bond—but it's all I have in me to do right now.

"Perhaps he can reflect on exactly why I felt the need to leave," I say. I mean for the words to come out harsh, but instead, they sound hollow and sad.

"What happened?" Wesley asks, eyebrows furrowing.

Leisel's brows draw together as she looks down at her feet, biting her lip. She's the reason I survived Camden's rage; she healed me after the fact.

"It doesn't matter," I tell Wes. "Suffice to say, my trust and faith were betrayed in a way that can't be undone."

I tense when I see Camden forcibly break through the witches holding him at bay. He calls out my name, a look of almost feral desperation in his eyes that tells me he's gearing up to fight anyone holding me back from him. That fight would be up against creatures of magic who can destroy him with little more than a thought, the idea of which doesn't sit well with me. No matter how I feel, I don't want him dead.

Reyna's hands start to crackle with blue magic as she stares at Camden, an evil smile curling her lips—one I'm sure she wears during battle—and I stop her by holding up a hand and shaking my head. She looks disappointed as the magic disappears from her palms.

I come to an abrupt understanding; no matter how much I don't want to speak with or be near Camden right now, he won't let up until I do. It might be in my best interest to just get it over with. If I don't now, I expect he'll start crashing on Wyatt's time talking to

Leisel, escalating in the way he's prone to doing when he doesn't get what he wants.

Camden stops ten feet away from me, chest heaving as he stares at me. "Sierra." My name sounds like both a plea and prayer on his lips, and despite myself, it sends a shiver down my spine.

I sigh. "If I give you five minutes, will you *please* leave me alone?"

His Adam's apple bobs as he swallows, giving me a single nod. I feel myself deflate as I say, "Fine."

Chapter Nine

I look to Odelia, who's staring at me with raised eyebrows and an expression that looks to be simultaneously impressed and questioning.

I call out, "Start preparations to head out, I'll be with you in a moment." Then I tell Wes, "Watch Leisel. She's your charge." He gives me a firm nod, which Wyatt frowns at, probably not liking the fact that somebody else is doing the job of protecting his mate.

The witches gather together by the fountain and Wes walks Leisel over to them. Wyatt wanders off to the other side of the town square, giving me the illusion of privacy with Camden even though I know there is none. That's fine by me; I feel more comfortable with people around us, ready to intervene should Camden go into another rage and try to finish what he started. I don't think he will; I can see his regret from his expression alone, but regret isn't enough to wipe away what he did.

Camden takes a few steps forward, but I halt him with a raised hand. "That's close enough, thanks."

"Sierra," he says, quietly, "I never meant to hurt you. I'm so sorry that I did."

I give a forced nonchalant shrug. "Yeah. Shit happens. That's the nature of shifters, right? Prone to rages where you might as well be rogue."

Pain seeps into Camden's expression, and I hate the fact that it brings me pain to see that. I hate everything about this situation; I hate that he's here right now when he should be tucked away in his castle outside Kinrith, the shifter capital on this continent. I hate everything right now, but I still can't manage to hate him.

"I don't have any excuse for my actions—I can't give you that. What I can give you is a vow to never hurt you again, so long as we both live."

I stare at him in silence for several moments before a low, cruel laugh bubbles out of my chest. "I thought matehood came with that vow innately, Camden. I thought that mythics protected their other halves, but you proved me wrong. I think a lot of literature on your kind will need to be rewritten, given the actions of their king."

I mean for my words to be harsh, but instead, they come out sounding sad and somewhat broken. My pain is evident in my tone, which I *despise* myself for. I hate that I feel so weak when it comes to him. The only other person I've ever been vulnerable for is my sister, and that's because she's the light of my life, as well as my life's purpose. For many years, I genuinely believed I was put on this earth to care for her, protect her, love her, and raise her—then Camden came along and it became clear that while my sister is one of my purposes in this world, she is not my only purpose.

For a while, I thought my purpose was to show shifters a better way, to help lead them in the darkness of the war that's been brewing ever since the mythic invasion. For the briefest sliver of a moment, I believed that my purpose was also to be a champion of both humans and even some mythics—to unite species who'd previously only known strife in an attempt to ensure their survival. Camden proved me wrong in the span of a few minutes, and that crushed me.

"It's a horrible excuse, but in that moment, I wasn't in my right mind. I didn't know my own strength; even in my rage I never would've killed you. I didn't even think I was hurting you—I just meant to scare you," Camden says, taking a step towards me. I take a step back, not wanting him any closer than he already is.

"You say you never would've killed me in the same breath as you didn't think you were hurting me," I point out flatly. "Which is it, Camden? Seems like you might not ever *intentionally* kill me, but intentions can get lost in translation. Right?"

Camden's eyes flutter closed briefly. "I forgot myself. I forgot my strength. It won't happen again."

Looking at Camden's expression of sheer regret and pain combined with hearing the earnestness in his words, I believe him. I believe that he didn't mean to hurt or kill me, that his rage robbed him of his ability to think clearly and monitor his strength. The biggest problem between mythics and their human mates is the fact that mythics, especially shifters, have a habit of forgetting their own strength. Granted, the bond helps keep them in check, but I can see how rage could overshadow even the power of a bond. Still, hearing his words doesn't take away what he did. It doesn't take away the fact that he set a precedent that I can't ignore.

"Fine," I say. "You went into a rage and took things farther than you intended. I survived that by a stroke of luck. What happens the next time I do something that sends you into a rage? It'll happen, Camden, I'm not kind or docile enough to get along with you at all times—I'll piss you off and probably send you into rages, which will lead us right back to where we are now."

"No," Camden cuts in emphatically. "Rage or not, I will never hurt you again."

I give a tired sigh. "You can't guarantee that." I feel the deep, consuming sorrow I've only just escaped from threatening to return, tainting my next words with a sullenness that feels like it takes root in my very core. "I lost a child, Camden, the existence of which had given me the shock of my life not long before it was taken from me. I thought the rogues would kill me along with my baby—instead, *you're* the one who nearly finished what they started. You lied to me when I asked you if I was at risk for pregnancy, then had everyone else around us keep it from me. Then, after I experienced a nice dissection via rogue shifter claw, you decided to blame me for the loss and try to...what? Scare me straight with a hand around my throat?"

Camden shakes his head. "I know you'd never get rid of the child now. I wasn't—"

"—thinking clearly, yeah," I cut in. "So you've said. Doesn't change the facts."

Camden falls silent, his expression turning inwards, pain lacing his features. Even now, with what he's done, I don't like the look of his pain. It makes some instinctual part of me want to fix him, to take the pain away, but I know I can't. The only thing that would take his pain away is my forgiveness, and I can't give him that. Not now, maybe not ever.

I saw a future for myself with Camden for a little while, saw us growing together and ruling together. He disabused me of that notion before it could really take root, which is part of what makes me so angry. I genuinely believe we could've had something good until he wrapped a hand around my throat and squeezed until my windpipe partially collapsed and I nearly died choking on my own blood.

"Just...tell me there's hope, please," Camden says, "Not now, not any time soon, but at some point, would you be able to forgive me?"

I take a moment to think over his words before responding. I can't stomach the thought of being with him right *now*, but I'm under no illusions that my sentiments will last forever. Already, part of me yearns to forgive Camden and get past this. While that part is nice and small now, experience has taught me it will grow until most of me wants to forgive Camden.

In the beginning of our relationship, I despised Camden. I vowed to him and myself that I'd never accept him, never be with him; it was only a matter of weeks before the bond battered at my resistance until there was little left. It wasn't *just* the bond that did away with my resistance though. It was also the fact that Camden and I could achieve a lot of good in this world together. I also came to see parts of him that I suspect few others have; a softness hidden under his armor, a capacity to care deeply and compromise even when he hated it.

I know there's some good in Camden. I know he has redeeming qualities, I know that had he not nearly killed me, I'd probably be by his side right now, and we might even grieve the life taken from *both* of us—that of our child—together. Camden is loyal to a fault, fiercely protective, wiser than his age indicates, and cunning as can be. All of those things serve as an enticement, if the occasional irritant, to me.

Realistically, I know I won't be apart from Camden forever. The bond might be muted and in tatters now, but the very same bond was very weak at the beginning of our relationship, yet still strong enough to make him feel magnetic to me. I just can't be with him right now; I'm still grieving and still raw, and still can't see a way past our conflict. I truly don't think that'll last forever, if we could get past my absolute hatred of shifters to be together, eventually we'll get past this too, but not now.

"I don't think there's a future for me without you in it somewhere," I admit quietly. "But no time soon. It might be years before I want to be near you again, Camden. Decades even. Or it could be months. I don't know. I lost my baby less than a week ago; today I lost two other people I cared for deeply. I'm not thinking clearly right now."

Camden's eyes shutter as he says, "Mariketa and Parker. Fuck. I'm sorry, I didn't even realize—I didn't put it together. I'm sorry you lost them. I promise to do everything in my power to avenge that."

I let out a mirthless laugh. "No need. You had no love for them, just as they had none for you or your kind. Their deaths aren't even wholly mine to avenge; that right belongs to their son, who returned from a hunt to find them decapitated."

That much is true; although their loss pains me greatly, I know it pains Wesley far more. I might have cared for them, even loved them, but they were *his* parents. I still remember the grief and anger I felt after the loss of mine. I remember wishing I could avenge them even though there was nothing that could be done. I couldn't blame Dad's cancer for taking him, just as I couldn't blame Mom for bleeding too much during birth—instead, I blamed mythics who took away the resources that might've ensured they lived.

Camden's jaw clenches but he nods. "When...when do you think we can speak again?"

If my tumultuous emotions were in charge on that front, the answer would be in a few years, once I've had appropriate time to cool down and move on. Unfortunately, logic has to take the wheel, because my dialogue with Camden isn't just relevant to us; it's relevant to the alliance between witches and shifters, one that will take constant coordination and cooperation to keep in check. I won't presume that Odelia would do all the talking on behalf of witches; eventually, she'll probably want my help, especially since Camden will be far more likely to give in to my requests than he would be hers.

"Soon I expect," I tell him truthfully, "since the war has officially begun, but we won't be speaking about us, Camden. I don't know when I'll be ready for that. Still, my anger and pain won't prevent me from carrying out my duties to the Nightshade witches and the survival of innocents."

Camden nods once. He doesn't look particularly pleased at my words, but he doesn't refute them either. Instead, he inhales a deep breath and says, "Alright. I'll accept that. When you're ready to talk about us, I'll be waiting. Until then, we'll both focus on our responsibilities to our people. I hope you know, Sierra, my people are still your people."

I raise my eyebrows at that. "Your people have a hatred of witches that drove some rogues to try to kill both me and my baby."

I understand that technically, after our bond was marked and consummated, I became queen to shifters. That didn't prevent some of them from trying to end my reign before it could begin.

Camden's jaw flexes and his gaze cuts to the side as he glares at cobblestone. "There's a small number of shifters who aren't pleased with our new alliance because they've been raised to see witches as a dangerous potential enemy. Many more of them felt that way until you used your power to kill Kyron who'd been terrorizing our population for decades. A lot of them changed their tune after that. I expect most of the remaining skeptics will change their minds after the witches complete wards on our territories, giving us a blanket of safety we've never before had."

That's a nice fantasy, but I'm not so quick to be optimistic. "Let's hope that's the case. Your five minutes are up, Camden, I need to return to coven headquarters."

"Where's that located?" Camden asks.

I almost smile faintly at his attempt to pull more information from me than I'd freely give. Instead of responding, I give him a stare that says, *nice try*.

"Believe it or not, I'm not asking for my sake," Camden says. "I'm asking so that I have somewhere to send letters for communication in case something happens before we speak again, and so that I know where to go if you ever call on me for aid. My warriors and I only have a general idea of where to go—specifics might be useful in the future."

I look to Odelia, who's hovering about twenty feet away, speaking with Reyna and pretending not to eavesdrop when I know she hears every word.

I turn back to Camden. "That information isn't mine to give." *I* don't even know the exact location, though I do know it's somewhere in the northern territories of this continent, within an expansive mountain range. "It's on my high priestess to decide whether or not to divulge that."

Confirming my suspicions that she's been eavesdropping all along, Odelia turns away from Reyna and walks up to me and Camden. She looks him up and down with a critical eye, distaste curling her upper lip.

"If I give you that information, what's to prevent you from trying to storm our territories to try to retrieve your Queen Alpha and the Princess Beta?"

"The fact that I will not do anything to upset my mate more than I already have," Camden says, his tone serious.

Odelia stares at him for several long moments before giving a nod. "I won't give you specifics, but I'll tell you a bit more than your warriors know. We reside in the Blaithe Mountain Range. If you need to send word, do it through Wyatt when he speaks with Leisel—shifters are not welcome on our territory. Only the warriors you sent may even get close to it. Do not share this information with anyone, and do not abuse it by trying to come to us either, or I will put you through a world of pain."

Camden's lips kick up at the corners. "I think we'll get along quite nicely."

Odelia barks out a laugh. "Perhaps in another life, wolf. For now, our alliance will be the only thing connecting us. Understand that should you break it, the spell binding it will kill you. Then I'll have my witch sisters resurrect you, temporarily pulling your soul back from the afterlife, just so I can torture you some more. Clear?"

Perversely, Camden smiles. "Very. It's been a pleasure, Odelia." His eyes flick to me and shutter with a mixture of longing and regret. "Sierra."

I incline my head. "Travel safely, Camden."

He smiles a sad smile. "You too. I'll miss you each day you're gone."

Despite myself, I'll miss him too, but I'll have plenty of things to distract me, such as war.

Camden walks away, going to the group of his gathered wolves. Odelia calls Maddy over and tells her to release the shield trapping the wolves in the town square. With a series of tactile gestures and a single word in Latin, the shimmery barrier surrounding the area drops.

I watch as Camden and his entourage mount their horses, and after one last lingering glance, ride away.

Chapter Ten

U pon our return, Odelia's first order of business is to call upon the Nightshade warlocks. Several men join me, Odelia, Reyna, Claire, Maddy, and Wesley in one of the larger rooms in the cavern system, which is strewn with couches and comfortable seats on one end and a large round stone table on the other. Leisel's off in her room, having said that she hasn't spent enough time with Chip today since she left him behind for our travels.

Four warlocks stroll into the room, one by one, and I look each up and down as they enter. The warlock at the head of the group has curly dark hair and deep mocha-colored skin. His eyes, an interesting color reminiscent of cinnamon sticks, flick from Odelia to me to Wesley. He pauses in the center of the room when he sees Wesley, his dark brows drawing together as he looks at my ward.

"Is that—"

"An earthly warlock, yes," Odelia responds before he can finish his question. "Quite a surprising find, especially since he marks the beginning of a new bloodline. I'm handing his training over to you, Rune. He knows nothing of magic. His only known power thus far is over earth and nature; his negative emotions can create earthquakes." Odelia looks to Wesley. "Wesley, this is Rune, my counterpart for the Nightshade warlocks. He's the most powerful warlock of our time, very capable, and very proficient in training young warlocks. You'll be in good hands with him."

Wesley looks over to me, a mixture of intrigue and fear shining in his eyes. I realize that the fear is because he doesn't want to be taken away from me and Leisel, the only familiar faces around him. I scoot closer to him on the couch we're both sitting on and wrap an arm around his shoulder.

"Can Wesley have a room near me and Leisel, and join us for meals?" I ask Odelia.

Odelia turns to Rune. "Will you keep your warlocks in check and cease with your ridiculous fights during meals if I invite you back to my table?"

Rune smiles, displaying pearly teeth, one of his front ones slightly crooked. "I'll do my best, but I make no promises. My men can be rowdy."

"I know that all too well," Odelia says dryly. She looks at one of the other warlocks in the room, a male with blond hair, fair skin, and eyes such a dark green they almost appear brown. "Bane, you're the one who starts the most fights; will you stop?"

Bane's eyes shift over to Wesley and he gives a nod. "For the sake of our new member, yes. For now."

Odelia turns back to me. "In that case, Wesley is free to join us outside of training hours, and I'll give him a room in the same hall as you and your sister."

"When are training hours for him?" I ask.

"The same as for you and your sister," Odelia responds. "We'll start after breakfast and continue on to dinner with a break taken for lunch. They'll be long, grueling, and arduous days, but you all have a great deal to catch up on before you're fit for battle."

"What about visiting human villages to give them protection?" I question.

Claire shifts in her cushioned seat not far from us. "That's a priority as much as training; we'll make a specific plan tonight. You will only be needed for however long it takes to convince them to trust us; after that, it's back to training for you."

I smile. "Will I just be training with magic or physical combat as well? I've heard the vampires favor blades as much as fangs and claws."

Reyna looks over to Bane. "He's our best trainer when it comes to edged weapons and our second-best fighter. He'll teach you the art of sword and blade fighting."

Bane rolls his eyes, sighing at Reyna. "You've beheaded one more vampire than me. *One.* That doesn't mean you're a better fighter."

Reyna smiles at him. "Maybe not, but the fact that I win when we spar does."

I look between the two of them, finding their interaction at once amusing and interesting. The ease with which they speak and banter tells me that the Nightshade witches and warlocks are close and very comfortable with each other. Moreover, they truly *trust* each other. I'm not sure what I was expecting, but I suppose seeing that they didn't eat meals together or always travel together led me to believe there wasn't such closeness between the witches and warlocks of this coven.

Bane's chest puffs out. "Since when does a draw mean a win?"

"Since the time I won three years ago. The draws since don't negate that win," Reyna shoots back.

When Bane starts storming across the room towards her, Reyna leaps to her feet. I startle as Bane waves his hand in the air and a *sword* appears in his grip out of nowhere. He tosses the sword to Reyna, who catches it by the hilt, giving Bane a bored look as another sword appears in his hand, this one for him.

"Really, Bane, you want to go again here and now?" Reyna taunts, swinging her sword in her grip, clipping the edge of the armchair she was sitting on. Feathers spill out of the cut on the leather, dropping to the floor in a pillowy white stream.

Wesley murmurs in my ear, "Are they all this insane?"

Reyna looks at Wesley over her shoulder. "Yes, young warlock, we are. Watch and learn. If you're lucky, some of our crazy will rub off on you."

Leisel chooses that moment to skip into the room, a bright smile on her face and Chip perched on her shoulder. She pauses in the entryway and stiffens when she sees Reyna and Bane facing off with each other, both of their swords at the ready.

Reyna's head swings to the doorway, and she chuckles at the look of sheer horror on my sister's face. "Don't fear, youngling, we're just sparring. Bane is a Nightshade warlock."

"How about we save sparring for another time and do it either outside or in one of the designated rooms?" Odelia says loudly.

Rune sighs. "You're no fun, O. Won't even let our members spar."

Odelia shrugs. "They can spar however much they want, but not in the common areas. Follow the rules or get exiled to your side of the cavern system; it's up to you."

Bane and Reyna exchange a glance before the swords disappear from their grips.

"Is making a sword appear out of thin air something that I'll be taught during training?" I ask.

Bane chuckles. "Sorry, sweetheart, that's a power you're either born with or you aren't." To Reyna, he says, "Some say I was born with a sword in my hand."

Reyna snorts. "And some say I shit gold."

Leisel skips her way over to me, climbs onto my lap, and then plants a kiss on Wes's cheek in greeting before turning her attention back to Chip who's in a playful mood. She tickles his furry stomach and he chatters loudly, curling around her finger before play-biting at her nails. The sight of Leisel playing with Chip is heartwarming and I exchange a smile with Wesley.

Both Leisel and Wes are surprising me with their resilience. I still feel like I'm somewhat in a slump after the sight I discovered in Aesara. Then again, Leisel was almost killed by a vampire when we were in Kinrith's castle, and she was just fine the next day. I can still see sadness in Wesley's eyes when I look at him—a great deal of sadness—but there's also hope that I imagine was absent the last few days.

Bane wraps an arm around Reyna's waist in a gesture that surprises me, pulling her close and drawing my attention to them, as I fully expect Reyna to tear him a new one for being so bold. "You know I wouldn't mind sheathing my sword in you anytime, Reyna."

My eyes bulge at the plain innuendo, and I cast a glance around the room to see if anyone else is surprised. They aren't—evidently, this sort of banter is also commonplace.

"Get a room," Claire tells them. "Preferably away from the two newest members of our coven, both of whom are *children*."

"I'm not a child," Wesley grumbles.

Leisel turns to me with her big doe-eyes and asks, "What does he mean, sheath his sword in her? Like stab her? Wouldn't that hurt?"

I scramble to come up with a response that doesn't taint her ears or pure mind. If I had it my way, Leisel would be abstinent and ignorant of sex for the rest of her life, but I know that's my overprotectiveness coming into play. Still, we're a few years away from the time when I give her *the talk* as my mother did to me the day I got my period, mere days before she went into labor and passed away.

"Um, he means that Reyna has a sword sheath in her room, which he would use."

Wes snorts. "*Riiiiight.*"

I slap the back of Wes's head and he shoots me a glare. Thankfully, Chip reclaims Leisel's attention, saving me from having to clarify or expound any further.

"We'll take the night off, considering the taxing events of the day," Odelia says. "Rune, you're in charge of showing Wesley around; take Sierra with you as well so she can see the other side of our mountain. Bane, watch the company before you start blathering like an idiot. Leisel, darling, you can either join Sierra, Wes, and Rune for a tour or you can help Claire—she's heading out into the forest in search of some herbs to replenish our stores."

Leisel's eyes light up at the option Odelia gave, but then shutter as she looks to Wesley. "Do you want me to come with you?" she asks him, to which Wesley shakes his head, murmuring that he'll be fine.

My heart warms. Leisel's ever the supporter, always thinking about people around her. I suppose that's the nature of a healer, and it's also one of the ways my sister's true *goodness* shines through.

Another warlock steps forward, one with light brown hair, eyes the color of a lake—an interesting hue of blue and green—and a well-muscled build. He says, "They also need to train with tactile combat spells." His eyes stray to me and glimmer with interest as he looks me up and down. "So you're the earthly witch and the shifter Queen."

I arch an eyebrow at him. "And you're the tactile combat magic specialist." He was mentioned earlier, I think his name is Cedrick. "If we're done stating the obvious, perhaps we could move on to more useful things, such as the tour we've been promised."

"Yes, we'll get to that now," Claire says, standing from her seat and stretching her arms over her head. "Cedrick, quit staring at Sierra. It's rude."

Cedrick doesn't remove his eyes from me as he says, "But she's pretty to stare at."

I blink a few times, belatedly realizing that he's flirting with me. I don't know how to handle or respond to that; I've never had to deal with flirtation. When I was living in Aesara, I didn't have time for boys as I was busy single-handedly running a farm and raising a child. Then I was snatched up by Camden, and he wasn't much for flirting; he's far too forward for that.

"Leave the poor girl alone, Cedrick," Odelia says. "She's had a bad time of it recently."

Cedrick takes a step towards me and offers me a smile that's at once slightly unnerving and very seductive. I know objectively I'm pretty, but I don't think I'm any great beauty—certainly not one that should be attracting such a hot gaze from a virtual stranger. Though, considering my separation from Camden, there's nothing *really* stopping me from taking an interest in others—perhaps turning my attention elsewhere will help temporarily free me of the pain that's been bogging me down ever since leaving Kinrith. I could do with a distraction, and I wouldn't be doing anything wrong by taking an interest in another.

Still, despite realizing that my options are open, I'm not in the mindset to seek out male company elsewhere. I wasn't lying when I told Camden that I don't see a future for myself without him in it somewhere; a distraction won't change that, and odds are it'll only create more problems between me and Camden, something I'm not interested in. I resolve to ignore Cedrick's interest and wait for it to pass; he's a handsome guy and I'm sure he also receives plenty of attention that'll distract him soon enough.

Rune claps his hands together. "Enough of that. Sierra, Wesley, you two are with me—let's give you the grand tour."

"I'll join," Cedrick says.

Considering he's going to be teaching me tactile combat magic, I should probably get used to being around him despite the strange, heated stares he's sending my way. I'm so unused to being the object of attention that I feel myself blush as I stand from the couch. Wes and Leisel follow suit. Leisel flits over to Claire, who takes her hand and leads her out of the room. Bane and Reyna head out as a unit, probably to find somewhere to either spar or fuck.

Rune waits until Wesley and I are beside him. Cedrick joins us, standing a mere foot away from me. I cast him another, more considerate glance, starting to wonder if I could find interest in him were circumstances different. Physically, he's attractive, but that isn't enough to really attract me to him; personalities are more important to me.

Case and point; I was physically attracted to Camden from the moment I met him, but my distaste for the glimpses of his personality I initially got—forceful, domineering, set in his ways—made it possible for me to ignore said attraction. It was only when I started to get to know him, the *real* him and not the facets of himself he's compelled to show his subjects, that the attraction became too intense for me to ignore.

The fact that my mind instinctively wanders over to Camden should be enough to deter me from thinking twice about Cedrick. It would've been if I weren't on such shaky footing with the Alpha; as it is, my thoughts about Camden are enough to piss me off to the point where I consider pursuing something with Cedrick just to help me get my mind off of my mate, but as soon as the thought crosses my mind, it's followed by guilt. I shouldn't be using other people to help me forget my problems.

I'm quiet as Rune leads us through the expansive cavern system, pointing out dozens of rooms and citing their purpose, both in the witch half of the mountain and the warlock half. Wesley seems fascinated by the mountain-dwelling that the Nightshade coven lives in, the sorrow in his eyes temporarily diminishing in favor of interest. Cedrick stays close to me the entire tour, though he doesn't speak anymore, and he stops staring at me after a little while, which I appreciate.

By the time Rune's shown us around the cave system, several hours must've passed; the mountain is huge. He leads us back to the balcony where witches take their meals in time for dinner. The cooks are just setting up platters of various foods, and I notice both witches and warlocks are mingling around the large table.

"Before Bane decided that food fights are the most interesting part of meals, we'd all eat together—witches and warlocks," Cedrick tells me. "Half of us would be here, the other half on the other balcony. It's nice to come back together."

Curious, I ask him, "How many members does this coven have?" I take a seat on the stone bench running along the length of the table, and Cedrick takes the spot next to me.

"Just over fifty in all. We're not the largest coven in this mountain range; we're actually one of the smallest, but we are the most powerful."

"How many covens are there in these mountains?" I ask.

"Dozens," Cedrick responds. "We have close to one hundred covens in Acuria, though not all of them are here. Witches and Warlocks claim the upper half of this continent, including northeast and northwest territories—we're not all confined to this mountain range, though a lot of us prefer to stick together here. The settlement is unofficially referred to as the Valley of Sorcerers."

"Sorcerers," I repeat. "Is that the term for the collective of witches and warlocks?"

Cedrick nods. "Yup. There are tens of thousands of us within covens of different sizes scattered around. The largest coven is a warrior coven that resides in the valley of this mountain range. They have about four thousand fighting witches and warlocks. They're our most capable coven physically, and yet even they yield to the Nightshade coven. Odelia has earned herself the title of Protector of Witches, just as Rune is Protector of Warlocks. We don't have kings and queens or monarchies, but we do have our own hierarchy. Protectors are our equivalent of kings and queens, I suppose, except their role isn't to rule but to protect and guide. There's the same structure in Sukarmir, with another guiding pair."

That's fascinating. "How were Odelia and Rune selected as protectors of witches in Acuria?" I ask.

Cedrick smiles. "They were chosen by the covens. Both Odelia and Rune have proven themselves several times over through fantastical feats, and they've both saved thousands of witches from horrible fates. Aside from being the most powerful witch and warlock on this side of the world, they also proved to be the most protective. All of the covens came together for a vote on who they'd look to for leadership a few years back; Odelia and Rune both won by a landslide."

I like that a lot. I appreciate that the two Protectors were chosen based on their merit instead of their bloodline. I can see how in shifter packs, dominance and power are hereditary, so monarchies are viable. Witches and Warlocks, however, are obviously different; fate chooses the most powerful rather than lineage, and the covens respond accordingly.

Leisel and Claire step out onto the balcony, drawing my attention away from Cedrick. Leisel has a bouquet of beautiful wildflowers in her hand, and she skips up to Odelia to present them to the high priestess. Odelia smiles warmly at her, accepting the flowers, and tucks Leisel's hair behind her ear before taking a blue flower and also tucking it behind Leisel's ear.

A feeling of profound gratitude washes over me as I watch the exchange. Leisel's been so wholly and readily accepted by this coven that it warms me. Not just accepted, but truly *embraced*; everyone who interacts with her seems to adore her which doesn't surprise me. My little sister is very lovable and radiates kindness and goodness that draws people to her like moths to a flame.

Dinner is a rowdy and enjoyable affair, with lots of talking, laughing, and shouting. Leisel and Wes sit on the other side of me, listening as I shoot more questions at Cedrick, who seems content to answer all of them. I expect him to grow irritated with my interrogation on the history of his kind and their customs and beliefs, but he seems to enjoy the fact that I'm eager to learn.

At the end of dinner, he tells me, "I'll see you after lunch tomorrow; we'll start on the basics of tactile combat magic. I look forward to working more closely with you. Sleep well, Sierra." With that, he leaves, presumably heading back to his side of the caves to ready for bed. The rest of the warlocks who joined us follow after him, leaving just the witches and Wesley at the table. I stand, taking Leisel's hand, prepared to take her to her room and open her mirror so she can speak to Wyatt for a bit before going to bed. Even though they just saw each other today, I'm committed to helping them maintain regular contact because I see how important that is to Leisel. I also motion for Wes to come with us so he can get settled in his new room as well.

Odelia calls out, "Rest well, you three. Tomorrow, the real work begins."

Chapter Eleven

The next day, first thing after breakfast, my training begins—as does Leisel's and Wesley's. They both seem content and trusting of the witches and warlocks surrounding them, which makes me comfortable leaving them for the day. Odelia takes me to a library—the largest room in the mountain, easily the size of three other rooms combined, the walls all lined with bookshelves. She picks out several large tomes, sets them up on a wooden table in the center of the room, and begins going over magical theory with me. She lectures me about the magical elements that need to come together to form a cohesive, viable, and successful spell. We spend two hours together, at the end of which she teaches me one of the simplest spells that all witches learn when they're young; a spell that fills a cup with water. It's a simple spell only requiring three words but understanding the function behind it—condensing water molecules in the air to form liquid—is fascinating. I realize that magic isn't capable of making something out of nothing; it draws on what already exists and reshapes it. Energy is recyclable, it can't be created or destroyed, only manipulated. The more skillful the manipulation, the greater the magic.

After the session, I pass Leisel in the hall on my way to one of the sparring rooms, where I'll be meeting with Claire. I blink when I see a small bird—a sparrow—on her shoulder, tweeting loudly.

"Where's Chip?" I ask my little sister as she stops beside me.

Leisel motions to the bird. "There. Claire did a spell that temporarily transforms him into a bird. It was *awesome*. He'll be back to a chipmunk in about an hour, but for now, I get to hang out with a bird."

Magic really is wondrous. I tap Leisel's nose and tell her, "Don't give Odelia too much trouble during your lesson, okay?"

Leisel's eyes sparkle with mischief. "I'll try."

I smile at her. "Good. Once you're done with the witches, you have some studying to do, sweet girl. We're not stopping school work just because we're now learning magic too."

Leisel's nose wrinkles. "Can I skip history?"

I shake my head, biting back another smile. "No, but you can do it first to get it out of the way. We'll go over your lessons before you talk to Wyatt tonight."

With that, we separate, Leisel heading in one direction and me heading in another. I meet Claire in one of the rooms on a lower level, a large space bare of anything but a soft mat set up on the floor, presumably to cushion falls as I learned yesterday this is one of the coven's sparring rooms.

Claire tips her chin at me in greeting when I enter. "Sierra. Ready to work?"

"I sure am," I respond. "Leisel seems to be far more amused than Chip is at his sudden transformation."

Claire grins. "Your sister is a joy to have around—such a sweetling."

I nod in agreement. "That she is. This world doesn't deserve her, and it's my job to shield her from it."

"Not alone," Claire says. "We'll help shield her as well now. Natural healers are the most important coven members during times of conflict; without them, we'd have lost many more lives in our battles over the years. She'll be well protected. It helps that she has an uncanny ability to make people adore her."

"She'll also be kept away from battle," I state, looking Claire straight in the eye. If Leisel wants to help heal witches and warlocks after battles, I won't prevent her from doing so, but there is no chance in hell I am allowing my sister near a battlefield.

"Of course she will," Claire agrees. "She's far too young to be exposed to warfare. I regret that she saw as much as she did in Aesara yesterday, though we did our best to keep her eyes off the carnage."

My stomach feels like it twists up in knots as I recall Mariketa and Parker, but I push away the pain in favor of focusing on the present. I'll grieve and avenge them outside of training hours; I can't let sorrow taint my progress.

"Today I'd like to start by learning about your fire," Claire tells me. "There isn't much written or known about the black flame, other than its extraordinary vigor and sheer magical power. It's one of the few magical abilities that's nearly unstoppable, something that no regular shield can protect from. Tell me about your fire."

I let out a breath before telling Claire everything I know about it. How it came out when I was merely a child after I'd gotten injured on a hunt with my father, how I spent the next years exhaustively trying to learn to control it and summon it at will, and how I all but retired it after mastering control over it because I saw it as too destructive to utilize. Claire listens closely, throwing in the occasional question, nodding along.

"How has your fire behaved since your miscarriage?" Claire asks once I'm done going over my history with my fire.

I blink at that, briefly looking down, pushing past the sorrow of the mention of my recent struggle. "I don't know, I haven't needed to summon it. Why do you ask?"

"Certain abilities are powerful enough that they're sentient. Magic itself is sentient. It can differentiate between wielders and sometimes even aid or harm those trying to use it, but the sentience of specific abilities is tied in with that of their wielders most of the time. Think of it as a tether between the magic and the wielder. With a select few abilities, however, the power itself is sentient, and the tether can be broken with trauma. My power over volcanoes is very rare, and it's a sentient gift—after I miscarried, I lost control of it. Had to relearn how to use and control it from ground zero, only this time, fighting against my own magic."

I feel myself grow cold as I take in her words and realize the possibility that my fire, the greatest hope to get through the war with minimal losses, might not be as stable as it once was. It's possible that what happened to Claire won't happen to me, but then... I have felt the rage of my fire recently and felt its volatility seeping into my veins. There have even been moments where it felt like the fire was a completely separate entity to me.

Claire must see the fear on my face because she quickly assures me, "That doesn't happen with everyone. Witches have miscarried with no magical ramifications before. I'm just informing you of my own experience. There's no guarantee that it'll mirror yours. Why don't you try summoning it? Just a small bit on the palm of your hand. We'll work from there."

A sense of trepidation that borders on fear washes over me. I inhale a deep breath, and call to my fire, as I have dozens—hundreds—of times before. I summon the flame that lives within me to the surface, pulling it forward. I feel it rising within me and am once again struck by the volatile energy it seems to emanate. Trying to get a better grip on it, I close my eyes and do my best to focus on it, focus on its properties and draw it out ever so gently.

Nothing happens. Anxiety starts to churn in my stomach as I try to pull it out again, only for nothing to happen again. For a moment, I'm thrust back in time to when I was facing down the rogues, desperately trying to call to my fire, panicking when it wouldn't rise. At the time, I understood that magical dips and surges were a common side effect of pregnancy, as I'd been told by the witches merely an hour before and the delay in my fire rising was exactly what allowed the rogues to hurt me as they did.

I shove away the memory, squeezing my eyes and clenching my fists as I try again and again to coax my fire out to no avail.

Finally, I open my eyes and meet Claire's gaze. She's wearing an expression that's a mixture of worry and understanding.

"It won't rise," I say, my words tinged with anxiety. "I feel it right under my skin, but it won't come out. Just like it didn't come out when I called on it to protect my baby."

Claire's lips purse as she inclines her head in understanding. "Have you ever had problems with summoning it since learning to do so on command?"

I shake my head. "Never until pregnancy. But I'm not pregnant anymore, the failure of my fucking fire is what ensured it, so why isn't it coming out now?"

"Because it doesn't want to," Claire says gently. "Remember, Sierra, the black flame is its own force. It's been harmonious with you for most of your life until conflict cost you your child. It's no wonder the fire doesn't want to be harmonious again—we'll work to get there. When you were first training it with your parents, you mentioned that anger made it rise?"

I wince, nodding. Getting upset enough always pulled my fire out of me, although that's a tricky game to play. My fire is dangerous enough when I'm calm; my anger tends to set it on overdrive, and the black flame in overdrive only means one thing: certain destruction.

"Yes, but that's pretty dangerous, so I try to avoid it."

Claire shrugs. "This room is warded against even the most unique and dangerous sorts of powers; even if your fire roars and rages around, it won't be able to escape this room. I need to see it to understand what work needs to be done, so I'm probably going to piss you off."

If she really believes that's the way, and so long as it's safe from harming others... "Okay. What if it attacks you?"

Claire smiles. "I'll manage. Now, try to summon it again."

I follow her instructions, making a noise of irritation when the fire pushes against the surface of my skin, but doesn't break it.

"It won't work," I tell her.

Claire arches an eyebrow at me, her expression condescending, and I understand that she's about to anger me in hopes of bringing out my fire. Her next words just confirm it.

"So, a witch whose only discernible and helpful power is now useless? That's what you're telling me? If you don't have the black flame, how do you intend to survive the coming battles?"

I feel my fire start to rile at that, shifting restlessly beneath my skin, starting to grow even more agitated. Although *I* understand she's just saying this as a part of our exercise, my fire doesn't.

Claire takes a few steps closer to me, then walks in a circle around me, her expression set in a cruel mask. "Summon the black flame, Sierra. Prove that you have value beyond being the King Alpha's mate."

That irks me because it reminds me that without my fire and magic, I don't have any use beyond being Camden's soulmate, which is not a realization I enjoy facing.

Claire steps closer. "Still nothing? Will your power be so dormant when enemies are knocking down our door, threatening you and your sister? Will it decide to hide away like a fucking coward then too?"

My fire pushes against my skin, *hard*, but not hard enough to break out quite yet. Gritting my teeth, I give Claire a nod, silently telling her to keep going. She might be pissing me off, but I understand that her words are serving a purpose. The flame within me doesn't seem to have the same understanding; it's getting more and more irritated by the moment.

"Not even a spark?" Claire questions mockingly, turning her back on me and walking to the far side of the room. Over her shoulder, she says, "How unfortunate. If you're the best we have, perhaps we deserve to die out."

That's what it takes to finally make my fire snap and burst out. I gasp as it travels over every inch of me, covering me in a black shroud tipped with gold, before traveling outward and shooting at Claire. I try to get control of my flame, slow it, or calm it, but it doesn't listen to my command. Like Claire said, right now my fire is entirely its own entity; its sentience is not tied in with mine. Whether or not I'm its wielder, it isn't listening to me.

Claire performs a series of elaborate gestures, says a few words in a language I'm not familiar with, and a shimmering shield forms around her just in time for my flames to reach her. They surround the shield, battering at it, but don't make their way through; considering the fact that most shields are useless against my fire, Claire must be using some serious power to keep herself safe.

"Come back," I murmur at my fire, holding my hands in front of me and trying to draw it back into me. My words and gestures have no effect; the fire continues savagely attacking Claire's shield, and I grow concerned as I see the shimmer of her shield start to dull down, as if my fire's successfully eating away at it.

"Sierra, now's a good time to bring your fire back," Claire calls out, her voice strained.

"I'm trying!" I call back. Then to my fire, "*Please* come back. She's not an enemy, she's a friend."

My words have no effect, and I truly grow scared as it continues roaring and raging, only growing more intense when it fails to get to Claire. Her expression grows alarmed, as well, and she shoots me a look filled with fear. Neither of us expected the black flame to behave this way.

My mother's words from long ago flit across my mind; *magic stems from your soul, my love. Should you wish to calm it, merely find calm in your soul.* They're followed by Wesley's words from yesterday, telling me about his ability to start earthquakes—how they'd only stopped when he calmed down. My fire might be sentient, but it's still a part of me; if the rest of me is calm, I can only hope it'll follow.

I close my eyes, inhale a deep breath, and pull one of my favorite memories to the forefront of my mind—a moment I dream about from time to time. It's a memory with my mother, when I was only Leisel's age. She was teaching me different aspects of painting. I was seated beside her in the spare room of our cabin as she glided her paintbrush over a canvas, demonstrating various strokes and techniques for me. My father came into the room moments later, armed with a glass of wine for her and a mug of tea for me. I remember the look of sheer adoration in his eyes as he kissed my mother on the lips, then scooped me up into his arms and demanded he be part of the painting lessons, taking my seat and situating me on his lap.

The roar around me dies down, the crackle and pops slowly becoming quieter before dying out altogether. Carefully, I crack open my eyes and breathe a sigh of relief when I see my fire has withdrawn, returning to its place within me.

Claire drops the shield around her, looking at me with wide eyes and an expression that's partly awed, partly afraid. Guilt hits me like a sledgehammer; Claire is trying to *help* me, and my fire nearly killed her for her efforts. The shield she had up would've only lasted a little longer; if I hadn't gotten control of myself when I did...

"I'm so sorry," I say quietly, wrapping my arms around my waist.

That snaps Claire out of her surprise and she glares at me. I internally prepare myself to be berated for losing control, possibly ostracized. I hate the idea that I've done something that could make any one of the Nightshade witches dislike me; I want to be on their good side, and my actions just now probably put me firmly on their bad side. Once Claire tells others what happened here, they might even ask me to leave out of fear.

Claire walks up to me and takes my arm in an iron grip. "*Never* apologize for your magic. That's insulting to you, your magic, and our goddess who bestowed it upon you."

I blink several times, staring at Claire with wide eyes. "You're not...I don't know, mad at me? Upset that I just nearly killed you?"

Claire lets out a laugh. "*Mad?* Sierra, I'm goddamn *relieved.* My power over volcanoes was barely functional for months after I lost my child; I could only draw the smallest stream of lava when I was seething mad. It was much later that it started going into rages. At least then it was useful, even if difficult to contain. The fact that your fire is clearly still fully functional, albeit stuck in a rage, is a good thing. That means you don't have to relearn how to use it, only how to control it."

I stare at her, wide-eyed. "I just nearly killed you."

"You think that's the first time shit's gone south while training magic?" Claire asks with an arched eyebrow. "You should ask Odelia about the time she nearly brought a mountain down on us. We're beings of magic, Sierra. There's a certain amount of volatility that's part of the package. If I didn't know the most ancient, strongest shields ever created, I wouldn't have volunteered to train you. The black flame is no joke, that much is for damn sure."

I'm a little taken aback by her easy acceptance of what just happened, but I suppose I shouldn't be. Like Claire pointed out, there must be some volatility that comes along with training witches; I'd be willing to bet everyone here who's taught another witch has seen and survived some weird shit in their time.

Claire smiles at me, and that smile lets me know there are no hard feelings. "So, you're fire's still strong; that's good. The next step is for you to get back to calling it at will, then we can focus on taming it at will. Ready to go again?"

I tilt my head at her. "You really are crazy, aren't you?"

"Don't insult me. I'm not *just* crazy, I'm insane. Kind of a side-effect of having powerful magic living inside you," Claire replies. "Now, let's get back to work."

Chapter Twelve

The next weeks pass in a blur. I train, spend time with Leisel and Wesley, train more, and then spend more time with Leisel and Wesley. Odelia and Claire turn out to be the nicest of my instructors; Cedrick likes to demonstrate tactile combat spells by using them on me—not at full power, but enough to leave some nasty bruises. Bane smacks me with his sparring sword, *hard,* each time I make a misstep. Reyna also teaches her combat magic by example, except she *does* send spells at me full-power. With her, either I throw up my shield to deflect or dodge the spells in time or end up with broken bones that Leisel then heals. My time with the Nightshade coven quickly proves to be intense and grueling, but despite the unsavory methods, I can see my training taking effect.

At the end of the first week, I manage to *not* end up flat on the ground, unable to even stand, after my sessions with Reyna or Bane. By the second week, I manage to disarm Bane once during sword fighting, and both Reyna and Cedrick get a taste of their own medicine as I start to pick up on spells—both spoken word and tactile ones. My time with Odelia proves to be very useful; lessons with her are a mixture of history, magical theory, and actual magical practices.

Claire's sessions are the most difficult, primarily because my fire fights me every step of the way. At the end of the second week, I can summon it on command nine times out of ten, but each time I summon it, the flames go berserk, attacking everything in the vicinity. Since the only thing ever in my vicinity is Claire, she jokingly tells me that she's getting a nice brush-up on her shielding techniques. At least a dozen times, I end up fearing for her life, and every time her response is a goddamn *laugh*.

Leisel and Wesley settle in surprisingly well with the coven, especially Wesley. The warlocks and witches join together for most meals, and I don't miss the fact that Wesley befriends some of the younger boys among the warlocks, as well as both Cedrick and Bane.

Leisel makes it impossible for people to *not* fall in love with her and is universally adored by all members of the coven. There are times when actual fights are started over who she'll spend her free time with; Claire nearly comes to blows with people several times, which only makes Leisel giggle with amusement. I joke that she must be part siren, but as I watch her ensnare everyone around her, I can't help but start to wonder if there's something more to her magnetism—some magical component fueling it.

Cedrick is strictly business during our training time, but outside of it, he's full of joking innuendos. We end up spending a good deal of time together, primarily because he knows the forest surrounding the mountains best, and Leisel *loves* spending time in the forest—as do I. Often, he ends up as our tour guide, showing us the best nooks and crannies in the nature surrounding us. We discover hot springs, a hidden waterfall, and even a naturally-formed slide that can take someone from the very top of the mountain to a pool of spring water in the valley at the bottom, all paved with smooth rock. My heart nearly stops the first time I get on it, especially since Leisel hops on excitedly before me and disappears from sight with a loud, exhilarated squeal.

I enjoy spending time with the coven far more than I thought I would. When I arrived, it was under the assumption that I'd be offered sanctuary and perhaps some lessons in magic. Instead, I've been pulled right into the large, dysfunctional, and highly entertaining coven that the Nightshade witches and warlocks are. They truly do strike me as a loud, rambunctious, not altogether sane family; they fight and argue and bicker, yet they also help and protect and love each other *fiercely*. If I've been reading them correctly, half of them also fuck like rabbits.

On the evening marking my third week with the coven, I decide to go out late at night to enjoy the cloudless sky and sketch for a bit. There aren't any painting supplies here and I haven't wanted to ask for them because I've already received so much from the coven, so I settle for taking a few blank scrolls of paper with me and a charcoal pencil.

On my way to the far-left edge of the cave system, where a door lets out directly into the forest, I run into Cedrick. It's nearing midnight and most coven members are already asleep at this hour, but he seems perfectly awake and aware as his eyes flit over me. Those blue-green orbs travel to the sack lugged over my shoulder holding my supplies, and he raises his eyebrows, stopping in front of me.

"You planning on making a run for it?"

I frown. "What? I'm the one who has sanctuary here, it wouldn't be in my interest to run away. Besides, if I left, I would have the courtesy to tell Odelia, and I would be taking both Leisel and Wesley with me."

Cedrick nods calmly. "Where you go, they go, huh? You're a natural-born protector."

The statement sounds like a compliment, and for some reason that's beyond me, I find myself blushing. "I wasn't always. I was actually a very happy only child to my parents; pure circumstance turned me into who I am today."

"No," Cedrick disagrees, shaking his head. "Destiny or fate, perhaps, but even then, protectors aren't made, they're born. Forces beyond their control then chip away at their exterior until the true protector within is revealed, but that's not a quality that can be learned, not truly."

I blink. "Oh. Thank you, I think."

"You're welcome," Cedrick responds. "Where are you heading with that sack?"

I feel my blush spread to my neck as I mutter, "Out to sketch for a little while."

"Sketch?" Cedrick asks, looking surprised. "Don't tell me that, on top of being possibly one of the most powerful witches alive, the woman who united witches and shifters, the Queen of shifters, and an extraordinarily capable protector, you're also an artist?"

I'm silent for a few seconds after he speaks because he just threw out a whole lot of big compliments in a casual tone, which makes me a bit tongue-tied. I like Cedrick, I could even say that if I weren't already mated I might be attracted to him, but I *am* mated. He's not an option for me.

I clear my throat. "I wouldn't call myself an artist. I do like to paint though. I learned it from my mother. When I can't paint, I sketch."

"You should've asked me sooner. I'll get you some supplies," Cedrick says.

I shift my weight, strangely uncomfortable with his kindness. "You don't have to do that. I don't want to ask for more than I already have."

"You're not asking, I'm offering," he responds. "So, where are we going to sketch?"

"We?" I ask, my tone faintly amused. "I don't remember inviting you."

"I invited myself. Since you'll be focused on drawing, figured you could use someone to watch your back." When I don't say anything, he rolls his eyes. "I'm not going to pounce on you, Sierra, but the woods are a dangerous place to be alone in the dark; we're not the only magical creatures living here."

Fair enough. I have heard that, although we're the only magical *people* living here, all the sorcery practiced in the Valley of Sorcerers has started to rub off on the animals here, making some of them far more dangerous.

"I was going to head over to that waterfall you showed me and Leisel last week."

"Alright, let's get going."

He walks with me to the end of the cavernous hallway, then opens the heavy stone door leading outside for me. As we emerge right into the forest, I inhale deeply, enjoying the fresh earthy scent that always lingers in the deep woods. Leaves rustle in the breeze and there are sounds of small night creatures scurrying around the forest floor as I head in the direction of the waterfall, Cedrick at my side. There's just enough moonlight filtering through the canopy of trees that we can see where we're going, but I still find the darkness comforting—I've always enjoyed forests at night.

"We shouldn't be spending so much time together," I say, the words abruptly pulled out of me mainly by guilt. I might not *like* Camden right now, quite the opposite, but I also understand I can't have anyone else. I might *technically* be able to, but I don't want to. My initial attraction to Cedrick fizzled out quickly when I realized that, although I don't want Camden right now, I also don't think I'll ever want anyone else.

"Why not?" Cedrick asks, sounding amused.

I give him a pointed look. "I'm mated, as you well know. I'm not available."

He shrugs, stepping over a log and holding out a hand to steady me when I nearly trip over it. "Mated or not, you can still have friends. Besides, your bond's currently hanging on by a thread from whatever that Alpha wolf did that made you run away, so I don't know that you have to stay loyal to him. Only a great betrayal can dim a bond—if he betrayed you, why stay loyal to him?"

Camden might have betrayed my trust, but I have no fears that he might turn to other women in my absence. He's loyal to the bone when it comes to the people he cares for; he fucked up massively because he was in a rage, but I don't think even a rage could make him stray.

"Fate has promised me to another," I say.

That draws a snort from Cedrick. "Fate has all of us promised to another if we're fortunate enough to meet them." He misses a beat. "Or unfortunate, in some cases. Regardless, just because I know fate has something in store for me doesn't mean I can't enjoy myself in the meantime."

"You know that you won't be enjoying yourself with me, though, right?" I prod. "I mean, our hikes are great and I've learned a lot from you, but I don't have anything to offer you other than friendship."

He bumps my shoulder with his. "So we'll be friends. You're allowed to have friends, right?"

The way he says the words rankles me, as if Camden's the ruler of me when he most certainly isn't. "People who try to tell me what I am and am not allowed to do usually regret doing so," I shoot back, my tone brusque.

That seems to amuse Cedrick. He smiles, as if enjoying a private joke, and says, "I don't doubt it, Sierra. You're fiery from within and without; I like that a lot."

I'm pretty sure he's still flirting with me, but I'm satisfied I got my message across, so I figure it's harmless. We walk on in companionable silence, our footsteps joining the cadence of the night. What I do appreciate about Cedrick is how simple it is to be in his company. He's generally easygoing, which is a welcomed change from the constant intensity I experienced around Camden. I wouldn't mind having him as a friend, as long as that's all he wants from me.

The sound of rushing water tips me off that we're getting close to our destination. A few minutes later, we emerge onto a rocky shore beneath a tall cliff, from which streams a foamy white rush of water, hitting the pool below. In the light of day, the water is crystal clear and gorgeous; at night it's far more imposing and even eerie but beautiful nonetheless.

I find a spot on the shore between the tree line and the edge of the pool, take a seat on a larger rock, and set my sack down beside me. Cedrick takes a seat on a rock not far from me as I pull out a book, prop it on my knees, open a scroll of paper on top of it, and then grab a pencil. I turn my gaze up to the sky where the brightly-shining moon is haloed by countless, glittering stars.

"I heard there was a time when the pollution on this planet was so thick you couldn't see the stars in some parts," Cedrick comments.

"That's an unfortunate truth," I tell him, focusing back on the waterfall and starting to draw an outline of the cliff and pool beneath. "Humans were careless with the planet they were gifted, to the point where they almost destroyed it. They would've truly destroyed it if mythics hadn't invaded the very day they did."

"Right, the doomsday invasion," Cedrick volleys back, nodding. "I heard the humans were gearing to launch a nuke the very hour shifters first opened a portal between Mythicacia and Earth."

I feel my stomach churn as I think of the sheer destruction a nuke would have wrought; Wyatt once told me that there would've been nothing left on this planet to draw Mythics here had the nuclear bomb gone off, which I fully believe. The fallout would've been catastrophic.

I'm torn between resenting humans for what they almost did and the great deals of damage they inflicted on this planet even before the almost-doomsday, and resenting mythics for invading and subjugating everyone already here. Neither side is entirely in the right.

"At least nature's been allowed to bloom once again," I murmur. "Maybe that's part of why more earthly witches and warlocks are being created; for a time, nature was dormant due to the abuse of humans. It isn't anymore."

"Possibly," Cedrick allows. "I think Reyna's theory is more likely; whatever's coming is so bad that this very planet and Mother Nature herself feels the need to create additional protection."

We're silent for several minutes as I sketch and Cedrick watches. I can feel his eyes on me, but it isn't uncomfortable, especially since I clarified that nothing more will ever happen between us.

"What's up with the vampires and dark faye?" I ask. "Are they all horrible? Or is it just the ruling few that are forcing the masses to go to war?"

Cedrick chuckles. "They're both creatures of the dark, with a naturally darker nature. There are those of them who choose to be good, but the culture they're raised in is violent and cruel, so few walk the garden path."

"So, there's an element of dark nature, but the final product is created by nurture?" I question.

Cedrick nods. "That's a good way of putting it. Some believe that if the vampires and darklings were offered a lighter path to walk, they might choose it, but that has never been attempted so there's no way to know for sure. It doesn't help that the royal vampire family are evil incarnate, and that the great houses of dark faye also prefer cruelty to kindness."

Wyatt told me that he believed vampires behaved the way they did because shifters gave them no other option. It's sad to think that the war we're currently in could be a product of bad blood between species, bred over generations. Still, sad or not, we're in the war now, and pitying the enemy won't get me anywhere. The fact of the matter is that vampires and dark faye—or darklings, as Cedrick called them—have made their positions clear. All we can do now is fight and hope for a positive outcome.

After another long stretch of silence, I finish the rough outline of the waterfall and get to work on shading. As I smudge the charcoal with the pads of my fingertips, I can't help but ask Cedrick, "Why are you nice to me?"

That seems to amuse him. "Are people usually mean to you?"

I shake my head, casting him a sidelong glance. "Not mean, necessarily, but I'm not exactly a warm and cuddly person, so I don't make friends too easily."

Cedrick shrugs. "I'm nice to you because I like you. I'm attracted to you, sure, but so are most of the single warlocks who've come across you—that's not why I want to be your friend. I find you very interesting, which is why I enjoy spending time with you. I also believe that you're our best hope of surviving the hybrids, so I figure being on your good side can't hurt."

Huh. I guess that's fair. I've never really had time in my life to pursue friendships; in Aesara, my focus was on Leisel and the farm. I grew close with Mariketa, Parker, and Wesley *because* of Leisel which was pure happenstance. I find that I like the concept of friendship more than I thought I would; being out here with Cedrick is more enjoyable than being out here alone.

I finish up my sketch, then put all the supplies back in the sack before standing and stretching my arms over my head. Cedrick stands as well, then walks alongside me as I follow a makeshift path through the forest, heading back in the direction of the caves.

"The vampires and darklings have been quiet in the last weeks because they've been mobilizing troops," Cedrick tells me as we walk. "I got intel tonight that they're readying to continue their attacks on the weakest villages in our continent, which happen to be the human villages. The consensus is that they're doing this as a fuck-you to the witch and wolf alliance; trying to instigate us. Odelia's heard whispers that they'll strike first at the villages bordering the sea, of which there are only a handful. We might get an opportunity to take that revenge you suggested to her, defending this continent by violently killing any invaders, sooner rather than later. Since we'd like to avoid human deaths in the process, tomorrow morning you'll be joining the witches as they visit the human village of Midlington to help convince villagers to accept the aid of witches."

I feel a frown furrow my brows. "Why are you only telling me this now? If I knew that I'd have prioritized getting a full night's rest."

"You needed to sketch to decompress," Cedrick responds. "You've been tense as a bow recently."

That's true, though I think everyone's been tense as a bow recently. Although battles haven't yet commenced, we are now officially at war. It's hard to be calm during wartime, especially when there's a constant fear for the safety of my sister and the fate of my own future hanging above my head.

When we approach the door that leads directly into the cave system, Cedrick opens it for me. Once we're inside and it's closed, he mutters a few words in Latin, and a faint blue glow creeps across the door, presumably magically sealing it.

"Thanks for the company," I tell him.

He nods. "See you in the morning. Sleep well, Sierra."

Chapter Thirteen

The following morning, after breakfast, Maddy teleports a group of witches and warlocks to the outskirts of Midlington, to the top of a hill overlooking the village. Midlington's on the southern end of this continent, a village that's right next to a large river hidden deep within an even larger forest that lets out to the open sea a few miles south. The climate is much warmer down here, and a pleasant breeze stirs the fine hairs at the back of my neck as I breathe away the worst of the nausea that accompanies teleportation.

There are about a dozen of us all in all, including Odelia, Claire, Reyna, and Bane, along with several others who joined us for support. Leisel stayed behind in the mountain, as I didn't want to risk exposing her to violence in the case that enemies show up or something goes wrong. Considering the tense times we live in, that's very much a possibility.

As the dizziness and nausea subside, I straighten and turn my gaze to the left, where I can see faint curls of smoke rising from the chimneys. This town is built much differently from Aesara. Whereas in Aesara there were primarily wooden establishments, here all of the buildings are made of stone. It makes sense that the houses and structures here are sturdier; this is a coastal village, likely prone to hurricanes and intense storms.

"I sent word last night to the council in this village that we'd be here to parlay with them in the morning," Odelia tells everyone. "They responded that they'll send an intermediary to speak with us."

"I look forward to speaking with them," I respond with total sincerity. I will do whatever it takes to avoid another catastrophe such as Aesara.

Just as I say the words, I make out the silhouette of a man walking up the hill that separates us from the village. From this distance, his posture—tensed shoulders, slumped back—indicate he is not happy to be sent to speak with a coven of witches. As he moves closer, I can make out his wrinkled features; he appears to be somewhere in his sixties, with deep furrows on his forehead, a black beard threaded with silver strands on his jaw, and short hair on top of his head.

He slows down as he approaches, appearing at once nervous and irritated. When he's ten feet away from us, he stops. I take a few steps forward to stand in front of the sorcerers with me and offer the human man what I hope is a warm smile even though it feels more like a grimace. I may have been the one to bring witches and shifters together for the first time in their history, but they needed each other for survival, so diplomacy wasn't terribly difficult then. To convince a human who naturally hates mythics to accept their help will be a much different task.

"Good morning," I greet the man. "My name is Sierra. I originate from Aesara, a village in the Midwest portion of Acuria." I pause to clear my throat. "I'm an earthly witch, though I lived with humans for most of my life."

"You can call me Samuel," the man says. "I know who you are, witch. You're a wolf in sheep's skin. A human hiding the mythic beneath."

Alrighty then. If he doesn't want to go through pleasantries, cutting to the chase is just fine by me. I often prefer direct conversations anyway.

"That's one way to look at me," I say with a nod. "Another way to look at me is the woman who put humanitarian aid on the agenda of both shifters and witches."

Samuel lets out a low, condescending laugh. "That so? You want to tell me you're all here to *help* us?"

I might be versed in dealing with hostility, but I do not appreciate his mocking tone.

"You don't seem to be in a talkative or friendly mood, which is fine," I say blithely. "I'll get to the point. Mythics are currently engaged in a war—witches and shifters against vampires and dark faye, as well as dark faye and vampire hybrids. It's a bloody, cruel war that's already laid waste to my home village. Aesara was burned, all the people within it were killed, and most of the women were raped before meeting gruesome ends. There was only one survivor, a boy who survived by a stroke of luck. Unless you wish the same fate to befall your home, you will allow me and my fellow coven members to place wards of protection around Midlington. If you're *very* smart and invested in survival, you'll also accept the help of shifters, who will send warriors to patrol the surrounding areas. I'm not here out of the kindness of my heart. I'm here because I don't believe humanity should go extinct, and that is exactly what you face in the coming weeks and months."

My speech renders the villager silent. His mouth closes with an audible click, his Adam's apple bobs as he swallows hard, and his features pale. I might feel bad about my harshness if I thought anything but very direct conversation would drive my point across. As is, I'm glad my words have shaken Samuel; perhaps he'll actually listen now.

After a long moment, he straightens. "Who's to say this isn't some sort of trick? You lot trying to get us to trust you and lower our defenses just so that *you* can destroy my village and kill everyone in it?"

I can't help myself; I laugh at that. Unlike his laugh, mine isn't cruel but genuinely amused. "If I wanted your village destroyed, I wouldn't waste time speaking with you. I'd use my magic to set it on fire from afar, then have the others behind me finish the job. There is literally no reason for me to waste time convincing you if my goal was your destruction. I don't like to waste time, and right now you are wasting mine. You don't trust mythics? I don't blame you. I didn't trust them for a long time either. I still don't trust most of them. What you can trust is logic. Logically, why would I be taking time from my day to parlay with you if I wanted you dead?" I speak to him in a low, measured tone, trying to keep myself calm even as my irritation starts to rise.

"It could be a trick, trying to lure me into a sense of safety," Samuel snaps.

I nod. "Right because that's at the top of my priorities. I'll be blunt; I don't give a shit about your feelings. Or anyone else's, for that matter. What I do give a shit about is the survival of your species; something I fought hard and sacrificed a great deal to ensure. If our interests to that end do not align, tell me and I'll stop wasting both our time. If you want to see your village burned and everyone within it dead, turn us away. If you want a chance at making it through the coming battles, speak now."

Samuel blows out a long breath and strokes his beard. He appears slightly less hostile than he did before. Instead, he looks lost in thought, probably weighing the merits of what I've said. If he uses an inch of logic, he'll come to see that I was being truthful when I pointed out that if I wanted to destroy Midlington, I wouldn't waste time here.

"Fine," he snaps. "Your witches can do their mumbo-jumbo. Shifters, however, are out of the fuckin' question. One of those dogs took my daughter from me, claimed her as his mate, and I haven't seen her since."

My heart clenches at that. I take a step forward, pleasantly surprised when the villager doesn't step back. "I have some sway with shifters," I tell him gently, which is putting it mildly. If I ask Camden to cut his heart out of his chest and give it to me right now, I think he would, though my request on this villager's behalf will be far milder. "If you tell me your daughter's name and the name of the pack that took her, I'll do my best to arrange a meeting between you and her."

Samuel blinks several times, his lips parting as hope starts to shine in his eyes, accompanied by doubt. He frowns at me, then says, "How?"

"I have contacts in high places," I say. "I can't guarantee anything, but I'll do my best."

Samuel looks down at his feet. "Lana. That's her name. She was snapped up by a warrior in the Red Moon pack two years ago. I don't even know if she's still alive."

"Say what you will of shifters, they are fiercely protective of their mates," I tell Samuel. "I'll do my best to find her. For now, if you could return to your village, we'll get to work setting up wards. Humans will be able to enter and exit the wards freely—you won't even know the barriers there—but no mythics will be able to breach the barrier unless invited in."

After a long look at me, Samuel nods again. "Just no shifters."

I'm not entirely surprised that he refuses to allow shifters near him and his fellow villagers; after all, shifters are seen by humans as monstrous creatures who bump in the night. What's more, this man lost his daughter to one. I nearly lost my mind when Wyatt found

Leisel to be his mate, and he hasn't put a hand on her or done anything but offer brotherly affection—I can certainly sympathize with Samuel.

Of course, that won't stop shifters from protecting this village as per our treaty—it'll just mean that they'll stay out of sight.

"Thank you," I tell Samuel. "I'm sure the others in your village will thank you as well once they see just what dangers currently lurk about."

Samuel snorts. "We'll see."

"Odelia, do you hear that?" Reyna asks, pulling my attention away from Samuel.

All of us fall silent, looking into the tree line in the distance. I turn over my shoulder, squinting my eyes.

"I don't hear anything," Odelia says in a worried tone.

That's when it hits me; there are no sounds at all. No birds chirping, no insects buzzing...the forest and all of the creatures within have gone silent. There's only ever been one other time when a forest was entirely silent around me; the evening I spent camping with the Rockwell Pack on our way into Kinrith. Animals, birds, and insects alike sensed the presence of dangerous predators and stayed still and quiet to protect themselves from drawing notice.

The silence now means that there are predators not far from us, even though I can't see anyone other than the witches and the human villager.

"Go back to the town, get everyone inside their homes," I tell Samuel.

He frowns. "Why? What's going on?"

My eyes stray to a single figure who steps out from the tree line, a tall man with silver hair and silver eyes with *red* pupils that I can see clearly even at this distance. Even from all the way over here, I can sense the staggering amounts of power rolling off him. That power reminds me keenly of the power I felt emanating from Kyron before I killed him, which tips me off that I'm facing down another member of the vampire royal family.

"Go, now, or I can't guarantee your protection," I snap at Samuel.

He doesn't ask again; instead, he takes off sprinting in the direction of the village.

"Is that another vampire royal?" I ask Odelia, stepping closer to her.

She nods. "Yes, it is. That is Actaeon, Rhaelar's younger brother. If he's here, that means there's likely a unit of his warriors not far behind."

Bane gives a feral grin. "Excellent. It's been too long since I slaughtered some vampires."

"I feel some dark faye lurking about too," Claire says with a hiss. "I think there might be a few darkling hybrids as well. I guess we'll finally get a taste of what battle with the hybrids might be like."

Reyna extends her hand to Bane, who high-fives it. They grin at each other, and Reyna says, "This ought to be fun."

I don't waste time asking them if they're entirely insane to be looking forward to the fight we're about to have because there's no time to spare, and I already know the answer is yes, they are both insane. I think that's part of both their charm and probably why Bane and Reyna are such good friends.

Several more figures emerge from the trees, but my eyes stay on Actaeon. He's my kill. I don't care whether or not he was personally there for the slaughter of Aesara; he's a member of the family that has cost me far too much.

I'm somewhat glad that Rhaelar isn't here, as I've already promised Wesley I wouldn't kill him. That's Wes's kill by right of blood and vengeance. Another vampire royal, however, is free game.

"Nobody touch Actaeon," I say, my words little more than a hiss. "He's mine."

Chapter Fourteen

"**Y**ou're not ready," Claire says.

I cut her a sharp glare. "Unless he's impervious to my fire, I'm fucking ready."

Claire glares right back at me. "Your black flame is out of control right now, Sierra. If you unleash it, there's every chance it'll kill everyone here, not just our opponents."

She makes a good point. I can't risk harming the sorcerers here with me, my allies, and my fire currently has a fifty-foot blast radius of sheer destruction. If I want to take down Actaeon, the black flame is my most likely means of doing so, but I can't do it here. I need to get him away from the rest of the people so I can destroy him in peace, without worrying about collateral damage.

"Fine," I concede. "I'll get him away from everyone else, run into the forest. Will you be able to take on the rest of them?"

Bane cracks his neck, his eyes taking on a somewhat crazed look. "Oh, yes. We'll take care of the rest of them."

I turn my gaze back to the tree line as more and more people emerge from it; just over a dozen in all. As there are only twelve witches and warlocks here, the opposition's numbers are a bit higher, but I don't doubt my coven's ability to destroy all of them—I've seen the magic harnessed on my side of the fight firsthand, and the level of power is nothing short of stunning. There's a reason the Nightshade coven is considered to be the most powerful of the sorcerer covens in Acuria, despite being relatively small.

The unit of enemies starts to creep forward, closing the distance between us. Bane snaps his fingers together, causing a glowing white sword to appear in his hand. He hands it to Reyna, before creating another for himself. Reyna swings the sword around in several elaborate, beautiful motions that almost seem like a dance of some sort before holding it out in front of her in preparation for battle as our enemies near.

Actaeon remains at the front of his pack. When only twenty feet are separating us, he halts, and a cruel smile spreads on his lips, showcasing elongated fangs.

"Well, now this is a *very* pleasant surprise," he drawls, his voice low and gravelly and filled with both delight and menace. "Here I thought this would be another boring slaughter of humans; I didn't presume I'd have the joy of killing witches as well. Nightshade witches, no less, along with the Queen of Mutts. This is turning out to be a lovely morning."

Odelia lets out a light, ringing laugh, running her eyes over the gathered vampires, dark faye, and hybrids. "You silly, silly creature." She turns to Reyna. "Will vampires ever cease to be amusing?"

Reyna shrugs, twirling her sword again. "I doubt it. They like to pretend they're the biggest and the baddest when they're really the lowest in the mythic food chain. I guess in their position, I'd have to pretend to be better too. You know, so I could sleep at night."

Claire nods. "Fortunately, we're not vampires. We don't have to pretend. It is kind of cute to watch though. Do you think the darkling hybrids will be the same or extra bitchy and narcissistic?"

Reyna nods. "Yeah, I'd take that bet. Ten silver coins, anyone?"

Actaeon's smile drops and he glowers at us, narrowing his eyes. "You won't be so confident once you're dead."

Reyna frowns. "Do you always state the obvious or is it not obvious to you that the dead don't have emotions?" She tilts her head to the side. "Do vampires lack common sense as well? It's not fun to battle with an unarmed opponent."

Her taunt is all it takes for our enemies to descend on us. Actaeon charges Reyna, while two people—a vampire marked by red eyes and a hybrid with strange purple eyes and pointed ears—run at me. I use a tactile combat spell I learned from Reyna to send both of them sailing through the air, landing on the far end of the field with pronounced cracks.

I wince with false sympathy, calling out, "That's gotta hurt." Before I can finish them off, Maddy appears behind them. She throws a dagger into the hybrid's chest while grabbing the vampire by the hair and smiling at him as she pulls another, longer blade from her boot and slowly draws it across his neck, watching as he chokes on his own blood. Once he's fallen to his knees, grasping at his neck, she takes off his head with one quick swipe of the blade. *Definitely not someone I'm going to cross.* As I've learned in my time with the coven, though darklings are killable with the usual methods, vampires need to be beheaded to truly die. Maddy wasn't lying when she said she was almost as good at killing vampires as Reyna and Bane.

An orb of smoky black magic flies at me; I duck underneath it, then use a tactile spell to send a bolt of lightning at the faye who threw it. He drops to the ground like a stone, his body seizing and convulsing, allowing another witch to dispatch him.

Chaos reigns around me as witches and warlocks face the enemy unit, cutting their way through them with surprising ease. The battle isn't truly *easy* though; there are some serious injuries sustained on my side, mostly thanks to the hybrids, who are eerily fast and very powerful both physically and magically. There are only three of them, and they all have glowing purple eyes and pointed ears like the dark faye, making them easy to distinguish

Maddy gets an orb of dark magic to her chest from a hybrid, knocking her unconscious. Another witch rushes to her side and covers her while she's out. A warlock's arm is nearly cut clean off before he shoves a dagger through the skull of his attacker. Odelia gets hit with a spell that causes a breakout of painful-looking blisters on her shoulder. Still, everyone continues fighting admirably.

Reyna and Bane team up, cackling and whooping each time they get another kill. Actaeon manages to block every attack against him, though his eyes remain on me, telling me that if I run, he'll chase.

So, that's exactly what I do. I turn to the side and sprint towards the forest on my right, utilizing every bit of strength and speed I have, needing to get away from those on my side of the fight before unleashing my power. Tree branches leave small scratches on me as I make my way further and further into the forest, leaping over logs, ducking under low-hanging branches, and trying to twist to avoid getting too scraped up. I hear Actaeon giving chase behind me and feel his presence closing in. Up ahead, I spot a clearing; I make my way towards it, satisfied that I'm far enough away from the battle to let out my black flame without injuring anyone I don't want to.

As I skid into the clearing, Actaeon catches up to me and his hand wraps around my arm, then forcibly throws me to the ground. The breath slams out of me as pain erupts all over my torso and I feel one of my ribs snap, but I don't let that deter me. I roll to my uninjured side to avoid his boot that's aimed for my head, then leap to my feet and spin around to face him.

Actaeon glares at me, teeth bared, claws extended. "You killed my brother."

I smile. "I did. One of the most satisfying moments of my life."

The vampire takes a step forward. "How?"

It's surprising that word *still* hasn't reached him of my fire. Or, perhaps it did, and he just didn't believe it. Either scenario seems likely; after all, if he knew about my fire and believed in its power, he wouldn't have allowed me to lead him away from his allies. This gives me the perfect opportunity to annihilate him.

"Painfully," I assure Actaeon. "It really was a fun slaughter, I'll give your little brother that. His death was prime amusement. Except for the fact that he was easy pickings; it's no fun when there's not a fight. Unlike you embarrassments to nature, I don't enjoy cutting down the weak."

"Which is precisely why you will lose," Actaeon snaps. "Your petty, useless morals will cost you your victory in our war." He takes a menacing step forward and I watch him carefully, slowly calling to my fire.

He extends his hand in a gesture so fast I barely track it and before I can move or make a sound, an orb of crackling golden magic slams into me, once again knocking me back to the ground. *Looks like Actaeon is one of the vamps who also has magic.* Would've been nice to know before he sent whatever spell that was at me because it feels like pure acid eating its way through my veins, sucking all the strength from me.

Actaeon tuts. "A single blow, and the queen's debilitated. How unfortunate for your people. You know, perhaps I won't kill you—maybe I should take you back with me. You may be weak, but your blood is powerful; you'd give me strong heirs."

Disgust washes over me in an intense wave. I didn't even want to bear Camden's child, though I'd decided to keep it; there's no fucking way I'll let this creature take me somewhere and try to impregnate me. It shouldn't be possible for him to impregnate me, but Odelia taught me that dark magic has a way of bending the laws of nature. Unfortunately, I'm so weak I can barely twitch a muscle, let alone move away.

That's fine. I don't need to move to kill him; all I need is to unleash the darkest part of myself and watch it consume him.

Actaeon takes slow steps closer to me, eyes traveling a path over my body. "That spell has you nice and docile, hmm? Perhaps I should take you now. An appetizer to the main course."

Even though my eyes are drooping with exhaustion, I force out a laugh. "You're as stupid as your brother if you think you can take me anywhere."

I let my eyes slide shut, inhaling a steadying breath, then call to my fire the way I've been learning to during sessions with Claire. Black flames burst to life on my skin and Actaeon freezes before an expression of shock edged with horror overtakes his pale features.

"That's not possible," he murmurs, taking a step back.

I force a laugh that feels like it rattles my lungs. Whatever spell he hit me with absolutely *sucks,* but it still isn't a match for my flames.

"The delusions never end with your kind, do they?" Before I can finish my sentence, my fire burns a path along the forest floor, incinerating ground and branches on its way to Actaeon. The foolish creature attempts to turn and run, but my flames are faster, rising like a terrifying tsunami high into the sky before diving down and encompassing Actaeon. They don't stop there, though, they continue traveling outward until they've breached the tree line at the edge of the clearing, where they begin disintegrating tree after tree, plant after plant, everything in their path. I *feel* their rage, feel their power, and both frighten me. With a deep breath, I attempt to rein them back in.

The flames feel my call to return but don't heed it, and I start to grow concerned as they continue spreading. I'm far enough from the others that they shouldn't be able to reach anyone, but if they keep going like this, they might.

Come back to me, I silently command, to no avail. Finally, I let my eyes slide shut, and try to calm myself, calm my own anger in hopes that my fire will follow my lead, as it usually does. Slowly, my breathing evens out and my heart slows as the worst of my fury seeps out of me. The roar from my fire subsides, and when I open my eyes, I see it's gone. *Training with Claire has certainly come in handy.*

I blink as I take in the scorched earth around me, piles of ashes where there used to be trees. As expected, my fire demolished everything in the near vicinity, not just Actaeon, before I managed to pull it back. I still have a long way to go to control the black flame again.

I roll over, minding my cracked rib, and force myself to my hands and knees, feeling as wobbly as a newborn foal. Whatever spell Actaeon hit me with took its toll before I killed him. It feels like it takes an eternity to get to my feet, and I fall flat on my back twice during the process. Once I'm finally steady, I start to stumble through the forest, heading towards the direction where I can hear battle cries echoing, traversing several meters of scorched ground before getting back to regular blooming land. When I emerge from the tree line once again, I see that the coven has soundly defeated our enemies. There are only two people left—one of them a vampire, the other a darkling hybrid.

It only takes me a moment to realize that these two men aren't alive because the Nightshade witches and warlocks can't defeat them, it's because the crazy sorcerers are playing with them. Reyna and Bane circle the vampire, both swiping out with their swords to leave shallow wounds on him, making him bare his fangs and swipe out with his claws to no avail.

About thirty feet away, Claire and Maddy, who's been revived from her bout of unconsciousness, have teamed up on the darkling, and are sending various spells sailing at him. Each one draws a hiss and curse from the dark faye, but each time he tries to retaliate with a spell of his own, Claire throws up a protective shield and *laughs* at him.

The rest of the coven members are gathered off to the side, watching with expressions ranging from amusement to genuine pleasure as they observe the vampire and darkling get tormented before being killed.

Odelia's eyes find me as I approach them and she offers me a smile, asking, "I presume Actaeon's dead?"

"Very," I confirm, walking closer. "He had magic, though—hit me with some sort of golden orb that feels like it sucked all the strength out of me. He also might've broken my rib."

Odelia's brows furrow as she thinks that over. "Hmm. I suspected the royal family was gifted, considering Kyron's teleportation abilities, but to wield actual magic instead of having a single gift is concerning. What did this golden orb feel like?"

"Acid injected into my veins," I respond, stopping beside the high priestess. "I'm still feeling the effects of it."

Odelia places a palm on my shoulder and I startle as a feeling of warmth, not unlike Leisel's healing, travels through me. It's not quite as strong a sensation as when Leisel heals, but when Odelia lifts her palm, it feels like most of my strength has returned and the lingering pain has abated.

"I'm not a natural healer, but I do know my tricks," Odelia tells me with a soft smile. Then she calls out, "Alright, Bane and Reyna, Claire and Maddy—enough playing with them, finish up so we can do our jobs and head home."

Reyna and Bane exchange a look of annoyance, while Claire groans aloud. The red-haired witch calls out, "You never let us have any fun, O."

Odelia arches an imperious eyebrow. "You've had twenty minutes for fun; now it's time for business. Finish them off."

Reyna tells Bane, "I get to kill him."

Bane promptly slashes his sword across the vampire's neck, separating his head from his shoulders, and smiles at Reyna. "So sad, too slow. Next time don't advertise your intentions, just do it."

Reyna narrows her eyes at Bane. "Oh, you *motherfucker.*"

I roll my eyes as the two cross swords, then quickly get into a violent fight, exchanging blows that make the air ring with the sound of metal hitting metal. Meanwhile, Claire tosses a stream of crackling blue magic at the faye, who promptly explodes. I blink at the sight. "Wow. Killing is just another form of recreation for them, isn't it?"

"Indeed it is," Odelia says to me with a nod, before addressing the rest of those gathered. "Now we see exactly what we're up against. Our enemies are on the rise in this continent once again; we're working against the clock to protect the villages that need protecting. Let's get to it; we haven't a moment to waste."

Over the next hour, I help the Nightshade witches and warlocks put up a magical barrier surrounding Midlington, not unlike the one I remember creating around Kinrith's castle with the help of Claude. Villagers within the town do their most to make us feel unwelcome with dirty looks and muttered curses, even though *we're* helping *them,* but Samuel helps keep them out of our way.

Once we're done, I pull Odelia aside, hit with a new thought. "What if we ask Samuel to speak with other human villages on our behalf? Vouch for us? I don't mind talking down some irate humans, but if we have to waste time doing that, there's a better chance our enemies will descend on the villages before we can protect them."

Odelia's eyebrows rise. "That sounds reasonable. Speak to him. If he agrees, I'll have Maddy teleport him to other villages before we go. If not, you've proven to be a very capable, if not sometimes blunt, diplomat."

I smile grimly. "When survival is on the line, convincing people of their need to work together becomes markedly less difficult."

I step through the shield and find Samuel outside of one of the stone buildings speaking with a group of villagers in hushed tones. After a brief aside, he agrees to rally other humans on our behalf—likely because he saw the darklings, vampires, and darkling hybrids attack not long ago, which would've given him a better understanding of exactly how much danger his kind is in. After a brief farewell and promise that I'll do my best to get him a meeting with his daughter, the Nightshade sorcerers return to our mountain.

Chapter Fifteen

*L*ucid dreaming is a very useful tool. I learned it when I was only a child, plagued by nightmares of shadows and monsters that would never leave me alone. Every night when I went to sleep, it was merely to fight another battle in my dreams. Eventually, I became afraid of sleeping. That is, until my mother taught me how to differentiate a dream from reality. Once I'd realized that I was sleeping, it became easy to take control of the dream. To this day, it still is.

Initially, I'd have to look into mirrors or search for other clues to make sure I was dreaming; years later, I've become adept at telling when I'm sleeping because dreamscapes are different from reality in the subtlest ways. Colors are slightly muted, objects are somewhat warped, and the atmosphere is always restless and filled with something tangibly off.

Looking around the living room of my cabin, it only takes me a moment to understand I'm asleep. The last time I was here, blood decorated the floor and walls, the furniture was overturned or rearranged, and I was looking at the corpses of Mariketa and Parker propped on the very couch I now sit on. I look into the flames flickering in the fireplace, black flames exactly like the ones that live within me, and immediately understand that I'm in a very strange dream.

I slowly stand from the couch and look around the living room of my cabin, only to stop short when I see a figure standing not far behind the *sofa. I have to blink several times as I take in the ethereal beauty of the woman standing in front of me. She's tall, standing somewhere around six feet, and has glittering silver eyes littered with golden specks, long black hair flowing over her shoulders, ruby red lips, and skin that's so fair it almost appears blue. From the energy radiating off of her, which is so forceful and magically powerful it's nearly suffocating, I understand that I'm currently faced with the sort of being I've never come across. Not just a being; a deity. And not just any deity...I think this is the goddess of magic herself, Hecate.*

I blink several times and reach up to rub at my eyes with disbelief, yet the figure remains. I've seen drawings of her in old books, though none come even close to reality.

"You disappoint me, child," Hecate says. Her voice washes over me, feeling like a hundred invisible needles prickling at my skin, making me wince.

Fear takes hold of me, but I manage to force words past stiff lips. "I'm sorry?"

Hecate continues staring at me. "Apologies will get you nowhere. What I need from you, what this world needs from you, is progress and power."

I'm not sure what to make of her words, so I continue staring at her. Hecate stares right back at me with a critical gaze, her dark brows furrowed and a faint expression of distaste on her face.

"You have power that I bestowed upon you, power that will save much of this world," she tells me. "Instead of using it, you squander it. Why?"

Assuming she could only be referring to the black flame, I say, "If you mean my fire, it's out of control. Dangerously so."

Hecate shakes her head. "The flame within you cannot ever be fully controlled, only wielded with precision."

"I can't wield it with precision," I reply, keeping my tone low. "It attacks anyone around me."

"As it should," Hecate snaps, seeming to grow irritated. "Everything that has happened to you has been with good reason. Your misfortunes have only served to make you stronger, and the most recent tragedy added fuel to your flames, as it was meant to."

My jaw drops as I take a step back. If I'm interpreting correctly, what the goddess before me is saying is that I was meant to miscarry; that my fire was meant to lose its sanity and become an unstoppable force. What happened was either a construct of fate, destiny, or the goddess before me.

"I was supposed to lose my baby?" I whisper.

"You are not ready to have a child. First, you must become master of yourself. To achieve that, this world needs to survive, and you are one half of the savior. Dark times linger on the horizon. Armies of both shadows and death are on the rise. You have the means to stop one of those armies, but the second must be subdued by another."

"Camden?" I ask, trying to think through her riddle-like words. I'm not sure what she means by armies of shadows and death, but I can imagine it isn't good. I also understand that my fire is meant to serve as a deterrent in the war against one army, but another army will fall to whatever the other half is. I can only assume that's my soulmate.

"No," Hecate replies. "Your mate is integral for your strength, as you are for his, but he cannot stop what's to come. Your bloodline produced the other half needed. She must be trained and prepared, as must you."

My bloodline. She. There's only one living being with my blood flowing through her veins, and that is my sister.

"What do you mean?" I ask, fear washing over me. I have every intention of keeping Leisel as far away from battles as possible, not putting her in the midst of a fight.

Hecate abruptly disappears, then reappears in front of me, making me gasp. She grabs my arm in her hand, and a cry of pain escapes me as a horrible burning and stabbing sensation spreads beneath her grip. She releases me just as quickly as she grabbed me, and the pain subsides into a dull throb. I look down at my arm, feeling my eyes bulge as I see a symbol burned into my skin: two crescent moons on either side of a full moon. The sigil of Hecate.

"True power cannot be caged, especially when it grieves, foolish girl. You are a warrior, my warrior, as my brand on your arm will remind you, and warriors do not wallow in their difficulties. They find a path forward. That is what you will do. Muster your fire, for you will need it. Only the black flame can defeat the forces of the dead, but a golden light is needed for the army of shadows. Both must come together if our kind is to survive the coming war."

Hecate reaches her hand up again and I instinctively flinch, but this time she merely runs an ice-cold finger down my cheek. "Train until exhaustion thrusts you into unconsciousness, then train more when you awaken. Perhaps then you will be prepared when the end nears. Open your eyes, young witch, or they will be closed forever."

* * *

Heart hammering in my chest, I claw my way back to consciousness, panting and dripping with sweat. It takes a moment to truly orient myself, especially in the pitch-black darkness of my room. Once I'm convinced I'm no longer asleep, speaking to the *goddess of magic herself*, I murmur a simple spell that creates an orb of light in front of me. I wince as the interior of my room is illuminated by bright white light that quickly fades into a more subdued gold. Only then do I realize that my arm is still throbbing. I pull up the sleeves of my sweater, wincing when I see that the mark Hecate gave me is burned into my skin in real life, not just in my dreams.

I need to talk to someone about the conversation I just had—I feel like there were a million hidden messages in Hecate's words, and I was only able to decipher a few. Enough to know that the war I'm in will be much more destructive than previously anticipated, especially if the patron goddess of witches takes enough concern to come to me in a dream.

I throw the covers off myself, stumble over to my chest of drawers to put on decent clothes, then leave my room, hoping to run into someone. I'm not keen to wake up any of the witches, especially the high priestess, but I will if I must—I'm anxious enough to wake up everyone in this dwelling if it'll get me answers. Luck appears to favor me tonight, as I hear voices coming from one of the sitting rooms used as a common area for witches. I make my way to the room, pausing in the doorway when I see Odelia, Claire, and Reyna all sitting around a wooden table with several maps and books laid out on it, quietly speaking amongst each other.

I clear my throat and all three turn to look at me, appearing mildly surprised at my intrusion.

Odelia frowns at my frazzled appearance. "Sierra, is everything alright?"

A choked laugh that sounds more like a wail escapes me. "No. I really don't think it is."

The witches exchange questioning glances with each other, though Odelia's eyes only glance at the others briefly before returning to me, narrowed with concern.

"She looks like she's seen a demon," Reyna says to Claire.

"Close," I reply. "I just shared a dream with Hecate."

After a beat of silence, Reyna lets out a long breath. "Oh. I thought it was something serious. Sierra, almost everyone here has imagined Hecate in one dream or another—that's pretty common, considering who and what we are. Even our subconscious minds long for our patron goddess."

I guess her skepticism is warranted—I can't be the only witch to have ever claimed to see our goddess in their sleep. While the others might've been dreaming up illusions, I know my experience was no illusion; the dull pain in my arm reminds me of that fact.

I shake my head. "I assure you, I imagined nothing."

I pull up the sleeve of my sweater, showing the burn Hecate left on me, the tri-moon mark. The room falls utterly silent for several moments before Odelia stands and briskly walks up to me, taking my arm in her hand, and drawing it closer so she can examine the burn. Her expression registers a mixture of shock and worry as she runs her thumb across the mark, drawing a hiss from me.

"This emanates a very strange, incredibly powerful magic," Odelia says, glancing over her shoulder at Reyna and Claire before focusing back on me. "You truly were visited by our goddess."

"It wasn't a fun visit," I tell her.

"Sit, tell us what was said," Odelia instructs, leading me over to the table.

The high priestess and two elders listen closely as I describe my conversation with the goddess of magic with as much detail as I can. I tell them about what she said about being disappointed in me, her riddle-like words of me being one half of this world's savior with the other half being my sister, and of the armies of both shadows and the dead on the rise. Once I'm done, they exchange grim looks with one another.

"Armies of the dead can only mean one thing; there's a necromancer among our enemies," Reyna says.

I stiffen at the word *necromancer* because only a small bit of literature exists about them, but that literature is indicative of great evil.

I look to Odelia. "I've read in copies of ancient books that there exists a single power that allows a magical being to raise people who've already died. Not resurrect, as in bring back their souls, but reanimate using a warped form of black magic. Is that what we're discussing?"

Odelia grimaces before giving me a nod. "Yes, unfortunately, it is. Necromancy is as rare as the black flame; it's a power that has to be god-bestowed, not even the fates are strong enough to give it. A necromancer is a very, *very* powerful being; with a bit of training, they can reanimate armies of corpses and skeletons, unifying them with a single consciousness tied into the necromancer's own and thus directing them at will. Hecate gave you a warning, Sierra, one that came at a rather opportune time in your training." She exhales heavily, reaching up to massage her temples, an expression of worry overtaking her features.

Claire adds, "The last time a Necromancer lived, it was a rogue warlock in Mythicacia. He raised armies of the dead that destroyed much of that realm—four covens had to come together to trap and kill him. No magic would work on the dead men he raised, so many coven members fell to the dead before one finally managed to kill the necromancer. Then, all the reanimated corpses returned to their natural state of death. Nobody knew there *was* a power that could fight the dead."

"That must be why Hecate actually came to you," Reyna murmurs, arms crossed and brows furrowed in contemplation. "She didn't want a repeat of what rendered our home realm essentially useless."

I listen with a mixture of interest and growing fear as the witches educate me on the perils and dangers of a necromancer. While it's fascinating to learn what prompted mythics to leave their native realm in search of a new one, it's equally daunting to know that history is now repeating itself, and only I have the power to stop it. In my eyes, I'm a nobody; an earthly witch who hid her power for her entire life while growing up on a farm, who now has the fate of the world resting on her shoulders. A fate that can only be combated by an out-of-control fire.

"Hecate also mentioned an army of shadows, yes?" Odelia asks me.

I nod.

She sighs, bracing her elbows on the table and dropping her head into her hands with a murmured, "*Fuck*."

"Shadow wielders are somewhat less rare than necromancers, but no less dangerous," Claire explains to me. "They're capable of creating shadow-beings with black magic that are controlled by the wielder's will, and those beings are very dangerous. They're sort of amorphous creatures that can kill with a touch; a shadow can be anything, including a very sharp knife that slices through opponents and can't be stopped because they're made of magical vapor."

"Fuck," I say, echoing Odelia's sentiment.

"Apparently, we were also given someone who can stop shadows; your sister," Reyna says. "I noticed she gives off a golden glow when she heals, which isn't common for healers. Evidently, that gold light is a power of its own that happens to manifest when she heals. We'll need to train her to distinguish the light from the healing, and she'll need to learn how to wield the light to chase away the shadows that'll doubtlessly come for us. Gods, we have a lot to do."

"First, I need to find out the identities of the shadow wielder and necromancer," Odelia says. "Presumably it's one of the triads—"

"Triads?" I question, frowning.

"The vampire, darkling, and darkling hybrid alliance," Claire tells me. "Calling them triads is nice and succinct so we don't have to refer to them by the vamp, darkling, and hybrid army each time we speak of them."

"Wouldn't it be one of the darkling hybrids?" I ask. "It seems like they'd be the most powerful of the triads."

Reyna shakes her head. "Not necessarily. I'd have thought so initially, but then there's been a pattern in the vampire royal family of those vamps having magical abilities. Kyron, the youngest, could teleport. Actaeon threw magic at you when you fought him yesterday. Now, there's only one royal left; the eldest, the king. I wouldn't be surprised if Rhaelar's either the necromancer or shadow wielder. Vampires and darklings are both creatures that respect and follow strength, not unlike most mythic species. Except most mythic species look to strength for the sake of protection, as in a monarch to lead them and keep them safe, while the nature of vamps and darklings is to follow the most powerful conqueror, not protector. They're power-hungry creatures, and I can't imagine the darkling hybrids are any different. If they're following Rhaelar, it means that he has some power worth a lot in the name of conquest."

Chapter Sixteen

I let out a long sigh, trying to wrap my head around everything. In essence, there is a virtually unstoppable army of creatures coming for witches and shifters in the name of conquest, and only my sister and I can fight their two most powerful members, whoever they are.

"Why me?" I ask. "Why Leisel? We might be earthly witches, but that's the only special thing about us."

Claire drums her fingers against the table, tilting her head to the side as she looks at me. "That's an excellent question. Tell me, can regular fire harm you?"

I blink at the sudden change in topic, but because our other topic of conversation nearly melted my brain in its complexity, I don't mind the switch. I nod. "Of course."

"That's interesting," Claire says with a low hum.

I blink. "How so?"

Claire exchanges a look with Reyna, whose eyebrows are raised with a puzzled expression. The two then look to Odelia, who raises her head from her hands, appearing more contemplative than surprised.

Reyna finally says, "Claire has power over volcanoes and lava—she's impervious to fire. We have another witch who's a natural fire-summoner, she is also immune to the effects of fire. The fact that you aren't just serves as confirmation."

"Confirmation of what?" I ask.

I don't like feeling that there's a secret about me floating around that I'm not privy to, and that's exactly what this feels like. It seems the two elders and the high priestess know something about me that I don't, and I'm eager to be let in on it.

"It's not absolute confirmation," Odelia remarks, casting a glance at Reyna. Then she turns to me. "Do you pray?"

I'm slightly frazzled at the abrupt change of topic yet again, but I figure this factors into whatever the witches are trying to confirm about me, so I nod. "Daily, to all the gods."

"What about to Hecate?" Claire asks.

I nod again. "Twice. My mother warned me to be selective when reaching out to the patron goddess of witches, to only bother her if I truly, *truly* needed her help."

"Tell us about those times," Odelia requests softly.

I frown, growing irritated. "Why does it matter?"

"Answer the question," Reyna snaps.

I cut her a glare. It's been a long night already, and I'm not in the mood to deal with Reyna's attitude. "Add on a please, and I just might."

Perversely, that makes Reyna smile. "Oh, I like you, Sierra. Your fire burns bright. *Please* tell us about the times you've prayed to Hecate, why you reached out, and if she responded."

"The first time was when Leisel caught pneumonia as a child," I say. "She was dying and I couldn't save her, so I reached out to Hecate. The following morning, Leisel was healed as if she was never sick. A week later, her own healing powers emerged. The second time was when I declared duelum to try to get out of my mating with Camden—I prayed to Hecate to ask for her help in my fight. She..." I trail off, unsure if I should reveal this next part because that could be viewed as cheating in my duel.

Then again, I didn't explicitly break the rules of duelum; I can't be held responsible for what the goddess of witches decided to do on my behalf. Besides, it soon became apparent that declaring duelum to the Alpha King and even winning my duel wasn't enough to escape him. In any case, I doubt the witches here will out my secret.

"Yes?" Odelia presses.

I blow out a breath. "When I dueled with Aspen, something strange happened. Time slowed down for everyone but me—everyone around me moved in slow motion while I was functioning at regular speed."

"Yeah, that *definitely* confirms it," Reyna says.

"Confirms what?" I press.

"Most witches have one or two discernible natural magical powers; the exact ones are often decided by the fates," Odelia explains. "Certain powers, however, are simply too powerful to be awarded by fate—they have to be bestowed by Hecate herself. The black flame is said to be one of those powers. For her to bestow it upon you indicates that you're favored by her. The fact that she gave you a proverbial leg up in your duel only confirms it; Hecate watches over you, Sierra. Now it's clear she's done so for a good reason—she must've known what was coming our way, and hedged her bets by giving you and Leisel the powers needed to combat the darkness that could tear this world apart."

That explains her comment during my dream about my power being bestowed by her. I was too caught up in the other things she said during my time with her to focus on that tidbit, but now that I am, things begin to make sense. Still, it feels a bit outlandish to imagine that *I* was chosen specifically by Hecate.

"Hecate doesn't respond to your prayers?" I ask the witches slowly.

"She did once," Claire says. "I prayed, asking her to give me enough strength to seek vengeance on those who destroyed my home; I managed to go three weeks without food or water and then detonate a volcano on a pack of rogues. The other times? No."

"Hecate is selective in her responses," Odelia says. "Prayers are our way of reaching out to her and looking for a connection; it's her choice whether or not to reach back. More often than not, she doesn't. The fact that she has with you several times is telling."

I let out an exhausted sigh, leaning back in my seat and running a hand through my hair. "Right. Okay. What happens now?"

Odelia's lips thin as she stares at me. "Now, I'll send my spies to find out precisely who the necromancer and shadow wielder are, while your training, along with your sister's, will shift to solely focus on readying your fire and her light."

Lovely. I look at Claire with an apologetic expression because our sessions have been as hard on me as they have on her.

"I'm sorry," I say. "I know training won't be easy."

She shrugs, not looking particularly bothered. Then her eyes drop back to my arm. "We're all members of Hecate's army; you happen to be a favored one, which is a great burden to bear. I'll do what I can to help, and hope you don't kill me in the process."

Her nonchalance is startling, but I suppose it shouldn't be. Claire's seen and done a great deal of insane things throughout her life; that much has already become clear to me. If there's anyone who can handle trying to help me with my fire, she's already proven it's her.

"Back to your conversation with our goddess," Odelia says, threading her fingers together and resting them on her stomach. Then, seeming restless, she stands and paces to the bookshelf in the corner of the room. "Alcohol first," she mutters.

I watch as she pulls on the spine of two books at once, and that particular shelf pops forward, revealing a hidden bar.

"That's...elaborate," I murmur.

"This is where we do elder meetings when the need arises, and that hidden bar has the best enchanted glasses magic can create," Reyna tells me. "Tell the glass what liquor you want, and they'll fill up and continue filling up each time they're emptied until you tell them to stop."

Odelia walks back over to us with four glasses in her hands, setting one in front of each of us before retaking her seat. She murmurs, "Bourbon," and her cup fills with an amber liquid.

Likewise, Reyna and Claire both vocalize their drinks of choice—red wine for Claire, vodka for Reyna—and a moment later they both have full cups.

I pick up my glass, feeling faint magical vibrations come from it. "White wine," I tell the glass, and it promptly fills up with a light golden liquid. I bring it to my nose and inhale, surprised at the rich fruity bouquet, before downing it all in one go. The wine is delicious, and the faint burn of the alcohol feels soothing as it slides down my throat, calming my nerves ever so slightly. No sooner do I set my cup down than it refills, bringing a smile to my lips. "Magic is...versatile."

"To say the least," Reyna mutters. "Some powers reanimate the dead and turn them into mindless creatures whose only goal is to kill; others can, apparently, kill those already dead; a strong enchantment can make the best glass for parties."

"Versatile indeed," Claire agrees, lifting her glass in salute before downing her wine.

"Back to your dream," Odelia says. "You mentioned that Hecate said your mate is important to your strength."

"I believe the word she used was integral," I say with a wince.

The apology Camden offered me in Aesara didn't have all that much meaning in the moment, as I was still intensely raw, but now I've had time to think and calm down somewhat. Not enough to forgive him, but enough to understand he was under enormous pressure already when I miscarried. His violence towards me was by no means acceptable, but I can see he was in a bad place and forgot himself. I don't think he'd ever do something like that again; his remorse and regret were very real. I've also had time to recognize that he didn't attempt to make excuses for himself when we spoke, only gave guarantees that history wouldn't repeat itself. I'm not ready to go back to him, to Kinrith, but I might be ready to speak to him again. Besides, the chasm in my chest created by our faulty bond is its own hindrance, one I'm growing tired of.

I can't ignore the very real possibility that events unfolded as they were meant to. After all, as much as it pains me, when Hecate told me I wasn't ready to be a mother, her words rang true. When she said that Camden is integral to my strength, I can't deny that also had a ring of truth to it. If we're really meant to fight an army that now includes shadow beings and corpses, it might be time to get back on speaking terms with Camden. If for nothing but the fact that we'll need to communicate to figure out how we'll defeat the triads.

"He will be integral, but not just to you and your power," Odelia says. "He has warriors that we need. Before you came in, Sierra, we were doing an accounting of the latest number of fighting triads, as found out by one of my deployed spies; right now, they outnumber us five to one. Shifters will even the odds significantly, giving us the advantage. We need to start training our witches and warlocks with the shifters who are in fighting shape."

I nod, because I know she's right. Our current situation transcends fights and grievances; this is a matter of survival, and even with my black flame and all the considerable magic wielded by the covens, we can't survive alone.

"I've been having weekly discussions with Camden via mirror portal regarding the growing concerns with the triads," Odelia informs me. "If you're ready, it might be for the best if you start speaking with him. He respects me but he reveres you."

"I didn't know you'd been talking with him regularly," I murmur, not liking the twinge of jealousy that travels through me. There's nothing to be jealous of; Odelia couldn't be less interested in my mate outside of technical conversation, as she has a healthy distrust for shifters. Still, some part of me doesn't like that she's been communicating with Camden instead of me.

"We've had a decent amount to coordinate, not the least of it being the battalion of his warriors surrounding this mountain range, serving as protection for all of us," Odelia says. "He's been very useful and has stuck to the terms of our alliance, even going above and beyond in some cases."

That doesn't surprise me. I know that Camden is loyal and sticks to his word—something I learned beyond a shadow of a doubt during my time in Kinrith before things went south. He protected his brother from their father when they were merely boys, protected his entire kind from threats, and when he says he'll do something, he does it—good or bad.

I also heard the stir from this coven and surrounding ones at the arrival of shifters; not all were pleased with the additional protection, though Odelia talked them down by assuring them that the wolves were under strict instruction to protect from a distance. Evidently, they don't even know the exact location of the coven bases; the wards Odelia has up protect us from the scent of a shifter. The stationed warriors only know to roam a general area and be prepared to act if called upon.

"It might be time for you to start parlaying with him directly," Reyna says. "He'll do whatever it takes to please you; the man is pussy-whipped to the max."

"If you're ready," Claire adds, casting a glare at Reyna. "You don't have to if you don't want to."

"I don't mind," I tell them. With things heating up as they are, it's time to start reconciling the rift with Camden. It'll take time to heal what's been broken between us, but I think it can be healed with great effort on both parts. "I'll reach out to him tomorrow."

Odelia nods. "Good. We should all get some sleep—it's very late, and we'll all have plenty to do come morning."

Chapter Seventeen

Camden

In wartime, it's shifter custom for the King Alpha to call upon all of his top generals, captains, and commanders to come to the capital of shifters to strategize. That's how it was in Mythicacia, and that's how it has remained. A few of the men and women in the room with me are Alphas of their own pack, though most prefer to stay in their territories and send their top commanders instead. It matters little to me whether those I'm speaking with are fellow Alphas or top warriors, as long as they have command over their troops, loyalty, and a knack for strategy.

Now, after spending yet another evening in the war room with Wyatt and top generals from different packs and different breeds—some wolf, some feline, and even a dragon shifter— who have traveled from around the world to join me to strategize, I dismiss the room to their respective guest houses on palace grounds. They file out and retire to their chambers for the evening leaving only two people behind with me. My brother and Claude.

Wyatt remains seated in one of the chairs around the war table where an extensive detailed map of this planet is meticulously painted. Figurines are resting atop several areas, indicating amassed troops belonging to vampire, dark faye, hybrid, witch, and shifter armies.

"Things are shaping up nicely," Wyatt says, reaching out to pick up a dark triangular figurine meant to represent vampires. "Things are looking promising, now that we have a surplus of magical power on our side."

I shake my head. "We don't have an accurate accounting of enemy troops yet; we're just guessing based on the regions where they're gathered. Aither has sent out some of his dragons to scout. They should be back to us with concrete numbers in the coming days." I drop into my seat, sighing. "Even so, that won't solve the riddle of exactly what kind of magical power we'll be facing from the dark faye and hybrids."

"Considerable," Claude says, pushing off the wall where he's been standing and silently observing through the course of my meeting, just as he has been every night since my call to loyal packs started bringing top shifters into our palace. "The darklings on their own are beings of great power, and the hybrid offspring between them and vampires are creatures we've never faced or fought."

"The witches had a scrap with some hybrids while warding coastal human villages," Wyatt says. "They didn't report any issues with facing them. They also managed to kill Actaeon, who's long been a menace to this world, not unlike his brothers."

Claude takes a seat at the table beside Wyatt, crossing his arms. "That's because the group of witches who did the warding are all Nightshade Coven members, making them extremely powerful in their own right. The rumors say that Sierra killed Actaeon with the black flame, which also incinerated a considerable stretch of forest. Not all witches are as powerful as the group that happened to be in the right place at the right time, and it stands to reason that our enemies didn't send all their most powerful members for something they assumed to be a routine raping and pillaging of a small human village. The fact that Actaeon was there merely speaks to the vampire royals' investment in our war, and that family's personal appreciation for hunting down the helpless."

My fists clench tightly and my claws extend, cutting into my palms and drawing blood. I crack my neck, fighting for a semblance of calm, as is always the case when I hear Sierra's name mentioned. I force my hands to relax, exhaling a deep breath. I miss my mate with a fierceness I hadn't anticipated; having her gone and the bond in pieces has been a growing strain on both me and my wolf. I haven't seen her or even heard from her since our meeting in Aesara three weeks ago. Not being able to even *talk* to her scrapes away pieces of me that I know won't return until she does.

"Fortunately, the only vampire royal who remains living is the king," Wyatt says. He casts a glance at the clock mounted above the doorway then stands from his seat. "I believe I'll be retiring now as well."

"Enjoy speaking with your mate," I tell him, unable to keep the resentment from my tone. I don't want to resent my brother, but what he has with Leisel—nightly communication—is something I'd kill to have with Sierra.

Wyatt gives a half-hearted grunt in response then briskly walks out of the room.

"Give it time, Camden," Claude advises. "Sierra cares for you, more deeply than either of you know. I sensed that when she was here during my interactions with her. I don't think that care would have disintegrated entirely."

"I almost killed her." The words are a dark, guttural admission, one that shames me every moment I'm awake, *and* in the rare times when I manage to sleep.

"Your actions were regrettable, brought on by a rage of losing your father and then losing your child. The stress of looming war that's plagued you in the last months couldn't have helped. You erred greatly, yes, but keep in mind there are very few faults that mates can't forgive. The bond between you and her isn't broken, merely hurt, which serves as a positive indicator that there's hope," Claude says.

I shake my head at him. "For someone who spent the initial days after her fleeing refusing to speak with me, you seem terribly forgiving now."

Claude lets out a long sigh. "That is the nature of love, Camden. You can be angry—*furious*—with the person you love, but that won't cause you to love them less. I love you and your brother as if you were my own. I will always support you, even when you may not deserve it." He stands from his seat, rounding the table to put a wrinkled hand on my shoulder. "You've proven yourself worthy of my support, Camden. Your recent contrition and solemnity have only gone to show that. Get some rest, if you can, tomorrow I'll be opening portals for arriving troops, which you'll be expected to greet."

His words are touching, as is the knowledge that Claude is still here. He has been with my family for generations, but I don't get the sense he was as close with my father, grandfather, or even great-grandfather as he is with Wyatt and me. He had a heavy hand in raising us, teaching us, guiding us. I know Wyatt cares for him as deeply as I do. He's certainly acted more of a father to us than our actual father ever deigned to. Our father may have been a good monarch, but he was not a good parent.

"Thank you," I tell Claude, gratitude coating my voice. "For everything. Truly."

Claude squeezes my shoulder before releasing me, bowing his head respectfully, and trails out of the room, leaving me alone with my thoughts. I pour myself a drink from the bar cart in the corner, take a seat at the head of the table, and scrub a hand over my face. No sooner have I taken a sip than another person walks into the room. I sense Aspen, one of my best warriors and a personal guard who often travels with me before I look up to see her.

She smiles at me, bowing her head before taking a seat to my right. The spot that rightfully belongs to Sierra which annoys me. Aspen has been seeking me out more and more often in the absence of my mate, which has begun to grow bothersome.

I've slept with Aspen on a few occasions in the past when nights got long and lonely and we were both pining for mates we didn't yet have. There was a very clear mutual agreement that, once one of us found our mate, that would be the end of any occasional fun to pass the time and chase away loneliness. She seemed to abide by that; she was respectful and deferential to Sierra when they met, didn't even hold it against Sierra when she won their duel and never tried to start anything with me again, instead treating me like her Alpha and King.

I'm not sure if she's looking for companionship or something more these last weeks, as she's been coming to find me at random hours of the day and night. Whatever the case, she should know I'm not interested.

"Aspen," I greet flatly. "What do you need?"

She clears her throat, stroking a hand through her blonde hair, which I notice she took care to style in waves.

"To see how you're doing," she says kindly.

I arch an eyebrow. "I am the same as I have been each time you've posed that question in the last weeks; fine."

"You aren't," she says, leaning forward, her presumptuousness surprising me. "You haven't been since Sierra left. Especially since we saw her in Aesara; everyone can sense there's something off."

I narrow my eyes at her. "What business is this of yours? My worries are not your concern. Only the safety of our pack is your concern, especially considering we are now officially at war."

Aspen's lips thin and her jaw clenches before she says, "If you need comfort, I am happy to provide it. We were good together, Camden. I respected that you found your mate and backed off, but then she *left*. She hasn't come back, and it doesn't seem like she's going to. You're hurting, and—"

"Enough," I say harshly, unwilling to listen to any more of this bullshit. "I do not need comfort from you. There is only one being in any realm that can fill the chasm in my chest, and that is my mate. Likewise, there will only be one person in the world who will be able to properly meet your needs, and it is not me. It never was. If you'd like to travel once the war is over and search for your mate, I will be happy to give you leave, but you will not look to me for comfort or whatever it is you want. I cannot provide it. I belong to another."

Instead of backing off as any sane shifter would when commanded by their Alpha and King, Aspen's features twist in anger. She says lowly, "Sierra doesn't want you. *I do*. I was willing to accept her as my queen and Alpha Female, but she isn't here. We can be together again, if only until she gets over herself and returns—"

"Get. Out," I growl, feeling my wolf push against my skin, absolutely enraged that one of our pack members would have the gall to come onto me during such a time. "If I ever hear you speak of *us* again, there will be consequences."

I use the commanding voice that forces any wolf belonging to my pack and just about all shifters to obey; a voice that makes Aspen lower her eyes in submission, stand, and scurry out of the room.

Irritated, I knock back the remainder of my drink, then storm back to my chambers. Nobody would have the gall to approach me in my personal space; they know better than that. Aspen shouldn't have approached me at *all* with such notions, and the fact that she did tells me I haven't been paying close enough attention.

In all fairness my thoughts have been geared towards two things recently: war and Sierra. Nothing else has really been able to make it through the fog clouding my mind because at this moment I only have two responsibilities that matter; a responsibility to protect my people, and a responsibility to somehow get my mate back. Everything else is just white noise, irritating and unnecessary.

Back in my chambers, I close the door behind me and lock it for good measure, not in the mood to deal with anyone else tonight. As they're prone to doing, my eyes stray to the blue cushioned sofa in front of the silver-encrusted fireplace with a small coffee table separating them. Some of my favorite moments with Sierra were spent there—we talked, even laughed, she comforted me in my time of grief following the death of my father and spent ample time giving my wolf the attention he's desperate for. On cue, my wolf lets out a loud whine, pawing at me, trying to get me to fix what is broken between us and our mate.

The creature is more elemental in his thinking; he understands my rage drove Sierra away, but her continued absence saddens and confounds him. He wants her back here *now* and doesn't have the capacity to understand that it'll take a great deal of effort from me to get her back. That or an act of the gods—some sort of damn miracle.

I let out a long sigh, figuring I should shift and give my wolf some freedom to roam about sometime soon. If shifters don't give their animals proper time to explore, the animals will get restless and disgruntled. Sharing one's soul with an animal has its complications, and it requires walking a delicate balance between man and wolf to maintain dominance over our inner animal. Without that dominance, we're at risk of turning rogue—losing ourselves to our animalistic instincts completely, which often leads to disaster. After all, animals are primarily creatures of instinct and survival; they don't really *do* logic.

I head to my bathroom, wanting to shower and at least *attempt* to get some rest, even though I don't have high hopes that sleep will come to me. As I'm splashing my face with cold water from the sink, trying to get my wits about me, I notice the mirror start to ripple. Instantly, I straighten and tense; the only time I've seen mirrors start to move like water is when witchcraft is being done to open either a portal or communication. Odelia's reached out to me regularly so we can share our gathered information on enemies and plan ahead, but she usually reaches out using mirrors in other rooms of the castle, most notably Sierra's old room, not *this* one.

A flash of red hair and golden eyes appears in the ripples as they start to slow and smooth over, revealing an image of *Sierra*.

She's seated in what looks to be a cavern of some sort. Her eyes are wide, she looks a little pale and her body is stiff in her seat like she might bolt at any moment or close our connection. It takes every ounce of my being to stay in place and not leap forward, pressing my hands against my mirror, trying to get closer to her even though there are thousands of miles separating us.

She looks good. Tired and a little wrung out—I also notice bruises along her arms that make me nervous—but good. Alive. Present. And in front of me, *finally*. I've been praying that there would be a moment I might find myself facing her through a mirror portal rather than the Nightshade high priestess, but I didn't expect it.

"Hello, Camden," she says uncertainly.

Chapter Eighteen

Camden

My wolf instantly goes on alert, pushing against my skin hard, trying to force a shift so he can get to her. I hold firm against him.

"Hi," I respond, not quite certain that this is actually happening and not a hallucination brought on by lack of sleep. In either case, I don't care; this is the closest I've been to Sierra in far too long. If it's a hallucination, it's one I never want to end.

"It's been a while," she says, a blush staining her cheeks as she looks me over. "You look like shit."

Definitely not a hallucination. Only the real Sierra, *my* Sierra, would be that blunt. I've always found that more endearing than rude.

A laugh rumbles out of me. "Thank you. I haven't slept much."

Something that might be empathy flits across her expression for a brief moment before she shutters it, inhaling a deep breath. It doesn't look like she's terribly comfortable with reaching out to me, but she isn't breaking the connection or running away, so I take that to be a good sign.

"I'm sorry to hear that," she murmurs, surprising me. I'd have thought any of my pain or misfortune would please her not upset her. The fact that she still seems to care gives me a great deal of hope that I hold onto tightly.

I shrug. "That's the nature of being a leader. Besides, I stressed you out so much you didn't sleep for something like four nights and then passed out—turnabout's fair play. Shifters don't require much sleep anyways." I'm rambling, trying to fill the awkward silence with something, and I'm pleased to see it doesn't drive her away—instead, a small smile forms on her lips.

"Fair enough. I, uh, figured it might be good if we start communicating directly rather than going through Odelia. The witches are under the assumption that you'll listen to me more than you'll listen to anyone else."

"They're right," I admit.

I'll parlay and coordinate with Odelia, I've come to have a great deal of respect for the high priestess, but I can say no to her if she pushes too far or says something I disagree with. Sierra has a much better chance of wrangling an agreement—I'll be the first to admit that. It's just about impossible to deny my mate anything.

Besides, I have more trust in Sierra than I do any of the other witches. I came to understand a great deal about her during her time in the palace; namely, she has a good heart and a moral compass that drives her to do the right thing, regardless of personal prejudice and sentiment. That's exactly what drove her to push me to make peace with the witches; she saw it as the best chance of survival for shifters, humans, and witches, so she set aside her personal dislike of mythics and got to work.

A small smile flits over her lips. "Yes, right. I'm reaching out to discuss some...new developments. Ones of a concerning nature."

Hearing the worry in her tone, I straighten. "What's wrong?" Whatever the problem is, I'll fix it.

She shakes her head. "Nothing with me personally. I, uh...this is going to sound ludicrous, which it absolutely is, but I had a visit from Hecate while sleeping. Not just that I imagined her in my dreams, she came to me."

Shock courses through me at that, along with a flicker of disbelief. Gods don't reach out to mortals; we're beneath their notice. They might care about the species they created as a whole, but not individuals. We're not significant enough to them. There have been a few moments in mythic history where a mythic claimed to have been visited by a god; most of those times were debunked. Not all of them though. Claude confirmed that on a few rare occasions and in times of great peril for a species, a patron god of that species might reach out to a member of it to pass on tidbits of wisdom or advice.

If there's anyone in this realm that could attract the attention of a god, I'd be willing to wager that's Sierra. That also indicates that witches are in greater danger than previously assumed.

"What did the goddess of magic want?" I ask.

"To pass on a message," Sierra responds. Then, she gives me a brief rundown of her encounter with her patron goddess, along with the implications of Hecate's cryptic warnings, which she later figured out with the help of other witches.

"A shadow wielder and a necromancer," I say once Sierra's done speaking, my voice faint. "*Fuck.*"

"Agreed. The upside is that the black flame can kill the reanimated dead, and apparently, Leisel's light can combat the shadows. The downside is that we have a very small amount of time to truly learn to control our powers. There's also a...complication with my fire."

That makes me tense and I lean forward, gripping the edges of the sink so hard the marble cracks under my hands. "What kind of complication?"

Pain seeps into her expression, turning her full lips down at the corners and making shadows creep into her eyes. One of her hands idly moves to rest on her stomach, which tips me off before she even speaks. "The"—she blinks several times, inhaling a deep breath—"the miscarriage. It messed with my fire. When the rogues confronted me, I tried to call on my flames again and again, but they wouldn't come forward until it was too late—apparently dips and surges are a common side effect of pregnancy in witches. The fact that a dip in my power cost me my child sort of sent my fire into a rage. It's powerful enough to have its own sentience, and it's been uncontrollable ever since I lost the baby. I've been working on training it, and at this point, I can call it at will, but when I do, it sort of goes berserk. Attacks everyone and everything around me." She swallows before raising her hand, showing me a symbol scarred into the flesh of her arm. "Hecate gave me this in the dream, a permanent reminder that I'm her warrior. Told me that everything happened as it should have, my fire is behaving the way it needs to, and that I simply need to figure it out and move forward—she wasn't much help when it came to controlling my fire. I don't think she feels I need to control it. Possibly because, as a deity, she doesn't see the harm in my fire laying waste to people on our side of the fight, as long as it kills the necromancer too."

I swallow hard, feeling a dark, deep sadness pull at both me and my wolf at the mention of our lost child. It was barely a child, only an embryo at that point, but it was still my baby. Someone I desperately wanted to meet, raise, and love alongside Sierra. The insanity of recent weeks has done a good job of distracting me from my loss, but thinking about it still brings me a great deal of sorrow. I can see that it does the same to Sierra.

"I'm so sorry I blamed you for our loss, Sierra," I tell her quietly, a deep shame radiating in my core.

Her loss is as heavy as mine, if not heavier because our baby was cut right out of her body while she was unable to do anything to stop it—that must've been a deeply traumatic experience. Afterward, when I should've held and comforted her and grieved with her, instead I blamed her and hurt her. Even if she comes to forgive me for that, I don't know that I'll ever forgive myself. "The miscarriage wasn't your fault. I know that. I was so blinded by rage at the loss that I wasn't thinking clearly, and I hurt you when I should've protected you."

Tears spark in her eyes as she glances to the side, before returning her gaze to me and giving her head a shake. "It's in the past. Nothing can be done about it now. According to Hecate, what happened was part of some fucked up celestial plan." Her teeth grit at that, and she appears to try to swallow down her rage.

I have to admit, I'm not particularly pleased that our tragedy was part of some greater plan regardless of how important or noble. I also understand that gods are gods; they'll act in the way they see fit to achieve their own ends with little regard for how it impacts a single individual. Besides, despite the horror of the situation, there's something cathartic about knowing that the loss wasn't for nothing. It was horrible and it led to a falling out I wish I could go back in time to change, but like Sierra said, it's in the past. All we can do is move forward.

"Odelia brought up the idea of starting to train our fighters together. Witches and shifters should start becoming accustomed to each other, especially since they will soon be sharing a battlefield, on the same side for the first time ever," Sierra says, switching the topic away from the past and towards the future.

I clear the darker thoughts from my head, instead focusing on the here and now. Historically, when witches and shifters shared a battlefield, they were on opposing sides. Losses were heavy on both ends, and the victory was always dismal regardless of the winner because many lives were taken in the carnage. It would be good to start teaching our people to work together rather than simply trying to eradicate each other.

"I'll arrange that on my end. Troops are still arriving from around the world, but there'll be a heavy concentration of them in Kinrith in the coming weeks. If Odelia could send her troops down here, we can start training them together," I offer.

Sierra nods. "I'll pass on the message."

For a long moment, we stare at each other, a thousand unspoken words passed between our gazes. She has a mixture of regret, pain, and a flicker of longing etched into her features, while I assume I have a similar expression, with more emphasis on longing.

"One more thing," Sierra says, and everything within me jumps to accommodate any request she might have.

"Name it," I reply. "Whatever you want that's in my power, it's yours."

She blinks a few times, a slight smile curling her lips before they flatten into a thin line. "When I visited the coastal village with my coven a few days ago, I spoke with a human who had a great deal of animosity towards shifters, stemming from the fact that his daughter was taken from him. Apparently, she's a mate to a shifter in the Red Moon pack. Her name is Lana, and her father, Samuel, is desperate to see or speak with her. He's really worried, Camden. When humans lose their kids to mythics, they never get to see them again. That makes a lot of them think that their children are being mistreated or abused and perpetuates their hatred and distrust of Mythics. To that end, I have two requests."

I feel my brows furrow as I think through her words. Humans have generally been too far beneath my notice for me to give them or their feelings a second thought; a problem that Sierra's presence had enlightened me to. She's brought a great deal of perspective to my life, and while I don't always love it, I can admit it's valuable. I try to imagine what it might be like if I had a daughter who was taken away from me for the purpose of mating, and I never saw or heard from her again—instantly, anger thickens my blood.

There's a reason shifters don't let human mates out of their sight; they're too protective, too keen to keep their mates with them at all times and not risk letting them go. Like me, shifters generally don't bother themselves with thinking about the thoughts or feelings of humans because they don't truly matter to us, which is a mistake. One that's been overlooked for far too long.

"You want me to arrange a meeting with Lana and her father, and you want me to write in some sort of law that guarantees humans contact with their family even after they're claimed and brought to pack territories," I guess.

Sierra's head tilts to the side, and she appears somewhat taken aback by my intuition. My problem has never been an inability to read people or a lack of empathy; it's that my empathy has only ever extended to my own kind...until now. If Sierra's presence in my life as my mate is an indicator of anything, it's that there are things that need to change, and the two of us are in the unique position to make those changes. There's a reason the gods paired us as they did, and I believe at least part of that is to bring reform that strengthens this world and its inhabitants.

"Yes," she agrees with a nod. "I get that humans don't really matter to Mythics—after all, why should they? They nearly destroyed this planet before your invasion and are currently the weakest people living on it. That being said, they *are* important. Aside from the fact that humans are mates to many mythics, I think everyone needs to understand that being more harmonious with the natives of this planet can benefit all of us. They know this planet, they've lived here much longer than you, they know history and hold secrets of nature that could be useful. In the grand scheme of things, they matter as much as any of you."

I nod slowly unable to disagree because she's right. Humans have suffered most under the reign of mythics; we beat them back and subjugated them until their numbers dropped from billions to maybe hundreds of thousands, if that. The reigning shifter monarch never actually gave out orders to kill humans, but my father and grandfather did nothing to protect them either because they didn't consider humans theirs to protect. To them, they were merely pests; it mattered little whether they lived or died.

"Agreed," I say simply. "I'll speak with the high council, get something drawn up. I'll also reach out to the Red Moon Alpha, and have him confirm Lana's presence and facilitate a meeting between her and her father."

Sierra's eyes brighten. "That would be great. Maybe...maybe it could be beneficial if you attended the meeting along with Odelia. Show solidarity, make it clear that the highest-ranking witch and shifter on this continent are willing to work with humans. Word could spread and the gesture might go a long way in opening some human minds. It won't fuel change overnight, but it'd be a good first step."

She's right, which, as I'm starting to realize, is a habit of hers. Sierra's a thinker, a planner, and someone who's already proven to be very gifted with diplomacy. She has a knack for uniting individuals who have always hated each other, probably because of her nature as an earthly witch; a human with magic that stems from the very fabric of nature on this planet. There are very few of those, so it's difficult not to listen to her. After all, witches and shifters have spent centuries on this planet, and *thousands* of years in our native realm hating and fighting each other until she brought us together. Granted, we need each other for the sake of survival, but I don't think anyone but she could've united us.

"I can agree to that, on one condition," I tell her. "You come along as well."

Sierra gives me a look that says *I can see right through you*. "You're making that a condition because you haven't seen me in weeks, aren't you?"

I shrug, giving her a half-smile. "I won't deny that. I miss you terribly as does my wolf. He's been sulking like a hormonal teenager for quite some time." I like how her face softens a little at my words, so I feel confident enough to go on. "That's not the only reason, though. When you speak, people listen. You have a unique perspective and a good way with words. With you around, I think it'll be a lot more difficult for Samuel to be hostile towards me and mine. Besides, you're the orchestrator of the meeting, don't you want to get the credit and make sure everything goes according to plan?"

She gives an eye roll. "You don't have to manipulate me with offers of getting thanks, that's not why I'm doing this. I'm doing it because it's *right*. I'll attend, though, to keep the peace and make sure things go smoothly. Samuel was very hesitant to even let my coven ward his town, thinking it was some sort of trick until I...well, bluntly told him if I wanted him dead he'd already be dead."

I feel my lips kick up in amusement. As much as Sierra can be a powerful diplomat, she's also blunt when the situation calls for it. She's never had a problem standing up to people when they're in the wrong, least of all me. This conversation is just another example of that.

"Of course you did," I say, amusement coating my tone. "I'll get back to you with word from the Red Moon Alpha soon. Could we...could we speak again like this? More often, I mean?" I've missed seeing her, hearing her voice, just having her in front of me, even if she's a great distance from me.

Sierra considers me for several long moments before inclining her head. "I think I'd like that, yes. I'm still angry with you, Cam. Really angry. But...we were both in a bad place the day I ran. It's probably time to start getting over our shit, if only for the sake of our people. *They* need us."

Cam. I haven't heard her call me that nickname in far too long, and the shiver that runs down my spine only affirms just how much I've missed it. I've missed *everything* about her, and I'm impatient to have her back. My wolf has gotten over the initial shock and exhilaration of seeing his mate and is now frantically urging me to try to claw my way through the mirror to get to her. I ignore him though, instead focusing on the hope her words bring. She's willing to speak to me again. I'll get to see her face to face, not just through a mirror, as soon as I arrange the meeting between Lana and her father, which puts that at the very top of my to-do list.

Something shifts and pulses in my chest intensely, forcing a gasp from me and nearly sending me tumbling sideways. I clutch the counter again, blinking several times, shocked when I realize what the sensation is; *the bond.* I haven't felt anything other than numbness and a horrible chasm every time I've tried to access the bond, but now I can feel it doing *something*. Starting to reform in the most minute basic way, but at least I can finally *feel* it.

I look back to Sierra, only to see her with a hand pressed over her chest, clutching it while gaping. She looks as shocked as I feel, and when she meets my eyes, there's a mixture of fear and hope shining in hers.

"You felt it too?" I question, even though I already know her response.

She nods. "Our bond. It's...doing something."

"Which is more than it's done for over a month," I say. I feel as much fear as I see painted over her features—fear of somehow fucking this up again, fear of not being enough for her.

"I think it might be trying to mend," she murmurs, a frown briefly creasing her brows.

"It must be responding to the fact that we're finally communicating," I realize.

"Huh. Well, there's that." She stiffens as I hear some yelling in the background that makes me concerned—like someone is having a shouting match outside her room. Her lips thin as she says, "You were right with one thing; witches *are* crazy. I have to go."

"Are you safe?" I ask, worry sparking within me.

She laughs. "Unless you count two coven members using the hallways as a sparring ground to win a bet as unsafe, I'm fine. This is a commonplace occurrence, don't worry. Leisel's a natural peacekeeper though, so I worry she'll get caught in the crossfire—I need to go."

"Can we speak tomorrow night again?" I ask. As an enticement, I add, "I should have heard back from the Red Moon Alpha by then; I could get a date and time for a meet to you."

She waves a hand, craning her neck to look at something out of frame. "Yes, that's fine. I'll reach out at the same time." With that, she leans forward, swipes her thumb over the corner of the mirror, and disappears.

Chapter Nineteen

Sierra

It isn't often one walks into a room to witness a witch and a warlock, both holding glowing swords, circling each other with kill-ready looks on their faces.

"*Take it back!* I am *not* sane!" Reyna shrieks.

Bane laughs, giving her sword a light strike with his. "Prove it, witchling. You seem to be all talk and no follow through."

"My string of darkling ears and vamp fangs is longer than yours!" Reyna shouts. "I was the one who *started* that tradition around here—what about that advertises sanity?"

Claire, seated on a sofa at the far end of the room, gives me a half-hearted wave. "Don't be alarmed, they get like this every once in a while."

Either the two sorcerers don't hear her or they simply choose to ignore her; Reyna and Bane continue glaring at each other. Well, Reyna's glaring, while Bane's biting his bottom lip in what appears to be an attempt to hold in a laugh. I blink as Claire picks up a bowl of candied nuts from the table in front of her and tosses a handful into her mouth, her attention glued to her fellow Nightshade sorcerers.

"Are you seriously kicking back with snacks like this is a damn theatrical performance?" I ask her.

She chews and swallows before replying, "Best entertainment we get around here." She tosses another handful back as Reyna slashes her sword through the air in a sweeping motion, nicking Bane's arm. He hisses at her, and then the two are on each other, trading strikes, the deafening sound of steel clashing against steel echoing through the cave. They don't just use swords; they also throw spells at each other, with Reyna demonstrating her powerful ability to use single-word spells, half of which she knows well enough to be able to speak them in her mind, that pack quite the punch—I hear several bones snap as the two go at each other.

I shake my head. "I'm going to find my sister and Wes; have fun with the two psychos."

"Thank you!" Reyna exclaims, momentarily pausing in her fight to point her sword at me. She delivers a kick to Bane's torso that sends him stumbling back several steps, crashing into a nearby table, and pointedly tells him, "See, *she* gets it! Sierra, out of the two of us, who do you believe possesses less sanity?"

"I believe I'll lose what little sanity I have if I stick around to watch," I mutter. Then, louder, "Ladies, you're both equally crazy. Now if you can stop fretting about whose dress is prettier and other menial nonsense, we have shit to do."

"This isn't menial! He insulted me!" Reyna exclaims.

"See what I mean?" Claire says through a mouthful of her candied nuts. "They're fucking hilarious."

I shake my head, walking out of the room. In my time with the witches, I have learned that they really *are* crazy; they treat combat like a fun sport rather than a necessity of life as a mythic, which is probably why they are so damn proficient with it.

And even though they can easily overtake opponents with magic, they find swordplay to be *entertaining*—something about the enjoyment of drawing blood from opponents.

I make my way out to the balcony where breakfast is served, finding the usual crowd of people gathered around the large stone table. Rune and Odelia are speaking with each other at the head of the table, ignoring their plates, while many other rambunctious conversations are also taking place. Leisel is seated on the bench, giggling as she weaves a braid into Maddy's hair, who's sitting beside Leisel. Wesley's sitting on the other side of her, speaking animatedly with Cedrick—presumably about tactile combat magic, which Wesley has proven to excel in.

I walk up to the table, mussing Wesley's hair in greeting, smiling when he shoots me a disgruntled look over his shoulder, before pressing a kiss to the top of Leisel's head.

She beams at me, greeting me with a loud, "*Goooooood morning*," and I blink as Chip leaps off of her shoulder and climbs up my arm before perching himself right up against my neck, rubbing his furry cheek against my skin in greeting. Reyna emerges onto the balcony as well, sporting a few new bruises and cuts—not looking put off whatsoever by them as she seats herself at the table and starts loading a plate. Claire and Bane follow behind her, also taking seats at the table and getting started on breakfast.

"You seem to be in high spirits today," Odelia observes, breaking her conversation with Rune to cast me a speculative glance.

I *am* in a better mood than I have been for several weeks, which can only be attributed to the fact that I spoke with Camden last night. We both got a good deal off of our chests, and the bond that's been weighing on me in its shattered state became a little lighter as it began to heal.

"Spoke with Camden last night. We agreed that some new laws need to be put in place that allow humans who have been claimed by shifters to have continued contact with their families. He'll be getting back to me tonight about Samuel's daughter, Lana, and hopefully we can set up a visit soon."

Odelia smiles at me, looking as pleased with this new development as I am. "You really are quite the diplomat, Sierra."

I shrug. "My status as both human and witch *and* shifter by mating affords me a lot of leeway and different perspectives. I can get humans and witches and shifters to listen simply because of what I am."

"That's only part of the puzzle though," Cedrick chimes in. "There's having the right to speak from multiple perspectives, and then there's actually getting people to *listen*. Don't sell yourself short; not everyone in your position can manage to do what you've done."

The high praise makes me blush a little. "I think the fact that everyone who I need to listen is facing war makes them more amenable to seeing reason. Circumstances are certainly favorable."

There's also the fact that I've spent my life reading up on the history of this world. Initially, because my parents insisted that history is one of the most important parts of education, and then because I missed my father's impassioned history rants so much, I felt continuing with reading up on and studying history was a way to make sure he lived on in memory. I devoured every biography and textbook I could get my hands on, and that's all been surprisingly helpful. In a way, without even realizing it, I've been preparing to take the role of a diplomat between species for practically my entire life.

"Are you going to be in contact with Camden regularly?" Odelia asks me, standing from her seat to approach me.

I nod. "I think so, yes. There's one caveat to setting up the meeting between Lana and her father; Camden would like both of us to be there along with him. He can represent shifters, you represent witches, and I represent humans."

Reyna, eavesdropping from where she's seated on the other side of the table, snorts. "Of course, he did—that's the best way to get an in-person meeting with you as soon as possible. Wolves are sneaky as fuck."

"Not as sneaky as witches though," Odelia freely admits. She gives me a long look up and down, her eyebrows raising. "The bond between you and him is different. Stronger. Almost like it's starting to heal."

I nod. "We had a good conversation. I felt the shift take place—I think it's beginning to mend."

"That's very good," Odelia says with a nod. "Especially since Hecate specified how important he'd be to your magical strength. Maybe the mending of the bond will help you gain more control over your fire."

"That would be very comforting," Claire says. "I'm good with shields, but even I occasionally tire of having to hold one up for my life each time we train."

I wince, shame overcoming me. "I'm sorry for that."

Reyna interjects, "Why? Fear of life is good for the soul. Reminds us of what we're fighting for."

"Just because *you* get a rush out of fear doesn't mean the rest of us do," Claire says on a sigh.

Reyna blinks. "You don't like being afraid? I fucking love it. Gets my blood pumping." She pauses. "It also gets me horny, which can be a bit of a drag, since I then need to find someone to alleviate—"

"Reyna," I cut her off. "There are children present."

Leisel looks at me. "What does horny mean?"

I stifle a wince. One of the less fun parts of living with witches is that they have no filter and aren't very versed in censoring themselves, so oftentimes they end up dropping sexual terminology around Leisel and I have to answer uncomfortable questions.

"It, um..." I trail off, trying to think on my feet. "It means someone's excited for battle."

Leisel frowns. "Isn't Reyna *always* excited for battle? She fights like it's her job."

Several laughs sound from the people seated around us, tuned into this exchange like it's the most entertaining thing in the world. Claire's lips are thinned to suppress a smile, though her eyes are sparkling with mirth. Reyna isn't even trying to suppress her smile—she's grinning like a loon, staring between Leisel and me, looking excited to see what's next. Wesley's shaking his head with exasperation, Cedrick's chuckling under his breath, and even Odelia looks like she's fighting a laugh.

"Yes, I do," Reyna confirms.

Leisel nods. "So you're always horny."

"Yep," Reyna says. Her fight against laughter fails as a snort escapes her.

"When will Camden reach out to you regarding the meeting?" Odelia asks me, smoothly changing the topic and giving me a reprieve.

"Tonight," I reply. "Same time as I reached out to him last night. Hopefully the meeting is set up soon."

"That eager to see him?" Odelia questions, her tone faintly teasing.

"Eager to take the first step to living harmoniously with the natives of this planet," I correct.

Odelia doesn't look like she entirely believes me and her expression advertises that fact.

I'm apprehensive to be near Camden again, as I'm still not exactly over the fact that I nearly lost my life to him, though I do understand he was in a rage, and I don't think that he'll repeat his actions. Beyond the fact that his apology last night rang with sincerity, there's also the fact that I could *see* his regret and determination in his expression. He really was sorry for what happened, and I believe he learned from his mistake. Still, that knowledge isn't enough to entirely put me at ease, because I don't think I'll ever be able to forget how he looked when he was choking me. He was so furious, so mindless, he didn't even realize what he was doing until it was too late.

I think that I'll be able to get over it eventually, but that'll take time. It isn't a simple matter—letting go of that memory won't be easy, but I am willing to try because the small part of me that missed Camden from the moment I left has been growing. Even while our bond was all but null and void, I still missed him, which is telling. Now that it's on the mend, I'm missing him more, and I'm no longer terribly irritated with myself for that fact.

"Right, then, eat up so we can get to training," Odelia tells me.

* * *

That evening, Camden reaches out to me with news that he's arranged a meeting for Lana, her mate, and her Alpha in Midlington, allowing Lana a visit with Samuel for the following day. So, the next morning, Maddy teleports me, Odelia, Claire, and Reyna back to Midlington, directly to the clearing where we appeared last time.

I'm not surprised to see that Camden's already here, along with Wyatt and a few other people I recognize as pack warriors. There's also a young blonde woman standing next to a tall dark-haired man—Lana and her mate, I presume. In Lana's arms is a *baby*, which immediately makes my heart clench. Had things been different, I might've soon held my own baby in my arms.

Camden is speaking to a tall man with graying hair, a graying beard, and silver-blue eyes, about twenty feet away from my entourage, not far from Lana and her mate. Camden looks up and his eyes meet mine moments after I appear. A slow smile spreads on his lips, and his eyes practically light up with pleasure, which makes something in my chest stir with positivity.

He straightens and motions to Lana and the man beside her, along with the man he's been talking to, before leading them over to us.

Stopping a few feet away, he gives a respectful nod to Odelia. "high priestess," he greets.

"King Alpha," she returns, forgoing the respectful nod.

I know that, while Odelia might be glad that things are on the mend between me and Camden and that he's willing to dedicate great deals of time and effort into both his alliance with her and his relationship with me, her protective nature of witches means she'll probably be even slower to forgive him than I will. After all, when he hurt me, she took it as a slight against her kind—as a personal offense against all witches, and I've learned that Odelia can hold a grudge like no other. She won't let that grudge affect business though, which only makes me respect her more.

"This is Bordat, Alpha of the Red Moon Pack, which resides in the eastern territories of this continent. Bordat, the high priestess Odelia is currently the greatest ally to shifters, so I hope you will treat her and her companions with the respect they deserve," Camden introduces. Then motioning to me, he says, "This is the earthly witch that word has been spreading about and my mate. She's the person who facilitated our alliance."

I have to admit, I like the praise and acknowledgment he's giving me along with Odelia. Apparently, Camden takes alliances as seriously as we do—otherwise, his tone wouldn't be warning all the unfamiliar wolves to conduct themselves respectfully or risk his wrath.

Bordat bows his head to Odelia, then nods at me, before flicking a brief, somewhat dismissive glance over Reyna and Claire. "It's a pleasure to meet you," he tells me, also glancing over to Odelia as he speaks. "Beside me is one of my best warriors, Korbin, and his mate, Lana, who is holding their nine-month-old pup, Galantia. We're all very glad to be here to facilitate a meeting between Lana and her father—she's missed him a great deal."

Despite his words, Bordat doesn't *sound* particularly happy to be facilitating such a meeting—in fact, he sounds like being here is a chore that he'd rather not take part in. When he said that Lana missed her father, he sounded like he couldn't care less, which rankles me—as a member of his pack, whether she's human or not, Lana should have his consideration and protection. It looks like it'll take some legwork to get other Alphas to prioritize their human pack member's needs, which I am more than happy to encourage.

Lana steps forward, giving me a teary-eyed smile. "I was told that you're the person who got the ball rolling on this meeting—I've been asking for quite some time to no avail. Thank you so much, my queen, I can't tell you how happy seeing my dad will make me."

Her mate, Korbin, nods along with her, before casting an irritated glance at their Alpha. I get the sense from that silent exchange that Korbin might've brought up Lana's request to their Alpha more than once only to be brushed off and denied, which I can imagine is frustrating. It's heartening that Korbin really does seem to care about Lana's familial connection, though it doesn't come as a great surprise—I know that, even when I was dead set on fighting him, Camden took steps to make me happy and comfortable in the palace because my happiness brought him contentment. I still remember and miss the painter's studio he had set up for me.

Galantia, who's been sleeping soundly, stirs and makes a few restless noises before blinking her eyes open. Those eyes find her mother almost instantly and brighten before a wide toothless smile overtakes her chubby cheeks. I can see both Odelia and Claire melt at the sight, while Reyna looks markedly uncomfortable in the presence of a baby. Galantia's eyes then shift around every gathered person with curiosity before landing on me, and she proceeds to stare directly at me with a penetrating gaze that feels like it reaches down into my very soul. My heart squeezes tighter, and it feels like an invisible hand wraps around my chest and lungs, making breathing difficult.

Slowly, Galantia's smile returns, and to my great surprise, she reaches her arms out in my direction with grabby hands. Lana gives a delighted laugh, looking from her daughter to me. "She doesn't take to people very often—she never reaches for anyone outside the family."

Korbin adds, "Gala's like me in that regard, I'm afraid."

Lana walks a few steps forward, closing the distance between us. "Would you like to hold her, Your Majesty?"

"As long as you agree to call me Sierra," I return, my voice slightly choked. "I'm not really one for titles. I'd like to be as much of a friend as I am a monarch."

Lana smiles widely, then gently extends her arms to me. I take Galantia in my arms, taking care to hold her properly, and stare down into her smiling eyes. The pup reaches one of her tiny fists up to grab a handful of my hair and yanks on it, making me wince a little before a chuckle escapes me.

"You're a strong one already, aren't you?" I coo at her, feeling my chest fill up with warmth.

"Don't we know it," Korbin grumbles. "I had to start shaving my beard after she yanked half of it out with that grip of hers."

Lana bumps him with her shoulder. "That's your fault. She gets her strength from your side of the family."

It's at once heartening and sad to see how close Lana and Korbin seem and how *happy* they appear together, along with their daughter. A longing ache pulses in my chest because a big part of me wants exactly what they have; family, happiness, a sense of peace and belonging. I might've had it, too, if fate hadn't decided to take my child from me before its time.

Seeing a few figures walk over the hill, I hand Galantia back to Lana, and then motion over her shoulder. "I think someone's here to see you."

Chapter Twenty

Lana gasps lightly before spinning around, just as Samuel and an old woman by his side come into view. He stops for a moment, dead still, as he looks from Lana to the baby she's holding, and back to his daughter. Samuel's eyes shift to Korbin as Lana hands Galantia off to her mate before taking off in a sprint to run to her father. The two collide in a tangle of limbs and exchange of watery smiles, tears streaming from both Lana and her father.

I feel my eyes flutter closed—seeing the father-daughter exchange makes me miss my father with a sudden violent ache. I have to admit there's even a bit of jealousy floating around within me—I'd kill to see Dad one last time, to introduce him to Leisel, the daughter he never got to meet, to hear his voice again. As much as seeing Lana's reunion brings me joy, it's also a reminder that she has things I never will, and some part of me can't help but envy her for it.

I squish that part vehemently, reminding myself that I have a great deal of memories with my family to keep me company, even if I no longer have the option of seeing them. As Lana brings her father over to the group of people and starts making introductions, I see that Samuel has clear reservations as he looks over the gathered wolves and witches, though he does seem to soften slightly at seeing me.

"Camden, while we have you, shall we discuss business?" Odelia says quietly.

Camden inclines his head. "Of course. Best to give the family some space for their reunion anyways."

As a group, the Rockwell wolves and Nightshade witches walk a few steps away from the others, far enough that our conversation won't be overheard.

Wyatt bumps my arm with his own. "Gotta say, I'm a little disappointed you didn't bring Leisel with you."

I shrug. "She has a busy schedule with training. Besides, you get to speak with her and see her nightly."

He wrinkles his nose. "Not the same as an in-person meeting."

"If you aren't enjoying the conversations my coven facilitates nightly, we don't need to go through the effort of opening up the connection," Odelia says sharply.

Claire points at Odelia. "What she said."

Wyatt quickly holds his hands out in front of him. "I'm not complaining, believe me—I'm more than happy to get to speak with her consistently. I didn't mean any disrespect."

"Next time we meet in person, I'll bring my sister," I assure him. I know Leisel has affection for Wyatt, and I get the sense that she sees him as something of a close friend and confidant. Wyatt gives me a grateful smile in turn.

"Onto business," Odelia says. "All fighting sorcerers are prepared to mobilize at a moment's notice, and portals have been created at each coven base that can be coded to any location within a matter of minutes. The triads have been quieter than usual, which is cause for concern, though I assume their lack of action means they're regrouping. After all, the vampire royal family has lost two of its three members, which I imagine to be disheartening to the masses."

"Good," I say. "Let them worry and stew; the more disheartened they are, the easier they'll be to beat."

Camden raises his eyebrows. "I like this vicious side of you." When I arch a brow at him, he amends, "When it isn't turned on me, that is."

"What are preparations like on your front?" Odelia asks him.

"Progressing," Camden replies. "I've called all the warrior packs and fighting shifters to the lands surrounding Kinrith, along with all the appropriate Alpha's and commanders. Once everyone's here, we'll have an army of about a hundred thousand shifters—including wolves, felines, and a small pack of dragons that have agreed to aid our cause. Some of those dragons are currently on scouting missions to count the enemy forces—so far the reports we've received put the triad's numbers at close to sixty thousand, though we'll hopefully get confirmed reports within the next days."

Odelia nods. "Excellent. I have fourteen thousand fighting witches, which means we'll soundly outnumber our enemies. The living ones, at least."

"Only fourteen thousand?" One of the warriors standing behind Camden pipes up, shooting Odelia a condescending look.

That makes every witch in the vicinity, including me, bristle. A moment later, a stream of crackling silver magic slams into the wolf who was stupid enough to speak, knocking him to the ground and making his body seize. That silver magic then splits from him and attacks the two other shifters on either side of him, also making them drop like stones.

I glance to my side, seeing Reyna with a hand extended in front of her and a *bored* expression on her face. "Yes, wolf, fourteen thousand. A single trained warrior of ours can muster up the power to take out three to five people without batting an eye, which means that one witch is equivalent to an average of four shifters. In shifter terms, that would put us close to sixty thousand. Now, take into account that there are several dozen of us who can take out ten to *fifty* enemies with the use of a single power, and our numbers are evened, wouldn't you say?"

I bite my lip, trying to hold in a smile as all the remaining wolves who stand cast Reyna glances of utter amazement tinged with fear. The wolves continue seizing on the ground, shaking, teeth chattering, and whatever spell she just hit them with is so intense I think I hear a few bones snap as well.

Camden licks his front teeth. "Your point has been taken. If you will please back off of my warriors?"

Reyna gives Camden a pointed stare that says *I don't take orders from you* before turning to Odelia who gives her a nod. With a sigh, Reyna drops her hand back to her side, and whatever spell was afflicting the warriors cuts off. The three appear dazed—one of them is passed out—and all look like they've seen better days.

Wyatt blinks several times, looking between the felled wolves and Reyna. "I...I have no words."

"Then shut the fuck up," Reyna returns dryly.

I stifle a smile then give Camden a shrug. "You were right when you said they're crazy. It's the kind of crazy you want—*need*—on your side of the battle though."

Camden inclines his head. "Evidently so. Roan, Saunders, stop embarrassing yourselves and get up. Wake up Leander as well."

One of the wolves—Saunders—stumbles back to his feet, gives his head a shake, then shoots Reyna a look brimming with hatred. "You cracked my fucking rib."

"Only one? Shame," Reyna scoffs.

"Ease up, Saunders, that one will annihilate you if you try her," Wyatt says mildly.

Saunders, however, doesn't appear to want to ease up—it looks like Reyna's little lesson really grated on his pride. He takes a menacing step forward, which I know is a mistake when a slow, excited smile spreads on Reyna's lips. That's the look she gets whenever she's about to tear into an opponent like they fucked her mother.

"That wasn't a fair fight. You took me off guard," Saunders snaps. "Do you have no honor at all?"

"Not even a drop when it comes to someone who's being condescending to me and mine," Reyna returns with a toothy smile. "You want to go again? This time I'll even let you take the first hit."

"No need for that," Camden interjects calmly. "Saunders, stand down, you'll only make even more of a fool of yourself. Odelia, thank you for the update. If I could have a moment with you privately to discuss some finer details?"

Odelia inclines her head at him, and the two pace away together, talking in hushed tones. I feel my brows knit at not being included in a conversation, but I figure whatever it is, Odelia or Camden will tell me later. I understand there's an element of leader posturing that's coming into play—Odelia is the leader of witches while Camden is the leader of wolves, so I understand they'll need to have some private discourse leader to leader. While I'm *technically* Queen of shifters, I suppose I'm currently on a leave of absence of sorts, considering the fact that I'm living and training with the Nightshade Coven, so I understand I don't get to be privy to the same details I would be if I was living in Kinrith with Camden.

There was a time when him holding anything from me would've hurt, courtesy of the bond—and while the bond is still in such a tenuous state, despite being on the mend, I find that I can see him through a much more logical lens rather than an emotional one. So, while he and Odelia enjoy their private talk about who knows what, I return my attention to the other shifters and witches gathered.

Saunders is continuing to glare at Reyna, looking like he's about a second away from lunging at her, which would be *very* ill-advised. Reyna might *look* relatively harmless, as she has a fairly slim build and appears more beautiful than lethal, but she is as deadly as it gets—I've learned that repeatedly by having her beat the shit out of me in our *training* sessions. Underestimating her would be a grave mistake.

"No magic, just a straight fight," Saunders says, proving that bulging muscles do not equate to intelligence.

"Think twice before challenging her, wolf. She's one of our best," Claire cautions.

"With magic, maybe. I don't think she'd get very far with fists," Saunders replies, looking far too arrogant and smug for his own good.

Reyna rolls her head around, cracking her neck, before stepping up to Saunders, not looking concerned at all. To be fair, I wouldn't be concerned if I was as proficient with hand-to-hand combat as she is—but Saunders clearly doesn't know that, and I have the vague sense she's about to teach him a painful lesson.

"I accept your challenge, mongrel. And since I meant what I said earlier, I'll even let you take the first hit."

The two step forward, taking up the space between the group of gathered shifters and witches. Saunders gives Reyna a calculated up and down, considering her, while Reyna looks distinctly uninterested, as if Saunders is beneath her notice.

"What, you want me to flash you before we start? Stop wasting my time and take the first hit, you pussy," Reyna taunts.

Claire shuffles closer to me then murmurs in my ear, "The shifter king won't get pissed if Reyna puts one of his best warriors out of commission, right?"

I shake my head. "No. This actually might be beneficial—shifters worship strength above all. If Reyna proves that she has it in spades, she'll get a lot of respect, and shifters will start thinking twice about picking on witches. Considering we'll be starting joint training soon, that might be for the best."

Claire smiles. "*Awesome.* I've always wanted to watch her take on a shifter without magic—ten silver coins says she'll have him knocked out cold within the first two minutes."

"No way. She likes to play with her prey—she's gonna take her time with this one," Maddy disagrees.

Our conversation is interrupted when Saunders swings his fist at Reyna's face in an impressively fast move, though the speed gets him nowhere. Reyna catches his fist, then twists his arm sharply to the side before bending it backward. Two cracks sound, most likely bone breaking, and Saunders rears back with a roar of pain. He doesn't let his injury slow or stop him—instead, he comes at Reyna with all the rage of a storm, using claws, kicks, and punches with his hammer fist. *None* of the hits land though; Reyna bobs and weaves to evade each blow before it can make contact, which just appears to piss Saunders off.

I glance over my shoulder in time to see Camden watching Reyna and Saunders with a look of concern. He murmurs something to Odelia, who throws her head back and laughs—whatever their exchange is, it appears to calm Camden and they return to conversing.

Hearing a feminine hiss, I switch my attention back to the fight in front of me and see that Saunders managed to draw some blood with a swipe of his claws, leaving a gash on Reyna's arm. Instead of appearing angered though, her hiss turns into a chuckle. Then she switches from defense to offense, and honestly, she moves so fast it's hard to track her with my eyes. She lands a punch to his chest that cracks several ribs, an uppercut to his chin that appears to daze him, and two consecutive kicks to his knee that dislocate it and force him to keel over.

Impressively, Saunders manages to get back on his feet, proving that Camden has tough warriors surrounding him—though they're not as tough as the witches surrounding me. Claire and Maddy start shouting encouragements for Reyna to *fuck the shifter up,* while the other shifters yell encouragements at their fellow wolf.

"I think she's almost done with him," Maddy says when Reyna lands a knee to Saunders groin that makes a high-pitched yelp escape him. "He's tiring, and she gets bored when they don't fight back."

True to Maddy's words, Saunders has gone from offense to defense. He's dazed, sporting many injuries—busted knee, busted groin, broken nose, broken arm—while Reyna only has the claw marks on her arm.

I wince when Reyna grabs onto Saunders' arm, the one that she's already broken, using one of her hands to pull it straight while driving her other fist under it, sending it crashing up into Saunders' elbow, shattering the bone and joint before releasing him. Saunders lets out a loud shout but is quick to retaliate, driving his other fist right into Reyna's ribs, which causes a few popping noises. Her features twist in pain, but she doesn't recoil or even stumble back; the only way to know the hit hurt is by her wheezed breath. Then she lands a kick to Saunders' solar plexus that has him sprawling out on the ground, panting and groaning.

Reyna crosses her arms and plants her feet as she stares at Saunders, giving him a pitying smile. "What were you saying about me not getting very far with fists?"

Saunders weakly tries to lift his good leg, presumably to sweep Reyna's feet out from under her—Reyna catches the leg and twists it, and another wince-worthy crack echoes through the air before she drops his leg, letting it fall limply to the ground.

"Enough, wolf. Submit, and I'll heal you," Reyna says flatly.

"She can heal?" I ask Claire.

"Most witches can heal with spells, but that sort of magic takes up a lot of power to anyone who isn't a natural-born healer," Claire replies.

Looking delighted, Maddy adds, "And healing spells hurt like a *bitch*. Yay!"

"Submit, Saunders. The fight's over," Wyatt calls out.

Through gritted teeth, Saunders growls, "I submit."

Reyna sniffs. "I thought you'd have more fight in you."

With that, she squats beside Saunders and hovers her hands over his broken arm before murmuring a chant under her breath—several cracks sound as the arm rights itself, and Saunders lets out another cry of pain. Reyna moves her hands along his body, healing every injury, each of which appears to hurt as it heals almost as much as it did when inflicted. Once she's done, I expect her to spit on Saunders or something equally rude—instead, I'm surprised when she extends a hand to him. He eyes her hand wearily before taking it and lets her pull him to his feet.

The two stare at each other for a moment, before Saunders admits, "You're fast as fuck."

Reyna inclines her head. "And you pack a mean punch with that hammer fist. Cracked three of my ribs with one blow; impressive."

Saunders appears surprised at her praise, raising his eyebrows. Then he inclines his head and says, "Lesson learned; don't piss off a witch."

Reyna grins. "Good. Then I won't have to repeat it." She extends her hand and Saunders gives it a shake before the two part ways, just in time for Camden and Odelia to stroll back to the group.

In the distance, Lana, Korbin, Bordat, Galantia, and Samuel are still speaking with each other, apparently having been too engrossed in the reunion to pay attention to the noises from the fight.

Camden comes up beside me, casting an unamused look at Saunders. "I believe I told you to stay out of it."

Saunders blanches, probably because he went against his Alpha's orders by fighting Reyna. After all, Camden bade the warrior to stand down, and he instead had the bright idea of challenging Reyna to a duel. I'm not exactly sure what the punishment is for going against the orders of an Alpha, as I wasn't around Camden long enough to see exactly how he deals with dissent among his inner circle, but I was around long enough to know Camden runs a tight ship.

Saunders bows his head with respect, and mutters, "Apologies, my King. I was merely testing the integrity of our allies."

I look to Camden, awaiting his response, wondering if it will be a mild admonishment or something more along the lines of a painful punishment. I feel my muscles tense as I stare at him and realize his reaction right now will serve as an important marker going forward. I got to know Camden to an extent during my time at Kinrith, but I was only there long enough to scratch the surface of him as a *person*. I know very little about him as a *ruler*, other than the fact that he's revered and respected by shifters everywhere. Right now, though, I find myself questioning if he's someone who leads with fear, like some of the worst—yet admittedly most effective—tyrants in human history, or if he rules with love, like some of the most adored rulers, or if he's like the wisest rulers and uses a mixture of both.

Camden narrows his eyes in contemplation as he stares at Saunders. After a long moment, he says, "Since you've already learned firsthand just what happens when you challenge a witch, I'll be putting you in a commanding position of joint training between our warriors and the witches, starting in the next weeks."

Saunders inclines his head, accepting his new task, before melting back into the group of warriors. I find myself staring at Camden with both interest and mild surprise; he didn't punish Saunders for disregarding him likely because he saw that Reyna already did. Instead, he put Saunders on a job that will teach him the value of uniting and working with witches, something that tells me that Camden is a wise ruler, after all.

Camden turns to me with raised eyebrows. "Do you think that's an appropriate response?"

I blink, mildly surprised that he'd think to ask me, though I suppose I shouldn't be. Even when I've been willfully ignorant of the fact, I have to admit that Camden has consistently made an effort to see things from my perspective and ask for my opinion. It shames me that I can't say I've done the same; there have been many occasions when I couldn't put myself in his shoes—or, more accurately, just didn't care to. While he's made big mistakes in our relationship, I can't say I've been entirely without fault. I've villainized him many times on account of his species, which isn't fair.

I appreciate that he considers my opinion because it goes to prove that he doesn't just care for me, he also respects my thoughts and sentiments. Feeling a small smile pull on my lips, I tell him, "That sounds fair to me." Then I turn my gaze to the wolf we're discussing. "Saunders, will you be able to work side by side with the witches? Let go of your prejudice even though we have fewer numbers to offer the war than your kind?"

Saunders meets my gaze for a moment before inclining his head in respect. "I will do my best to bring unity to our rallied troops, my queen. I apologize for any affront I may have brought you."

I nod. "Thank you." I turn towards Odelia, who's watching my exchanges with a small smile pulling on her lips. "Who should we put in charge of joined training on our side?" I ask.

"Our most successful, not to mention powerful when it comes to combat, is Reyna. Since she's already proven her worth in the eyes of shifters, I think it'd be fair to put her on the task," Odelia tells me. She turns to Reyna, whose lips are pursed with displeasure, standing with her arms crossed over her chest. "Do you have any objections?"

When Reyna opens her mouth, probably to respond that she *does* have objections, Claire takes the liberty of giving her hair a tug. "Don't be difficult for the sake of being difficult. Take the deal, use the opportunity to beat some sense into as many wolves as you feel like, in whichever painful manner you believe suits your task."

Reyna's eyes brighten minutely at the prospect of having future chances to fuck with shifters. After a long moment of darting glances between the shifters, a slow evil-looking smile spreads on her lips. "Yeah, I'm down for being in charge of training on our side. I want to see how many shifters I can get to cry."

Claire shakes her head with a sigh but doesn't bother to say anything or protest. We both know Reyna well enough to understand that she functions on her own time, with her own convictions and reasons, and there's little point in an outsider trying to change her. It'll only end up amusing her and frustrating them.

"Very well, that's settled," Odelia says. "Now, Sierra, if you'd like to bid farewell to the shifter-human couple and their daughter, now would be a good time—we should be getting back soon."

"I'm having one of my lawmakers work on a fundamental right for humans to maintain contact with family members who have been claimed by mythics; he'll probably have the legal script ready tonight if you'd like to go through it during our usual time with the mirror portal."

"Usual time," Maddy repeats, interest creeping into her tone. "Now that, I'm interested in."

Saving me from explaining that I've agreed to speak nightly with Camden, and the many questions that would surely follow, Lana approaches along with her mate and daughter in tow. Once again, her daughter's bright eyes fixate directly on me, and she gives another toothless smile. Again, my heart squeezes in my chest, this time accompanied by a healthy dose of sadness. The little girl is adorable and the sight of her smile is damn heartwarming, but it also brings me a pinch of pain because I would be only a few months away from holding my own child had the attack not taken place.

Judging by the look Camden casts me, one edged with melancholy and regret, he's thinking along the same lines.

Lana laughs as little Galantia reaches for me again. "I'm sorry, my Qu—Sierra, she's normally not so drawn to strangers."

I swallow hard, accepting Galantia as Lana passes her over, settling her on my hip and enjoying the sweet baby scent she gives off, trying to push away personal sorrows and just enjoy the act of holding a little bundle of joy in my hands.

"It's no problem," I assure Lana. "I love children."

My voice cracks a little on the last word, and I clear my throat before turning my attention back to Galantia as she takes a fistful of my hair, staring at it wide-eyed. I tap her nose with my free hand and murmur, "You're just the sweetest little thing, aren't you? With a curious mind, I can tell." I look to her parents. "Odds are you'll have a scholar on your hands before long."

Lana chuckles. "Let's hope." She pauses, casting a glance back at the village. "My father had to return, and I wanted to thank you once again for orchestrating this visit."

I incline my head. "It's truly no bother. Was he happy to meet his granddaughter?"

"Overjoyed," Lana tells me with a wide smile. "Truly, I've never seen him smile so widely. I know this is probably the last time I'll see him—"

"Nonsense," I cut her off quickly, bouncing Galantia up and down as she starts to stir restlessly. "I'm currently working with Camden to put together some laws that allow humans regular contact and visitation with their families. You have my word that your father will have the opportunity to watch his granddaughter grow. If all goes well, you'll be able to visit him here, and he'll be able to visit your pack."

"Is that so?" Bordat asks testily, arching an eyebrow at me.

I give him a very direct, bold gaze that dares him to continue questioning me. "It is so, Alpha," I say, keeping my voice calm. "That is, unless you have an issue with keeping families together. If you'd rather continue sewing discontent in your pack members, I'm sure that's something you can take to the high court—the counselors will, no doubt, be greatly pleased to spend their time listening to such protests."

Camden lets out a puff of laughter beside me, Wyatt coughs to hide his own laugh, and Bordat averts his gaze to the ground, obviously deciding that challenging me further isn't worth the hassle. I don't know what his problem is with taking simple steps to allow his human pack members, people he is sworn to protect and aid, to have contact with their families, but I will not allow any interference. His problems aren't my concern; the well-being of all shifters, witches, and humans is.

"My apologies," the Alpha murmurs wisely.

"Accepted. I trust I'll have your full cooperation with future steps to facilitate contact between humans and their family members. After all, if you were separated from your family, I imagine you'd be rather desperate to see them?" I say, my tone icily polite.

Bordat appears to deflate at that. "I wouldn't be able to survive it. Of course you'll have my cooperation."

"Excellent," I respond. I brush a kiss over Galantia's head, giving her one last smile before returning her to Lana. "I'm afraid I need to get back, but we'll be in touch. I wish you all the best with your daughter and life, and if there's anything you should need, feel free to reach out to me. I'll always have time to listen to concerns as any decent leader would." I give their Alpha one last pointed glance that makes both Lana and her mate crack smiles.

"I'll speak to you tonight?" Camden asks.

I give him a nod. "Yes." As I watch the family walk away, I say to him, "Thank you for this. It means a great deal."

He gives me a smile in turn. "It's no bother, Sierra, I'm happy to help."

Curiously, I ask him, "What were you discussing with Odelia?"

"Evacuation measures in the case of an attack," he replies candidly. I find I like how open he is, and willing to answer my questions. If they were posed by anyone else, I doubt he'd be so accommodating. "In the event that enemy forces break through Kinrith wards, Odelia invited our people to retreat to your territory. Likewise, if you're under an attack you can't prevail over, you will also be welcome to retreat to Kinrith. At this point, it seems wise to plan for any and all eventualities."

It certainly is. Seeing Odelia subtly beckon me over, I say, "This has been lovely. I'll speak with you tonight?"

"Tonight," Camden agrees.

Chapter Twenty-One

Camden

*B*ack in the childhood home of Sierra's cabin, I find myself walking through the small, quaint space, marveling about the fact that it's where she grew up. As I turn my head towards the fireplace, I notice something distinct; there is a fire burning. A black fire, though it gives off no heat.

Knowing that something is off here, I inhale deeply through my nose, only to be greeted with absolutely no scent. Nothing. My mind flickers back to the conversation I had with Sierra via mirror portal recently; one where she told me she was visited by her goddess in a dream.

Several anomalies hit me at once. The house without scents...one where the smell of death and decay should assault me, considering the horrors that took place here not long ago. The black fire and the fact that the atmosphere seems almost muted are all indicators that I'm not awake.

I have an easy enough time remembering my dreams, especially recent ones which are of war, death, and Sierra. The worst ones are about war leading to me losing Sierra. Since this is a dream without war, *death, or Sierra, I understand quite quickly that, while I am dreaming, this is no normal dream.*

"Wolf," a strange, echoing voice calls out from the far end of the cabin, causing me to spin around. I blink several times as I come face to face with a tall glowing creature. She has fair skin that seems to glow with a faint blue, long black hair, and gleaming silver eyes... it only takes a moment of looking at her to understand that, impossibly, I am being visited by the very goddess who gave Sierra the power to wield an incredible all-powerful fire.

"Hecate," I respond.

Claude's many tales of witchcraft and dealing with deities come in handy; I instinctively drop to one knee and bow my head. The old witch doctor was quite clear that gods are big on being shown respect from mortals, and that they have touchy tempers and the predisposition to destroy things when they're bored. If offended, destruction wouldn't start to scrape the surface of what they might end up doing—it'd be more along the lines of painful annihilation after a prolonged bout of torture.

If I'd received a visit from the god of shifters, I might not be quite so wary or deferential, as the creator of my kind has visited my ancestors in centuries past, and the tales of those visits say they were positive. This isn't my god, however, meaning I need to tread very carefully.

"Rise, Alpha, we do not have time for formalities," Hecate says, her tone somewhat impatient.

Startled, I stand, meeting her eyes. She gives me a long look up and down, then proceeds to walk in a circle around me, examining every inch of me. Then she stops directly in front of me and presses an ice-cold hand to my chest startling me. That shock is quickly superseded by a feeling of electrical currents slamming through my system and centering on my chest, drawing a shout of pain from me—this pain is like no other I felt before. My muscles seize and my body shakes as whatever magic the goddess sends into me tears through my system, blinding me. As abruptly as it began, the pain disappears, and I realize I've fallen to the ground when I feel the cold wood beneath me. Small tremors run through my body in the aftermath of the pain, and I struggle to get my breathing back under control.

"Your soul is strong," the goddess says. "As expected and as needed. Get up, wolf, I didn't harm you; I merely need a sense of your power and how it might amplify that of my Favored."

Feeling as weak as a newborn babe, I once again force myself to my feet, stumbling slightly and blinking multiple times. Hecate doesn't sound apologetic in the least for my pain, though I wouldn't expect her to; I am not one of her kin, and apparently, the only importance I have to her is through my relationship with Sierra.

"I also gave a little...acceleration, shall we call it, to your bond. It is taking too long to mend, and you and my witch must be united to face the dangers fast approaching," Hecate goes on.

As soon as she says the words, I become aware of the subtle shift in my chest; the hole that's been there, and that has filled in the most minute, incremental way through my recent interactions with Sierra, now feels a good deal smaller and like it's continuing to fill much faster than before. I don't know if Sierra will be pleased by this development, as I presume this acceleration goes both ways and she'll be feeling this same change through her end of the bond, though she should understand as well as I do that gods aren't much for the concept of consent. They do what they want, when they want, often functioning to meet their own ends with few cares as to how their actions might impact mortals. It's fortunate that this goddess seems to have some regard for Sierra, even going as far as to refer to my Sierra as her witch, which antagonizes me on a fundamental level, though I keep my frustration locked up tight.

"You betrayed one of my Favored," Hecate says, her tone flat. "Usually, that is an automatic death sentence, however, we live in unusual times. You and my witch were bound for a reason; your god and I did not take the orchestration of such a union lightly, which is fortunate for you. Otherwise, I would've punished you already and freed my Favored from you."

The fuck? *The way Hecate is speaking almost makes it sound like the match between Sierra and I wasn't arranged by fate alone but by two gods, mine and hers. That's beyond shocking to me because, as I'm being reminded of presently, gods don't usually give much of a shit about mortals. Hecate certainly thought nothing of putting me through the sort of pain I've never before experienced, yet she evidently had a hand in making Sierra my soulmate, and vice versa.*

"Danger is afoot. Dark times approach from other continents, and enemies slink closer every day. You will mobilize and prepare your army, wolf, and you will heal the rift between you and my Favored. A time will come all too soon when the Valley of Sorcerers will be attacked. When that happens, it will fall to you to invite the living sorcerers to your home and protect them. You will prove to Sierra that she can trust and rely on you, you will bond to her, and you will strengthen her. She needs every drop of power for the battle to come, and you are essential to that." Hecate holds out her palm, and a clear crystal appears on it, one that crackles with magical power—something even I can sense. "You will give her this as a gift once you are fully bonded—attach it to a necklace or ring. It will connect the two of you on a level superseding what even soulmates can achieve, and connect your powers. You will not betray or harm her again, ever, *lest I decide your usefulness has run its course. Now awaken, Alpha, and prepare."*

She steps forward, shoves the crystal directly into my chest, and pushes me with such vigor that I slam into the ground, only for my eyes to open.

Greeted by darkness and the familiar scents of my bedroom, still faintly laced with Sierra's scent from the moments she spent here many weeks ago, I pant and gasp, feeling my heart race in my chest at the speed of a galloping stallion. I scramble out of bed, falling to the cold stone floor with a faint *oomph*, finding that whatever Hecate did to me in my dream has left me weak while awake.

Something clatters to the ground beside me—a faint, glowing stone. *The crystal*, I realize, one that Hecate managed to transport when she literally shoved me out of my sleep.

Claude. I need to find Claude. He'll have a better idea of how to deal with whatever the fuck just transpired; I'm beyond disoriented and filled with confusion, though I understand that my union with Sierra is a necessity on a celestial level. I also have a vague understanding that something bad is about to befall the Valley of Sorcerers, and I need to reach out to them to warn them, for which I need magic. After a minute or two of catching my breath and blinking the fog away from my mind, I rise to my feet, and turn on the lights in my room, squinting as they nearly blind me. Then I stumble out of my bedroom and through my chambers before opening the door to the hall outside of my personal quarters. At the end of my hallway, I find two stationed guards, who both stiffen at my approach.

"Get Claude," I tell one of them sharply. "Bring him to me *now*." To the other, I command, "Wake my brother and bring him here as well." If the Valley of Sorcerers is in danger, Leisel is in danger, which Wyatt needs to be apprised of. I also need his help to finish drawing troops to Kinrith and its surrounding areas immediately—I must heed all the instructions from Hecate because I can't imagine she would take the effort to come to me in a dream if circumstances weren't dire.

As the guards take off sprinting down the hallway, I call out, "Change of plans—bring them to the War Room." I need to dress, stow away the crystal somewhere safe, and start figuring out what I'm going to do.

It kills me that I have no easy way of reaching Sierra; even if Claude opens a mirror portal, there's no guarantee there will be anyone on the other end waiting to listen. The protective instinct to keep my mate safe rears inside of me, agitating my wolf as much as it does me, causing him to pace and chuff irritably within me, pushing for supremacy. Silently communicating to him that he will not have as great a chance of warning our mate and keeping her safe as I will, I return to my chamber and try to think through the mindfuck I just experienced.

* * *

"*Fuck!*" Wyatt roars as I finish telling him and Claude of our forthcoming challenges. He turns wide, wild-looking eyes to our witch doctor and says, "Reach the witches by whatever means necessary and *warn them.*"

Claude looks at me. "Did Hecate specify what exactly would happen?"

I shake my head, stabbing a hand through my hair. "No, she was very vague."

"Typical of a deity," Claude murmurs, nodding. "Nevertheless, if she thought it important to reach out to you, true chaos is about to descend on our allies. I'll do my best to reach them." With that, he shuffles out of the room.

"Take a breath," I tell Wyatt, watching as he clutches his head in his hands. The prolonged separation from his mate has grated on both him and his wolf, even though they see her daily. Although he didn't snap at Sierra for not bringing her sister along for our meeting a few weeks ago, I can tell he was close. While Leisel is not mature and therefore Wyatt has no romantic sentiments towards her, he does still have a primal drive to protect her and ensure her comfort and happiness—distance makes that difficult. The fact that she's now in an unknown amount of danger only makes matters worse.

"I *can't* fucking breathe," Wyatt snaps, giving his head a hard shake, and starts pacing the length of the table. "I don't know how the fuck you're managing to stand there all calm and collected. *Our mates are in grave danger.*"

"They are also surrounded by witches with the sort of power and training that we cannot fathom," I say. Of course, I am no less frantic internally than Wyatt, but I have a long day of informing my commanders and captains that they need to get the remaining troops to Kinrith *now*, instead of over the next two weeks as agreed upon, ahead of me, which means I need to keep a level head.

According to Hecate, we will soon be playing host to witches, which means that joint training will need to be in full throttle immediately. As anxious as I am, I can't afford to be a mess right now; I need to be a ruler. I also need to trust the fact that Sierra excels at protecting both herself and her sister—she told me that her fire's currently rogue, which in most cases is a very bad and dangerous thing, but right now it could mean that she'll be able to protect herself against whatever danger Hecate alluded to.

"That's not enough!" Wyatt roars. "*We* should be there to protect them! How is that not eating at you?"

"It eats at me every second of every day," I snap, my tone terse. "However, instead of engaging in disastrous thinking, I'm choosing to focus my energy on what I *can* do rather than what I can't. If Claude's attempts to contact the witches fail, I'll still be speaking with Sierra tonight, as will you with Leisel—we can warn them then."

"What if the attack happens today?" Wyatt demands. "What if it's happening as we speak and they're in fucking danger?"

I've already considered that dreaded possibility, though I try not to give it much credence because that particular line of thinking is cripplingly terrifying, and I need to remain strong right now. "Then we need to be prepared to receive and aid them. Get your head screwed on straight, Wyatt, and help me. Whether it's in an hour or in the next days, we're about to have tens of thousands of witches at our doorstep. We've already had to build towns for troops; now we'll have to do the same for sorcerers and figure out a way to keep our people from harming them. Many shifters are still wary of sorcerers, and generally speaking, shifters respond to fear with violence. That cannot happen. We need them as much as they need us."

I watch as Wyatt inhales several deep breaths, opening and shutting his eyes several times, and then appears to collect himself. He straightens, the inhibiting rage clears from his eyes, and he gives a nod.

"Fine. Right. I'll...I'll get in touch with the top men staying on our grounds, figure out how we can accelerate the process of getting all the fighting men and women here."

He stands and strides out of the room, at the same time that a familiar person strides in. Not, Claude, unfortunately, which only serves to irritate me.

"What do you want, Aspen?"

She blinks a few times before bowing her head respectfully, stopping a few feet away from me. "I heard commotion through the palace grapevine; I thought I might come check on you."

Check on me? As if we're lovers or even *friends?* I've taken Aspen off my personal detail and have no intention of letting her close to me unless necessary. Her access to the castle itself should be limited, as I've made it clear to my top guards that I don't want to see her roaming the halls anymore, but I suppose in this moment of chaos she could've snuck by. She is still a captain in my army, which gives her certain leeway among my ranks, though I've tried to scale it back.

"You are not in a position to check on me. You are no more than a member of my pack, one whose behavior has been bordering on insolent for far too long. Go back to your duties, Aspen, I do not have time for you right now."

Her brows draw together and she shifts nervously from foot to foot, though she doesn't do the smart thing by *fucking leaving*. Instead, she says, "I heard there might be some witches coming to stay with us soon. Don't you need help arranging accommodations?"

There's a note in her tone that causes me to stiffen. Aspen has never been a fan of sorcerers; in fact, she repeatedly verbalized that we should distrust them, though she's been kept in line by Claude and Wyatt. That doesn't mean that she couldn't cause problems by sewing distrust amongst my ranks at a time when our very survival depends on working with sorcerers and not against them. Her offer to *help* is entirely disingenuous, and I believe she might make it her mission to make the lives of witches difficult when they retreat here. That is not something that I will permit; no *fucking* way. I will ensure that everyone does their utmost to make the sorcerers comfortable, and I will not have Aspen sabotage that out of petty jealousy.

"Listen to me very carefully," I tell her slowly. "You will focus on your duties. You will not start telling people they should worry about the presence of witches and warlocks. You will not plant seeds of doubt with anyone about my mate. You will act in a manner befitting of your station as a high-ranking warrior, a *captain,* or that station will be revoked."

Aspen balks, her features paling. "I haven't done anything like that. Even if I was worried about the presence of witches and warlocks, leagues of sorcerers, would that really be punishable? After all, it is in our best interest to keep an eye on them. They're known to be a destructive bunch. Sierra could've killed me during our duel, and she wasn't utilizing magic then."

Done with this bullshit, I say, "You will not refer to your Queen by her name but by her title—"

"She hasn't been *acting* like a queen," Aspen bursts out, daring to interrupt me.

"Enough!" I roar. "You do not interrupt me. I don't know where you got the godsdamned gall to address me with such familiarity or to try to cause problems, but you have no right. None whatsoever. Sierra is my mate and our Queen. You are a good warrior who I had the bad sense to occasionally share a bed with. You have no meaning to me. Continue conducting yourself in such an outrageous way, and I will ensure you do not have meaning to anyone anymore. Keep your mouth shut and your head down, and stay the *fuck* out of my castle."

Claude rushes into the room, his tan features wrinkled with worry. He pauses in the entryway, looking from me to Aspen, then sighs. "My dear child, I do hope you haven't been trying to spread more of your nonsense about witchcraft."

His words clue me in to the fact that Aspen has already started creating problems for me—or tried to, at least. Evidently, Claude kept her in check, likely by treating her like the child she's behaving as. I didn't realize my desire for Sierra would've impacted an old bedmate like this, but I don't have time for it.

"Get out," I repeat, raising my voice at Aspen. "Do not come back. You need something, you go to your commander. Not to me, Claude, or Wyatt, but the commander of your unit." I use the tone that compels submissions from all shifters, and it appears to work. Aspen scurries out of the room while Claude focuses on me, his lips thinning. "We can speak of Aspen's problems another time. For now, I used every portal key we know to try to contact the witches, but couldn't reach any of them. Not in any of the three usual locations—Odelia's office, Sierra's chambers, and Leisel's chambers. It's morning, so it could be that they're all at breakfast and not in their respective rooms."

It could also be that whatever danger Hecate spoke of has befallen them, and there is absolute *shit* I can do about it. I can't reach Sierra, so I can't warn her—all I can do is pray and hope that she defeats whatever's coming her way.

A slithering sensation moves through my chest, and a faint echo of contentment passes through me, making me frown. There is absolutely nothing about me that's content at this moment...and that's when it hits me. Once marked and consummated, the bond between mates connects the two souls deeply enough that they get echoes of each other's emotions. In the week after we consummated, before I fucked things up between us, I'd get echoes of Sierra's emotions—whatever strange magic Hecate performed on my bond, *accelerating* it as she said, must have reactivated some of the parts of it that have lain dormant. I can't feel her emotions like I did back then, the small sense I got just now was faint, but at least I can feel *something*. And it might just serve as a gauge of Sierra's welfare.

Chapter Twenty-Two

Sierra

Gathered in one of the many common areas of the Nightshade Coven's cavern system, I find myself bemused as I glance around all the seemingly mismatched, bickering people. Reyna and Bane are, as usual, taunting each other for the hell of it—from my observations, that taunting will soon turn into fighting, and then evolve into fucking. Loudly. Odelia and Rune are speaking by a stone archway, which I know is used as this coven's portal base. Cedrick's sitting beside me, chatting with me lightly about what I need to work on with tactile combat magic, though he's reluctantly impressed with my progress. We're going over specific hand gestures together—slowly, of course, or this room would be shattered to pieces—to work on my technique.

A sort of shift in my chest makes my fingers falter, and I blink several times, blowing out a long breath.

"What's wrong?" Cedrick asks. "You're doing well with this variation—you just need to adjust the position of your thumbs."

I shake my head. "Not that. My bond with Camden...it's been particularly active today."

He frowns. "What do you mean?"

Cedrick and I have become closer friends through our training and the time we spend outside of it together, so I have no problem confiding in him.

"The bond has been slowly healing in the last weeks as I've been speaking with him and we've been working together for some preparations, but before now that healing has been an incremental drip. Now it feels like a small, albeit steady, stream of healing. Like something's accelerated it," I explain.

Cedrick's brows furrow. "Huh," he says, breaking his hand formation and reaching out to run his hand through his hair. "Did seeing him during your meeting in Midlington two weeks ago really affect you so positively?"

"I don't think it's that," I reply, relaxing against the back of the couch. "I was personally quite pleased with the outcome of that meeting, but it didn't serve to accelerate or slow the bond's healing. The bond seems to work in its own time; positive forward motion with me and Camden ensures that the healing drip continues, but it hasn't made it speed up the way it now feels like it has."

Cedrick opens his mouth to respond but is cut off when Claire sprints into the room, chest heaving, a look of panic etched onto her features. Instantly, everyone is on high alert because it takes a hell of a lot to jar Claire. The woman is as steady as it gets.

"Outlying covens just sent me a report of a black fog rolling over our territory," Claire says, panting and flushed. "Scouts also reported seeing a male with silver hair and silver eyes making his way through our valley, along with another dark-haired male whom the fog is spilling out of. It looks like Rhaelar and his shadow wielder have decided to make an appearance."

The mention of Rhaelar's name alarms me—if he's here and he has the shadow wielder with him, it can only mean he's preparing to attack, to try to wipe out the witches...or at least weaken their numbers.

"It gets worse," Claire says, still breathing heavily. "Alongside the shadows are walking *corpses* and *skeletons*. I think...I think Rhaelar's the necromancer, and he's brought an army to our territories—an army that we haven't warded against."

Oh, fuck. That means everyone in the Valley of Sorcerers is now in terrible danger—thousands of witches and warlocks. Odelia must think the same thing because she swiftly begins barking orders at everyone in the room, as does Rune.

"Maddy, engage evacuation protocols; go to each coven base, open their portals, and code them to take us straight to Kinrith. Reyna, go with her, rally everyone, and make them leave—we aren't safe here anymore, but our warriors might want to fight. Claire, you know what to do." Odelia rattles off the orders quickly and succinctly, wearing an expression of worry melded with fear and outrage.

"Bane, go with Maddy and Reyna," Rune says. "Make sure our warlocks also know we need to get out rather than fight. The rest of you, disperse and engage our doomsday warding mechanism. Also, send word to the covens outside of our valley to evacuate, in case Rhaelar and his shadow wielder decide to go after them when we escape. That is, if they haven't already—" He cuts off with a curse, shaking his head. "Our wards can't stop the dead or shadows, but they can slow them and give us time to get out of here." He turns to Odelia. "How the *fuck* did they find us?"

"I don't know," Odelia says. "Could've been a tracking spell of some sort—whatever the case, we're not prepared to face the dead and shadows. We only have two members with powers who can fight those threats, and they aren't ready."

"I can unleash my fire on the dead once everyone's evacuated," I say.

Odelia shakes her head. "No, there's no sense putting you in danger when the smart move is to leave. When Rhaelar and his shadow wielder realize there's nobody here to terrorize, they should crawl right back to whatever hole they've been hiding in. Then we can get to work warding Kinrith against black magic so they can't pull this move again. Go get your sister and Wesley; bring them here. Once Maddy's opened portals for other covens and returned, she'll open the one here and we'll send them straight through so they're out of danger. She'll be rounding up children to get them through portals first—they're our priority."

I nod, standing and quickly making my way through the caves to the balcony where Leisel and Wesley are known to spend their free time together. I expect the hallways to be a place of sheer mayhem but am proven wrong; while it's clear every witch and warlock knows we're under attack and evacuating, they don't run or scream—they walk or jog at a brisk pace to their destinations, most looking scared or furious, but all appearing to still have their good sense about them. I get the vague feeling that this isn't the first time the population of sorcerers on this continent has had to up and run.

When I get to the balcony, I don't see Leisel or Wesley there, which makes my heart start to race. What I do see, however, is the thick fog Claire spoke of rolling over the valley in the distance. I also see groups of people running away from the fog, presumably to get to the nearest portal. I don't take time to watch the chaos unfold though. My heart racing, I turn back to the hall, this time jogging in the direction of the recreation room where Leisel and Wes sometimes hole up to read together. I shoulder through many witches and warlocks, all heading in the opposite direction, feeling my fear pick up. I need to find Leisel and Wes before they get caught up in the storm that Rhaelar and the shadow wielder are creating.

They aren't in the recreation room either, which means they have to be in their bedrooms, hopefully together. I sprint to the hallway where all three of our bedrooms reside. There are only a few stragglers in the halls, all briskly making their way toward the opposite side of the mountain range where evacuations are probably underway while I'm frantically trying to find my sister and my ward to get them out of the way of danger.

I don't bother knocking on Leisel's door, especially when I *feel* her presence on the other side of it—I burst in, letting out a breath of relief when I see Leisel and Wes seated on the floor, hands joined, with a floating orb of golden light hovering above them—a creation of Leisel's, no doubt. It appears they're practicing magic together.

"Leisel, Wesley, get up," I half-shout, my voice filled with strain and worry. "The mountain range is under attack, we need to get out."

Leisel snaps her eyes open while Wes instantly jumps to his feet, not wasting time. He pulls Leisel up along with him, giving me a wide-eyed look. "What's going on?"

"A necromancer and shadow wielder are here with an army of shadows and the dead," I say, walking forward and taking Leisel's hand. "We're evacuating to Kinrith. There isn't time to explain, kids, we need to fucking *go*. Gods, when I couldn't find you two, I nearly had a heart attack."

"We were just practicing separating my healing from my light," Leisel says, her tone wobbly.

Realizing that I snapped at her, I pull Leisel close and press a kiss to the top of her head. "I know, sweet girl, and it looks like you're making great progress. Now, please, let's *go*."

As a unit, the three of us rush out into the hallway. I direct them to the coven's common room where Maddy should be activating a portal as we speak—Wesley sprints ahead and I run to keep up with him, but Leisel isn't as fast as us, stumbling and tripping over herself. Not having time for delays, I sweep her into my arms, holding her to me with an arm around her waist before picking up my speed. We get to the other side of the cavern system in a matter of minutes, in time to see that Maddy's already opened a portal in the stone archway that stands in the center of this room—I see the telling shimmer of magic within it.

"Dear gods, *there you are*," Odelia says, looking frantic. "All the Nightshade members have already made their way through, and the outlying covens are evacuated. Reyna's rounding up stragglers along with Maddy and the others, they'll be here any moment."

I set Leisel on her feet right in front of the stone archway. Wesley peers into it with wide eyes and an expression of wonder, looking a bit awed, probably because the portal is giving off palpable amounts of magic. It fills the room and makes the fine hairs on my arms and the back of my neck stand on end.

"Wesley, take Leisel and go through, *now*," I say, pushing Leisel into his arms. He takes her hand in his, holding her close.

"Leisel, sweetheart, this portal will take you right to Kinrith's castle—find Wyatt, he'll protect you," Odelia says.

Leisel looks between me, Odelia, and Claire, who's sitting cross-legged on the stone floor, hands pressed to the stone and eyes shut. "What about you all?"

"We'll be right behind you, my love," I say. "We just need to make sure everyone's gotten out."

With that, I give Wesley a none-too-gentle shove, and tell him, "*Go. She's your responsibility now, protect her with everything you have."

He gives me a firm nod. "I will." With that, he pulls Leisel through the archway, and the two disappear.

"You should go too," Odelia tells me. "We need you alive and safe for the battles to come."

I shake my head. "I'm the only person who can combat the dead, I'm staying until everyone else has gone in case my fire comes in handy. How are evacuations going?"

At that moment, Maddy reappears with Reyna, Rune, Bane, and Cedrick in tow. They all appear worried and out of breath.

"Everyone's out, we're good," Maddy says.

"A few of our warriors wanted to stay and fight, so I shoved them through the portals and shut the portals behind them so they can't come back, and Rhaelar and the dark fucker can't follow," Reyna says.

Odelia gives a nod of satisfaction before turning to Claire. "How close are you?" she calls out to the redheaded witch.

"Close," Claire mumbles. "Turning a mountain into a volcano isn't an easy godsdamned task, but I'm getting there. A few more minutes and this range will be flooded with lava."

That's when it hits me; Claire's strange actions and the reason she's stayed behind. She's going to use her power to create and activate volcanoes, which just might bring a fiery death on Rhaelar and his shadow wielder. Even a vampire can't survive a torrent of lava; if Claire can drown both people in lava, the war will effectively be over, because without shadows and armies of the dead, our opposition will lose their two greatest weapons.

"We lost a few dozen sorcerers in the outermost territories to shadows and corpses," Maddy says, her voice sounding faintly choked. "The warrior wolves that were protecting the outskirts of the Blaithe mountains too. Gods, Odelia, the shadows are like nothing I've seen before. The creatures they create can turn from fog to humanoid in the span of a millisecond, kill someone, then go right back to fog. And the corpses and skeletons...they're inhumanly fast and just *won't die*."

Odelia curses, then turns to Rune. The two of them walk to the edge of the room, engaging in a hushed conversation while Cedrick says, "*Fuck*, the talisman storage. We need to clear it out and take as many talismans with us as we can. There are some ancient artifacts—a stone that'll be integral in warding against the dead. I'll be back."

Rune pauses in his conversation with Odelia to say, "Now isn't the time for heroic bullshit, Ced. I can feel Rhaelar, his dead, and the shadow wielder moving closer, we need to stick together. Fuck the talismans."

"If we don't get the stone, we won't be able to properly ward, and this will happen again. I'll be right back," Cedrick snaps, and before anyone can protest, he takes off in a run out of the room, and I hear his footsteps echoing through the stone cavern.

"*Fuck*," Rune roars. "I'm going with him—Claire, how close are you to detonation?"

Just as he asks the question, I feel a faint rumble in the ground beneath our feet, as if something within the mountain is shifting and rearranging—something like lava breaking through the earth's core and starting to travel upwards, to the peak of this mountain.

"Very fucking close, which means you need to hurry," Claire says, her voice strained. There's sweat beaded on her forehead and dripping down her brow. Abruptly, she stands. "Reyna, I need a clear visual of the valley."

Reyna jogs to the far side of the room, holds her hands out in front of her, performs a series of tactile gestures while mumbling under her breath, and the rock wall in front of her *explodes* outwards, startling the hell out of me, and letting out an actual shockwave that sends a burst of power through the entire room. With a few simple gestures, she managed to create an actual explosion—sometimes, I forget just how powerful her witchcraft is because she prefers to use swords to cut through her enemies. Times like this, though, I'm reminded that she is a force unto herself, and the reason she enjoys swordplay is because she likes drawing blood from opponents with blades, not because her magic won't cut it.

I peer out into the mountain range, feeling my throat clog with fear when I see that the dark fog is now encompassing the entire valley and crawling up the sides of mountains, covering forests and fields with what looks like thick black smoke. I also hear the faint echo of inhuman wails, moans, and groans from down below, as well as see clunky figures moving with abnormal speed—the army of reanimated dead presumably.

Claire walks right up to the opening and holds her hands out in front of her. The trembling of the ground beneath us increases, and awe overcomes me as I see smoke starting to pour from several mountain peaks. Avalanches also start to fall, great rockslides that start from the very top of the mountains and quickly bulldoze their way down.

"Rhaelar's the necromancer," Maddy says. "I saw him at work...he—" She cuts off as her voice gets choked up. "He reanimated all the sorcerers that died. They can't use magic, but they then tried to attack the remaining ones. Managed to tear another two witches right in half."

I glance to my side, seeing Odelia's expression shadowed with both pain and determination. As the designated and fairly elected Protector of Witches, I imagine any loss of life will weigh heavily on her.

It's weighing on Maddy too—the witch is putting up a brave front, but I can see she's rattled by what she saw down in the valley while trying to get her fellow witches to safety.

Claire winces and lets out a hissing breath, hunching over, before once again straightening. I startle when I see her eyes have turned from their usual green to a reddish-orange color, and her hair has brightened as well. Her skin also takes on a glow that starts as golden and turns a brighter orange, right before a loud explosion sounds in the distance, and I see one of the mountain peaks giving off the heaviest smoke *erupt*. From the eruption comes a thick cloud of noxious fumes that rise high into the atmosphere, along with a *fountain* of lava that also shoots high into the air before collapsing onto the mountain and rushing down the side of it, careening towards the valley below with stunning speed.

"There's one," Claire says, her voice choked. "Now let's get the rest of these bitches going—I'll save the Nightshade mountain for last."

Chapter Twenty-Three

"**D**on't overextend yourself too much," Odelia says, her tone warning. "Too much magic will consume you fatally, don't let that happen."

Claire groans. "I won't." A few hand gestures from her precede three more peaks exploding simultaneously, also quickly sending rushing streams of lava down their sides that quickly start to gather in the valley, overwhelming the dark fog and replacing the groans of the reanimated dead with the loud sounds of the lava boiling and hissing, destroying everything it comes into contact with.

The dark fog doesn't dissipate though. It merely rests on top of the river of lava steadily rising in the valley, which I take to mean that the shadow wielder isn't dead.

"Cedrick and Rune need to get back here *now*," Odelia hisses. "Claire's almost done with all the other mountains in this range, and I can feel ours starting to heat—we need to get out of here."

As if summoned by her words, loud footsteps echoing down the hall precede Rune running into the entrance of the room, a brown sack lugged over his shoulder filled with bulky items that clink and clatter. Without preamble or wasting any time, he runs straight up to the portal.

"Cedrick's right behind me, I'm taking the talismans through." Not waiting for a response, he jumps through the portal, telling me that whatever items and talismans he has with him must be very powerful and very sacred, meriting his total attention and protection.

A moment later, Odelia lets out a muttered, *"Fuck."*

Before I can ask her what's wrong, Cedrick slowly walks into the cavernous opening of the room, but he isn't alone. He's being held in a chokehold by a silver-haired, tall man with blood-red pupils surrounded by silver irises and gleaming fangs bared in a feral smile.

Instantly, the ground beneath our feet ceases its trembling, signaling that Claire's stopped the process of turning this mountain into a volcano.

"Well, allow me to be the first to say how lovely a reunion this is," Rhaelar drawls.

I tense, feeling my fire roil beneath my skin, drawn forward by the vampire king who radiates an otherworldly power that somehow feels *wrong.* He has magic, powerful magic, but something about it is off—ingenuine, almost, like the power he's wielding wasn't his to begin with.

Cedrick looks perfectly calm despite having long sharp claws held up to his neck, as if this is a commonplace occurrence rather than a situation where his life is very much at stake and his death almost seems assured.

Rhaelar's eyes shift over every witch gathered alongside me—Reyna, Claire, and Odelia—all of whom watch him silently with expressions ranging from fear to pure unadulterated rage. Odelia appears strained most of all—after just having heard that her numbers have been reduced by several dozen witches, she's now seeing a warlock who's part of *her coven* in a perilous position.

"Ah, the volcano witch," Rhaelar says as his eyes land on Claire, who's glaring at him. "Your little trick was most impressive—I didn't know these mountains were dormant volcanoes."

Claire's voice is deceptively casual. "Because they weren't until now."

Rhaelar appears most interested in this, his eyes brightening. "Well, it appears you have quite the gift. Shame you're choosing to waste it on sorcerers. If you joined my ranks, we could do a great deal together."

At that, Claire lets out a loud, boisterous laugh that would seem genuine if she wasn't giving Rhaelar a glare that raises goosebumps on my arms from the sheer ferocity of it. "You think I have any inclination to join you, vampire? How many of my kind have you killed?"

"Not enough, evidently," Rhaelar responds casually. "That's just fine. Death will come for you all soon enough. First, I will take Acuria—all the sorcerers and mongrels on it will fall under my reign or die. Then we'll move onto the rest of this world until it's purged of weakness and entirely under my control." After that disturbing declaration, his eyes turn to me, darkening. "You're the one who wields the black flame—I can feel it."

I offer him a bloodthirsty smile. "And yet, here you are, facing me. Doesn't seem like the best course of action, does it?"

Rhaelar chuckles, a rattly noise that's deeply discomforting. "In most circumstances, it would be quite foolish, but seeing as word has it your fire's out of control and I'm holding a warlock tightly against me, I don't see any danger from you. Unleash your fire, and who's to say it won't kill both me and one of your own?"

He's right. Somehow, he's heard that I have the black flame, and unlike his younger brother, he actually believes it—possibly because, as he said, he can feel it. What's more, he's heard that my hold on my fire is tenuous at best, though he obviously doesn't know just how tenuous or he'd have said my flame would kill everyone in this room rather than just him and Cedrick. In either scenario, I can't safely let out my fire while there's anyone else in proximity. It might kill Rhaelar, but it'll kill everyone else, too.

"It appears we're at a stalemate then," I say, trying to keep my fear from my tone. "How's this; release the warlock, and you'll live to fight another day. Don't and...well, my flame happens to have a knack for going after vampires."

Rhaelar's features twist in rage at my insinuation. "Yes, you've been the downfall of *both* of my brothers." He gives his head a hard shake. "Actaeon didn't believe the rumors that you had the black flame, the fool outright dismissed him. Otherwise, he wouldn't have faced you to destroy that quaint little village."

I shrug. "A theme I'm seeing with vamps is you underestimating your opponents, and then getting dead for it."

"A mistake I don't intend to repeat," Rhaelar growls, one of his claws pricking into Cedrick's skin and sending a drop of blood running down his neck. I feel my heart clench at the sight; Cedrick's become a good friend during my time in the coven, and I have no idea how to get him out of danger right now. I refuse to unleash my flame with people still in this room, so I'm effectively powerless to help him.

"Ah-ah, I wouldn't go throwing any spells at me," Rhaelar says, eyes flicking to Reyna. I glance over to see that her hands are flexing by her sides, building some sort of crackling purple magic in her palms. "After all, even if that spell hits me instead of him, I'll tear this warlock's throat out before it can reach me. Down, witchling."

Reyna bares her teeth at him. "What's your game here, vamp? You hurt Cedrick, we kill you. I assume your shadow wielder got caught up in the lava, like your skeletons, otherwise he'd be here. Your only way out is to release Cedrick and run like hell—that way you might live to fight another day."

Rhaelar scoffs. "I sent Ernesh home when the third eruption of lava started—I won't risk one of my greatest assets, but I also couldn't resist getting my hand on at least *one* Nightshade sorcerer. I would've preferred it to be the Queen of Mutts—after all, she has taken my family from me. I suppose taking one of her coven members from her might be the best I'll get today. I can live with that."

I exchange an uneasy glance with Claire. Rhaelar seems to be out for blood because I've killed his two other brothers already, a slight against him he's eager to return. I can only thank the gods that Leisel's away from here, out of reach, or I have no doubt Rhaelar would've gone for her throat instead. Blood for blood, like the note he left in Aesara said.

"How about a trade?" I ask, thinking on my feet. "You want me. Let Cedrick go and you can have me."

"So you can burn me to ash as soon as I've let him go? Not likely," Rhaelar snaps.

"Sierra," Cedrick says quietly. "Do it. If my death means his, fucking take it."

That request feels like a sledgehammer to my system, and it reinforces just how desperate every sorcerer is to see Rhaelar dead—enough so that one of the strongest warlocks currently living seems okay with losing his life.

"No way," I say, shaking my head at the same time that Claire, Odelia, and Reyna all make loud protests along the lines of *fuck no*. Staring at Rhaelar, I vow, "Soon, I will watch you die a slow death, screaming in agony. I am going to *destroy* you."

Rhaelar smiles again. "Lovely, then. I suppose I'll just take a nice long drink from young Cedrick here, then teleport away before you can stop me. The rest of you will get what's coming to you soon enough."

That makes panic unfurl within me, and I *desperately* try to think of some way to save Cedrick. He doesn't deserve to die, but right now, his death seems like a goddamn forgone conclusion.

Pain stabs inside my head, reminiscent of a horrible headache, making me wince, just before I hear Claire's voice say, *Cedrick, when the vamp pierces your neck, use whatever trick works to shove him back and duck down to the ground. I'll shield you. Sierra, that's when you let out your black flame. As for the rest of you, get to the portal as soon as you see me throw up my shields.*

It takes a moment for me to realize that Claire isn't speaking aloud—somehow, she's telepathically communicating to everyone in this room except Rhaelar and presenting us with a highly dangerous plan. One that just might work. My headache disappears as quickly as it appeared, and I take that to be an indication that the telekinetic connection has been broken. I cast a quick glance at Odelia, seeing her give a nearly imperceptible nod, just as Rhaelar grips Cedrick's head with one hand and his shoulder with the other. He shoves his head to the side to expose his neck, and a moment later, his fangs rip through Cedrick's skin—grimacing in pain, Cedrick uses his moment of distraction as an opportunity to bring his hands together in front of him, perform some tactile spell at *lightning* speed, then drop to the ground, slamming his hands against the stone. A shockwave rolls off him that knocks all of us to the ground, including Rhaelar. I scramble back to my feet in time to see Reyna and Odelia leaping through the portal, right as a shimmery glow appears over both Claire and Cedrick, both of whom are flattened to the ground.

I call to my fire, letting it burst out of me, directing it towards Rhaelar—the second before it reaches him, the motherfucker disappears into thin air, which only enrages my flame more, sending it into a fury rushing around the room, battering at walls and the shields protecting Cedrick and Claire.

Claire calls out in a strained voice, "Fucker fled. Pull back the fire, Sierra."

With a loud curse, I give my head a hard shake, trying to breathe deeply and ease the fury in my veins, which proves difficult. Rhaelar was there—*right fucking there* in front of me. I could've killed him, had I just been a second faster or more skilled, the war would have been over. Mariketa, Parker, and all of Aesara would be avenged. I turn my head to the ceiling and let out a roared, "Fuck!" unable to contain myself or my fury. With that fury, my fire rages hotter and higher, egged on by my negative emotions.

"Sierra!" Claire yells. "Pull it back *now!*"

The thing is, I don't know if I want to. Right now I need to destroy *something*, somehow. Otherwise, I might just boil over and explode. Revenge was in sight and I lost it. I'll have to tell Wesley that his parents' deaths have not been paid for, that I failed. He might've forgiven my killing Rhaelar, since the vamp was right here in front of me, even though I promised Wes that kill; I don't think my ward will forgive my letting Rhaelar get away. It seems that I have a propensity for failing in *everything;* each time I come close to succeeding in something, it's yanked away at the last moment. My mating with Camden, being an actual mother, protecting Leisel and Wesley, *avenging my village,* taking care of my parents—I've failed in it all, repeatedly. I can't seem to shake the thought that, if my track record is of any indication, I'll also fail to prevail in the upcoming war. My fire's as rogue as any insane wolf, I am woefully unprepared to be the greatest asset to my side of the battle. I can't do *anything* right, not really.

A loud, pained roar finally draws me from my thoughts. I gasp when I realize that pained shout comes from Cedrick, brought on because my fire has eaten almost all the way through his shield and singed his skin. In the span of a heartbeat, my anger disappears, replaced by fear—a second later, my fire recedes. Claire drops the shields around her and Cedrick with a groan, then sprints to Cedrick to examine him. His arm has a dark, ugly-looking burn that's causing blisters and what looks like skin decay; much to my horror, that decay spreads steadily, darkening his skin and creating more blisters and sores that look extremely painful.

"We need to get him to Leisel," Claire grits out, casting me a look with furrowed brows that I translate to mean, *you've really done it now.*

"I'm sorry," I whisper, horrified at myself. "I—I didn't mean to—"

"Not now," Claire barks. "Help me get him up and through the portal."

Chapter Twenty-Four

When I tumble out of the portal, helping Claire heft the weight of Cedrick, who's significantly bigger and heavier than both of us, I stumble upon a very interesting and once in a lifetime scene. The portal leads directly to the courtyard in front of Kinrith's castle, and there are thousands of witches scattered around the space, surrounding gardens, and grassy meadows, many injured in one way or another, talking amongst themselves and helping each other. What truly makes the scene strange, however, is the fact that countless shifters are intermingling with them. From royal guards to pack warriors to average shifter civilians who I assume come from the city of Kinrith, the wolves are standing with the sorcerers. Moreover, they are actively *aiding* them. A few carts are set up around the courtyard with food, clothes, and other basic necessities, and shifters are walking about, giving these offerings to the injured and frazzled witches.

It almost looks as if the shifters somehow knew of our impending arrival and prepared for it. While I notice wary looks on several shifters' faces, I don't see anyone appear unwelcoming—if anything the wariness is mixed with interest. This tells me that, in my absence, Camden has gotten his people in line and made clear they are to treat my kind with respect.

My attention quickly shifts to finding Leisel and Wesley. I spot Leisel perched on the edge of the fountain in the center of the courtyard, pressed up against Wyatt on one side with Wesley flanking her other side. In front of them, on a small cloth, is an offering of bread, cured meats, and a cup of water Wesley holds, which looks like it came from the cart a few feet away from them.

Leisel notices me as soon as I notice her, and she runs up to me and throws her arms around my waist. I release Cedrick after helping Claire lower him to the cobblestone ground, and pick Leisel up in my arms, breathing in her scent, assuring myself that she's well and unharmed.

"You okay, my love?" I ask her, pulling back to cup her cheek and looking over every inch of her.

She nods. "Wyatt and Camden were here when I came out. Camden said something about a dream with Hecate that warned him we were in danger and would need to come here—he said he tried reaching out to tell us, but nobody was around the mirrors at the right time."

That would explain the surprisingly well-organized way the sorcerers have been received. Relief and gratitude fill me, but it's quickly tempered by the low groan Cedrick releases on the ground beside me. Leisel's attention snaps to him and she gasps as she takes in the blistering burns on his body. Without prompting, she drops down to the ground beside him, places her hands on his injured arm—drawing a loud cry of pain from him that makes her wince—and heals him. It doesn't go unnoticed that her healing him is a lot slower going from when she heals anyone else—the process takes several infinitely long minutes rather than its usual seconds, and the entire time I feel like an absolute piece of shit for injuring my coven member. I didn't mean to hurt him; I simply lost control of my emotions, which in turn fueled the rage of my fire until it managed to eat through a shield and do serious damage. Cedrick's lucky to be alive, and that knowledge eats at me.

I hurt one of my friends, someone I like and respect a great deal, someone who's taught me some of the most powerful combat magic there is and has trained me, never asking for anything in return. I'm furious with myself for that fact and ready to permanently lock away my fire, though I know I can't. It's needed in the upcoming battles.

Still...looking at the tens of thousands of people gathered around me, it becomes clear that I need a better way to control my power, and I need it yesterday. If I don't, it'll continue spreading unchecked, hurting unknown amounts of people on my side.

I look at Claire, wringing my hands in front of me. "I'm sorry," I tell her. "I didn't mean to—"

"Not now," she says abruptly, giving her head a hard shake. When she looks at me, it's with an ire that I've never seen before—one that makes me want to cower away from her glare because in this moment she doesn't look like the witch who's become my close friend through my time at the coven. She looks like a stranger who I've slighted and is trying to hold back from harming me in turn.

Odelia appears beside us, taking stock of the situation with sharp eyes. She looks at Leisel beside a newly healed and passed out Cedrick, Claire's murderous expression, and my shame, and seems to put the facts together quickly.

"Your fire got out of control," she guesses with a sigh.

"Godsdamned understatement," Claire snaps. "Her fire nearly killed Ced."

I brace for the same condemnation from Odelia that I'm receiving from Claire, but don't get it. Instead, Odelia looks upon me with a soft, sympathetic, understanding expression. "It was a tense situation. You were stressed, which fueled the rage of your flames. I'm assuming Rhaelar got away?"

I nod. "That's when I sort of lost it."

"*Sort of?*" Claire says harshly. "You nearly killed Cedrick!"

Her words cut like a knife, making me wince. The shame curdling in my stomach, making my insides feel like they're twisted up in knots, amplifies tenfold. Claire has never batted an eye at my fire during training, but that's because it never hurt anyone. Her shields were always enough to protect her, if only in the nick of time. Now that it has caused damage to one of our coven members, her previous leniency is nowhere to be seen. Instead, she's aiming daggers at me with her eyes. If looks could kill, my cold corpse would be rotting in the ground. I hate the fact that my actions and my emotions have strained our friendship so much that she's no longer looking at me like a friend. She's looking at me like an enemy to be taken out.

Odelia gives Claire a harsh look. "That won't help us now. Control yourself, Claire. Sierra didn't do anything intentionally. She'd never harm one of us."

"The evidence right here proves otherwise," Claire snaps. "He could've *died.*"

"People actually died when you were regaining control of your gift, or have you forgotten?" Odelia says sharply.

Claire sucks in a breath at that, blinking several times, and her expression of fury deflates into uncertainty as she casts me another look. Then she rises to her feet and murmurs about finding Reyna before stalking away.

Odelia turns to me. "The guilt you're feeling is senseless, young witch. Every Nightshade member has experienced the downsides of having great power, and we've all harmed—if not killed—others in the course of our training. Magic is volatile and fickle like that. Don't blame yourself." Someone calls her name from the crowd, and she says, "We will speak more on the matter later. For now, find your mate, catch up with him—I have plenty of dealings to see to."

She strides away, her pace brisk, right as Wyatt and Wesley vacate their spots at the fountain in favor of approaching Leisel and me. I pull Wes in for a hug, then give him a good long look over, ensuring he wasn't hurt in the ordeal, and then turn my attention to Wyatt. Before I can greet him, he also—surprisingly—pulls me in for a strong, albeit quick, embrace, before stepping back.

"I've been worried sick," he tells me. "We knew something bad was coming your way because of Camden's dream, but we didn't know what it was. Leisel, Wes, and Odelia filled me in—I'm so fucking sorry the Valley of Sorcerers was invaded and had to be destroyed."

My eyes shift downwards, and for the first time, I realize there's no going back to that place—at least no time soon. The mountains turned into volcanoes and exploded, burying the caverns and villages. While I only stayed there for a while, I came to adore the magical, nature-heavy area, and I feel the loss. I can't imagine how other witches are feeling right now—they're probably all grieving the loss of their home and the little slice of paradise.

"Thank you," I murmur, "but I don't deserve your sorrow—I was only there for a matter of weeks. The other sorcerers here lived there for years, nearly centuries in some cases. They'll be grieving the hardest. The wolves protecting it also fell, so I also have to convey my condolences to you. I truly am sorry we couldn't protect them, Wyatt."

Wyatt nods, casting a gaze around the many people. "That shifter unit knew the risks of wartime; they died with honor by protecting our allies." He clears his throat. "We'll do our best to ensure your comfort while you have refuge with us. Once the war's over, we'll happily help sorcerers find a new, sustainable home, hopefully one as meaningful as the last one." He pauses, eyes straying to Cedrick. "Since we expected you, we've been setting up accommodations for your numbers. Houses are being built in the near vicinity, and in the meantime, there are many abandoned mansions and smaller palaces on the Crown's territory—we'll set up as many of your people as we can there, and the rest will go to properties a bit farther away."

Gratitude fills me, and I smile at him. "Thank you. How did you arrange this all so quickly? I assume Camden had his vision last night since we spoke not long before that."

Wyatt gives a short laugh. "When Cam sets his mind to something, he makes it happen. Your goddess told him the sorcerers would need refuge here, so as soon as he woke up—while having Claude try to contact you—he got on top of that. He's at one of the larger palaces right now, overseeing that it'll be fit to receive as many witches and warlocks as possible. He should be back shortly."

I nod. "If you could see that Leisel and Wesley have somewhere to go away from this chaos, I'd appreciate it."

Wyatt inclines his head. "Of course. I'll take Leisel to her old wing of the castle—Greta and Cara are very much looking forward to seeing her again. As for Wesley, I can have the empty room on the other side of Leisel's room made up for him, so the three of you can be close. That is, if you'd like to stay in this castle. If not, I'll find accommodations for you three elsewhere."

He doesn't sound pleased at his latter offer, likely because he wants to be as close to Leisel as possible, but the fact that he still makes the offer warms me to him further. Wyatt's always been considerate of the opinions and sentiments of those he holds in high regard, and this is a reminder of that.

"The main castle sounds fine, thank you. Leisel, Wes, are you two okay with that?"

They both nod, and I don't miss the way Leisel's eyes sparkle with excitement. "I'm gonna show Wesley the library."

Wes wrinkles his nose at that—he's less of a literary person than Leisel—but doesn't disagree. "I'm not leaving Leisel," he says.

It's heartwarming to see how close they are, and how protective Wesley is of Leisel. Although she already has me and Wyatt, I fear her kind and somewhat gentle nature means that she'll be susceptible to the cruelty of others. The more people there are to protect her, the better.

"Go on, then," I tell them, surprised by how easy it is to trust their safety and comfort in Kinrith. Aside from that horrid incident when Camden went into a rage, I was never anything less than entirely safe and physically comfortable while with him—he always saw to that. My tumultuous emotions are what made my time here difficult, and I find that although my emotional state is nowhere near good right now, I feel better for being here, where I know those who matter to me will be protected. "Just don't leave the palace without company," I add on, earning nods from Leisel and Wesley.

As the three turn and walk into the grand entrance, I stay by Cedrick's side, kneeling next to him protectively, even though I'm not sure the reaction I'll get when he wakes up. He told me to kill him if it meant killing Rhaelar, but I don't know if he'll be so lenient that I accidentally almost killed him in Rhaelar's absence. I watch people mill around me, barely sparing Cedrick and me any glances, all the while keeping close to the unconscious warlock until he starts to stir just a few minutes later.

"*Fuuuuuck,*" he groans, eyes fluttering open. His eyes then widen as he shoots into a sitting position, looking around him with an expression of distrust and confusion bordering on panic.

"Easy," I tell him. "We're in Kinrith. The wolves mean you no harm, you're safe. We're taking refuge here for the time being."

Cedrick blinks several times before turning to look at me. I brace myself for the anger and rejection I'll undoubtedly get from him, almost flinching prematurely, but it doesn't come. After a long moment, he says, "Well, your fire hurts like nothing I've ever felt. At least that means our enemies haven't and won't die pleasant deaths."

I feel my head jerk back at his words, shock quickly turning to a jaded sort of hope as I tilt my head to the side, wondering if my fire might've somehow messed with his head.

"You aren't...angry?" I ask

He frowns. "Angry at what? Oh, the Valley of Sorcerers falling? Yeah, I'm pissed about that, but I guess it was only a matter of time before that slice of paradise was destroyed. War is rarely kind enough to leave homes intact."

I shake my head. "No—I mean, yes, the destruction Rhaelar and his shadow wielder wrought was awful, but I'm not talking about that. My fire burned you. I nearly killed you—a second longer and I *would've* killed you. You could've died just as easily if we hadn't gotten you to Leisel."

Cedrick's expression smooths out at my words. "Oh, that? No, I'm not upset. You'd be surprised how many times I've been seriously injured while training fellow sorcerers—it's a pretty common occurrence. You didn't even come the closest to killing me."

I stare at him, wondering if he has a few screws loose. "Claire looked ready to destroy me for what I did. You should be too. Cedrick, you were nearly gone from this world because of *me*."

He *rolls his eyes* and pushes to his feet, somewhat unsteadily. I rise, too, unsure of what to make of his reaction. "Claire's just in a protective tizzy after everything that went down. It's not like you actually meant me harm, Sierra. I *told* you to kill me when Rhaelar had me, and you refused. That means that my protection matters to you—you went against my demand to ensure it. Just because your raging fire came at me doesn't mean *you* did. It just means we'll need to figure out a way to help you control it. We'll find something—I promise you—but don't beat yourself up over me. I'm fine and I'm not upset with you or blaming you."

When I still look at him incredulously, he wraps an arm around my back and pulls me in for a hug. "Seriously, Sierra, no hard feelings on my part. We're good," he murmurs into my hair.

That's when a goosebump-raising growl sounds a few feet away from us, at the same time that the bond starts to tingle in my chest, signaling that Camden's close. I turn to look over my shoulders, and my eyes lock with my mate's familiar silvery-blue ones.

Shit.

Chapter Twenty-Five

I release Cedrick, a tad too quickly, which I belatedly realize only makes this look more suspicious even though there's nothing more than friendship between us. Camden has no way of knowing that though, since we haven't exactly discussed him during our nightly chats. I've told him a bit about coven life, but I've kept details on specific coven members to myself, primarily because I didn't want to break Odelia's confidence by divulging anything.

"Cam," I greet. "I don't believe you've met my coven member and friend, Cedrick."

My use of Camden's nickname, one only Wyatt and I ever use to refer to him, appears to relax him minutely. Still, Camden stalks up to me with all the territorial possessiveness that shifters naturally have over their mates, and without asking, wraps a hard arm around my waist to tug me into him.

I gasp when it feels like electricity travels from his skin to mine, lighting my body up and making our bond pulse in my chest with warmth and what I suspect is approval. While at any other time, I might push Camden away and slap him for good measure for his presumptuousness with physical contact, I don't feel the need to right now. I've had a shit day, and I understand that it would probably bother me to see Camden embracing a female, so I can't blame him for his actions. Surprising both of us, I lean into him, also wrapping an arm around him and resting my head on his chest. I'm exhausted from facing off against Rhaelar, using my fire, and then experiencing Claire's abrupt shift and condemnation towards me—Camden's the very personification of strength, which I can very much use right now.

"I heard about your dream with Hecate," I tell him as he blinks down at me with apparent surprise. "Thank you for organizing all of this. What can I do to help?"

His features soften slightly and his attention to Cedrick all but disappears as he focuses on me. He wraps his other arm around me, pulling me snugly against his chest, and rests his chin on my head. "You can let me hold you like this for a bit. I nearly lost my fucking mind when Hecate warned me that danger was coming to you and I couldn't reach you—it took ten years off my life, at least."

A puff of laughter escapes me. "Since your lifespan could be centuries-long, I don't think a decade will cost you too much. I'm okay. Rattled, without a doubt, but okay." Noticing that Camden's once again casting a dark look at Cedrick, I add, "Now, if you could please stop glaring at Cedrick, I'd appreciate it. I used my fire to try to get Rhaelar, and instead got Cedrick with it—that led to some anger amongst others, and Cedrick was assuring me he wasn't angry with me. There's nothing untoward going on between us."

Camden pulls his head back to look down into my eyes, and whatever he sees must appease him because he nods. When he flicks a glance at Cedrick, his eyes are still jaded, but no longer murderous.

"There's an aid station set up that way, with witches swarming it—including that crazy combat one," Cam says, tilting his head to the left of him.

In my peripheral vision, I see Cedrick take the hint and walk away, leaving me with Cam. Although there's a great deal of people wandering around us, in this moment it feels like there's just us. I haven't touched Camden like this in what feels like an eternity, though it's only been a few months, and I'm surprised by how...*natural* it feels to embrace him. I'm reminded as to how well we fit together, like two halves of a whole.

"Wyatt took your sister inside?" he questions.

I nod against his chest. "And my ward. Wesley's being set up in the same hallway as me and Leisel."

I don't bother asking if that's okay with him because he should know I wouldn't allow anything else—if he has a problem with that I'll gladly tell him to fuck off. If Camden has a problem with that, I'll gladly tell him to fuck off.

He doesn't make any comment though. Instead, he continues holding me tightly like I'm the most precious thing in the world—and I realize I am to him. I've missed that feeling and I've missed him, as loathe as I might've been to admit it. Something's changed between us in the last weeks, aided by the strengthening of our bond. I feel like there could be a new beginning between us and feel hopeful despite the horrible day I've had.

Quietly, I murmur, "If you ever hurt me again, I will burn you alive."

A soft chuckle escapes Camden. "If I ever hurt you again, you won't get the chance; I'll throw myself off the nearest cliff to keep you safe. But I won't, Sierra. Never again."

I believe him. For quite some time I was reluctant to accept that he made a mistake that he quickly realized he couldn't afford to make again; I saw his actions as setting a dangerous precedent for our future, and I ran. Now though, I don't see things in such a black and white manner—I can see the picture as a whole. He was hurt and grieving, then my—*our*—loss brought him more pain and grief which fogged his mind with rage. If the same thing happened again, I don't think he'd attack me. I think he'd keep his thoughts in line just enough to walk away until he cooled down. After all, past experiences do serve as excellent teachings for the future. Nobody should be judged by the worst thing they've done, me included.

Cedrick could've decided that my burning him set a precedent for me doing so again, even though *my* emotions were in a rage that led to me losing what little control of my fire I had and instead fed into it. He understood that I wasn't in my right mind, and easily moved past it. After that ordeal, there's no way not to reflect on my situation with Camden because there are certainly some parallels.

"How did you get all of this set up so quickly?" I ask Camden, somewhat confounded. He'd have only had a matter of hours to prepare for a mass influx of witches and warlocks, yet he appears to have done a very effective job of readying to receive us, complete with housing in the works, aid and food stations, and shifters that are actually mingling with sorcerers rather than fighting them.

"I'm me," Camden responds simply. When I pull back to give him an entirely unamused look, he smiles. "I'm the king, Sierra. When I want something done, people around me work quite fast to make it happen."

I step out of his arms, which makes him frown, and look around. "Apparently you run a pretty tight ship. Having all of this ready for your allies...it'll certainly bolster your alliance with Odelia."

Camden's frown deepens. "I didn't do all of this for her, I did it for you. You're the one who matters to me. You're the one who made this alliance possible. If it wasn't for you, I probably wouldn't have put in half the effort."

I try to ignore how his words seem to burrow under my skin, warming me from the inside out. The fact that he says them in a surly, almost irritated tone instead of a warm and kind one makes them more meaningful, because I can tell he's being genuine. He *did* put in all this effort for me. Camden has a strong sense of integrity, so he still would've helped the witches simply for the sake of his alliance, but my being part of the equation made him go above and beyond.

"Well, thank you," I murmur. "Now, what can I do to help?"

He gives me a long look up and down. "You look exhausted, so you can rest."

A smile pulls at my lips. I am exhausted, it's been a particularly trying day, but I'm too keyed up to rest. "I'd rather help."

He lets out a sigh of irritation but doesn't protest, which I appreciate. "Odelia's off with Reyna and a few warlocks, discussing wards. She intends to put shadow and necromancer-proof wards around a very large span of land, large enough to protect not just the crown's territory but everywhere that warriors, troops, and war-aid groups are staying, which is about a fifty-mile stretch, considering I keep some packs apart since they don't like each other very much. You could help her coordinate that."

I nod, recalling the bag of talismans Rune took through the portal. The reason Cedrick ended up captured is because he went after those talismans, one of which is apparently the most powerful warding tool currently in existence.

"I'll go find them," I tell him. "I'm sure you have your own kingly duties to oversee as well."

Camden also nods, but he looks reluctant to part with me. "Unfortunately, otherwise I'd be at your side. I've organized a welcoming dinner for the top sorcerers—I can't include every single witch and warlock, but all the Priestesses, Priests, and a few elders from each coven are invited to the castle's dining hall tonight, along with all my top commanders. Everyone should get used to each other. I'll see you there?"

"I'm not a priestess or an elder," I point out, somewhat playfully.

Camden pulls a half-smile. "No, but you're my queen. Now that you've returned, though the circumstances of your return are unfortunate, everyone should get acquainted with you." When he sees my apprehension, since I am *not* particularly excited to step back into the role I ran away from, he adds, "Bordat will be there, along with Korbin, who's his top warrior, and his mate Lana. I'm sure they'll all be pleased to see you again."

I chuckle at that. "Actually, I think Bordat would like to gut me, since I challenged his authority pretty directly. Word has it Alpha's don't like that."

Camden shakes his head. "You're wrong. Shifters respect strength, both physical and strength of character—you've proven repeatedly you're very powerful magically and have a character worthy of a ruler. Certainly a better conscience than I do. Bordat might not have liked the way you put him in his place initially, but he respected it, probably because he realized you were right to do so. Besides, Lana and Korbin have both been spreading word of your kindness and fairness around their pack, which has traveled to others. You'll be a very welcome addition, and many people will want to meet you. They have for some time, but circumstances made that impossible."

Once again, the praise he delivers is spoken in that kind of irritated tone, like he's annoyed that I'm not seeing things clearly, which only endears me.

"I'll be there," I tell him softly. "I'll also be back in the castle, staying with Leisel and Wesley." After a pause, I add, "Odelia will most likely bring Reyna, who delighted in beating the shit out of your warrior, and has absolutely no filter. Will that be a problem?"

"No. Again, my kind respects strength and power, and she proved she has leagues of both. Saunders wasn't the happiest initially, but now he chuckles over the incident, and is looking forward to training troops alongside her. The magic of sorcerers will greatly compliment the strength of shifters—there's no denying that."

He's right, and that's our greatest hope in this war. The combined strength of our species, working together to protect the nation as a whole. I don't think training will be entirely clean, and I definitely foresee fights breaking out, but my observations of shifters thus far are in line with what Camden is saying—they don't hold grudges over fights. As a naturally physical species, they settle a lot of problems through violent means, and then are content to move forward.

I shrug. "Just don't complain when she manages to offend at least half the people in attendance—it's a gift of hers." With that, I turn and walk off, heading in the direction that Odelia went earlier.

I find her not far away, predictably speaking with Rune, Bane, and Reyna with a serious expression on her face. There are a few other witches gathered around, and there's a slight shimmer surrounding the group that appears to be a shield of some sort. When Reyna spots me, she waves me to her, and I step through the barrier without any resistance, which is surprising—generally, shields keep people out.

"Sound barrier," Reyna explains at my look of confusion. "We don't want all our secrets spilled to the mongrels."

Odelia sighs at her. "Since we're taking refuge with the shifters, can you not treat them with a touch more respect?"

Reyna blinks. "I am being respectful. I haven't lashed out at anyone or started any fights. Yet."

Bane shakes his head at her, an amused smile curling his lips. "What she means is your persistence in calling shifters mongrels, beasts, and other such terms."

Reyna tilts her head to the side. "Why wouldn't I call them what they are?" She motions to Odelia. "She's repeatedly told me that honesty is an important quality, and I'm exercising it."

"Calling them mongrels and beasts isn't honest, it's derogatory and rude," Rune says with admirable patience. "After all, how do you feel when people call us abominations or perversions of the natural order?"

Reyna shrugs. "I don't much care one way or the other, but for the sake of defending our kind, I do generally beat whoever dares use such terms to a pulp." After a pause, she gives a nod of understanding. "Right, so when I call shifters by what they really are, I should be prepared for a fight. That's cool with me—I like blowing off steam."

Rune sighs. "That's not what she meant—you know what, never mind. Trying to get through to you is more hopeless than trying to move a mountain with my bare hands."

Reyna grins. "So glad you understand."

I let out a low laugh of amusement, surprised to be laughing at a time like this, after the day I've had. Reyna, with all her quirks and social ineptness, can pull a laugh out of any spectator at the worst of times. Having her at the dinner tonight will certainly be entertaining, though I have no doubt she'll create some messes Odelia will then need to clean up with the power of diplomacy.

I'll probably be expected to aid in that, as my return to Kinrith does indeed connote my return to my station as Queen. I'm not sure where that puts me with the Nightshade Coven or sorcerers as a whole—how can I be a coven member *and* the Queen of shifters? That's something I'll need to discuss with Odelia at a later time. For now...

"Should we get started on warding the area?" I ask. "I doubt Rhaelar will attack twice in one day. He'll need to regroup, but if he could get to us at the Valley of Sorcerers, which is hidden and only known to a few, he can easily get to us in Kinrith, which exists on every map."

"Yes, we'll be getting started on wards here immediately, especially now that all the witches in Acuria have arrived," Odelia says with a nod. "The good news is the witches who were already here and warded Kinrith and its surrounding lands have built a solid base for us to work off of; we'll only need to improve on it using our stone, not start from scratch. The difficult part is that the stone itself contains the sort of power that only a few sorcerers in existence can safely channel without being killed from the sheer overload of magic. The people standing in this circle, along with a handful of others, are the only ones who can safely handle such power. Sierra, I know you've had a difficult day, more so than many of us...are you in the right frame of mind to help right now?"

"Keep in mind that the power from the stone needs to be channeled entirely clean," Rune advises me. "There can't be any negative emotions tainting your system—you have to lock all that shit down while working with it."

I pause before responding, considering his words. I'm not in the best frame of mind, especially after my encounter with Claire and feeling her anger that bordered on hatred. Cedrick's easy acceptance of what had happened helped; the fact that he wasn't upset whatsoever sort of soothed the burn Claire left behind, but I'm still a little downcast. Just because my emotions aren't in the best place though, doesn't mean I can afford to sit back—it's quite clear that the witches and warlocks as a whole need me right now. The fact that I have the black flame, which is a deity-bestowed power, means I should be able to handle whatever's in the stone Cedrick risked his life to retrieve, meaning I really am needed for the warding. I can't, however, risk my emotions making a mess of things or putting myself or others in danger.

"If you can give me an hour to get my sister and Wesley settled and cool down, I should be good," I say after a long moment of thinking. "Leisel has an uncanny way of serving as a calming beacon to me."

Odelia smiles, the gesture filled with both understanding and warmth. "Yes, that child serves as a calming beacon to all of us, truth be told. There is something very special about her—light and healing power aside. Of course, Sierra, go to your family, ensure they're alright. I'll also take the time to get as many of my witches settled as possible."

Rune agrees, "I'll do the same with my warlocks. Shall we meet back here in an hour? The ritual itself should take less than an hour—it's a quick, albeit very delicate and tricky, bit of casting. We'll have enough time to wash and prepare for the banquet that the shifters are throwing in our honor."

"Sounds good to me," Reyna says. "I'm assuming that, since she's kind of throwing a magical tantrum at the moment, Claire will be excluded from the ritual?"

Odelia shakes her head. "Absolutely not, we need her as much as we need Sierra. I'll calm her, help her see reason, and we can make sure she's casting far enough away from Sierra that neither of them gets irate."

I wince, feeling horrible that I've created such unrest and a lack of unity within the Nightshade Coven. I never thought I'd be at odds with Claire; then again, I'd never before injured a coven member.

"I'm sorry to be making such problems," I say, my tone coated in shame.

"Don't be," Odelia says simply.

Rune adds, "Every person who will be using the power of the stone to cast wards along with us has had accidents, some of them have even caused fatalities at one point or another. Magic is a fickle, volatile force, especially when it's powerful. Nobody here will fault you for what happened, especially since it's clear you pulled back in time, and Cedrick is healed. Think nothing more of the matter."

Chapter Twenty-Six

R egardless of Rune's assurances, I find myself thinking on the matter a great deal as I part ways from the coven and make my way into the castle, winding up familiar staircases and walking through hallways filled with memories—some good, some bad.

My mind replays the moment when I fed into my fire rather than doing my best to control it on a loop, as if determined to torture myself. My thoughts only clear when I enter Leisel's old bedchamber, greeted with the warming sight of my sister sitting on her bed across from Wesley, reading a passage from a book out loud to him, with Chip dozing on a pillow not far from her. The two look up at my entrance and Leisel climbs off the bed before skipping right up to me and wrapping her arms around my waist in a hug.

I hold her to me with one hand and use the other to stroke through her somewhat unruly strawberry-blonde locks, breathing her in and reminding myself that we're here, away from danger, as safe as we can be for the time being. Wesley also gets off the bed, and promptly joins our hug, wrapping his arms around both me and Leisel as if sensing my need for comfort. His time with my sister must be rubbing off on him—I've noticed he's become more attuned to the emotions of others in recent weeks. That could just as easily be attributed to the fact that, although Wes puts on a brave face, he's still grieving the death of his parents. He lost them mere months ago and his life was swiftly turned upside down. While being with the coven has kept him well-occupied, I still see shadows in his eyes.

"I'm so glad you two are alright," I murmur, holding them both tightly.

"Thanks to you," Wes says. "You got us out of there in time, saving the day."

A breath of somewhat sardonic laughter escapes me. "I'm not a hero, Wes."

Leisel makes a noise of disagreement. "You're my hero, Sierra. You should know that already."

"Mine too," Wes mumbles into my hair. "You saved my life in Aesara and gave me purpose when I lost it. I heard what happened with Cedrick—you shouldn't blame yourself. You've done a lot more good than harm."

Feeling my heart warm and fill until it's practically bursting, I say, "I love you guys so much."

"I love you too," Leisel says, nuzzling closer to me.

Then she nudges Wes and he also grumbles, "Obviously, I love you both too. You're the only family I've got left—I'd do anything for you."

Gods, I don't deserve these two, but I'm beyond grateful to have them in my life. After several minutes of just standing there and hugging, we separate in time for Greta—Leisel's nanny during her time at the castle—and Cara—Greta's mate and my lady's maid—to make an entrance. They greet the three of us, and Cara even gives me a hug, telling me how much she's missed my presence in the castle. Greta instantly starts fussing over Wesley and Leisel, reminding me just what a phenomenal caretaker she is. After hearing that we haven't eaten since breakfast, an incensed Greta calls up for sandwiches. Then she and Cara retreat, and I enjoy a quick bite with Leisel and Wes before having to make my way back down to the courtyard.

By the time I make it down there, I find that the area has been mostly cleared of the copious number of people who were here merely an hour ago leaving just a few dozen stragglers, mostly shifters, who are helping pack up the carts and clean up the area.

I'm feeling significantly lighter and better after spending time with Wesley and Leisel, especially after their encouraging words and the true feeling of family that comes with them. I greet Odelia and Reyna who are standing by the fountain along with Maddy and an unfamiliar warlock.

"Rune's already in position with the others," Odelia says, clutching a wooden box engraved with sigils in her hands. In front of her, on the ground, is a map of Kinrith, along with surrounding villages and towns. A large circle is drawn around the area. "They've made their way to the far sides of the territory we'll be warding. Maddy, Oberin, Reyna, grab horses from the stables and ride to the starred points on the map—you'll be casting from there. Sierra, you're with me—we'll head into the forest until we're in the center of the area that we'll be warding. That's where we'll be working from, sending energy outwards to the witches casting at the edge of the existing shield. I'll be teaching as we go along, but basically, our ritual will consist of a built-on version of Merlin's Shield."

She taught me about Merlin's Shield during one of our sessions together—it's a very effective warding method, the basis of which I learned when I first shielded the Crown's territory under the guidance of Claude. While working with Claude, I had to expend at least a liter of my own blood, but the warding technique Odelia taught me only requires a drop of blood, which is then magically replicated and stretched in the creation of individual sigils that create a net around a designated area of land, and upon completion, turn into a shield.

Reyna, Maddy, and Oberin take long looks at the maps, particularly at the points that have been marked with stars, before giving Odelia a nod of agreement and walking at a brisk pace toward the palace stables. Meanwhile, Odelia threads her arm through mine and starts leading me toward the tree line that marks the entrance to the forest.

"I was a late bloomer," Odelia says, breaking the silence. At my look of confusion, she elaborates, "Magically, that is. Most witches start to develop their specific gifts when puberty sets in—around ten or eleven. For warlocks, it's a tad later, around twelve or thirteen. My power and discipline was magical discovery; I had an affinity for altering existing spells and creating new ones, a very rare gift for witches, but not one that came with great deals of power. It was only when I was eighteen that my power hit a surprising growth spurt; one that was too strong for me to handle and came along too quick." As we break through the trees and make our way into the forest, she continues speaking, accompanied by the sounds of chirping birds and buzzing insects.

"I grew up with Rune, both of us members of the Nightshade Coven from a young age. We sparred together often and enjoyed each other's company. When my power expanded and I started developing new gifts, he insisted that we continue sparring, even though our priestess at the time had cautioned against it. One day, during one of our practice fights, my magic went out of control as a new ability developed; the ability to create and wield lightning naturally, without the use of a spell. I hit him with a high-voltage strike entirely by accident, one that stopped his heart. Luckily, I was very proficient in the healing arts despite not being a natural healer and had already devised a spell that could restart any being's heart—something that would revive anyone so long as their soul hadn't yet departed. It worked. Rune came back to life, and the crazy bastard laughed. He was always a bit on the unhinged side. I, however, wasn't so amused.

"I hid myself away, going to an isolated part of the cavern system and set up wards in the room that prevented any power from escaping them and causing destruction. I starved myself to weaken my power, then trained myself relentlessly, refusing the offers of aid from others unless I was so weak I couldn't possibly be a danger to them. The result was I nearly killed myself from malnourishment—the high priestess at the time stepped in, insisted on training me herself, and helped me integrate back with the coven. It was one of the lowest points in my life, save when our coven was stormed by dark faye and they killed a third of our members, including my high priestess."

Holy shit. Odelia wasn't kidding when she said all sorcerers of great power have stories of seriously injuring or in some cases killing someone by accident; apparently, Odelia herself actually killed Rune, though she quickly brought him back to life. Then she nearly killed herself. I can see why she's telling me this; it's a pretty unambiguous way of telling me not to be too hard on myself because my struggles are entirely normal.

"Wow," I murmur, unsure of what else there is to say. Despite having to be an extrovert simply because of her position amongst witches, Odelia is a fairly private person. She doesn't talk about herself very often, and now I understand why—she has a complex past. tempted to ask more about the dark faye attack that took the old Nightshade high priestess, but I also don't want to be intrusive or disrespectful. I get the sense that she'll tell me more when she's ready to tell me more; I'm lucky she's been so open with me already.

It does make me feel significantly better to know that one of the most powerful witches in existence has shared my struggles and makes me feel less alone in my experience. After all, if Odelia once lost control to the point of killing the man who's now the Protector of Warlocks, it's hard to judge myself too harshly in comparison.

"Yes," Odelia murmurs, squeezing my arm. "We've all experienced our difficulties, so do not be too upset with yourself. Unlike me, you pulled back in time, otherwise Cedrick would be mere ashes. You've done very well in your short time with us, learned nearly a lifetime's worth of knowledge and have become proficient with many different forms of magic as well as combat. Have pride in what you have achieved—I don't know of anyone else who has done so much in such a small amount of time."

I grimace. "I don't think I excelled because I'm terribly gifted, more so because I didn't have another choice. It was learn and grow as fast as possible, or risk not being able to protect my sister and ward in the difficult times we're experiencing—that's not something I could allow."

Odelia inclines her head. "Motivation is indeed important, but it isn't enough—immense raw talent and power is needed to learn as much as you have to the point of mastery. You might not be a master quite yet, but you are more proficient than most."

She slows to a stop beside a sprawling oak that emanates a strange, potent sort of energy, unwinding her arm from mine. The tree is so tall the tops of its branches disappear into the sky, with hundreds of branches of different lengths and widths shooting from the trunk. It's probably centuries old, and upon taking a few steps closer, I realize there isn't just energy coming from it, there's magic. Powerful, vibrant magic that makes the air around it nearly buzz.

"We've reached the center point of the warding circle," Odelia informs me, turning the box in her hands over. "You feel the magic in the air, yes?"

I nod. "All nature has some magic and energy, as I've learned, but this tree...there's something special about it."

Odelia smiles. "Yes, well, the witch doctor—Claude, if I'm not mistaken—carved sigils into the base of this tree when mythics first came to this land; sigils that made it an epicenter for magic and, with time, transformed it into a tree of life. From my understanding, he often comes here for meditation and rituals—the tree and surrounding lands are therefore saturated with magic. Ideal for the ritual we're about to do, as we'll have plenty of power from our surroundings to draw on."

I watch as she creaks open the lid of the wooden box, revealing a smooth, black stone that radiates the sort of power I've never felt—a power that prickles and stings my skin as it fills the air, instantly making me wary. Whatever magic that stone has, I can see why Odelia insisted that only the most powerful sorcerers handle it; I have no doubt touching it directly would be painful, and enough to kill most others.

"Emerson's stone," Odelia tells me, looking down at the rock. "This has been passed down through the most powerful high priestesses for centuries; it originates from Mythicacia, our old home. Each witch who has had possession of it did rituals to infuse it with different types of power; the unique thing about this stone is it serves as a talisman that can hold unlimited amounts of power, whereas most talismans can only hold so much. After so many generations and hundreds of high priestesses, this stone is possibly the single most powerful talisman in existence. It's also entirely self-sustaining; when it came into my possession, I did a ritual with Rune that ensured that the stone would forever automatically regenerate any power drawn from it."

I blink several times, taking a step closer, surprised that the air around the stone has thickened and is crackling with so much magic it makes me wince. "If it ever fell into the wrong hands…"

"It would be useless," Odelia assures me. "The stone also has self-protection magic; only a Nightshade high priestess or someone working alongside one would be able to handle and draw from it. The stone's a living thing at this point, Sierra. It can differentiate friend from foe and it's coded to my lineage. Not blood lineage, but magical lineage."

Magic truly is a thing of wonders, capable of doing almost anything. In a way, it's daunting to be around such power; I worry if I mishandle it, that could have horrible repercussions or cause a negative ripple effect, which means I'll be following Odelia's instructions to the letter.

"Merlin's Shield is primarily tactile in nature," Odelia tells me as she gently withdraws the stone from the box and holds it in the palm of her hand. "We'll be adding a few variations to it, and I'll need you to follow along with my gestures and chants precisely."

I can see that there's a small aura around the stone, as there is with all living things, which means this rock truly is alive. The aura, which is initially grey, quickly changes to a silver so vibrant it's almost painful to look at, then morphs into a silvery-blue which makes Odelia smile.

When she glances at me and sees my puzzled expression, she explains, "The aura indicates the stone's…*mood*, for lack of a better term. The dark grey means it's resting, silver means it's taking the measure of whoever's holding it, and the silver-blue means it's accepted its wielder and is willing to work with them."

"What would it look like if it rejected whoever's holding it?"

Odelia smiles. "It would turn a dark red, then send out a burst of power that would liquefy their organs and stop their heart—a defensive mechanism infused into it by the last high priestess who wielded it. Give me your hand."

I blink. "You...want *me* to hold it? What if it decides it doesn't like me? I'm not a Nightshade high priestess."

Odelia lifts a shoulder in a delicate half-shrug. "Then it has been a pleasure knowing you, Sierra."

My lips part. "What—I don't want to be killed by a damn stone of all things!"

"I was only joking," Odelia says with a chuckle, shaking her head in amusement. "If the stone simply doesn't want you holding it, it'll first heat up until it's hot enough to burn skin, making an unwelcomed person drop it. It's if that person continues to try to use it the defense will be triggered. So, if it gets hot, simply give it back to me. You're in my presence, working with me, which the stone should recognize. Now really, Sierra, there's no need to fear; hold out your hand."

Somewhat reluctantly, I close the distance between us and slowly extend my hand to Odelia. She gently transfers the stone to my hand and I suck in a sharp breath of air as pure, invigorating power courses through my system, feeling almost like a shock of electricity from a faulty light switch, only *much* more intense. It makes goosebumps break out across my skin, but I try to ignore the sensation in favor of watching the stone's aura. It turns black as soon as it makes contact with my palm, which makes me nervous. After a few seconds, it once again transforms to that bright silver, before settling into the same silver-blue hue it had in Odelia's grasp.

She smiles. "See? Nothing to worry about. Now, for both of us to draw from the stone simultaneously, we'd either both need to be holding it—which we can't do since our hands are needed for the casting—or create an energy tether to it. You might feel a slight tug on your chest; don't be alarmed." Odelia's eyes flutter closed as she chants something under her breath, then opens them again and touches two fingers to the stone before moving them to my chest. A sharp yank at my solar plexus nearly startles me enough to drop the stone, but I stop myself just in time and watch with amazement as a faint shimmering thread is created between me and the stone, hovering in the air. A crackling sensation of power quickly takes up residence in my chest, and I can practically feel the stone pushing magic into me. Odelia takes the stone from me and repeats her chant and gesture, creating her own tether, before bending down and setting it on the ground. Two nearly invisible threads stem from it, one connecting to Odelia's chest and the other to mine.

"Let's begin," Odelia says. "The others just got into position—I can feel them. Start with the opening variation to Merlin's shield, go through the three stages of it, and then follow along with me for the additions."

Inhaling a deep breath, I hold my hands out in front of me, fingertips to the sky and palms facing outwards. Then, in tandem with Odelia, I begin going through the gestures. As my hands move together and apart, fingers intertwining and separating in the way I learned from Odelia, a drop of blood is drawn from both of our palms with magic alone, hovering midair between us. That blood then starts giving birth to several different glowing red sigils, and I watch with amazement as those sigils quickly seep into the forest floor, creating a red glow visible just beneath the surface. Then they shoot outwards, traveling beneath the dirt and leaving a trail of glowing red as they disappear from sight, no doubt heading towards the sorcerers hovering at the edge of the warded territory, waiting to receive the sigils and incorporate them into a shield that'll protect everything within from everything outside of it. With each new sigil created and sent out, there's a pulse in my chest as the stone continues feeding me magic. The power from the stone is more than I've ever felt or channeled—even more concentrated than that of my fire, which makes me wary, but also brings on a sense of awe.

As we come to the end of Merlin's Shield and start on the additions, Odelia catches my eyes and slows the gestures of her hands so it's possible for me to follow along. My tether with the stone starts to crackle with greater amounts of power, as the newly created sigils are *much* stronger and more potent than those that came before and also glow brighter. My fire starts to rile within me, and I can sense its interest in the ritual, although it doesn't try to rise up and interfere, most likely because it doesn't perceive any danger to me.

The longer I cast with Odelia, the more taxing it becomes and the more I feel myself growing tired. Although I'm aided by the stone, I'm still expending great deals of personal energy, and that takes its toll.

"The next part is the final variation—watch your thumb and pinkie positions carefully," Odelia advises me.

Through a series of movements, I watch as a single sigil is created between us—a conglomeration of intricate swirls connected in what almost looks like a trifecta, glowing such a bright red it's almost painful to look at. That sigil then clones itself into six separate sigils, drawing *immense* power from me that the stone can't replace at once, and then melts into the ground before following the existing paths of previous sigils and rushing away from us.

"That'll do it," Odelia says, sounding a bit out of breath. "Assuming the others hovering at the edges of the shield do their jobs properly, which they should, Kinrith will now be protected from even the power of a shadow wielder and necromancer—the blackest of magics. I don't think your fire itself could penetrate through."

"Good," I murmur, a bit drowsily. "Rhaelar won't be able to pull his stunt again." Seeing the flicker of pain in Odelia's eyes, I add, "I'm sorry the valley had to be destroyed, and that we lost sorcerers."

Odelia shrugs, though the gesture is halfhearted. "We'll find a new home once the war's over, and the fallen will be grieved by their loved ones. We've had to relocate before; that's the nature of being part of a species that is hunted out of fear by others. Now, let's get back to the castle—I believe we have a banquet to prepare for."

Chapter Twenty-Seven

When I return to my chambers in the castle, my first order of business is to check on Leisel and Wesley, both of whom are in their respective rooms. Leisel grumbles a bit at being left out of tonight's festivities, though Wes has promised to keep her company and help her continue to practice with her light-creating powers, which only appeases her minutely. After giving her a kiss and explaining that tonight is an adults-only event not suited for youngsters, I leave her and Wes in the care of Greta and retreat to my chambers where Cara is waiting with an excited smile. Her black hair is pulled back into its usual bun, and she bounces on her toes, her hazel eyes glimmering with anticipation. Even her smooth walnut skin appears to be vibrating and glowing—I think she's looking forward to the banquet more than anyone who'll be in attendance.

I sigh. "I suppose your exhilaration stems from the fact that you're about to put me in a pretty dress and do my hair some fancy way for the banquet?"

Cara nods eagerly. "I have the perfect dress picked out, and I already know how I'll do your hair—you'll be the most beautiful woman there."

I grimace. I know I'm relatively pretty, but I've never been one to draw extra attention to myself—I spent most of my life covered in horse manure and dirt from the farm, which I never minded all that much. In fact, I prefer it to getting all dressed up in something that will likely draw eyes to me, even more than already will naturally be trained in my direction for the simple fact that I am Camden's mate.

"I don't think that'll be the case since there'll be plenty of witches in attendance. They're ethereal in their beauty, hard to outdo."

Cara's eyes sparkle. "Oh, trust me, you'll outdo them. You're already beautiful but you'll be jaw-dropping by the time I'm done. Let's get started, shall we?"

Just under an hour later, it becomes apparent that Cara really wasn't kidding when she said she'd make me look stunning. As I stand in front of the full-length mirror in my closet, staring at myself with parted lips, I have to wonder if Cara's a fairy godmother of sorts. The silk dress she chose is blood-red with a neckline that shows a good glimpse of cleavage. It's floor-length and molds to my body from the straps holding up the deep v-neckline to just above my knees where it flares out in a ruffle of satin and silk encrusted with glittering stones, several of which dust the floor. My hair is styled in a regal, elaborate updo with a few stray curled strands framing my face. My lips are painted the same color as my dress, and Cara even put some makeup on my eyes, smokey pigments that bring out the gold of my irises along with a cream that darkens and lengthens my eyelashes. I feel like a real-life princess—no, a queen, and I barely recognize myself.

"Do you like it?" Cara asks from behind me, and I see her reflection bouncing on her toes once again, a pleased smile lighting her face.

"I love it," I reply sincerely, giving my head a shake. Going from a farm girl to *this* is kind of a shock. I already knew Cara has an eye for fashion, as she proved one of my first conscious nights in the castle when she dressed me for dinner, but she's outdone herself now and I realize she was holding back before. "I barely recognize myself."

She tsks. "Don't be silly. You still look like you, just a dolled-up version. The king will be beside himself—everyone will." A conspiratorial gleam lights her eyes as I turn to her. "I think he might want to lock you up in his chambers to keep you to himself."

The fact that her words send a path of heat scorching through my body as images of just what I might do with Camden in that scenario flash in my mind means I truly have come a long way with him because there's no fear. No flash of his past mistakes, only a low humming arousal that I immediately try to tamp down because now is *not* the time.

I clear my throat. "Whether or not he wants to is beside the point; I believe I'll have a lot of mingling to do tonight." I don't bother to suppress the shudder of distaste that the thought of mingling sends through me because I'm not a terribly sociable person by nature.

I may have learned recently that I'm a decent diplomat, but half of that is attributed to the wealth of reading I've done on world history and politics, and the other half has to do with the fact that when I'm fighting for what I believe in, I can be very passionate. I truly believed that an alliance between witches and shifters was the only way to win the war we're now in, so I put my everything into making a solid treaty. I also believed that humans who mated into their packs deserved the inherent right to maintain contact with their families, so I have fought and will continue to fight for that. I certainly think the triads all need to die, and I'm willing to bleed to make that a reality.

Cara smiles softly. "The King Alpha is very experienced in that department, he'll guide you. Besides, word has it you've proven to be quite the diplomat, so I don't think you'll have too much trouble. Speaking of the king, he should be here any moment to collect you—"

She cuts off as a few banging knocks sound at the door before saying, "And that'll be him. I'll get the door so you can take a moment to steel yourself. I'll warn you that, as Queen, you'll be expected to speak with all the top generals and Alphas dedicating troops to our army, so it will probably be a long night."

With that, she walks off, and I hear Cara open the door before telling Camden that I'll be out in a moment.

I slip on the black, strappy heels with red soles she left for me, taking a second to balance myself on the foot-destroying contraptions, before straightening my spine, squaring my shoulders, and striding out of the closet. Camden is leaning against the side of the doorway, arms crossed over his chest, one ankle crossed over the other, and looking at once devastatingly handsome and terribly at ease despite the rigor of the upcoming night. He's wearing a flattering black tuxedo that must be custom-made for him, with the way the jacket stretches across his broad shoulders, accentuating his muscular frame. He looks divine and edible, his aristocratic facial features framed beautifully by his chestnut hair which is styled into a side part.

The moment I step into the room, his eyes are glued to me, then momentarily widen before the silver-blue orbs flare with heat. He opens and closes his mouth a few times, looking uncharacteristically lost for words, before saying faintly, "Holy shit."

I motion to Cara. "She's the mastermind."

Cara beams at that but shakes her head. "I'm good, but you're a very beautiful subject to work on. I barely had to do anything to bring the full force of that beauty to the surface."

"Remind me to give you a raise," Camden tells Cara, which makes her blush profusely as she bows her head.

Then he slowly unfurls from his position against the doorframe and prowls forward, gliding towards me, all intense masculinity and confidence that turns my insides to a puddle of goop. He stops directly in front of me until there's less than an inch of space between our bodies and slowly slides a hand across my waist to settle it at my lower back.

"I'd really like to kiss you right now," he murmurs.

Cara gasps. "Not now, Your Majesty, or you'll ruin the rouge on her lips! Save the kissing for *afterward*."

A light laugh escapes me as I smile at Cara, though heat curls my insides and my lips start to tingle, as if aching for the feel of Camden's against them. The close proximity and contact also make the bond pulse with faint approval and pleasure, growing even stronger in my chest. I think it approves of the fact that Camden stated his intention in almost a questioning way rather than steamrolling me because I know that it takes a lot of effort on his part to stop himself. Shifters are tactile creatures, incredibly physical, and matehood makes them even more tactile and in need of touch, so I know Camden's restraint is for my benefit and at a personal cost of discomfort.

"If you behave, you can later," I tell him softly. Then I tell Cara, "Thank you for your help. I'll see you tomorrow."

Cara takes her cue to scurry out of the room, just as the door adjoining my room to Leisel's opens, and I hear a soft gasp come from it. Seeing my sister in her doorway, lips parted and eyes wide as she stares at me, I step away from Camden and hold out my arms to her. She trots right up to them and throws herself into my embrace before leaning back to pat the top of my head and run her little hand over my cheek with an expression of wonder. "You look so gorgeous," she tells me, blinking several times. "When I grow up, I want to look just like you."

Greta, standing in Leisel's room and holding a book, gives me an approving nod. "You look very regal and graceful, Your Majesty. My mate did an excellent job."

"Thank you," I tell Greta, before tapping Leisel's nose. "When you grow up you'll be a beauty of your own, my love. Now, give me a kiss, and head to bed. Has Wesley also gone down for the night?"

She shakes her head. "No, he's in the room with the map on the table, talking to Claude about something. Greta will make sure he goes to sleep after I do." She leans up on her tiptoes and kisses my cheek. "Goodnight, Sierra, I love you."

My heart warms. "I love you too, sweet girl. Goodnight, sweet dreams. Kiss Chip for me."

She giggles before skipping back into her room and closing the door behind her, leaving me alone with Camden. I straighten and turn back to him, clearing my throat awkwardly. "I suppose we should get going?" Glancing at the grandfather clock propped against the wall, I feel my brows furrow. "Looks like the banquet started about ten minutes ago."

Camden nods. "It's customary for rulers to be a little late, so everyone's gathered once we make our way in. I'm not sure how I feel about anyone else seeing you in this dress; people might get the idea to try to steal you away from me. You're irresistible."

I feel my cheeks warm. "Flattery won't get you anywhere, Cam."

"It's not flattery, it's honesty," he assures me. "You're so gorgeous, I can barely breathe, but it's not just your beauty that's enchanting. It's your personality, your *goodness* beneath the steel armor, your intelligence and wit—all of it wrapped up in a very pretty package. Who *wouldn't* want you for themselves?"

My blush spreads further, creeping down my neck, and I tuck a flyaway curl of hair behind my ear. "Maybe anyone who doesn't want to risk getting burned alive by a god-bestowed power?"

Camden shakes his head with an amused smile. "Don't forget that shifters revere strength and power, my beautiful mate. It's almost like a religion to us as much as matehood is. You have a surplus of power that's as much a lure as the rest of you. In any case, if anyone gets negative ideas in their heads, I'll just rip their throats out."

It probably says something bad about me that I find his words arousing, the fact that he's so possessive over me that the thought of me being with someone else would make him resort to violence. Especially since, now, I truly believe that his violence will never be turned on me—not even if he goes into a rage again. The last time he was in a rage, I've come to understand that not only was he not in his right mind, but he also truly didn't understand his strength; he does now, and I don't think he'll ever forget it again. Not with me.

"Really, we should go," I tell him. "Odelia will be expecting me, and Reyna's bound to start stirring some shit promptly, which means we'll probably have some ruffled feathers to smooth over."

Camden offers me his arm, which I slip mine through, before letting out a soft sigh of contentment. "I've missed this," I admit, somewhat quietly as he leads me out of the room.

"Good, because I've been a fucking shell without you," Camden replies. "I've missed you so much I felt like there's been a tight, constricting band around my chest for the last months to accompany the chasm within it."

Another pulse of approval, and this time affection, travels through the bond, warming my chest and bringing a smile to my lips. "That chasm isn't there anymore for either of us," I observe. "It has started filling up quickly. I woke up this morning to find that the drip of the bond healing had turned into a steady stream."

Camden nods. "Ah, yes, that. When Hecate came to me last night, she also did something to the bond—kicked it into gear, I think." He tells me about his dream in detail, including the crystal Hecate gave him and all the details of their conversation. "I don't think she likes me very much, but she accepts the necessity of my presence in your life."

I nod slowly. "Well, you are a necessity to me. Not just to my power, but to me as a person as well. It took me a long time to realize how well-matched we are since we're opposites in many ways, but we really do fit together in a sense that I don't think anyone would have expected or anticipated. We suit each other well, complete each other."

Camden gives me a smile filled with so much affection and a glimmer that I might even call love. "We agree on that point, and I'm very glad you finally see it."

As we stop in front of an ornately carved wooden double-door entrance on the first floor that I know leads to the ballroom, with two guards standing in front of it, Camden asks, "You ready?"

I nod. "Just...don't get mad if I go for people's throats if they irritate me or talk down to sorcerers."

"You won't have to," Camden replies calmly. "I'll throw them out myself, though I really don't think that'll be an issue. There's great respect for you across the shifter communities."

He nods to the guards, who promptly swing open the doors, then leads me through. The room is bustling with people, though it's so large that it doesn't feel cramped—the hundred or so guests fit comfortably in the large space. There's a magnificent chandelier hanging from the high vaulted ceiling with orbs of light sitting atop crystal spindles, casting a gorgeous rainbow kaleidoscope of colors around the room. The walls and floors are made up of a crème shade of marble, and lining three of the four walls are tables bursting with food. There are also waiters weaving through the crowd with silver platters holding either champagne or an array of finger foods, offering them to the guests.

This event is very formal; all the women are wearing gowns, and all the men are wearing fine suits or tuxedoes as they mingle with each other, talking and laughing. I'm surprised to see that several witches and warlocks are chatting with shifters, no animosity or anger coming from them—merely curiosity. It really does look like all the guests are keeping a firmly open mind about interspecies mingling, even though—as far as I know—this is the first time in history that sorcerers and shifters are sharing a space without trying to kill each other. I smile when I see Odelia and Reyna speaking with Lana and Korbin. Baby Galantia is absent, probably with a nanny for the night, and the interspecies couple looks very at home together, happy beyond words. Then I notice another addition speaking with them, whose presence shocks me—*Samuel*, Lana's father.

Chapter Twenty-Eight

"Is that Samuel? Of Midlington?" I ask Camden, my tone sounding as startled as I feel.

"Ah, yes. I invited a few humans to this event, along with family members of humans who are here with their mates, to get the Alphas and top members of packs accustomed to the new laws that have been instated. The ones stating that humans who mate into shifter packs will henceforth have the right to maintain contact with their families, and Alphas of said packs are responsible for facilitating that contact."

I blink several times as tears sting the backs of my eyelids, feeling awed. Camden's taking this issue seriously, and I know that's due to my influence. He listened to me, heard me, and wants to work with me because he knows I'm right. This right here is profoundly meaningful; I know it will have a ripple effect. Many of the humans I see in the room look somewhat wary and unsure, but also pleasantly surprised. Samuel looks as happy as can be, especially when a maid walks over to him and hands him a sleeping baby Galantia, who he promptly takes into his arms and holds close, looking down at her with a soft smile and a touch of wonder in his eyes.

This tri-species banquet is a very powerful statement, especially since it's being hosted by two rulers; nobody will be able to ignore the new laws, and anyone who sees Samuel with his daughter and granddaughter will understand the value of keeping families together, the warmth that it can bring into lives.

"Thank you," I say to Camden, my voice faintly choked up.

Camden unwinds his arm from mine, only to slide it around my waist, resting his hand on my hip and giving it a squeeze. "I thought you might appreciate this. It was also the easiest way to hammer the message into my fellow Alpha's heads; if they don't adhere to the new laws after this, they can't claim ignorance—it'll be direct insubordination, which they all know I punish harshly."

Lana spots me from where she stands towards the center of the room, wearing a beautiful silver dress, and her eyes light up. She tugs on Korbin's arm and also motions to her father before walking right up to me and Camden. Once in front of us, she gives a light curtsey, the deference of the action making me slightly uncomfortable, while Korbin bows and Samuel also gives a slight bow.

"Your Majesties," Lana greets brightly. "Thank you for hosting such a beautiful event and thank you for inviting my father and daughter. I couldn't be happier to have them here."

I smile at her. "We're pleased to have you. Korbin, good to see you. Samuel, it's lovely to see you as well—I trust you've had the opportunity to get better acquainted with your granddaughter?"

Samuel nods, his eyes warming as he stares down at little Galantia. Then his gaze slides back to me. "When you offered to set up a meeting between me and my daughter, I didn't dare trust it would happen, but it did because you made sure of it. Then when I heard of the laws shifting to allow me and other humans contact with our family members who had been claimed by packs, I laughed in disbelief, assuming it would go nowhere. I'm very, *very* happy to have been proven wrong. I owe you an apology and my gratitude. You've returned the only family I have left to me. Thank you, my queen."

The way he says *my* queen rather than Your Majesty is a sign of acceptance from him to me, acceptance that I hope will be echoed by other humans because, despite my status as a witch, I'm still human. My power comes from this earth. I will always fight for them, to make life better and more just for them, and hearing the fact that it worked, seeing Samuel's gratitude fills me with joy. It serves as a reminder that I'm capable of making changes that have a positive impact, especially when I work with Camden.

"I'm just glad I was able to help," I tell him, blinking back the tears threatening to fall. "Thank you for coming. If you have any problems in the future, or Lana's Alpha makes contact difficult, please reach out and inform me. I'll ensure the problem is taken care of."

Lana's smile widens. "Oh, Bordat wouldn't dare interfere, especially after tonight. None of them will, or they know they'll be susceptible to your mate, the *king's* infamous wrath. Nobody wants to deal with that." Sliding a look at Camden, she adds on, "Respectfully, Your Majesty."

Camden shrugs, unoffended and unconcerned. "A healthy dose of fear keeps the masses in line. Please, enjoy your evening."

Korbin gives us another nod before ushering his mate and father-in-law away.

That's when Odelia approaches us along with Claire, Reyna, Bane, Rune, and Cedrick. Odelia and Rune stand at the front of the group, and Odelia offers Camden a gracious smile that doesn't appear to meet her eyes. She also doesn't curtsey, merely inclines her head, which is her subtle way of making it clear that she sees herself as Camden's equal, not his subordinate. Rune, on the other hand, doesn't even nod; he merely stares at Camden coolly, his eyes assessing.

"Quite a presentation you've put together, Camden," Odelia says mildly, glancing around the room. "I do commend your inclusion of so many witches *and* some humans. It seems we're all gelling together better than one might've expected."

"If only someone had come up with the simple idea of diplomacy sooner, we could've avoided much strife. Even aided each other in times past," Rune says.

"That's a nice way of putting *if only the wolves would have pulled their heads out of their royal asses and grown a pair sooner*," Reyna comments.

"Reyna," Odelia says calmly, her tone faintly admonishing. Reyna rolls her eyes but keeps quiet, while I fight to hold back a smile.

"I am grateful for your support in our time of need. The gesture will be returned in the future," Odelia tells Camden, folding her hands in front of her. Her eyes turn to me, and a warm smile graces her lips. "Thank you for encouraging your mate to do the right thing. It's been long overdue."

"It has," Camden agrees mildly, accepting responsibility for not making efforts to reach out and reconcile with the witches and warlocks sooner. "We should all be grateful that the gods paired me with a woman such as Sierra, or else we wouldn't be here now. I hope you enjoy the banquet."

"As long as your wolves stop eyeing my witches like pieces of meat to either burn or use, we won't have a problem," Reyna murmurs, her eyes sliding to the side. I follow her line of vision and find an unfamiliar wolf—one with silver-blue eyes, marking him as an Alpha—staring at her with a look of interest and intent. She glares at him, arching an eyebrow that dares him to fuck with her at his own peril.

"I think we'll peruse the spread of delicacies you've put out for us," Odelia says regally. "Sierra, we'll speak more tomorrow. Camden, enjoy your evening."

"Same to you," Camden replies, watching as they stroll off, heading towards one of the white satin-covered tables lining the walls. "I still don't think they like me very much," he says to me.

I shrug. "Sorcerers are insular; they're prone to disliking anyone who isn't their own. Don't take it personally."

Camden nods. "Well, let's get some mingling out of the way—then I have a nice dinner set up for us in my private chambers."

I raise an eyebrow at him. "We're not staying here to eat?"

Camden shakes his head. "No. You once told me you don't like large crowds; I won't make you stay here any longer than manners dictate. We'll stay for about an hour, speak with all the relevant people, then take our leave. I plan on feeding you dinner, then you can feed me dessert."

I try to ignore the explicit images and thoughts that his words send sailing through my mind, but it's damn near impossible. Impossible to ignore his raw sexual appeal, the way he calls to parts of me I didn't even know existed before him. Parts that crave him despite all the baggage between us. No, *especially* in spite of all the baggage, because I now understand we can overcome a great deal together. Camden's proven himself to be an excellent partner in many respects and much of the previously broken trust between us has been healed. Enough for me to be looking forward to what will come after our mingling tonight.

Camden and I begin walking around the room, getting segued multiple times by many different people—some of them Alphas, some commanders of armies here to represent their forces and Alphas—and I speak with each of them, passing on my gratitude and respect for their allegiance, trying to make it clear that I hold their troops in high regards and that I, along with the sorcerers, will do what it takes to protect as many as we can.

One hour quickly turns into two, as it seems everyone wants a chance to speak with me and Camden. I get quite tired of being stared at like a unique specimen that all in attendance are trying to figure out, but I maintain my diplomatic smile and try not to react to being treated like some sort of rare exhibit. In a way, I am a rare exhibit; an earthly witch mated to the king of shifters, making me their queen while I'm not even a member of their species.

Camden senses my irritation, whether through the bond or otherwise, I'm not sure, and offers me touches that convey both support and desire throughout the evening. When his arm isn't firmly around me, cupping my hip, it's at my lower back, nearly brushing my ass. He gives me light kisses on my cheek and leans unnecessarily close when telling me the names of relevant figures so I don't make a fool of myself, his warm breath gusting over my neck. All the contact may seem innocent to any onlookers, typical between mates, but it serves the purpose of riling me up. My nipples are pebbled into hard, sensitive peaks, as if my entire body is anticipating the attention that Camden will soon give it. Attention I crave more with every passing minute until I can barely stand it.

I feel him tense just after we've finished talking with a Beta who's bringing a troop of warriors ten thousand strong to our cause, right before a familiar woman stops in front of us: Aspen.

I remember her from the time I dueled with her, though I barely saw her after that—her duties towards Camden only went as far as accompanying him when he left Kinrith, from what I recall. I did see her briefly in Aesara a while back, where she glared at me, but I ignored her presence and cruel looks because my attention was firmly on the destruction of my home village.

"My King," she says to Camden, giving a deep curtsey that gives a clear view of her cleavage, which is practically spilling out of the plunging v-neck of her navy-blue dress that borders on outright scandalous. Then she tips a look at me and greets, "Sierra."

I feel my eyebrows lift. Every person I've spoken to tonight, barring the sorcerers, have referred to me by my title as queen, not my name, so Aspen calling me by my name feels like a deliberate provocation and a sign of disrespect. She was respectful towards me before and after our duel; I guess that's since dissipated.

As I look between her and Camden, I become aware of something else; when she looks at him, it's with greed and lust in her eyes, and when he looks at her, it's with faint irritation and distaste. Something about it makes me wonder if they might've shared a bed at one point or another; I know for a fact that Camden wasn't celibate while waiting for me. The thought of him sleeping with her irritates me in a way I never anticipated; it's like a force of sheer jealousy unfurls in my chest, making me want to take this bitch by the hair and bash her pretty, seamless face against the nearest surface.

I blink at her. "I'm sorry, who are you?" I ask as if I don't remember her, returning her disrespect with some of my own.

Aspen's upper lip curls. "One of the captains in your mate's army," she says, unnecessarily loudly, her tone threaded through with superiority. She says *your mate's* army instead of *the crown's* army or *your* army, the way everyone else has been speaking of the forces so far, which only pisses me off further, though I don't let that show. I remind myself that I'm here in my capacity as a ruler, and making a scene won't help my image, which I imagine took a bit of a hit when

I disappeared without a word. Nobody's brought it up, but I've seen curiosity in people's gazes.

Seems the best course of action here will be to kill her with kindness, even if she is wearing a fuck-me dress, red lipstick, and dark makeup, all of which accentuate her already pretty features to make them stunning.

"Ah, of course," I say with a small smile, as if I'm embarrassed for not remembering her. "You're Aspen—my apologies. Our duel wasn't too long ago, but a great deal has happened since then. You fought well—it's heartening to know there's such talent in our army."

Her eyes darken at my mention of our duel because she knows as well as I do that I beat her. She got a few considerable kicks in, gave me injuries that I might've never recovered from if my sister wasn't a healer, but ultimately she yielded. I recall the fact that time slowed during the duel to my advantage, and as Aspen casts Camden another sultry look, I think I finally get why Hecate did something so advantageous for me in that particular moment; my goddess must not like Aspen very much, considering Hecate herself played a part in pairing us together and Aspen seems to know my mate in an intimate sense.

"What are you doing here, Captain?" Camden asks her crisply, his eyes shuttered. "You weren't invited, and you are not welcome. I made it very clear when you barged into the war room this morning that you did not have free leave to wander the castle as you pleased and should remain focused on your duties."

I don't like the fact that they spoke this morning, but the way Camden characterizes that conversation—the fact that she barged in and he sent her away—placates me minutely. In all the time I've had my struggles with Camden, I never entertained the idea that one of those struggles might be a woman from his past since shifters revere matehood. They're social and sexual creatures by nature, so few of them make it to the time they find their mates without indulging in carnal pleasures, but those indulgences are always meaningless, and from what I've heard, all unmated shifters who take care of each other's needs have an unspoken agreement that their time together is purely physical, because each and every one of them has a mate out there, waiting for them.

"I came to pay my respects, of course," Aspen says innocently.

"Then pay your respect and do not waste our time with petty games. Curtsey to Sierra, acknowledge her as queen, and then you may leave. If you do not, I will assume you do not value your captainship as much as you've led me to believe. That would be a great shame, considering how hard you fought for it—to throw something so honorable away for a meaningless feud that only exists in your head."

Oh, I fucking *love* that, the way Camden stepped in to defend me and put Aspen in her place. He draws me closer to him as he speaks, his hand flexing on my hip possessively, and I place a palm flat on his chest, giving him a grateful smile that makes Aspen hiss under her breath.

At this point, her theatrics and aura of anger are drawing some attention from the room—Reyna's sizing Aspen up as if wondering how fun she might be to toy with, Odelia's lips are pursed with distaste, and several shifters gathered around throw Aspen looks of disgust for her antics, probably having heard her previous comments that drip with disrespect and feigned superiority.

Aspen notices this, casting a look around her, and seems surprised at the glares she's receiving, as if she expected support from the people around her. I'm not sure why, since many of them are here with mates—not all of whom are wolves—so they understand just how sacred the bond is, and naturally frown upon anyone who tries to disturb it.

Finally, she says, "You might act the part and hang off the king's arm, but that does not make you queen."

I shrug. "And you may act the part of a harlot, trying to get the attention of a mated male, but that doesn't mean he is going to give you a second glance. Coming here to disrespect me doesn't make you look powerful or respectable, Aspen. In fact, it just makes you pathetic."

"Leave," Camden says through gritted teeth, his voice low and filled with authority—a tone that'll compel any and all who rank below him into submission. There's a stifling amount of dominance coming off him, aimed at Aspen—the sort of dominance that's impossible for a less-dominant wolf to ignore. I can feel the fury pouring off him in waves; anger that Aspen dared to challenge me here and now.

Aspen's head instinctually bows at Camden's tone as she stiffens before turning and walking towards the entrance, every move stiff and mechanical. I watch her go, feeling a mixture of irritation at the fact that she knows Camden in the sexual sense, turned on because Camden defended and protected me quite ferociously, and overall befuddled. Camden turns to me, using his free hand to cup my cheek.

"Are you alright?" he asks quietly.

I nod. "Do you know her...that way?"

Camden flicks a gaze around before pulling me closer. He murmurs into my ear, "Too many shifters with good hearing around; I promise I'll tell you everything once we're gone. Okay?"

I nod at him. I'm not going to punish him for Aspen being a bitch, but I think it would also be beneficial to find out if there's anyone else around who might try to interfere with my claim to him. Because even in the times when I couldn't get far enough away from him, Camden has always been mine. Just like I'll always be his.

Chapter Twenty-Nine

After speaking with Wyatt, Camden and I take our leave, heading to his personal chambers. I look around the familiar space, seeing that nothing has changed about it, save for a few new claw marks around the fireplace's mantle. On the table in the corner lies an inviting spread of dishes, presumably taken from the feast downstairs. Camden leads me by my hand over to the table, draws out my chair, and helps me into it before taking a seat beside me. He loads food onto my plate and pours me wine, and I watch him with a mixture of wariness and curiosity. Wariness, because I want to hear about what the hell Aspen's problem is, and curiosity, because I can sense Camden's contentment through our bond, which I attribute to him enjoying the simple act of taking care of me.

Once he's done with my plate, he puts food on his own.

"Are you going to tell me about you and Aspen?" I ask him as he's pouring himself a drink, unable to hold my tongue any longer. I was not pleased by the display earlier, just like I'm not pleased with his stalling.

Camden's eyes fall to my plate, and he says, "After we've eaten, I will, I promise. I don't like the idea of you going hungry—it unsettles both me and my wolf."

Understanding that this is a primal drive for him, which means he most likely won't budge, I eat the contents of my plate quickly, barely tasting the food, too lost in thought and nauseated by the way Aspen looked at Camden earlier—as if she was his to look at.

Once we're done, Camden leads me over to the couch, sits down, and pulls me onto his lap. I'm not sure I love this position but I can sense his need to be close to me and to touch me, so I don't fight or protest. Instead, I stare at him expectantly.

"I don't usually get involved with people who are part of my circle or army," he tells me. "Mixing business with pleasure is a good way to tempt fate to make life difficult. The one exception to that was Aspen, who was very persistent. A few years ago, I hit a low point while waiting for my mate—for you—and was less discerning than usual. We shared a bed a few times, though I made it abundantly clear that I was only acting for physical release and nothing more. She seemed on board with that, said she was also waiting for her mate and was simply seeking something with no strings attached. She stuck by her word even when I met you—congratulated me and swore fealty to both of us. When you left, though, it left many things in my kingdom uncertain. I was committed to getting you back, but Aspen seemed to see your abandonment as final and as an opportunity to seek more with me. She's approached me several times, disparaging you for leaving and trying to encourage me to abandon you. Each time I've sent her away, making it clear that you are the only woman for me, and that she was being disrespectful and ridiculous."

I like the fact that he sent her away, but I don't like Aspen's audacity in trying to come for a *mated man*. Even if I'd never come back, even with the previous state of our bond, Aspen should understand as any mythic does that once mated, there is no going back, especially not for shifters who revere matehood in an almost religious sense. More and more I'm seeing her as a conniving bitch and a potential threat.

"This morning, after I had my dream with Hecate and convened my council for preparations, Aspen again showed up. This time, it seemed her angle was different; I got the sense that she wants to sew discontent with my people and make them afraid of the idea of our alliance with sorcerers. Run a campaign against sorcerers, so to speak, create distrust and apprehension. I told her that if she did, she would face dire consequences, and she stormed off. I did not invite her to the banquet tonight, Sierra—she's not even high-ranking enough to have attended. I believe her goal was to throw you off, try to get you to snap in front of the masses, which could have made them doubt you. Your reaction, or lack thereof, tripped her up and made her look weak and ridiculous instead." He pauses as a small grin lifts his lips. "You played your role seamlessly tonight, and I have to admit that seeing you play with Aspen and belittle her was very attractive. If I hadn't been so worried as to your reaction and thoughts or the idea of you being upset, I would've been hard as a rock in front of everyone—I'm glad that didn't happen."

I shake my head, smiling faintly. "You wolves and your sexuality. Completely insufferable. I won't lie, I don't like that there's someone around you who knows what it's like to be with you—"

"Then I'll kick her out of the army or demote her so she no longer has any right to be near me," Camden cuts me off, saying that like it's the simplest thing in the world. "I could send her to another pack if that'd make you more comfortable."

I blink at him, realizing now more than ever just how much my comfort and security, both physical and emotional, is a priority for him. Aspen's obviously a competent warrior or she wouldn't be a captain, let alone a member of his personal traveling guard, yet he's willing to give up a good warrior simply at the idea that having her around could bring me some discomfort, which endears me to him. I wind my arms around his neck, nestling closer to him, breathing in his heady masculine scent.

"Thank you," I tell him, "but that's not necessary. There's no need to deprive your army. If Aspen tries to come at me again, I'll delight in reminding her exactly why that's a bad idea. Ideally in a way that makes her look like an idiot in front of many people, as she did tonight."

A smirk lifts Camden's lips before he skims them up the column of my neck, sending a shiver of pleasure and anticipation down my spine. "I like this side of you; the vindictive, clever side that prefers tact over force. It's deeply arousing."

I shake my head. "I'm your mate, Camden, I'm pretty sure anything I do is going to be deeply arousing to you."

He lifts his head, eyes clashing with mine, burning a brighter, icier blue that makes heat sweep through me. "Say that again," he demands, and I feel the unmistakable outline of his erection start to grow and harden against my stomach. It's the first time he's heard me call him my mate since leaving and it obviously has a deeper effect on him than anticipated.

I blink at him coyly. "Anything I do is going to be deeply arousing to you."

A low growl comes out of him. "Not that, the other part. Tell me you're my mate again, Sierra, tell me I'm yours and that you're mine."

I raise my hands to plunge my fingers into his soft, silky hair, enjoying the texture of it as it sifts through my fingers. "You're my mate, Camden. Mine. And I'm yours."

"Damn fucking right I am," he says, his voice a husky rumble that raises goosebumps on my arms. "Don't you ever forget that, and don't you *ever* leave me again."

I lean my forehead against his. "It killed me to leave you, but I was afraid. Besides, I think the distance helped us grow, even though it was painful. I needed to trust you again, needed you to prove your loyalty, and you did. Brilliantly. I'm back to stay, Cam, unless you do something to drive me away."

"I won't," he vows. "Never again. I'd kill myself before hurting you again. Now open those pretty lips, I want to taste what's mine."

Smiling, I shift my head sideways and close my lips over his. He fists a hand in my hair, at the base of my skull, and uses it to shift my position to his liking. My lips part on a gasp at the prickle of pain with his gesture, and he uses the opportunity to sweep his tongue into my mouth, groaning against my lips. His hold around me becomes steel-like, almost bruising, and I revel in that as much as I revel in the way he's ravishing my mouth. There's no tact to our kiss; it's feral, demonstrating his need for me, which matches my need for him. I moan when he nips at my bottom lip, clutching him tighter, and that soft noise seems to set him off entirely.

His hands travel to the zipper at the top of my dress, pawing at it, before impatiently gripping the silk between two hands and tearing it apart. As the loud noise of the seam splitting echoes through the room, I pull my mouth from his and frown at him. "I loved this dress."

"I'll have another made for you," Camden growls, eyes blazing. "It was in my way."

He pushes the straps off my arms, leaving my top half entirely bare and as his burning gaze falls on my breasts, I can feel his erection harden even more against my stomach. He places his hands on my bare back and lowers his head to one of my nipples, suckling on it hard enough to elicit another, louder moan from me. Though we were only together fully just once during my time in Kinrith, he learned the things I like most, and as he licks and sucks and nibbles I realize that he hasn't forgotten a single thing. His mouth is hot and deliciously wet, and every scrape of teeth and lave of his tongue creates an answering tug in my core.

"You're wearing too many clothes," I moan, desperate to feel his bare skin on mine. "That's a problem for me. Fix it."

He pulls back long enough to shuck his jacket and rip his shirt, sending buttons flying in every direction, and then he's back on me. Our lips collide in a frenzy of passion as his hands rise to caress and mold my breasts, pinching and twisting my nipples exactly the way that drives me insane. In no time at all, I'm grinding on his erection, cursing the material of my dress and his pants for separating us. He seems to share the sentiment because he abruptly stands, holding me tightly, and one more tug on the skirt of my dress along with a rip precedes the rest of the fabric falling off me, leaving me in only panties made of lace. My legs wrap around Camden's waist as he walks us through the living room of his chambers, down a hallway, and into his bedroom. He drops me on the bed, claws off his pants and boxers, and then climbs on top of me, his bare cock nudging against my abdomen insistently.

As he drinks deeply from my mouth again, one hand braced beside my shoulder, the other lowers and his fingers slide along the aching flesh between my legs, pulling a whine from me. I need him inside me, but he seems to be in the mood to take his time.

He stares down at me with pure reverence in his eyes, seeming awed at the sight of me here, probably because we both assumed not too long ago that I'd never return to this place and never accept him again.

"You're so goddamn beautiful," he says, shifting back to stare down at me with affection and hunger warring in his gaze. "So perfect. My Queen. *Mine*." As he speaks, he continues sliding his fingers through my slit below, winding me tighter and making my toes curl. Unlike the last time we were in this position, I'm not under the influence of a blood moon—it's purely him that's arousing me, making me desperate to feel him inside me as well as all around me.

"I've missed your body, your taste," he tells me, brushing his lips against mine. "I think I'm going to taste this pussy now. *My* pussy, really, considering only I'll ever be able to have it."

I feel a slight frown furrow my brows. "It's my pussy, not yours."

Camden rumbles out a low, amused chuckle. "It might be attached to your body, Sierra, but every inch of it belongs to me. Just like every inch belongs to you."

I curl my hand around his rock-hard cock, drawing a hiss out of him. "That means this is my cock."

"It is," he agrees. "Always has been." He spears two fingers inside of me, making my back arch with a groan. I release him, my hands curling into fists and rising to scratch at his back, which draws a noise of satisfaction from Camden as he gives me a rather wolfish grin. He adds a third finger inside of me, seeming to revel in my gasp and the way my eyes flutter shut as pleasure winds me higher and brings his thumb up to slowly rub my clit. Enough to drive me half out of my mind, but not enough to get me off—the pressure is too gentle, his rhythm too slow, and his fingers inside me are mostly still.

"Camden," I grate out, wriggling my body, trying to get him to *move*.

"Yes?" he purrs, pressing down on my clit a little harder.

"*Get moving*," I growl.

He grins. "Anything my queen wants, but first, I need you to tell me this pussy belongs to me—that every inch of you belongs to me. That *you* belong to me."

It registers through the haze of lust fogging my mind that Camden needs this confirmation from me, needs to hear the words from me to settle the uncertainty in him. I don't want to deny him that, but I also don't like the fact that he's not getting me off when I am *so* godsdamned close already. "Get to work making me come and I'll scream it," I say, my voice breathless.

Camden doesn't respond verbally—instead, he moves so quickly it's a blur. Before I can inhale my next breath, he's settled between my thighs, with my legs hooked over his shoulders and his hot breath on my pussy. His fingers are still inside me, still far too fucking still, and the look he gives me is filled with so much lust, anticipation, and reverence, it makes the knot of tension at my core wind even tighter.

I whimper when he pulls his fingers out of me, ready to threaten him with bodily harm if that's what it takes for him to get going, but apparently, that's not necessary. He spears his tongue inside me, fucking me with it, before using it to lap up my wetness and travel higher on my slit, swirling over my clit, making my toes curl. He spends the next several minutes, or what could be hours, building me towards an orgasm slowly and leisurely, though everything about him is tense and his noises are ones filled with pleasure, as if he's enjoying this as much as I am. I wind my fingers into his hair, my moans and groans growing louder, my eyes closed and head thrown back as he finds and exploits every sensitive spot I have. His fingers thrust back inside me, this time *four* of them, stretching my channel to the point where it almost hurts. I know he's preparing me to take his cock inside me, which is thicker and longer and will definitely be a stretch, though it's one I look forward to.

"Tell me you're mine," he murmurs against my aching flesh, laving his tongue over my clit again.

"I'm yours," I say hoarsely, ready to do whatever he wants if it means I get to come.

"Yes, you are," he agrees, his voice a low-pitched growl. "Now show me those pretty eyes and scream my name as you come."

I force my eyes open, not having realized they closed at some point during his sensual torment, in time for him to fix his lips around my clit and suckle gently. My back bows as pleasure so intense it's almost *too* intense whips through my entire body, and the knot of tension within me simply detonates. I do cry his name as my body quivers and my channel convulses around his fingers. With a growl of pure pleasure, he thrusts and suckles harder, drawing another, louder cry from me. I writhe on the bed as I ride my orgasm and he wrings every drop of pleasure from me until my body falls back on the bed, exhausted and well sated.

Still, it's not enough; I know the only thing that will satisfy me is feeling him inside me. I tug at his hair, drawing him up my body and he comes willingly, sealing his lips over mine and thrusting his tongue into my mouth, letting me taste myself on him. I hook my legs around his waist, making his cock grind against my hypersensitive flesh and drawing a noise I didn't think I was capable of making from me. I gasp as suddenly he flips me around, leaving me face down on the bed, before dragging me to my knees with a grip on my hips. I prop up on my elbows to avoid suffocation and glance over my shoulder at him, growing a touch afraid at the feral need in his eyes. He drags his nails, which have sharpened into claws, over my ass, not hard enough to break the skin but hard enough to sting a little, and the pain adds a rapturous edge to the pleasure. I wriggle my ass as an enticement, needing to feel his cock already, which makes him hiss. Turning my eyes to the intricately engraved headboard, I shimmy my ass again, and then my mouth opens on a silent scream as he abruptly plunges his full thick length inside of me, forcing his way into my swollen channel and making me squeeze my eyes shut as I struggle to accommodate his girth. It stretches and stings a little, but I'm too far gone with pleasure to notice, and the feeling of him buried in me almost feels like coming home.

"Sheer. Fucking. Heaven," he growls, withdrawing his length part of the way only to slam back into me with such strength the headboard bangs against the stone wall and stars burst in my vision. He sets a pace so quick that the friction almost burns as he thrusts in and out of me, gripping my hips so tightly I know I'll have bruises in the morning. I claw at the bedsheets and moan and yelp, so swept up in sensation I'm half out of my mind. Just when I'm on the verge of another orgasm, he withdraws, making me whine with disappointment, then flips me over again, leaving me on my back, hikes one of my legs up high around his waist, and thrusts back into me all while staring into my eyes.

"Never leave me again," he growls. "I can take abandonment from anyone else, but not you." Each word is punctuated by a hard thrust, and my eyes flutter shut from the sheer, overwhelming force. It's not just the physical sensation that's too much; it's also the emotional. I can feel the bond shifting and rearranging itself in my chest, strengthening the longer our bodies are connected until I can feel his pleasure almost as if it's my own—until I can feel *him* intimately, like we're entwined at a fundamental level.

"I won't," I cry out, tossing my head from side to side and scratching my nails down his back so hard I feel blood well up under my fingers, which just makes him growl with satisfaction and fuck me harder.

"No, you fucking won't," Camden says, his voice gravelly and immovable. "Never. We were always meant to be; it was always us, Sierra. You complete me."

"And you complete me," I moan, my voice somewhat hoarse from all the loud noises that have been escaping me. I force my eyes open, seeing both desperation and uncertainty in Camden's gaze, a completely unguarded look that I've only ever seen the last time we had sex. That time was different; he was taking advantage of my need that was stoked in the light of the blood moon and used it to claim and mark me. I wasn't prepared for it, and that led to a series of events that broke us. Now, we're back together, and our union is much steadier and more stable. I can see that he's not sure of that though, along with the very deep-seated fear that he'll lose me again. I clutch his neck, bringing his head towards me, and turn my head to the side, revealing the faded, barely visible scar of the mark he gave me last time we were in this position. I didn't want it then; I definitely want it now, to be connected to him. I didn't realize the uncertainty my mark fading and bond going dormant caused both of us, but I think we both need what I'm about to offer.

"Mark me again," I breathe out. When Camden hesitates. I dig my fingers into the nape of his neck and cry, "Do it!"

That's all the invitation he needs. He sinks his elongated canines into my skin, and the sharp stab of pain quickly morphs into soul-wrenching pleasure. I orgasm with full-body convulsions and a scream that echoes around the chambers; Camden's thrusts stutter before he goes still, withdrawing his teeth from my neck and letting out a low noise of pain.

Realizing that he's holding back from coming while I'm still in the throes, I understand he doesn't want a repeat of last time—impregnating me without my knowledge. "Come," I tell him. "I'll take a draft that keeps us safe tomorrow; fucking *come*, Camden."

With a few more harsh thrusts, he does, spilling himself inside me with a groan that sounds like a mixture of pain and pleasure. Then he falls on top of me, both of us sweaty and breathing hard. I gently push him to his back, then roll on top of him as I catch my breath, fitting our bodies together. My cheek rests against his heart, which I hear hammering away beneath my ear, my chest is pressed against his torso, and our legs are tangled together. I let out a long, deep sigh of contentment, feeling the call of sleep pull at me and letting my eyes flutter closed.

That clears right up when Camden grips my waist and shifts me so that my legs are on either side of him, and I feel his cock stiffening against me again, which makes my eyes snap open as I stare down at him with surprise.

"We're not done," he tells me, his voice final and immovable. "I've waited far too fucking long to feel you again; one time isn't going to cut it, Sierra. I'm going to fuck you until we're both too exhausted to move, probably until the first rays of dawn break on the sky."

Then he makes good on his promise.

Chapter Thirty

I awaken the next morning to an empty bedroom, which immediately makes me frown and sit up. Then I hiss; my entire body is sore, especially the place between my legs, and the countless aches and pains serve as an excellent reminder that Camden lived up to his word last night. Bright light filters through the windows, casting a mid-morning glow over the room. By the time he was finally satisfied last night, I'd come so many times I lost count, and the first rays of dawn were indeed brightening the sky with a dim blue and pink. The clock ticking away at the edge of the room shows that it's nearly noon, which means I got a few good hours of sleep in. My mood is bright, and I realize that's because of the strength of the bond in my chest—it feels steady and whole in a way it never did before, which only makes Camden's absence more poignant and painful.

Waking up to him gone feels vaguely like...abandonment, though I'm not sure why and I know the sentiment is ridiculous. I suppose that, after the night we shared, I expected Camden to cling to me, not to just simply leave before I awoke. Trying to hide my sullenness, I search through Camden's wardrobe until I find a shirt to put on, since he destroyed my dress last night, then tentatively head out of the bedroom. Walking through the hallway leading out to the living room of his chambers, I smile faintly when I see several of my old paintings hanging on the walls. When I first found out Camden had taken them from my home in Aesara without my permission, I was nothing short of outraged, feeling that he didn't deserve him.

Now, with Aesara burned to ashes along with all the people I knew growing up, I'm grateful that Camden brought the paintings here. If they'd remained in the house where Mari and Parker were gruesomely murdered, then set up in a display, I couldn't have ever looked at them again.

I emerge into the living room, feeling yet another pang when I see that Camden is nowhere to be found. Pathetically, I can't stop myself from wondering if I somehow displeased him last night. I thought the sex was amazing, and that asking him to mark me again was the right way to go, but I guess it couldn't have been truly extraordinary if he had more important things to tend to first thing in the morning.

I silently admonish myself for my clinginess and decide to carry on with business as I should. It's late enough in the morning that Leisel should already be awake—no doubt she'll have continued with her habit of waking Wesley up to hang out with her. I should be there for both of them. Resolved to pretend my chest isn't aching, I turn to head back to Camden's room and find a pair of pants to borrow, only to pause when the door to his chambers opens and Cam comes striding inside, a cup of coffee in his hand which he's stirring with a spoon.

He pauses at seeing me in the middle of the room, and his eyes darken with lust when they travel over his borrowed shirt, then descend further to my bare legs.

"Where were you?" I ask pathetically. "I woke up alone."

Camden blinks then frowns as he approaches me. "I wanted to be waiting for you with coffee and breakfast when you woke up. I didn't expect you to be up so early." He hands me the mug. "When I saw that the servants were lagging today, I checked down with the kitchen—apparently Odelia's invited herself along with several choice members of her coven to the castle for an early lunch and discussions, so the cooks were running a bit behind readying everything. Someone will come around with food in a couple of minutes, but I figured I'd at least get you your fix of caffeine. I recall you once mentioning you turn into a monster without your morning coffee."

Just like that, the bond within me settles, as do I. I let out a sigh that leeches much of the tension from my body and lean into Camden, accepting the mug. My eyebrows raise when I take a sip and realize he made it exactly how I like it, with milk and honey, and I give him a nod of gratitude. "Thank you. I was worried that last night wasn't to your liking, so you had taken off."

Camden lets out a puff of astonished laughter. "*Not to my liking?* Sierra, it was fucking amazing. My wolf's calm for the first time since you left, and I'm elated to see my mark on your neck and feel the vibrancy of our bond." He leans down, resting his forehead against my own. "It makes it all the more difficult for you to leave me."

I feel a reluctant smile pull on my lips. "You're going to be dreadfully possessive now, aren't you?"

"I always have been, now I just don't need to hide it," he responds, rubbing his nose against mine before stepping back. He reaches into his pocket, procuring a glass bottle with a cork containing a strange-looking green slush. "The witches must have anticipated our reunion, because Odelia gave this to one of the castle servants and instructed them to leave it outside my door. There was a note attached about it being a draft you'll want in the morning."

I feel my lips twitch. The Nightshade witches are a nosy bunch, always butting into each other's business, but they're also supportive and very caring of their own. I remember mentioning to Odelia in passing that I'd need some form of birth control to stop myself from getting pregnant again before I was ready to; apparently, she got right on it.

I take the bottle from him, walk it along with my coffee over to the table, and set them both down. As I'm examining the draft Odelia sent, a knock sounds on the door; Camden growls out, "Set the breakfast tray on the ground and *go*."

When he casts another look at my bare legs, I realize why he's being so growly; he doesn't want anyone else to see me in any state of undress. *Typical territorial wolf.* After waiting a few moments, Camden cautiously opens the door, glancing up and down the hall before picking up a wooden tray from the ground and kicking the door closed behind him. Scents of fruit, ham, and freshly baked bread fill the room, a mouthwatering aroma. As Camden sets the tray on the table, I uncork the vial and sniff the contents, then have to suppress a gag. It smells like swamp water and I'm sure it won't taste any more pleasant.

Shaking my head, I hold my breath and down the contents of the vial in three gulps, grimacing when I confirm that it tastes as unpleasant as it smells. I wash it down with coffee, shaking my head.

Camden watches me with his brows drawn, looking contemplative and not altogether happy. "Do you want children of your own?"

I blink at him. I've always figured I'd eventually be a mother, though I was so swept up in raising Leisel as a daughter that I never got around to thinking of the mechanics or preparing for that eventuality.

"Of course I do. I love children—they're delightful." When I see tension leech out from Camden's posture and expression, I gently remind him, "I wanted to keep our baby even though I wasn't prepared for it and you weren't exactly honest with me about the possibility of pregnancy. I'd sworn to protect it just before the rogue attack."

Shame shadows Camden's features, and he glances away for a moment. A lump of sorrow wedges itself in my chest, and it takes me a moment to realize the emotion's not just emanating from me, but from both of us. Camden lost a child as much as I did that day, and the loss sent him spiraling into a rage. I don't think that memory will ever not be painful to look back on, but it no longer infuriates me as it once did. I reach across the table, taking his hand and giving it a squeeze.

"We'll have a family together, eventually. I'm sure of that. Just not now—I'm still young, and now that you've marked me again and our bond is strong, I'm quite sure my aging will slow to a crawl. We have time."

Camden's eyes meet mine, brightening a bit at my words. He squeezes back, turning our hands over so his covers mine. "Yes, we have plenty of time. Besides, with the danger looming, right now isn't a choice time for a royal pregnancy, no matter how much I want to see your belly swell with the life I've put in it."

His words have the surprising dual effect of both endearing me and arousing me, as if the thought of him getting me pregnant is a turn-on. I shelf that thought for later consideration.

"Come on, we should eat. We have a busy day ahead of us, and I'll need to go check on Leisel and Wes soon."

Once Camden has filled a plate with food for himself, we both eat in comfortable silence. I drink two cups of coffee, feeling refreshed and more awake by the time I'm done, and quietly marveling at the new strength of our bond and just how much stronger and more powerful it makes *me* feel.

My thoughts stray to my sister and Wesley, both of whom are firmly a part of my self-made family, and I eye Camden, wondering if he can accept both of their presences easily. Yesterday he had no problem with them staying in the same wing as me in the castle, but that could be more of a courtesy than a genuine welcome.

"In terms of my sister and Wesley..." I trail off, taking a sip of water and trying to gather my thoughts as Camden looks up from his buttered bread with raised eyebrows. "They're part of my family, which makes them members of yours through our mating. I don't know what your general thoughts on children are, let alone accepting kids that aren't related to you by blood—"

"Sierra," Camden cuts me off calmly. "I've seen firsthand that you're more of a mother than sister to Leisel. I adore that about you. I can also see that Wesley means a great deal to you, and that you take him being your ward very seriously. I fully accept both of them; I'm happy to have them here. I think they'll bring warmth to the castle that's been absent since...well, since my mother passed away. I wouldn't profess to be a father to them, especially not to Leisel, simply because she'll eventually be mating with my brother, but I'd like to be a figure they can trust and rely on, like you are. I'll be there for them as much as they need or want me."

His words warm me from the inside out. I toss my fork into the bowl, stand, and then plop down onto Camden's lap, which seems to *delight* him. He sets down his bread and his arms come around my waist, and pleasure pulses through our bond as he nuzzles my hair. When he begins stroking his fingers through it, I let out a faint hum of enjoyment.

"You know that having kids here will shift the castle dynamics, right? I mean, if their behavior in the coven was anything to go by, then they'll be running around the halls screaming at the tops of their lungs and playing tag and hide and seek—"

"LEISEL, WHERE ARE YOU?" Wesley's voice echoes through the castle from what sounds like a few halls away, cutting me off. A moment later, the door to Camden's room quietly creaks open as Leisel scurries inside, then closes behind her. My sister is panting, red-faced, and out of breath, with a wide smile on her face.

When she sees that she's in Camden's room, she blinks, and then her cheeks turn red as she grows abashed. "Um...I may have played a trick on Wes, and he's kind of upset, though it was *really* funny, so I was running for a place to hide. I'm sorry, I didn't realize I was in the king's part of the castle—"

"It's not a bother," Camden says, sounding genuinely amused and not at all upset. "You're welcome to hide in here whenever you need. I can't promise that you won't earn a scolding from Greta, but I don't mind."

Leisel beams at that, eyes brightening, then tenses when angry-sounding footsteps pound down this hallway. I stand from my seat and offer her a hand, saying, "I'm going to borrow a pair of pants from Camden before heading back to our rooms. There's also something I'd like the show you." As Leisel takes my hand, I glance at Camden over my shoulder. "Do you still have the key to the art studio?" Leisel immediately perks up at those last two words and turns a gaze gleaming with excitement toward Cam.

"It's unlocked, the key's on the table inside," Camden says. "I'll tell Wes I heard you run in a different direction for now. Sierra, the meeting with witches is in the war room in two hours; there'll be lunch served afterward."

Chapter Thirty-One

After getting Leisel and Wesley to reconcile and returning to my room to dress for the day, I spend the next hours with them, both of whom decide to join me in the painter's studio in Camden's chambers. Leisel's watched me draw and paint countless times, but Wesley never has, so I outline the basics of sketching for both of them, using a few pieces of loose paper still strewn on the small wooden table by the window, then watch as they both work on their own sketches, murmuring amongst each other. Camden returns from a meeting with Claude as the kids are both working on the dynamics of shading, and he leans in the doorway with his arms crossed, watching the two work side by side.

I quirk an eyebrow as I cross the room to him. "I suppose you're reconsidering the placement of this art studio, aren't you?"

He chuckles. "Not at all. They actually remind me a bit of me and Wyatt when we were younger—we'd be at each other's throats one minute, then getting along wonderfully and stirring up mischief the next. It's refreshing. They're welcome here whenever you three would like, except, of course, in the evenings." His voice lowers as his eyes drop to my lips. "When the moon's high, you're mine—I won't share you."

I smile, pleasantly surprised at his willingness to accommodate Wesley and Leisel, and not at all shocked at his possessiveness over me in the late hours. I wouldn't be surprised if we spend half our nights fumbling in his bed, lost in the throes of pleasure.

I glance over at Leisel and Wes. "Alright, you two, off to our wing of the castle. Greta's expecting you and tutors will be waiting. I've got some business to take care of."

Leisel leaps into my arms for a hug, smiling when I smack kisses over her cheeks, and Wes grumbles when I ruffle his hair. He also pauses for a long moment to look at Camden, after Leisel's skipped out of the room.

"A lot of the sorcerers think you're a monster," he says slowly, "but you seem alright. If you hurt Sierra, though, we're gonna have a problem—I don't give a shit if you're king."

My eyebrows raise as I blink at Wes, surprised by his protectiveness of me. It feels like *I'm* supposed to be the one protective of *him*, but he seems equally invested in my wellbeing—enough so to stare down the Alpha of Alpha's without flinching or looking away.

I look to Camden, somewhat afraid that Wes's direct challenge will cause the Alpha wolf in him to feel the need for a show of power and dominance over the young boy who has the gall to threaten him. If Cam lashes out, I'll be honor-bound to protect Wesley, and the thought of that gives me absolutely no pleasure. For the first time in our relationship, we're on solid footing; I don't want anything to jeopardize that.

"I have no intention of hurting Sierra," Camden says in all serious-ness. "If I do, you have permission to take whatever retribution you deem fit for such an offense. Sound fair?"

My lips part at the exchange, and Wesley is equally surprised, eyes widening. I think he expected there to be a conflict and was prepared to fight in the name of my honor; now, Camden's giving him free rein to retaliate. Something strange happens in my chest—something that I fear might be even more permanent than the bond connecting us, a feeling I've never quite felt for Camden before. Full of affection, reverence, respect, and a burning need to keep him.

Wesley's quick to recover, puffing out his chest and giving Camden a nod. "We have a deal." He tips his head at me before walking out of the room. I wait until I hear the door to Cam's chambers slam shut before turning to my mate, not even trying to hide my surprise.

He tilts his head to the side. "What, you thought I'd retaliate against a child who's protective over you?" He lets out a laugh, shaking his head as his hands slide around my waist. "The more people you have invested in your wellbeing, the safer you are, so I won't begrudge them. Besides, Wesley seems like a good kid and your sister loves him, so I'll afford him some leeway."

"I didn't expect you to be so domesticated," I tell him, winding my arms around his neck and pressing close.

"Oh, love, I'm not domesticated, as you damn well know." He lifts me up in his arms, hooking my legs around his waist, and I let out a squeal.

"We have a meeting to get to—"

"They can wait. I didn't get a taste of you this morning, which has left me hungry," he growls as he carries me back into the bedroom. I trail my lips along his neck, then do the same with my teeth, my toes curling when I feel his erection press right up against my core.

"Strip," Camden tells me in a no-nonsense tone that brooks no argument. I'm not in a particularly defiant mood, especially since I know his touch brings incredible pleasure. I slip out of my dark brown pants and the accompanying crème blouse while Camden wanders into his closet, returning a moment later holding something very sparkly, shiny, and attention-grabbing in his hands.

I discovered my first day in this castle that I share an acquisitiveness with witches born of other realms—anything glittery and pretty will grab my attention and never fails to make my heart speed up. Camden holds up a necklace to me that practically drips with jewels, and my eyes widen as I stare at it, pausing in unfastening my bra.

"I meant to give you this last night, but we were running late and the dress you were wearing briefly cleared my mind of all thoughts," Camden says, kneeling on the bed and leaning over me to clasp the beautiful piece made of blue and white jewels set in a delicate chain around my neck.

"Cam, it's gorgeous," I breathe, running my hands over the cool stones. The necklace is tight, clinging to my neck, with a few loose jewels that fall lower at the center, tickling the space between my breasts.

"Only the best for you," he says, leaning back to examine it, a slow smile spreading on his lips. "When I had it made, I resolved to see you wearing nothing but this necklace—we're going to make that a reality before we get to the meeting."

After delivering two earth-shattering orgasms, Camden helps me pull my clothes back on with an expression of pure smug masculine pride, then escorts me to the war room of the castle, where a group of people are already gathered, seated at the table. Reyna, Bane, Odelia, Rune, Claire, and Wyatt all have seats around the table. The setup vaguely reminds me of the last time I was in a room in this castle with Claire, Odelia, and Reyna. At the time we were negotiating terms for a potential alliance between shifters and witches; we've come such a long way since then, it feels like that meeting was years ago rather than a mere few months.

"You two took your time," Reyna purrs sarcastically, giving me a knowing smile. Then, her eyes catch on my necklace and widen. "Holy mother of diamonds—" She cuts off as she gives Camden a narrow-eyed look. "You're not trying to buy our witch's affection, are you?"

"He knows better than that," I reply on Camden's behalf.

"It's merely a token of my affection," Camden adds, leading me by my hand over to the head of the table, helping me into my seat before taking his own. "Now, we have several orders of business to get through, but first I'd like to inquire as to whether your accommodations have been sufficient."

"More than," Rune says with a nod.

"Your hospitality is appreciated and will not be forgotten," Odelia adds.

"Excellent," Camden replies, inclining his head. "First order of business; I'd like to get started on the joint training that will begin later this afternoon, after our meeting. Reyna, you will be leading the training sessions along with Saunders, if you're still amenable." When Reyna nods, he goes on. "The purpose is to teach your kind and mine to work together; to create a cohesiveness that will be necessary in battle. We have enhanced strength and speed, you have magical powers of many varieties; the two can serve as amplifiers for each other, all the more so with practice."

For a little while, he discusses technicalities with the group, asking for the sorcerer's input, along with his brother's, an admirable amount of times. He makes it clear that he sees our alliance as a partnership and doesn't want to make decisions without getting Odelia and Rune's input. Then he goes on to discuss several other matters—Odelia also tosses a few topic points into the mix. By the time we're wrapping up, nearly two hours have passed.

Claude rushes into the room as we're all standing, readying to head to a sitting room for a casual lunch, looking out of breath. "The dark faye," he pants, wide-eyed. "There's a clan of them at our borders, outside the shield. They seek an audience with the leaders of the shifters and sorcerers."

After a moment of stunned silence, Camden bangs his fist on the map table with a curse, looking infuriated at the news Claude delivers. Reyna, Odelia, Rune, Claire, and Bane don't appear to be faring much better; they're equally angered by the fact that the dark faye have the audacity to show up outside the shield, demanding an audience.

Reyna cricks her neck to the side. "Well, it's been too long since I got to kill some darklings, so I guess them showing up here isn't all bad. I always say a few kills are a great warmup for training, anyways."

Claude grimaces. "I'm not sure they're here for nefarious reasons. When I spoke with their leader, Kazimir, he told me that he wasn't here for battle, he was here with the proposition of an alliance between his clan and us."

Reyna barks out a laugh. "He's fucking lying. Faye are sneaky like that; misrepresenting their intentions so that they can stab you in the back the first chance they get."

"I'm not so sure about that," says Claude, shaking his head. "I didn't sense deception from him, and he's only brought about twenty people with him; a small clan. I truly think he might be here to make peace, not instigate a war."

Wyatt lets out a thoughtful hum. "That wouldn't be the most preposterous thing in the world. After all, it's quite possible that not all the darklings are happy that they've been pledged to fight for vampires; the two species have been at odds with each other many times throughout mythic history, so a faye wouldn't naturally be happy to bleed for the sake of a vampire. It could be that some are, in fact, so against the idea that they'd be willing to come to us."

"Or it could be that they're using an alliance as a front to destroy us from the inside," Reyna snaps, to which several gathered people nod.

Camden lets out a sigh, deflating slightly. "Either of those scenarios is possible, though I'm inclined to assume they're here as enemies. It makes sense, however, that we should hear them out—if we don't like what they have to say or doubt their intentions, we can kill them. Simple as that."

"I do not like dark faye as a whole, given that they are responsible for the deaths of too many of my kind," Odelia starts, "But I also understand better than most that it is unfair to judge a whole species by the actions of some. Someone find Maddy—she has the ability to search through a being's thoughts and memories along with teleportation. If the faye allow her to search their minds and she finds that they aren't intending to double cross us...well, as much as I dislike the idea, they could be useful. Darklings are powerful, and if this group has been privy to the war efforts of our enemies they could have valuable information. We still haven't been able to get a concrete accounting of how many troops they have, especially since many have gone underground where we can't reach them."

She's right. I haven't had any personal dealings with the darklings outside of the battle on the outskirts of Midlington, but it's difficult to assume that all of them are bad. Most, perhaps, but not all. After all, I spent my life villainizing mythics—shifters especially—only to come to Kinrith and discover that they weren't all monsters. Some of them treated humans monstrously and almost all overlooked our existence and value, leaving us to the mercy of rogues and the many problems that arose out of lack of resources, but Camden has helped me change much of that.

"Let's talk to them," I say. Looking to Claude, I ask, "If you'll lead the way?"

"You should stay here, Sierra," Camden says. "I don't want you in danger."

His words are so preposterous they almost cause me to laugh out loud. After all, I'll be part of the upcoming battle because my ability to wield my fire is the only thing that can return the dead to their natural state, combating Rhaelar's power to reanimate them into a mindless army. The fact that Camden wants me to stay here isn't just galling though, it's also painful. We shared a meaningful night just last night, came together for the first time since I left, and now he's trying to cut me out. It hurts more than I expected and that pain quickly translates into anger. I glare at him, only to feel a flicker of fear travel through our bond, telling me that he's truly afraid of something happening to me, softening my ire ever so slightly. Reminding myself that snapping at him won't help, I instead reach out to take his hand. He clasps mine tightly, giving me a beseeching look.

"I appreciate your wish to protect me, but I am quite capable of defending myself and inflicting great deals of damage. If a fight breaks out, I'll be fine."

"I think we'll start heading to the dark Faye," Rune says with an eye roll, "You two can catch up when you're done sorting this out." With that, everyone files out of the room, led by Claude.

"There's no guarantee of that," Camden says irritably. "We don't know much about dark faye, other than the fact that their magical capabilities can rival even that of sorcerers. You need to be careful, Sierra. I wouldn't survive it if something bad happened to you."

The vulnerability in his latter words softens me further, and I give his hand a squeeze. "Soon enough we'll be fighting against legions of dark faye and vampires; if the ones here mean us harm, I'd consider that good practice. I really do understand that you want me safe, but I can't cater to that. Staying behind isn't who I am as a person, and my position as ruler wouldn't permit it. I've learned a great deal in my time with the coven, I can take care of myself. Or do you not trust that I'm capable of defending myself?"

"Of course I trust it. I know how powerful you are," Camden snaps. "I just wish you weren't in a position to have to use your power. I wish that we lived in a calmer, kinder world where we could stay in bed all day to cuddle and fuck."

I feel a smile pull at my lips. "Unfortunately, the world of mythics is not a calm or kind place—it has constant conflict, as I've come to learn. Fortunately, I was gifted with power that gives me the strength to handle that. Besides, we might not be able to stay in bed all day to engage in the listed activities, but nothing is preventing us from doing them all night."

Camden's eyes start to heat up, and he lets out a soft chuckle. "I'll hold you to that." With a long sigh, he stands, also pulling me to my feet. "Fine, let's see what those pricks have to say. Then I'm confining you to my chambers for the rest of the day and night, where I intend to have my wicked way with you."

My smile widens. I'm still tingling from my earlier orgasms, and I do not mind that Camden's appetite is insatiable when it comes to me. "Behave, and I just might let you."

We walk out of the room and then the castle at a brisk pace. In the courtyard, I spot the group of people that'll be going to greet the darklings, with Maddy among them. She gives me a bright smile as I approach, a smile that doesn't dim when her eyes flick over to Camden.

Once we're close enough, she says, "I offered to teleport everyone to the place where Claude said they're waiting, near the evacuated town a few miles away. I figure that'll save us some time. If the dark fuckers are here to harm, I want at least one kill reserved for me; anyone who tries to get in the way of that risks taking the darkling's place."

I laugh, giving Maddy a wide smile. "You're so bright and bubbly, it's often easy to forget that you're as bloodthirsty and battle-hungry as the rest of the Nightshade sorcerers."

She beams. "I like the way people underestimate me; it gives me a helpful edge. Now, everyone please join hands. I'll teleport us a little ways away from the faye, then once the newbies have recovered we can go to them."

Saunders, who was apparently called to join us, frowns, narrowing his eyes at her. I don't miss the spark of interest in those eyes as he stares at her, or the charge of sexual tension in the air.

"What do you mean, recovered?" he asks, stepping closer to her.

Maddy giggles. "Oh, you'll see. Come on, people, I don't have all day. I was mid-spar with a few sorcerers, and I *love* taking out several at once." She shakes her head with amusement. "They always think teaming up on me will make it possible to take me out, yet end up confused when they're the ones on the ground, gasping for breath. So weird."

Saunders' eyebrows raise, even as he follows instructions and we all join hands. "You...*you* can take out several sorcerers at once? You look like a strong gust of wind could blow you over."

Reyna bares her teeth in a bloodthirsty smile at him. "I thought you'd already learned the perils of underestimating a witch, soldier."

"I have, but she's tiny," Saunders says, sounding almost irritated with the latter words, like he doesn't like how small Maddy is for some unknown reason.

Maddy just rolls her eyes at him as she takes Odelia's hand on one side and Rune's on the other. "Size isn't everything, big guy. Alrighty, let's get out of here."

Chapter Thirty-Two

I brace for the familiar, unpleasant sensation of teleporting, just as my surroundings blur and my stomach drops. As usual, the process is over in a blink, leaving us in front of an old town with mostly wooden buildings, and I realize that I'm not nauseous at all this time, just a bit dizzy, which means I'm getting used to teleportation. The rest of the witches are also fine. The shifters, however, are a different story. Camden only stays upright because I grab his shoulder to steady him, still looking off-kilter. Saunders tumbles to the grassy ground and promptly vomits, making Maddy giggle again. Wyatt looks a little green, though he refrains from throwing up, and the rest of the wolves need several minutes to gather themselves.

Once they have and everyone is back on their feet, Claude leads us through the town's center and out the other side, where a group of twenty faye are waiting just outside the faintly shimmering barrier of the shield, speaking quietly amongst each other.

The power coming from the group hits me first; it's not like the magic I've become accustomed to feeling while living with the coven. There's something darker about it. Not necessarily in a sinister way, not like the black magic I felt from Rhaelar and Ernesh; it's actually more reminiscent of the power my fire gives off. Volatile and destructive if misused or not properly wielded.

As soon as the clan hears our approaching footsteps, a male steps to the front of the group. He has skin so pale it almost looks dead, though it has a faint glow that leaves no doubt he's alive. With pitch-black hair, a strong frame, and midnight-blue eyes, he cuts quite an imposing figure, standing at a similar height to Camden. The power crackling from him is also the strongest in the group, which makes me think that this must be Kazimir.

He measures us with sharp eyes, before a slow, not altogether welcoming smile spreads on his full lips. I notice that his eyes linger on Claire for a few beats longer than the rest of us—possibly because he senses the heat from her magic, which is the first thing I noticed about her myself.

Camden and I naturally flock to the front of our group, and we stop when there is just under ten feet of space separating us from the darklings.

"Your Majesties," the frontman greets, inclining his head with respect. "I am—"

"Kazimir, I presume," Camden interrupts him. "I understand you're seeking an audience with us and a potential alliance."

"You understand correctly," Kazimir says, before turning his eyes to me. "You're the one who has the black flame—I can feel its power emanating from you. Many had thought the tales of you were lies, even when the vampire king, Rhaelar, confirmed them. I must say, you embarrassed him in a rather spectacular fashion, as did the one who decided to turn the mountains surrounding your home into volcanoes." Again, his eyes flit to Claire, who's standing beside Reyna. "That would be you."

Claire yawns. "If we're done stating the obvious, there's some business to get to."

"Indeed there is," I agree. "Our witch doctor told us you seek an alliance. My first question is why on earth would you want such a thing when you have a powerful army being built between your kind, the vampires, and the darkling hybrids that have been bred between you—a force that intends to rule this world should they succeed."

Kazimir's features harden. "If the aforementioned army succeeds, this world will be rendered uninhabitable, just as the last one was. Necromancy rots everything with its perverted power; everything from the corpses it reanimates to the ground beneath our feet. If it spreads too far, it will be the end of this world. I was alive when the last necromancer tore apart Mythicacia and we were forced to search for a new home; I do not believe we will be so fortunate as to find a better, more abundant world yet again."

"Is that the only reason you want to switch sides?" I ask, wondering if there's something more to his presence here and wanting to test Kazimir's mettle. "Because necromancy threatens this world? While that's true and it is a great concern, my concern is that your kind have a propensity for hunting down and killing off *my* kind. Sorcerers have suffered from your attacks for generations—"

"I have never, in my many centuries of life, permitted the persecution of fellow magical beings. Sorcerers and faye are alike in some respects; primarily that magic chose *us* as its vessels. To hunt each other is an insult to the fabric of magic itself, which I do not indulge in. In fact, I have punished members of my clan who thought to make sport out of harming fellow creatures of magic. Do not judge me on the mistakes of my kin, Your Majesty, for I am not them."

"You profess to be oh-so different?" Odelia questions, steel in her voice.

"I do," Kazimir says with a nod. "I have no interest in harming you. As I've said, that would be an insult to magic, and I do not insult my maker in such ways. We may pray to different gods and have different creators, but we are similar in many ways. Hecate is a dark goddess, as is ours, Nyx. I do not believe the two would condone us being at each other's throats. Sorcerers and shifters recently made peace with each other for the first time in history to band together and overcome a greater evil; I only wish to do the same."

"Two entire species banded together. It may have started with a single coven and a pack, but the members who signed and sealed the alliance were spokespeople for their species as a whole," I point out sharply. "The situation is different with you, as you do not speak for all darklings across the globe, you only speak for yourselves. If we were even to entertain the possibility of such an alliance, you do understand that you'd be obligated to go to war with your own kind, do you not?"

"They are not my kind anymore," Kazimir says, his tone resolute. "I am from a noble lineage, although the other nobles expelled dark faye from their ranks once the dark ones rose up and abandoned our species as a whole. I was sucked into this war through no will or intent of my own, and I do not want to go through with it. Not only do I not believe in the cause, I do not find the actions of other darklings any more acceptable than you do. Recent circumstances are what have landed me and the trusted members of my clan at your gates, but thoughts of such an alliance are not new to me. Several decades ago there was a vote amongst nobles on whether or not we should reach out to sorcerers—unfortunately, just before the day the heads of noble families voted, another darkling clan went after the Nightshade Coven in protest, causing much harm. Most nobles didn't think it was the right time to try to reconcile, but I was one of the few who maintained advocacy for building a bridge between our people."

That's interesting. Kazimir's voice rings with conviction and sincerity, though I'm conscious of the fact that someone who's walked the world as long as he has—centuries, if he is to be believed—has likely learned how to deceive quite well. Still, if he speaks the truth, I can't *not* consider his proposal; it would be detrimental to me and mine.

"If what you say is true, you wouldn't mind allowing one of my witches to search through your mind and confirm it," Odelia says crisply.

Kazimir appears hesitant at that, which could be an indicator of guilt *or* could stem from the fact that nobody would enjoy having their minds rummaged through. I certainly wouldn't freely submit myself to it unless I had a very compelling reason. The fact that he's here with offers of alliance and tales of valor should give him enough reason.

"Very well," Kazimir says. "I would ask that the searcher takes care not to wander too deep in my thoughts and memories—I've lived a long time, it would be easy to get lost in them."

"That, and you likely have many faye secrets hidden away in your head," Claire comments, once again drawing Kazimir's attention to her. And, once again, I notice he watches her a little too intently, as if he's seeing some new thing that he wants to explore and uncover. Claire merely arches an imperious brow at his steady gaze, which is intense enough to crumble a lesser woman.

"Indeed," Kazimir agrees, still staring at her. Then, more softly, he adds, "And I can sense you have plenty of your own secrets, little witch, so I'd be willing to wager that you'd have similar reservations."

Claire rolls her eyes in response, not bothering to give a verbal answer.

Maddy steps forward, exchanging a look filled with hidden meaning with Odelia, before turning to Kazimir. "I have neither the time nor the care to search through everything; my focal point will be the memories pertaining to witches, and others that will confirm or deny what you've already told us."

"Of course, she will also search the mind of every darkling you brought with you," Claire adds.

Kazimir's lips curve. "Of course," he agrees, a taunting note to his tone.

I don't bother telling him that taunting or in any way irritating Claire is a good way for him to get drowned in lava or otherwise fucked up, because he'll learn as much in due time, whether he's permitted to stay and an alliance is created, or if we find he's lying and kill him.

Maddy crosses the thin barrier of the shield protecting us from the faye and walks right up to Kazimir as if she doesn't have a care or worry in the world, which pulls a low growl from Saunders.

Reyna tosses him a frown. "Got something to say, wolf?"

Saunders blinks, turning to look at Reyna. "Just that your fellow witch has no damn sense of self-preservation, apparently."

"Why have self-preservation when she could take out Kazimir without even blinking?" Reyna questions, tilting her head to the side, appearing genuinely confused.

I watch as Maddy takes Kazimir's hand in her own, then reaches up and rests a palm on his forehead. Her eyes flutter closed, and a faint gasp escapes her. Kazimir's eyes remain open and he watches her steadily, as if ready to attack if she oversteps—something that will get him killed. A moment later, she releases him, and tells Odelia, "He speaks the truth. He *was* a noble that got cast out a few months ago when the other darklings rebelled, he *did* want to reach out to us many years ago for an alliance and never lost hope it'd one day happen, and he absolutely despises the triad alliance—in fact, he wants to help kill the dark faye that he considers traitors."

Odelia makes a faint hum. "Check the rest of them while we confer."

Odelia walks up to me, placing a hand on my arm. "Sierra, I would recommend that we might invite your sister out here. I do not know the full scope of power in dark faye, but I do know that Kazimir is as powerful as I am—he could have fabricated memories to back up his story, though I don't believe he has. Your sister has an affinity for *feeling* when people lie—she'd act as an extra layer of confirmation for us."

I tense at that. "I don't want Leisel out here, especially if Kazimir might still mean us harm." Leisel is someone I will always protect at all costs, it goes against my nature to instead put her in the line of fire.

"I don't think he does, but it never hurts to be sure," Odelia responds.

I pause as I consider, casting a glance back to Maddy as she moves on to the next darkling and also declares him as honest and in line with Kazimir's thinking. If we're really to consider letting these people onto our side of the fight, we could use every drop of confirmation possible, and I've seen firsthand that Leisel is very good at perceiving lies. It couldn't hurt to have her double-check, especially if she'll be safe.

"Fine," I agree, somewhat reluctantly. "Once Maddy's done, I'll ask her to bring Leisel."

Odelia nods. "Sound decision."

One by one, Maddy scans the minds of each faye accompanying Kazimir, and one by one she declares that they're all in line with their leader—none of them have any love for other darklings. In fact, they're all differing levels of pissed for being dragged into a war that wasn't of their choosing and doesn't line up with their personal convictions. Once she's done, she retreats inside the shield and Odelia sends her for Leisel; of course, Wyatt insists on accompanying them to explain to Leisel why we'd like her presence, which I don't protest. I once took great issue with Wyatt having any contact with my sister, let alone unmonitored, but I've seen time and time again that all he feels towards her is a sibling-like affection and a drive to protect her, both of which I respect and appreciate. I've learned to compartmentalize the fact that in many, *many* years that will change, and I'll consider that when the time comes.

While Maddy and Wyatt are off retrieving my sister, Odelia questions Kazimir further.

"You understand that the odds are that we'll be wiping out the majority of your species?" she asks, arching a challenging brow at him.

"I do," Kazimir confirms. "I've never had much to do with my fellow dark faye—they're too volatile for my taste. I will tell you that my clan is not the only clan that has abandoned the triads, as you've named your opposition, though I am the only one who's bothered to come fight for your side. There are a few hundred, perhaps a few thousand, others who have split off and gone into hiding, wanting to sit the war out. Most of them are somewhat like me, with no rancor or ill will towards sorcerers; some come from expelled noble lineages and have no interest in fighting a battle that will destroy this world. Others simply don't wish to die for a cause they don't believe in. I wouldn't recommend killing the ones who wish to live in peace, and there are a few I will insist you leave alone merely because they aided my escape, but the rest you can choose whether or not to hunt."

Odelia stares at him for several moments, looking confounded at his easy acceptance of the fact that she intends to kill many of his fellow darklings. Before she can respond, Maddy reappears with Leisel and Wyatt in tow. Wyatt tumbles to the ground, pale as a sheet, while Leisel is as steady as she can be, landing on her feet. My sister then pats

Wyatt's head in a hilariously patronizing gesture and advises, "Breathe through it, the nausea will subside soon enough." Then she strolls up to me and gives me a beaming smile, before turning her attention to the darklings. She appears curious as she looks at them, and Kazimir looks equally curious as he stares at her, tilting his head to the side.

"You're a very powerful natural-born healer," he observes.

Leisel shrugs. "I like helping people and animals. Why are you here?"

I chuckle at Leisel's bluntness, which she has undoubtedly inherited from me.

"I'm here for an alliance with your friends," Kazimir says. "I don't mean anyone within that shield any harm."

Leisel takes a few steps towards him, and I instinctively grab her hand and walk forward with her as she steps out of the shield, unwilling to let her near the darklings without protection.

"Are you going to hurt us by word or deed?" Leisel asks.

Kazimir's lips quirk. "You're well-spoken for such a young one. No, witchling, I won't hurt anyone here by word or deed—though my words may occasionally offend, I truly mean no harm. I want to help you all."

Leisel hums thoughtfully, before turning to me. "He's being honest," she assures me. "The rest of them...they're loyal to him and trust him, so I don't think they're going to hurt us, either."

I blink a few times as I stare down at her, a touch confounded. Being able to tell if someone's lying is one thing, but sensing feelings in others such as loyalty and trust goes beyond that. I think there's much more to Leisel's powers than just healing and being able to conjure a light; something that's coming through more and more with each passing day.

I stroke a hand through her hair, smiling down at her. "Thank you, sweet girl."

She smiles back at me, then turns to look at Wyatt, who's managed to get to his feet. She skips back to him and takes his hand, saying, "We can walk back if you want since you didn't seem to like teleporting so much."

Still looking a little green, Wyatt shakes his head. "The walk is several hours, Leisel, you'll get tired. If you want, though, you can ride my wolf back. It'll be faster."

My sister's eyes light up with interest and excitement while I stiffen in place. "I don't think that would be a very good idea. It sounds dangerous."

Camden steps through the shield, placing a hand on my arm. "We can reserve a wolf ride for another time." When Leisel pouts, nose wrinkling, he smiles. "It's kind of fun seeing Wyatt get all green and nauseated for such a big bad wolf, no?"

Leisel perks right up at that, releasing a giggle. "Yeah, you're right."

Wyatt makes a noise of disbelief. "You're supposed to be on my side."

"I totally am," Leisel replies, casting him an innocent glance. "It'll be faster, like you said." Then to Maddy, "Should we go now?"

"Let the leaders confer for a little while, the rest of you return," Odelia says. "Reyna and Saunders, I do believe you have training to get to."

"*Fuck* yeah, we do," Reyna says, bouncing on her toes. "I'm so gonna enjoy showing the wolves how dumb they are to step up to us, just like I had fun beating Saunders silly."

"That description's unnecessary," Saunders mutters, frowning.

I feel a grin pull at my lips at the confirmation that these witches, warlocks, and shifters are actually intermixing quite well—teasing and all.

"I have matters to attend to amongst the sorcerers—a few squabbles that ought to be settled with the threat of lava," Claire mutters, frowning at Kazimir when she sees that he's still watching her with narrowed eyes, as if she's an object of intrigue. "You leaders have fun talking with our once enemy and perhaps newfound allies."

Chapter Thirty-Three

After everyone's been teleported away, save for Odelia, Rune, Camden, and me, I turn back to Kazimir and his kin. It's difficult to view people that I've been taught to see as enemies in the last months as allies; then again, sorcerers and shifters were at odds with each other for thousands of years and they came together for the sake of this war. Perhaps it is time to do the same with some darklings as well.

"What can you tell us of the triads?" Camden asks without preamble.

"What would you like to know?" Kazimir responds. "I am an open book, so to speak. I have no love for that alliance, no love for their illogical thinking and sheer mania."

"Everything," Camden says emphatically.

"Their numbers, their strengths, their weaknesses, their plans of attack. If Rhaelar and that shadow bastard, Ernesh, have any weaknesses," Odelia clarifies succinctly.

Kazimir inclines his head. "Very well. In terms of numbers, they have about eighty-five thousand. Fifty-five thousand of those are vampires. Twenty thousand are dark faye, all disposable, mindless creatures. The other ten thousand are hybrids. That being said, you must not underestimate Ernesh's power; he can raise an army of shadows with hundreds of thousands of figures. He's a hybrid who has the strengths of both the vampires and dark faye; the power to feed on lifeblood like a vampire and the magic of a darkling. When he tires, he'll drain someone of blood and be back to full strength; Rhaelar throws soldiers at him like sacrifices. I've observed them training together; bodies pile up. As for Ernesh's weakness, he is not well trained in combat. If you can get past the shadows to him, he would be an easy kill.

"Rhaelar's weakness is twofold; first, his anger. His fury helps strengthen his magic, but it also makes him reckless. He rails over the loss of his siblings to an earth-witch in regular bouts of madness. Second of all, his power of necromancy is not natural—it is god-bestowed, and a rather recent development. He petitioned the patron god of vampires and war, Ares, for greater power a few years ago. Ares, the mindless deity who finds amusement in destruction, granted it. As it is not a born power, not one that was bestowed at birth, Rhaelar's necromancy ability is finite—if he uses it too much too fast, he will lose it."

That's a fascinating revelation, and it also reminds me of what Odelia told me, about necromancy being a god-bestowed power. Rhaelar's power now makes a great deal of sense—I remember getting the sense that it was unnatural when I met him during his invasion of the Valley of Sorcerers. Now, I understand why; Rhaelar wasn't born with the gift, he was given it later in life.

"Now, in terms of plans of attack, they intend to carry a full-scale assault in three weeks time, something that's been planned for quite a while now," Kazimir goes on. "They'll land on the western coast of this continent using a fleet of ships, raiding and destroying coastal villages and every other village and town they might come by as they make their way further inland towards Kinrith. Rhaelar and Ernesh both have the ability to teleport, but they cannot teleport more than two or three people at a time and weaken by doing so. Thus, they will not use those powers to cart their army here—they also wish for you to see them coming, a point of pride."

"Three weeks," Camden murmurs, frowning. "That's a very short time to prepare."

"For you, perhaps, but the triads have been preparing for years," Kazimir says calmly. "A small group of them have been rallying forces and steadily readying the masses for even longer—maybe decades. War was always going to happen between shifters and vampires; your kinds are natural enemies. The unexpected was when my kin decided the join." The way he says kin is with derision, I notice, as if he's ashamed to be a dark faye due to the actions of his brethren.

To an extent, I can empathize with him. For a long time I resented being an earthly witch because it isolated me from the people who lived around me. I could never truly be myself, never fully immerse myself into the society surrounding me for fear of discovery; for fear of what would be done to me even though I wasn't a mythic. Having magical blood, as I've learned, is enough to turn humans against a person.

"It would seem you and your clan are quite a remarkable exception," I tell Kazimir. "If you were truly raised in a society of violence and prejudice yet chose to stray from it, chose to do the right thing despite the disdain of those around you for being different...well, that's respectable."

Kazimir's eyebrows raise as he regards me, and it is as if he's truly seeing me for the first time. Not a crown or a ruler or a mate or even the wielder of the black flame, but as an actual person.

"Indeed," Kazimir agrees. "You're an unusual one, Your Majesty. Great power without great hubris is a rarity these days. I can see why so many people from vastly different species and walks of life all take to you."

"Thank you. And, please, call me Sierra." I turn to Odelia. "The barrier could serve as a final test of sorts. It's meant to protect from anyone who has ill intent, correct?"

"Yes," Odelia says with a nod. "It requires both an invitation and pure intent to be passed. There is a good chance it would cause great harm to someone invited in who carries intent to harm the people within it."

Excellent. I take several steps back, farther into the bounds of the shield protecting Kinrith, and extend a hand towards the darklings.

"Do come in." Although I trust the mixture of Maddy's mind-searching and Leisel's ability to sense not just lies but emotions with a depth such as loyalty, this will be a final test. If any of the darklings are kept out of the wards or simply disintegrate upon entry, we'll know if there's need to worry about betrayal.

The first to step through the shimmering shield, Kazimir has a small smirk on his lips, as if amused by this final test. One by one his fellow clan members follow, several of them carrying bags presumably filled with their belongings taken when they made their escape, and all make it safely through.

Camden nods. "If you're still standing by now, you *must* intend to help us. Very well. You all can make yourselves at home in the village just behind us. You'll be meeting with Wyatt soon; he'll decide where you're best put during the war and get any more pertinent information from you."

Turning towards Odelia, I say, "Perhaps you could see if witches might be amenable to taking some time to train with this clan in the coming days. I'm sure they'll have useful abilities—"

"I assure you, we very much do," Kazimir says. "If your people are amenable, I'd prefer to integrate sooner rather than later. As you know, distance and separation can give room for negative speculation, and I want it very clear that we are not here to harm. We are here to help."

"We could organize some sort of dinner in the coming nights," Odelia murmurs. "Start gelling our people together."

"I could host it in the castle," Camden says, though he doesn't sound terribly pleased at his own offer. "We can decide on training and other things once we see how everyone does together."

"We're not going to fuckin' bite them," one of the clan members, a man with a shaved head and tattoos over his exposed arms and neck, says. "We're not the godsdamned wolves here."

"Yes, but they do not know you," I remind him. "None of us do. We may know that you are indeed here to help and get away from the triads as you claim you are, but that doesn't make us know you as people, which is a pretty damn important first step."

"Very true," Kazimir says calmly. "Let us know the details for the dinner, and in the meantime I'll help my people set up temporary camp here. If I might first have a word with you, Sierra, I believe there's a matter I can help you with."

"Not without me," Camden growls.

Kazimir shrugs. "Very well." Turning to the rest of his men, he says, "Go on into the village, familiarize yourself and choose your housing. I'll be with you shortly."

"If you don't mind, I believe we'll all stay for whatever it is you have to tell my witch," Odelia says with a toothy smile.

"You mean my mate," Camden says with a frown.

Odelia waves a dismissive hand at that. "Whatever you say, wolf. Sierra will always be a treasured member of my coven."

Hearing her words warm me, as I've been questioning my standing with her coven since my return to my position as queen, and I smile at Odelia with gratitude.

After the others make their way toward the houses not far away, murmuring amongst themselves, Kazimir addresses me.

"The black flame is incredibly volatile in you right now—I can feel it. Have you been having problems with calling to or wielding it?"

I blink several times, trying to keep surprise from my features. Whatever Kazimir's powers are, they must be quite extensive if he can not only sense magical abilities within others but sense them well enough to tell if they're *volatile,* as he put it. I can also feel great power coming from him, which means I am rather glad I won't be on the opposite side of a battlefield from him. I daresay that the triads might've lost one of their most powerful players when Kazimir deserted and decided to take a stand with us.

I turn to Odelia with raised eyebrows. She stares at Kazimir with a sharp gaze that silently warns him to tread carefully. Though it's now confirmed that he's our ally, I don't know that he's trustworthy enough to reveal something like my difficulty with my fire. Odelia gives me a small, barely perceptible nod. Camden bands an arm around my waist and tugs me close to him, protectively, as if seeing Kazimir's question as a threat. I place a calming hand on Cam's chest before turning back to Kazimir.

"Yes, I have been having issues with the black flame. A few months ago, I..." I give my head a shake at the memories of my encounter with rogues, finding it as difficult as ever to speak about it, especially in the presence of a person I don't know. Still, if Odelia trusts him, I have no reason not to; she's proven to be an excellent judge of character. "I miscarried. An encounter with rogue shifters ended with me getting an abdominal dissection with their claws. My fire was faulty at the time, an apparent side effect of pregnant witches; it didn't come forth in time to save my baby. Since then, it's proven difficult to control. I can summon it at will, now, but it sort of goes rogue every time I do—spreading indiscriminately, attacking everything in its vicinity."

Kazimir nods. "I've heard of similar problems with some particularly powerful noble faye females who lost children before they were born—their magic quite simply stopped heeding them, for it was strong enough to have its own sentience."

He doesn't say *I'm sorry for your loss* as many would and for some reason I find that a lot easier to deal with than the sympathy I've received from others. Although I'm still not over the loss entirely—I don't truly think I ever will be—I am at a point where I'm tired of feeling wretched about it or having others convey their sorrows on my behalf. The way Kazimir simply accepts the fact rather than dwelling on it is somewhat cold, without a doubt, and hints to a modest emotional range, but it's also nice to not dwell on it.

"What did they do in those cases?" I ask him. "Is there a way to...fix it?"

"A complete fix? No. But there are temporary ways to tie the sentience of an ability into the sentience of its wielder; blending two consciousnesses in a way. Powers like the black flame are their own living, breathing forms of magic; they're prone to agreeing with their wielders, but that takes a measure of trust. When the trust is broken, a power can go rogue. What I've seen women do is use wearable enchanted talismans to control their powers. I could look into creating one for you so that you can wield the black flame without risking mass destruction."

At his words, everything within me comes alight with hope. After hurting Cedrick yesterday, though it was an accident, I've absolutely dreaded calling to my fire again, which I know I'll need to do in coming battles. To be able to do so safely, without worrying about harming my friends and allies, would be a great help.

"That would be most helpful, thank you," I say earnestly.

Kazimir shrugs. "It's not an entirely selfless act, as I'd rather not get burned to a crisp by one of the few powers in this world that can destroy me. I will warn you that the talismans often decrease the potency of abilities; you'll only be able to wield it at a short distance, and you won't be able to use its full potential."

"That's better than fearing to use it at all," I respond. Even if there are downsides and limitations, at this point I prize control of my flame above all else. As long as it isn't reduced to tiny flickers that have no real power to do anything, I'll figure out the barriers.

"Will the talisman be harmful in any way? Cause any short or long term damage to the power?" Odelia asks.

Kazimir shakes his head. "Aside from acting as a slight muting agent, and only for so long as it's being worn, the talisman will not produce any ill effects. It's entirely safe to use—I've seen it several times, I assure you."

As someone calls his name from the village at the same time that Maddy reappears not far from us, Kazimir gives all of us a polite nod. "I believe we all have business to attend to. I hope to see you soon."

"We'll visit in the morning," Rune says, an assurance intermixed with a subtle threat, as if warning Kazimir to be on his best behavior, which only makes Kazimir smirk.

"The water is still running in all of the homes. I'll have food sent for you all," Camden says. "We'll reconvene soon."

"I look forward to it, thank you," Kazimir says. He turns for the village, then pauses, facing us once again. "I do hope you understand that I seek to build a long-term alliance between *all* of us. The triad threat is not the only one that will be coming here in the future; it's just the closest and most prevalent one at present. Other dark forces will threaten this world. I believe that your people have the best chance of protecting this beautiful planet from those forces, and I'd like to join in that fight."

"What do you mean?" I ask him, frowning. "What could be worse than a necromancer and shadow wielder banding together to try to take over this world, along with quite the army to help them?"

Kazimir's smile is mirthless and his eyes darken. "Ah, as you'll come to see, young witch, those are threats coming *from* this world. We live on a planet that is one among many, and ours is particularly desirable for its many resources and near-universal habitability. Others will want it in the future, and when they can't take it, they might wish to destroy it—a petty mindset often seen amongst beings of great power."

"What do you mean specifically?" Rune barks.

"Nothing in the immediate future aside from the triads. You must know that I have lived for a very long time and walked amongst many worlds during that time—not just Mythicacia and Earth. From what I know, probability dictates that there will be more threats in the future, perhaps more *severe* threats. I don't know when or how. I don't have a great many details; you'd need to find an oracle to tell you such things. What I do know is the more powerful beings banded together with commitment to protect this world the better. I look forward to seeing you all again soon. For now, I must get my clan settled."

Chapter Thirty-Four

Dinner that evening is a much quieter and less formal affair. Seated in the dining room, Leisel, Wesley, Camden, Wyatt and I all enjoy a meal. I'm amused to watch Leisel and Wes squabbling as young siblings might, complete with flicking small morsels of food at each other when they think nobody's looking. Wyatt and I enjoy a debate over the merits of different ancient philosophers in this realm until Camden gets irritated at being left out and pulls me directly onto his lap to include himself in the conversation.

After Greta's come to take the young ones to bed, Wyatt excuses himself while Camden asks me if I'll spend some time with his wolf, who's evidently been pushing for contact with me. Since I've always liked his wolf, for a time much more than I liked Camden himself, I agree. He takes me to a courtyard behind the castle, with a stone fountain of a Pegasus standing tall, sending trickles of water from the creature's mouth to the stone basin below. The moon and star's reflection in the water ripple and glisten in the most entrancing way.

"I hope the talisman Kazimir spoke of can be created, and that it works," I murmur, staring into the fountain as Camden begins to strip off his clothing.

I might have been embarrassed at his nudity out in the open if I hadn't already spent ample time staring at his naked body and if I didn't know that shifters are far less modest about nudity than humans—considering they shift together frequently.

"Is that what's been troubling you?" Camden asks, pausing in unbuttoning his pants and walking up to me.

I turn my gaze from the fountain to him, feeling my lips quirk at the riveting display of his six-pack which I have every intention of memorizing with my lips at some point in the near future. The power in just his physique is enamoring.

"Have I seemed troubled?" I ask him as he winds his arms around my waist to hold me close, and I reach up with my hands to rest them on his shoulders.

"You've only been here for a day, but the only time I haven't seen shadows in your eyes is when they're instead glazed over with lust."

I feel my lips quirk. "Well, you are very skilled at temporarily clearing my mind of all thoughts; I'll admit this freely."

"Kind of you," Camden responds with a half-smile. Then his lips thin and his eyebrows draw together. "Truly, I would like to know what's been on your mind. I can feel that your mind and emotions are weighed through our bond, remember? Tell me about your worries. I can help alleviate them, if only by sharing the burden."

I look back to the fountain. "Aside from us being on the cusp of a war so terrifying I don't want to imagine the possibility of what will become of this world if our side loses, my fire has been problematic for me for far too long. Just yesterday I nearly killed Cedrick with it—he's been a good friend to me, and I hate the fact that I hurt him. I hate even more that it caused a rift between me and Claire. She's been a steady friend to me ever since arriving at the coven, a listening ear and someone who helped me learn to summon fire on command. It's never bothered her when I've *almost* hurt her during our training sessions because she had a powerful shield protecting her and I always pulled back in time. When I failed to do so during the fight yesterday and she condemned me afterward...it hurt." I let out a long sigh, shaking my head, grimacing at the pain that's still fresh in my system.

"I always sort of assumed that I wasn't a social person by nature, but after living with the Nightshades I realized that my issue was never trouble with making friends, it was with feeling safe enough in an environment to make friends. Claire and I became close, so her rejection sucks. Odelia told me that her reaction was more a product of her own past troubles than actual anger towards me, but still. She didn't speak to me today and barely even looked in my direction. I am *very* hopeful that Kazimir manages to create something that'll help me control my fire, but I also fear what might happen if he doesn't. I also want to reconcile with Claire and comfort the sorcerers since they've just lost their home. I want to keep Leisel away from the battles even though I know that won't be possible since her light is the only way to chase away Ernesh's shadows and...there's just a lot on my mind."

Camden nods slowly, taking several moments to process everything I've told him. "You didn't see it, but Claire cast apologetic, somewhat ashamed looks in your direction several times earlier when your back was turned or you were looking away. I have faith your friendship will remain despite your fight yesterday. As for Leisel, Odelia told me her light summoning is key as much as your fire—we can't keep her away, but we can make sure she is the single most protected person during any battle. I'm sure sorcerers and shifters put together will be able to figure out something sufficient for her safety. In terms of Kazimir and the talisman he spoke of...I think he'll come through for us. For one thing, this is his chance to prove himself as a valuable ally; for another, I don't think that male is the type to talk about something unless he can deliver. Now, I'm not going to mention Cedrick for the simple fact that seeing another man touch you, even if it was innocent, is enough to send me to a dark place during the best of times."

A soft puff of laughter escapes me as I shake my head. "Typical man. You're lucky you're cute, otherwise I might think you're too much to deal with."

"Cute?" Camden appears genuinely offended. "Try *devastatingly sexy* or *ridiculously attractive*. Cute refers to babies and small animals—not to an Alpha wolf and *King*."

I blink coyly. "Would you prefer adorable instead?" I reach up to pinch his cheek. "You are the most adorable thing I've ever seen—*ow!*" I cut off with a yelp when he turns and nips my thumb, hard enough to leave a mark.

"You're a jerk." When I try to withdraw my hand, he grasps my wrist and then licks my finger before sucking it into his mouth. I feel my eyes droop at the memory of him suckling some other choice places on my body last night, which I'm quite sure is his intent.

He releases my thumb with a final kiss. "There, I kissed it better." The heat in his eyes promises that he'll continue kissing me better quite soon. "In the future, refrain from addressing me by adjectives similar to *cute* and *adorable*."

I'm a little tongue tied, so I merely say, "Uh-huh."

Camden's smile comes on slow and sensual as he trails a finger from my cheek to my neck, splaying his hand in the center of it. There's no pressure behind the grip, nothing that constricts my airflow, but the gesture is possessive and dominant enough to make my breath hitch. He slowly strokes his thumb along the column of my neck, and I dig my fingers into his shoulder, fighting to not sway under the tsunami of arousal that sweeps through me as my body primes itself for his touch. There was a time when him putting a hand on my throat would've made me run in the opposite direction; my reactions tell me beyond a shadow of a doubt that we're past that time.

"I can feel your pulse fluttering away here, racing so fast," Camden says, stroking his thumb back and forward over a spot on my neck. I never thought a mere touch like this could be so deeply arousing, but I'm learning more and more about the world of sensuality and pleasure the longer I spend with Camden.

"Stop looking at me like that and it might calm down," I manage to say, even as I lean into his touch.

"Stop looking at you like what? Like I'm going to devour you?" Camden asks, arching an eyebrow. He leans down until his lips hover right over mine, and excitement sets me on fire. I feel blood well up beneath my nails, and Camden's hiss accompanies my realization that I've been gripping his skin so hard I broke it. Strangely, that sends even more arousal scorching a path through me along with a feeling of satisfaction. He marked me, so it's only fair that I get to mark him too.

"I am going to devour you, Sierra," he tells me. He leans even closer so that our lips are brushing with each of his words. "Repeatedly, for a very long time to come. I can't get enough of you and I don't think I ever will." Abruptly, he steps away, releasing my neck and leaving me gasping and swaying on my feet, feeling like I might topple over. *Dear gods, the man is potent.*

"First, though, my wolf's going to get some time with you so he can finally calm down." Camden strips his pants and boxers, leaving no doubt that touching me aroused him as much as it did me—his cock is hard as a steel rod and the tip glimmers with moisture. I have to admire his self-control. I'm a second away from making the expression *leading a man around by his cock*— something I heard often around my coven—into a reality.

Before I can act, Camden shifts—for a second or two the sickening cracks of bones breaking and reshaping sound through the air, making me wince. A moment later, Camden's large wolf with a black coat of fur stands in front of me, panting happily. I've interacted with this beast a few times before; usually he's far more gentle than Camden, lying down and waiting for my verbal permission to come close or even letting me come to him. Today, possibly because I haven't seen him in quite some time, there is no such consideration. I sink down onto the ground beside the fountain just as the wolf practically leaps atop me, letting out barks of exhilaration, panting and licking my face.

"Okay, yes, I've missed you too," I say, burying my hands in his soft black fur and petting the beast. "Wolf—I can barely breathe. If you lay down next to me, I'll be better equipped to pet you."

The beast instantly flops down beside me. Head resting on his front paws, grey-tipped ears perked up, the wolf gives me adorable pleading eyes and even a small whine when I don't move quickly enough. Shaking my head at the sheer absurdity that such a hardened man has such a playful, affection-seeking wolf within him, I make good on my promise, giving the wolf plenty of cuddles and speaking to him in a low voice about everything and nothing. He lets out a rumble that's eerily close to a feline purr, luxuriating in my attention as much as I enjoy giving it. I must sit with the overgrown wolf for the better part of an hour, stroking and doting on him, before he finally stands and stretches his front paws before shaking out his fur. After nudging my cheek with his nose one last time, he trots back to Camden's pile of clothes.

Not two seconds later Camden the man stands before me again, quickly pulling on his clothing while saying, "Now maybe he'll stop pushing to come out every time I'm around you—that wolf has been a menace recently."

I smile. "He's adorable—don't give me that look, I called your *wolf* adorable, not you."

"Careful of the thin ice you tread on," Camden says suavely. He extends his hand to me and just as I take it to stand, he swings me up in his arms in a princess-hold, drawing a gasp from me.

"Excuse me, Cam, but I am perfectly capable of walking on my own," I say loudly when he starts walking to the entrance of the castle, striding through halls heedless of the servants who look at him as if he's grown two heads.

"Quite so, but I like carrying you more. You like it too." He lowers his voice. "Besides, considering what I'm planning on doing to you when we get back to our rooms, you'll be glad of the respite. If all goes well, you won't be able to walk properly come morning."

As soon as he gets me back to his chambers, he starts making good on his promise. We don't even make it into the bedroom; instead, he sets me down against the wall by the door as soon as he's slammed it shut, pins me against it with his weight, and practically devours me with the force of his kiss. His teeth, tongue, and lips drink from my mouth until I'm too dizzy to stay upright on my own, feeling weak in the knees. When he feels me sway against him, Camden simply hoists me up into his strong arms and wraps my legs around his waist, continuing to kiss me. I sink my nails into his shoulders, probably leaving scratch marks, and dig my heels into his back.

"Fuck," he mutters, pulling away from my lips to bury his head in the crook of my neck while I thread my fingers through his silky hair, holding him to me. "I'm going to godsdamned *devour* you, Sierra. You're about to get so fucked—" He cuts off with a hiss when I turn my head and nip his earlobe with my teeth none too gently.

"Less talking, more moving," I murmur.

One of his hands rises to wrap around my neck getting me even more fired up than I already am. Then, abruptly, it disappears and Camden swears under his breath, pulling back to look at me and gently setting me on my feet.

"I'm sorry—I wasn't thinking just now, or earlier in the courtyard... it's just... instinct," he murmurs apologetically.

Startled, I realize that I wasn't bothered by him taking me by the throat as much as he was—I was too far gone in sensation to think as to how badly his hand on my throat ended months ago. I'm *still* pretty swept up in sensation, but the jar from the past gives room for rational thought.

"Don't be sorry," I tell him, leaning forward to plant a kiss on his lips. "I know you didn't realize your strength, and I know you won't hurt me again. If your instincts are driving you...let them. I like the way it feels. You won't take it too far."

It's only as I speak the words that I realize just how much I mean them, just how much I've come to trust Camden—more than I ever did before. I want him to behave the way he wants to; I know I can handle it, and I believe wholeheartedly that he'd never hurt me again. I don't think he actually meant to hurt me the last time, and he's learned to monitor his strength in the harshest possible way. Besides...these days I know a few tricks of my own to stop him if he takes things too far—living with a coven of battle-hungry witches and being trained by some of the most powerful sorcerers alive, has taught me a great deal.

Camden's brows furrow as he looks down at me, as if I'm confounding him with my trust, and his eyes take on a glimmer of warmth that humbles me. "You have no idea how much your trust means to me," he murmurs, ghosting his lips over mine again. "I won't betray it."

"I know you won't," I assure him. "Now, please stop talking and let's get to the fun part. I expect to receive an orgasm soon."

His lips quirk. "Well, I can't leave my woman unsatisfied, now can I?"

I feel a rip of material at my waist, and then my pants are suddenly in tatters around my ankles. Blinking, I realize he clawed them off of me. While that might be cause concern for most, I find his desire for me and impatience to get to me, to the extent that he won't even take the time to remove my pants, scorching hot.

Two thick fingers slam into me at once and my moan intermixes with Camden's hiss of pleasure.

"Already soaking wet for me," he murmurs. "That's my good girl. I want you wetter, though; I want to see *how* wet you can get before I eat this pretty little pussy, then plant it on my cock."

I moan my agreement as his fingers scissor inside of me, stretching my inner muscles in preparation. He adds a third finger, then starts thrusting them in and out of me slowly, leisurely, leaning his body weight against me to trap me firmly against the wall as he pleasures me. It's *too* slow, though, too lax, and after a moment I realize his gentle pace is deliberate. He's toying with me, giving me enough friction to set me on fire but not enough friction to get me off, and that's driving me out of my mind.

"Cam," I murmur, digging my nails into his back, scratching at it as I rise up on my toes, trying to grind myself into his hand and get what I need to reach my orgasm. My eyes flutter shut as he gives me a few fast, aggressive thrusts before returning to that maddeningly slow pace.

"What do you want, Sierra?" His voice is a quiet rumble. "Tell me what you want and it's yours, beautiful girl."

"I want—*ah*," I cut off with a louder moan as his thumb rises to circle my clit and my eyes snap open and widen.

"Hmm?" he taunts with another hard thrust before taking his thumb away and once again giving me slow thrusts with his fingers that make me want to sob with frustration. My entire body is tense in preparation to come; my core is tingling and my body is burning up with need for him.

"To come," I rush out. "Please make me come."

"As you wish." Even as he says the words, he pulls his fingers away and something akin to a sob leaves my mouth as I give him a look of utter betrayal that just makes him smile faintly as he scoops me into his arms again. I wrap my legs around him, shamelessly grinding into his erection as he starts walking somewhere. He lets out a low groan and spanks my ass, murmuring an admonishment for my impatience.

"It's your fault," I reply, the stinging on my ass only prompting me to grind against him harder. I can feel the thick length of his cock through his pants, and I want it inside of me already—I'm not in any mood to wait, not after the way he brought me to the cusp.

"Sierra, I'm going to fall over if you keep doing that—" He cuts off with a hiss as I grind on him harder. "Fuck this."

He changes direction, and a moment later I feel the soft cushion of the couch beneath my ass. I blink through my blurry vision, brought on through a pleasure-induced haze, to see that he's set me on the couch in front of the fireplace and is lowering to his knees in front of me. *Wow*. I don't think I've ever envisioned him getting on his knees for anyone—he's too much of an Alpha, a *King* for that—but here he is kneeling in front of me, staring up at me like I'm the answer to a life full of turmoil. Even while his gaze is reverent, his touch is anything but. He yanks my legs apart, pressing the outside of my knees to the side of the couch, leaving me achingly vulnerable and open to his stare.

The position is a bit of a stretch on my muscles but I don't truly feel the pain; not with the way his gaze is locked onto my pussy with such hunger and intensity it's almost frightening.

He leans forward, putting his mouth on the most sensitive part of me. I half-expect him to be teasing and slow again or to try to get me to ask for an orgasm again; he doesn't. Instead, with a growl, he devours my sensitive flesh just like he promised he would, sending me flying into a powerful orgasm that draws a loud moan of abandon from me, leaving me shaking. Before my first orgasm has subsided, he yanks me by my hips off of the couch and lowers me onto the soft rug, tearing off his own clothes with the same impatience he ripped my pants with, while I hurriedly yank off my shirt and bra. In moments, both of us are naked, and he's lowering his head to suck one of my nipples deep into his mouth with a groan of pleasure. I scratch at his scalp, then tug at his head as he starts sliding his cock along my slit, dragging his heavy length over my sensitized clit again and again while I whimper and whine.

"Fuck me already!" I snap when I feel the telling tingle of an orgasm creep up on me yet again. I don't want to come again until he's inside me.

He bites my nipple, drawing a yelp from me then looks up and says, "I'll fuck you when I'm ready to, Sierra, and not beforehand. I want to feel you come as soon as I'm inside you, so that's what's going to happen."

"I'm already there!" I gasp when another heavy drag makes my inner muscles clench around nothing but air, making me realize just how empty I am and crave to feel him stretching me even more.

He shakes his head. "Uh-uh, not yet. Be my good girl that I know you are and take it."

When I open my mouth to protest again, he wraps a hand around my neck; my eyes roll into the back of my head and my body falls limp under the dominant hold. His cock plunges into me, abruptly and mercilessly, just as I start to orgasm. Then he thrusts in and out of me like a madman, riding me through my orgasm, as I make a loud symphony of noises—broken moans, pleas for him to go faster and harder, things I'm sure I'll be embarrassed of when I'm capable of rational thought again. He doesn't stop or slow down once my orgasm subsides. Instead, he grunts and swears and continues to fuck me, leaning down to kiss me as he does. At this point, my inner walls feel overly sensitized and each drag of his cock in and out makes me acutely aware of his length, thickness, each ridge and vein along the pulsing of his cock inside of me. Although I feel pretty tapped from my two orgasms already, I nonetheless feel a third start to build inside of me, driving me half out of my mind because the pleasure becomes too much, the sensations too acute.

Camden pulls out of me only long enough to flip me onto my hands and knees, then he pushes right back into me and fucks me with smooth, harsh strokes that take my breath away. My breasts swing with each of his thrusts and he pushes my upper half down onto the rug. My sensitive nipples drag along the material of the carpet, making me moan even louder.

"Cam, please," I whine softly when I feel my pleasure reaching a crest yet again. This orgasm threatens to be the strongest one yet, threatens to tear my entire existence away with its intensity, which is somewhat frightening.

Camden's relentless—he reaches around my front with one hand while the other holds me down by the back of my neck and starts to circle his fingers over my clit. I whimper and try to wriggle away, the stimulation too much to handle. He chuckles and holds me in place more firmly, not giving me reprieve or escape, even as I start to beg him with barely intelligible words, not even sure what I'm asking for. My fingers scratch at the carpet, gathering wool beneath my fingernails as I nearly sob. I feel Camden tensing behind me before his motions over my clit speed up.

"Come again," he commands me. "Now—*fuck*," he cuts off as I come yet again with a choked scream. I feel like my body *erupts* with pleasure, making my eyes roll back into my head, toes curl, and causing all my muscles to spasm sporadically as my channel clenches around his cock repeatedly. After a few final thrusts he also goes still, achieving his own orgasm, but I'm too caught up in the throes to pay that much notice. Even as his cock starts to soften inside of me, I keep coming, seeming unable to control my body or get my orgasm to subside. It feels like an eternity later when my whole body suddenly goes lax and my orgasm ends, leaving me sapped of strength and breathless, with my heart hammering away in my chest I think it might just burst out.

"Now *that* was godsdamned amazing," Camden says, his voice thick with pleasure and approval. He's also breathing heavily behind me, but apparently he has much more strength remaining than I do, because not a moment later he lifts me into his arms. My head lolls against his chest, my eyes fluttering as he walks us to the bedroom before gently setting me down on the bed, brushing my hair away from my forehead as he does. He retreats into the bathroom instead of joining me, making me frown. I want him to hold me like he usually does. I crave skin to skin contact with him.

He must feel my confusion and displeasure through the bond because I hear him call out, "I'm just getting a washcloth to get you cleaned up, love, I'm not abandoning you."

I still don't fully relax until he returns a minute later with a warm cloth in his hand, cleaning me up just like he promised to. Then, tossing it aside, he joins me in bed, pulling me half on top of him and wrapping his arms around me, pressing a kiss to the top of my head and stroking his hand up and down my back. He reaches over to his bedside table, opening the drawer and withdrawing a dangling rose-gold chain, to which a crystal is attached. *Must be the crystal Hecate gave him.* As he fastens it around my neck, I feel a warmth in my chest, followed by the bond between us shifting around and feeling like it somehow cements into place, takes on a permanence.

"There," Camden murmurs. "Bound forever. Don't take this off—something feels profoundly right."

"I won't," I promise drowsily, loving the feeling of connection between myself and Camden, which the crystal only seems to strengthen.

It doesn't take long for me to drift off, so I think I might actually be sleeping when I hear him start to murmur soft words of praise and adoration to me. Most of them are too quiet to make out; it's the final thing I think I hear him say that *almost* wakes me up, though my mind and body are too tired to stay conscious.

"I love you, my beautiful mate. I'd fight the whole world to have you—I *will* fight the whole world to keep you safe. Nothing could ever separate me from you again."

Chapter Thirty-Five

I awaken to the sound of a low moan and a feeling of unbelievable pleasure coursing through my body. It takes me a moment to get my bearings and understands what's going on; Camden's between my legs, lazily lapping away at my pussy like it's his favorite meal, and I'm laid on my back with my legs hooked over his shoulders, letting out sleepy moans and whimpers. Already on the cusp of an orgasm, it doesn't take long before I come in his mouth, back arching and hips bucking, hands reaching down to grasp his hair as I grind against him, too caught up in the moment to question just how odd this situation is—to literally be woken up by an orgasm. Once it's subsided, Camden kisses a trail up my body before propping his elbows on either side of my head and smiling at me.

"Good morning," he greets.

"Off to a good start," I agree, accepting the kiss he leans down to give me. "Should I be prepared for wakeup calls like that more often?" I ask once he's pulled back.

"It'd be wise. If you're in my bed, I'm assuming I have free access to you." He pauses. "Any objections?"

I shake my head. "None." After a pause, as rational thought starts to return to me, I say, "I never got around to asking last night if you heard how Reyna's first joint training session went."

"Well, I presume," Camden responds, "I'll get a full report from Wyatt soon, but since I haven't heard anything yet, that means there were no disasters."

"That's definitely a plus," I say, winding my arms around his neck. "Reyna can be a little much."

Camden snorts softly. "That's a nice way of saying she takes a certain joy in breaking someone's will to live. Saunders was railing over the way she beat him senseless for days after the fact, even though it caused her to earn his respect."

Reyna does tend to act as a blow to someone's senses, even if she doesn't decide to go on the offensive and beat the shit out of them. She's also the reason my general combat and spoken-word magical combat abilities have vastly improved in a relatively short time span. She does not pull her proverbial punches, *ever*, and as much as it sucks to always walk away from sparring with her with broken bones or harsh bruises, her methods are proven to work. Pitiless and some might say cruel but terribly effective.

"We should get up and get started for the day," I say on a yawn. "I need caffeine, and we need to check on our newest allies and guests. I assume the dark faye won't be staying in that evacuated town forever."

"You assume correctly," Camden says. "I'd like to keep them relatively close for now, just to keep an eye on them, but in the future—if they prove as useful as Kazimir seems to think they will, I'll offer them land somewhere in Aesara, if they would like it. Maybe they'll want to settle somewhere else—no way to know for sure."

"You don't trust Kazimir, even after he passed a ridiculous amount of tests," I observe. To be fair, I don't entirely trust him either, but at least I trust that he doesn't mean us any harm.

"I don't know the man. All I know is what I've heard of dark faye, and the reports aren't good. I'm not prone to trusting anyone, Sierra.

The number of people I trust completely in this world can be counted on one hand."

I suppose that being a ruler, that's a fair stance. Having lived with a fair share of secrets for my entire life, I'm also not the most trusting of people; something that Camden and I have in common. The more I get to know him, the more I realize we have a great deal of things in common, despite the vastly different lives we've led.

The words I might've heard him say just as I was falling asleep last night, or possibly the words I heard in my dreams, float across my mind—his declaration of love for me. I feel my cheeks warm as I stare up at him, wondering if they were real or just a product of my desires. In either case, I can't deny that I've certainly been falling for him. I only arrived in Kinrith days ago, befuddled and worried for my people, but he's made my time here enjoyable despite the current stresses heaped on both of our shoulders, and has put aside ample time to spend with me, which I can imagine is no easy feat for a ruler who's currently at war.

"If you keep looking at me like that, we won't be making it out of this bed today," Camden informs me. "Which wouldn't be good, considering we both have a great deal of duties to attend to."

I bite my lip, nodding. "Yeah, um, let's go get breakfast."

No sooner have I showered and set up at the table in the living room, which has already been set with a beautiful, mouthwatering breakfast spread, than the door opens with both Leisel and Wesley walking through without having the courtesy to knock. *At least I'm fully clothed this time*, courtesy of Camden presumptuously moving a good deal of the clothing that once sat in *my* closet to *his*. I think he was being serious when he referred to his chambers as *our* rooms last night.

Greta hurries in after my sister, who wastes no time walking up to the table and plucking a strawberry from the bowl of fruit I'm eating, then holding it up for Chip, who's perched on her shoulder.

Wesley follows behind and takes a seat on one of the empty chairs at the table as if he's been invited. I guess the kids are used to having free access to my time in the mornings and aren't keen to give that up despite the change of scenery. I have to say I don't want to give it up either; I'd miss having them both around at any hour of the day or night.

"Your Majesty, I am so sorry, they disappeared before I could stop them—"

"It's fine, Greta," I cut her off with a wave of my hand, leaning in to kiss Leisel's forehead in greeting. Chip leaps off her shoulder and onto the table, then promptly begins picking through a selection of nuts in a bowl, pocketing several in his cheek. Leisel giggles while I smile, giving her pet a little stroke along his furry head.

Camden walks into the room not a moment later, righting the collar of his shirt. He flicks a glance over Leisel, Wesley, Greta, and Chip, then shrugs and drops into his usual seat, slapping Wesley's back and nodding at Leisel in greeting as he does.

"Your Majesty, I'll ensure my charges don't interrupt your morning time again," Greta assures Camden, showing that my protests fell on deaf ears.

"You'll do no such thing," Camden says. "They're welcome here, though I appreciate your concern. As long as they don't appear in the middle of the night, I don't have any problems with some extra company during my morning hours."

"But, Your Majesty, you've always enjoyed your privacy—"

"Before I had people I was happy to spend time with," Camden cuts her off with a wave of his hand. "Truly, Greta, this isn't a problem; go have breakfast with your mate while I enjoy some with mine. I'll send the kids back your way within an hour or so."

"They'll be better behaved by that point," I say firmly, looking at both Leisel and Wesley as I do so. Leisel gives me her brilliant smile while Wesley merely shrugs, unwilling to concede.

Greta's displeasure is visible and she hovers in place after being dismissed. "Are you sure?"

"Positive," Camden tells her. "Go keep Cara company. I'm sure she'll enjoy it. Thank you for checking in."

Reluctantly, Greta turns and sulks out, closing the door behind her.

Leisel crosses her eyes. "She's really big on etiquette."

Camden chuckles. "She always has been. She runs a very tight ship, but she also cares deeply for her charges."

Wesley and Leisel help us devour the majority of the food on the table, letting very little go to waste. Especially Wesley, who has a ravenous appetite and seems to be able to eat an infinite amount of food at all times.

Afterward, Leisel says they have classes set up with tutors and kisses me on the cheek before leading a grumbling Wesley out of the room by his hand.

"Maybe we should move breakfasts somewhere else and invite Wyatt," I suggest once the kids are gone. "I don't know how you did things beforehand, but I think a more family-oriented environment could be good for us."

Camden's eyes warm as he sips his coffee. "I'd like that," he agrees. His brows briefly furrow as his eyes glaze and he looks lost in thought. "Wyatt and I haven't spent as much time together as I would've wished since our mother passed away. With her, we'd eat together as a family and do many things together when time allowed. Without her, my father became wholly focused on duties, and since Wyatt and I had wildly different expectations and schedules within the castle, we couldn't really get as much time together as we once did. I didn't realize I missed the family time until very recently."

My heart clenches for this ruthless wolf who's given up so much for the sake of his position and for the sake of his people. Love, connection, friendship, family…he's lacked so much without seeing what he was missing because he didn't know anything else. I want to fix that for him, and I'm resolved to.

"Well, we'll just have to remedy that, won't we?" I ask him lightly. "Wes and Leisel won't settle for anything less than regular breakfasts now that they see you're okay with it, and I'm sure Wyatt would like to join as well. Even during wartime, there has to be room for the things we enjoy in life."

"You really do enjoy being a provider and nurturer for those you consider your own, don't you?" Camden questions in turn. "You're so good with children, it's a little startling."

I shrug. "I wasn't always the best with them—I grew up as an only child, very used to getting all of my parent's attention, but then they passed away and Leisel only had me so I didn't have much of a choice except to become what she needed. I found through difficult experiences that I very much enjoyed taking a leading role in her life, raising her and making sure she always had what she needed and as much of what she wanted as I could give her. Then when I found Wes in Aesara…" I trail off, shaking my head. "His parents were the ones who truly taught me how to care for Leisel when I was a broken mess after my mother died on the birthing bed. They did so much for both me and my sister and were so good to us, finding him as the sole survivor sort of felt like an opportunity to repay all their kindnesses over the years. Taking him in wasn't just a responsibility or the honorable thing to do, it truly felt—*feels*—like an honor. It helps that he's always been good friends with Leisel, and I've known him since he was born, but even without that I would've taken him as my ward."

"He's a good kid, from what I've seen," Camden remarks. "A rarity, considering earthly warlocks are as in short supply as earthly witches. How's his magical progress?"

"Coming along very quickly," I tell him, not bothering to hide the pride in my tone. "Wes can cause ground-shaking earthquakes with a mere thought these days, and he's picking up on the other magical arts quickly. He also helps Leisel train with her light; they do cooperative magic together all the time." I pause, a new thought dawning. "Is Wyatt...displeased in any way with their friendship? I know wolves are possessive of their mates, and even though Wyatt's no more than a brother to her now—"

"Not at all...at least not that he's told me or I've sensed," Camden cuts me off. "I think he's of the same opinion that I am; the more people that feel protective of his mate, the better."

I feel my eyebrows rise. "You didn't seem to feel that way when I was hugging Cedrick not long ago."

"I don't like seeing another man's hands on you, especially one who I can tell is attracted to you," Camden responds, his voice little more than a low growl. "You're mine, Sierra, absolutely nothing can change that. As long as he doesn't try anything, I'll be cordial, but I can't say I'll like anyone who likes you too much."

I smile a little, somewhat amused at his possessiveness. I can't fault him for it though, since I feel equally possessive of him when it comes to Aspen. Seeing her look at him during the banquet with a covetous gaze...I wanted to claw that bitch's eyes out. Then again, she and Camden have a history as I found out, whereas Cedrick and I have never had anything more than friendship between us. He admitted to being attracted to me, but he was also respectful when I made it clear I didn't consider myself available to anyone.

"Cedrick's helped me a lot with magic," I tell Camden. "All of my tactile magical combat abilities come from him. When it comes time for battle and I can hold my own, a big chunk of that will be owed to him. Some of it will also be owed to Reyna, Odelia, and even Bane—though he really is an asshole—but Cedrick's been pretty patient and supportive with me."

"You're not making a case for him," Camden says flatly. "I don't like the sparkle of fondness in your eyes when you talk about him."

I roll my eyes. "It's *friendly* fondness and nothing more. You're the only one I'm fond of romantically; the only one I've ever been fond of romantically. You don't have to worry about Cedrick as competition; he isn't."

"Good," Camden says with a nod. "Now, what do you mean about Bane being an asshole? Do I need to worry about him?"

I chuckle, shaking my head. The almost petulant protectiveness in his tone, like he can't stand the thought of anyone else bringing me even the most minor irritation, is perversely endearing. "No, Cam, you don't need to worry about him. He's trained me in swords and blades, and he has not been nice with his training. He's not as bad as Reyna, who thinks pain is the best teacher and doesn't consider our session over until I have a body covered with bruises or some broken bones, but he's not gentle either. Odelia and Claire are my nicest instructors."

Camden's eyebrows raise. "The sorcerers trained you in swordsmanship as well? What *haven't* you learned with them?"

I shrug. "We're at war, Cam. They all want me to be able to protect myself and my kind, all the more so since I possess one of two powers that will be integral if we're to survive this war. Living with them was harsh, the training was harsh, but I also learned a lot about myself, my endurance, and my capabilities in fighting."

"We should spar sometime with blades," Camden suggests. "I'd like to see what you've learned."

I shrug. "As long as you don't bitch when you land on your ass, I'm game."

He frowns at that. "Don't get cocky. I was trained in swords by the best swordsmen of our time."

"And I was trained by absolutely ruthless warriors who have lived lives having to fight for their survival," I retort. "We'll see who prevails; the witch or the bitch—sorry, I mean wolf."

Camden growls, though it's playful. "You're going to pay for that comment..." Then he scoops me into his arms and carries me away.

Chapter Thirty-Six

Not too long later, Camden and I convene in the courtyard with Odelia and Rune, who nod at us.

"Shall we expect lateness to be a regular occurrence with the two of you?" Odelia questions with a pleasant smile.

"I just got my mate back, you'll have to forgive me for not being eager to share her," Camden says, entirely unabashed.

I ignore the small thrill that his words send through me in favor of focusing on the most pressing item on our agenda today, and one I'm looking forward to; meeting with Kazimir again. I spot Maddy walking towards us along with Saunders, Reyna, and Claire in the distance, at the same time that Wyatt strolls out of the castle, going over a swath of papers in his hands.

"Excellent timing," Odelia says as Maddy approaches.

The slim witch is pretending to ignore Saunders, who's ranting at her for some offense. Reyna, on the other hand, is cracking her knuckles with a bloodthirsty look in her eyes that I find all too familiar.

"Let's make this quick. I have an army of wolves to beat into shape," Reyna says.

Wyatt, coming to a stop beside Camden, winces. "Did you have to instruct your witches to go full force on them during drills?"

Reyna blinks. "Why would I have done anything else?"

"Maybe because Aspen's now leading a rally against you calling you insane, given that dozens of wolves ended up with broken bones and serious injuries at the end of the six-hour session you led yesterday."

Reyna tilts her head to the side, appearing genuinely confused. "I fixed them all up afterward, what's the problem? Do you not want your warriors to be prepared to fight properly? It's not *my* fault they howled like bitches rather than fighting back. Give me a few weeks with them and they'll learn fast."

"I'll have to agree with Reyna on this one," Odelia cuts in, even as she shoots Reyna a censuring look. "The harder they train, the better they become."

Wyatt nods, conceding. "Very well. If you could at least refrain from calling them pathetic dogs or mangy mutts as you work, Aspen would have less to complain about."

"Aspen should not be complaining at all," Camden says, silky menace in his voice. "Wyatt, do have it passed on to her that if she doesn't like the methods that the witches *under our protection* use, she's welcome to leave the army, her captainship, and her place in the upcoming battle. I'm sure we'll manage just fine without her."

Reyna blinks at him. "Huh. You might not be so terrible after all."

"Right, onto our business for the day; I'd like to convene with Kazimir to see how he's settling and if he's made any progress on the talisman he spoke of not long ago," Camden says.

"I can go retrieve him," Maddy says brightly.

Odelia raises her eyebrows at Camden, silently asking if he's alright with bringing someone who was an enemy to us just yesterday directly to the castle.

Camden shrugs. "The guards around the village the darklings are currently inhabiting haven't mentioned seeing any foul play—I suppose we might as well get used to having that strange clan around. I'm fine with him coming here."

"He's calculating, but he's also smart," I observe. "I don't think Kazimir is going to try to hurt us for the simple fact that he sees us as useful, just as we see him as useful. As long as we remain useful to each other, I don't foresee any betrayals or great problems."

"Agreed," Odelia says with a nod, then tips her chin at Maddy. "Go ahead."

"I'm coming with you," Saunders says. "It isn't safe for such a little thing to be alone with darklings."

Maddy turns her gaze towards him slowly, her bright energy instantaneously switching to dangerous as she regards Sanders. "I am not a *thing*, and I am most capable of handling myself. I've fought darklings before, wolf; you'll just be dead weight I can do without."

"Dead weight?" Saunders repeats with disbelief. "I—"

"Take him," Rune interjects with an impatient wave of his hand. "It's always best to go into potentially unstable territory with backup, and despite his faults, Saunders has enhanced senses that you don't. He also seems invested in your protection." Rune gives a weighted pause. "We can discuss why that's the case at a later time. For now, we need to get things moving."

Maddy rolls her eyes, grabs Saunders' shoulder, and they disappear together.

Odelia, Rune, Reyna, and Claire start talking about some occurrence amongst the sorcerers this morning, while I turn to Camden, silently speculating. The glimmer of possessiveness in Saunders' eyes when he regards Maddy is rather familiar, and part of me has to wonder...

I rise on my tiptoes and murmur in Camden's ear, "Could they be—"

"Possibly. I'm not sure—time will tell."

I blink several times. "But...she's a witch and he's a wolf."

"I know, sweetheart," he murmurs. "That describes us as well. I've considered the possibility that interspecies mates are so rare because different species aren't known for mingling. Conceptually it should be possible for members of differing species to be fated to each other, though not terribly common since fate generally makes sensible pairings, and I've only seen her cross lines when it's truly necessary and makes sense. To have a mate that's *other* is...very complicated."

"It is," I agree quietly, then kiss his neck. "But if things are meant to work out, I think they will."

His arms wrap around my waist, hauling me closer, and my arms instinctually wrap around his neck. A loud throat clearing behind us breaks us up. I glance over my shoulder to see Odelia staring at me pointedly. Rune's looking away, Reyna's giving me a smirk, and Claire looks markedly uncomfortable. I release Camden with a sigh, though he doesn't follow suit; he raises one hand to wind into my hair and takes my mouth in a deep, passionate kiss in front of them until my toes curl in my shoes and I'm sagging against him. Only then does he release me, keeping an arm around my waist to hold me steady. I give my head a shake to clear it, then feel my cheeks burn as I realize the message behind Camden's possessive display; his territory, his rules.

"If I want to kiss my mate, I will, regardless of the time or place," Camden says immovably. "Or the company," he says a bit louder, turning his head towards the left. I follow his gaze to see that Cedrick's walking up to us along with Bane, which is probably why Camden kissed me as passionately as he did.

Cedrick holds his hands up in a mock display of surrender. "I'm not an interloper. Regardless of how tempting your mate may be."

Camden's growl intermixes with my groan. "Ced, please…don't. Camden's in a possessive mood."

Cedrick shrugs. "He should be confident enough in the foundation of your relationship not to worry about little old me, now, shouldn't he?"

I feel Camden tense up beside me, rising to Cedrick's taunt. Before he can go full Alpha though, Maddy reappears with both Kazimir and Saunders in tow. Saunders appears ill from the teleporting while Kazimir is entirely unphased.

He's dressed formally in a navy blue suit complete with a damn *handkerchief* in the breast pocket, apparently favoring one of the styles of this planet's eras past—the polished gentleman. He's also holding a blue bag in his hand, which I glance over with a flicker of hope, wondering if he might've already made the talisman we spoke of. His ice-blue eyes take in everyone surrounding him and he says, "I do believe some introductions are in order."

After Odelia has made said introductions, Kazimir nods. "Pleasure to meet you all. Odelia, Rune, Camden, Sierra—good to see you again. Thank you for trusting me to be closer to your home," he says cordially, though he doesn't sound particularly thankful—just bored. I get the sense that, if he wanted to, he could've been in and out of the castle without anyone noticing.

Kazimir's gaze lands on Claire, and once again, he lingers on her, giving a slow blink as they regard each other. Claire's brows furrow as she tilts her head to the side. "You have a problem, bringer of darkness?"

"I don't bring the darkness," Kazimir says smoothly. "I *am* the darkness. Important distinction. If I ever do have a problem, I won't need to say so; you'll know." His eyes swivel back to me, and he holds up the bag. "I went over the details of the talisman creation. I have the spell prepared, along with most of the ingredients. All I need is some gold to create it; it's the one thing I didn't have the foresight to bring."

"You brought a great deal of supplies with you," Odelia says calmly. "Some things that even I've never seen; interesting herbs that don't look like they come from our world." I realize the comment is a way of telling Kazimir that she has eyes on him; he seems to note this as well, though it doesn't seem to bother him because he merely smiles indulgently.

"I've walked the worlds for quite some time—I'm a collector of the rare and unique." Again, his eyes flick over to Claire, though much more briefly this time, almost as if he can't stop himself from looking at her. To me, he says, "Which is fortunate, considering I have all we need for the spell and enchantment. I will need several strong practitioners to aid me in the creation, and somebody well-versed in harnessing the natural energy of this realm specifically."

"I believe I could help with that," a new voice calls out. I turn in time to see Claude strolling towards us from the entrance of the castle, approaching us at a steady pace. He stops beside Wyatt to give him a nod, then briefly squeezes Camden's shoulder before giving me a respectful formal bow. Finally, he addresses Kazimir. "I'm trained extensively in the energies of this realm, magical and otherwise. I've spent the last two centuries studying it."

"Very good," Kazimir says with a nod, eyeing Claude with interest. Then to Camden, "Get me some gold, and we can get to work."

"I'll arrange it," Camden agrees.

"We can work in my spell room," Claude offers. "I've long since wished to witness the magic of a dark faye. Your powers are said to be very unique and rather vast."

Kazimir nods once again. "Indeed. Aside from a naturalist, the spell also requires three other powerful sorcerers, and the black flame wielder, as I'll require her blood to bind the talisman to her power."

"Rune and I will be happy to help," Odelia says with a prim smile, though I think we all get the sense she isn't *happy to help*. She'd merely like to observe Kazimir just like Claude.

"I'll join too," Claire adds.

"Excellent," Kazimir says. "Let's get to it then. Witch doctor, please do lead the way."

I'm unsure how he can tell that Claude's a witch doctor; it's a title awarded to those with very specific training and dual heritage. Kazimir seems to be a magical being of great power; perhaps he can discern such things as a result of said power.

Wyatt hangs back with Saunders, Maddy, Cedrick, and Reyna, while the rest of us follow Claude through the castle to his little nook in one of the towers. His spell-casting room is made of two rooms; one larger, one smaller, with shelves filled with supplies and herbs built into the walls and taking up most available surfaces. In the center of the bigger room is a large wooden circular table, on which Kazimir places his bag before starting to draw out supplies. Jars filled with odd-looking herbs, some of which glow, glass vials with strange liquids, all of which glow, and several stones are set on the table. Then he picks through Claude's personal stores of spell ingredients, adding several to the mix, while Camden calls for a bar of gold to be brought up. Surprisingly, it takes less than half an hour for his order to be fulfilled. A servant brings in the bar of gold and places it on the table along with everything else.

Camden stays close to me as Kazimir makes preparations for the ritual. Even when Kazimir suggests that the room won't be suitable for non-magic wielders, Camden merely growls at him in warning, palming my waist and making it very clear that he is not leaving me alone.

The ritual is elaborate and takes several hours. All the ingredients have to be purified and set with specific intent one by one and then bound together. The gold is melted by a spell, melded with my blood, and then mixed with all the herbs and liquids in a quartz bowl.

Finally, for the last step, Kazimir tells me to hold out my hand over the table, citing that he'll need to pour the mixture over my wrist for the talisman to take shape properly and be molded into a cuff that'll stay on.

"Absolutely not," Camden growls possessively. "You are not pouring a boiling, molten mixture over my mate's hand. It'll burn her to the fucking bone; nobody gets to break her skin or harm her."

Kazimir appears as though he's holding back an eye roll. "Do you really think I'd wish your mate harm? I want this talisman to succeed as much as anyone, wolf, as I don't particularly fancy getting burned to a crisp when she lets out her fire. The liquid is bound with her blood; it will not harm her. It will merely take shape."

"From what I've observed so far, he should be right," Odelia interjects with a nod. "I've never seen this exact creation before, but talismans don't harm their wielders when bound with blood; it goes against their very magical essence. Nobody in this room wants to harm Sierra, Camden."

I squeeze Cam's shoulder. "It'll be fine."

Camden's hand drops to grip my hip and give it a squeeze. I can feel through the bond his sheer panic at the idea of any harm coming to me, but he manages to rein it in, though just barely. He gives me a nod, and I hold out my wrist over the table, stifling trepidation so that Camden doesn't feel it through the bond and put a stop to this prematurely.

Kazimir tips the bubbling bowl over my wrist. I wince preemptively, then feel my eyes widen when the liquid touches my skin, but only brings me the barest feeling of warmth, accompanied by a strange shift that takes place within me. I feel my fire roiling inside of me, rising to the surface, as the liquid wraps around my wrist and holds there rather than dripping down onto the table. My fire seems intrigued by this talisman and drawn to it; it rises to test it, and I feel a nearly seismic shift within me when the talisman grabs hold of my fire and redirects it back to me.

For the first time in months, my fire calms. It feels as though the power is finally under my call, rather than the call of its own rage. I let out a soft gasp at the sensation, and at the sight of the gold hardening onto my skin into what appears like a fashionable bracelet, shining and engraved with sigils that shimmer in the light of the room.

"I think...I think it's working," I breathe out, stunned.

I withdraw my wrist as Kazimir sets the bowl back on the table, running the fingers of my other hand over the cuff, which has now cooled. It's about two inches long and reminds me of the ancient jewelry I've read about in textbooks, molded by gold to fit the hands of kings and pharaohs, queens and empresses. It's *beautiful*, and the power emanating from it is very strong. Stabilizing too.

"Of course it is, I made it," Kazimir says bluntly.

Claire sighs. "Check the hubris, darkling, we still need to test it." Kazimir turns to look at her again, but she ignores him in favor of looking at me. "Why don't we try to train with it?"

Her offer is quiet and almost tenuous, two things I'm entirely unused to hearing from Claire, and I realize it's an apology of sorts. She wouldn't be making the offer to train with me if she hadn't gotten past my accidentally harming Cedrick. The look she gives me is contrite and though she doesn't offer a verbal apology, I don't entirely expect her to. Instead, she's doing something more meaningful by offering to literally put herself in the line of fire for me.

I feel a smile tug at my lips. "I'd like that."

Chapter Thirty-Seven

Training with Claire passes smoothly. For the first time in *months*, my fire is *finally* under my control. The only side effect is that I can't send out blasts farther than twenty feet, but I can now fashion the bursts of power in ways I haven't been able to before. I can send out concentrated streams, orbs, and even walls of it. I can summon it on command and push it back on command. I exhale a deep breath of relief upon the realization that my power is once again my own, bound with my sentience and consciousness. When I call on it too much, the cuff starts to heat up with warning, which is all I need to pull it back.

After an hour of practice in the woods surrounding the castle grounds, Claire walks with me back to the castle where we're due for a meeting with Kazimir in the courtyard. Evidently, he has spies spread out amongst the ranks of the triads, and he's awaiting a report on the latest troop movement from them.

"I'm sorry about the way I reacted to Cedrick," Claire tells me as we stroll together.

I'm surprised at the verbal apology since she's already given a better one by showing her trust in me once again.

"Don't be," I say. "I was furious with myself for losing control like that. I can't blame you for being furious with me as well. I went too far, got too angry, and Cedrick nearly paid for that with his life. That was very painful, as I've grown fond of him."

Claire nods. "I know that. I've seen that you two are good friends; I knew you'd never hurt him. My anger was more at myself and my own past than at you. I want to make that clear. After I miscarried quite some time ago, once I had gained control of my volcanic abilities and my power came out of its dormancy, it went raging, not unlike yours. It caused a great deal of harm, and seeing Cedrick hurt by a rogue power brought a lot of bad memories back for me. I felt horrible for giving you a verbal smackdown just hours later, when I was settling into the room in the house Camden's temporarily given us—well, castle, really, but that's beside the point. I wanted to apologize that night, but I was ashamed. Yesterday we were busy. So...now that we have a moment alone, I truly am sorry. I won't blame you for things you don't deserve blame for going forward."

I smile at her, humbled. I get the sense that Claire hasn't uttered many apologies in her life because she's fairly level-headed. She has plenty of attitude, but unlike Reyna, she keeps a lid on where and when she lets it loose.

"Thank you," I tell her. "Apology accepted."

She nods. "Good. Now, let's go see what that weird darkling has to say."

"The weird darkling seems to have a thing for staring at you," I comment. "I mean, *really* staring, like he's trying to stare into your soul or something."

"It's probably him sensing my volcanic powers," Claire says with a shrug. "Rumor has it faye are big on magical powers that have to do with nature, they're fascinated by them. Also, I'm fucking gorgeous, so of course he stares at me—who wouldn't?"

A startled laugh bursts out of me. "You definitely are."

Upon convening in the courtyard once again, which is becoming a regular meetup for the so-called top dogs of the species currently congregated in Kinrith, I immediately note the grim expressions on everyone's faces. Camden appears furious and deeply worried as he speaks rapidly to Wyatt and Claude, looking like he's doling out instructions. Odelia and Rune are conferring. Cedrick, Reyna, and Bane stand together, also talking quietly with furrowed eyebrows.

Camden pauses his conversation when he sees my approach, and when he waves me over, I go to him.

"What's going on?" I ask him, frowning at the worried expression on his face, along with the feeling of anxiety pulsing down our bond.

"It would appear that Kazimir's abandonment caused the triads to move up their plans of invasion," he says. "The darkling got word from his spies, and Odelia just received word from her tenuous allies, the sirens. Apparently, the triads are already making the voyage across the sea. Their ships are magical by design, very powerful, very fast. We'll try to sabotage as many of them as we can whilst they're vulnerable at sea, but most of them will make landfall within the next days. They'll start raping and pillaging coastal villages—thankfully, evacuations were already underway. We'll just need to speed things along and start making way for the coast immediately."

"Oh, dear gods," I murmur, fear taking hold of me at the thought of impending war coming much faster than we'd have hoped.

There's a significant difference between a few weeks and a few days...we've barely had any time to train our troops together. I just regained control over my fire with the help of the talisman. Leisel's work on her light summoning is good, but I don't know if it's good enough. She'll have to be on the battleground with us since the radius of her light even at full power is limited, and I'll constantly be worrying about her being in danger while fending off the reanimated corpses and skeletons Rhaelar will send our way.

"I'd like to cut them off before they're too far inland. There's a field a hundred miles in from the coast, bordering a large forest, that should do for battle—we'll have some geographical advantages," Camden says. "We need to go to the war room and start planning immediately; I'll be summoning my captains and commanders to get troop movements underway."

"Maddy can help teleport people to the battleground," Odelia says. "If we had the right materials here I could make a portal, but that isn't an option—we don't have the resources or time to gather them. We do have an amplifying talisman that will help Maddy teleport hundreds of people at once—close to a thousand. It'll be taxing on her, and she'll need at least twelve hours rest afterward, but theoretically, we can get all the troops, shifters and sorcerers alike, into position in a day."

"Another day to set up traps," Wyatt says. "I'd like to take care of as many enemy troops as possible before we meet in a battle."

"While you set those up we can have our people work on warding the coastline and affecting the weather and sea currents, so that the triads land in the correct place," Rune adds, nodding. "Perhaps the sirens would be willing to help us on that front. I'll reach out to their king. Once the course for the triads is set and we've executed whatever sabotage we can, we'll familiarize ourselves with the land and run trainings for the remainder of our time."

"We need to construct an absolutely safe space for Leisel," I blurt, unable to take my mind from my sister. "Her presence is a necessity, I understand this, but I can't just leave her out in the open. Wesley will insist on being there, both to protect Leisel and so that he can avenge his parents."

I already promised Wesley I'd allow him to participate in coming battles, and that he'd be the one to kill Rhaelar, though I didn't promise to let him be an *active* participant. If I can sequester him and Leisel away somewhere near the battle, where Leisel can help without being in the direct path of harm, I might actually be able to focus on the battle rather than being distracted by her. I can't stand the thought of any harm coming to her; she's too precious, and not just to me but to this very world.

Camden squeezes my shoulder. "Already thought of, Sierra. There's a stone tower on the end of the battlefield."

"Which can be reinforced with powerful wards," Odelia interjects. "We'll put the young witch and warlock there with a small guard of protectors. Even if the rest of us should fall, they will survive—I'll ensure it."

"As will I," I say resolutely, heart pounding in my chest.

In a way, it's almost cathartic to know that this war will be over so soon; win or lose, it'll have reached its conclusion within a matter of days. As long as Leisel and Wes survive the fallout, I'll be able to live, *or rest*, in peace. For months there have been minor battles; Rhaelar sending groups of his men to attack villages, attacking the Valley of Sorcerers, driving witches and warlocks from their homes, not giving us a moment's rest or reprieve...it's time to put an end to the madness.

"Will your counterparts in Sukarmir be joining the fight?" Kazimir asks Odelia. "The more magical creatures aiding us, the better our odds."

Odelia shakes her head. "No. They're focused on defending their own territory right now, for which I don't blame them."

Kazimir raises his eyebrows at that but doesn't press her for more details.

"We have a great deal of work to do," Camden comments. "Let's get to it."

While Camden and many of the higher-ups in the warrior shifter hierarchy, as well as elders in the sorcerer covens, convene in the castle's war room, I go to Leisel and Wesley, heart heavy as I deliver the news to them. There are several evacuated villages in proximity to the battle-field, which is where troops will be taken, and where we'll be heading to stay until battle.

Wesley, as expected, demands to be part of the action, though he's appeased when I tell him I need him to protect Leisel. Leisel, on the other hand, seems frightened but resolute in the role she has to play and the fact that her abilities are needed for even the faintest hope of survival. Throughout the entire exchange, I'm stuck fighting back tears, my heart heavy with worry for these two younglings that I adore beyond comprehension. I can't lose them. I hate putting them in harm's way, which is why I'll do everything in my power to keep them safe. I know I'll fight doubly as hard because I'll be fighting for them as much as anyone.

Leisel immediately insists on continuing to practice using her light with Wes. Evidently, the two serve as amplifiers to each other's powers, possibly due to them both being sorcerers birthed by the magic of this earth, possibly because their close friendship and emotional bond serve as a conduit of some sort for their power. Though I've made clear to Wes that he will not be entering battle or even utilizing his earth-shaking abilities during the fight, since an earthquake would affect our troops as much as the opposition, his presence will certainly help Leisel.

As I watch them go into Leisel's room to practice, Greta enters my chambers, facing me directly.

"Greta," I greet, feeling tired and weary, needing to join the gathering in the war room. "What can I do for you?"

"Your Majesty," she says with a bow of her head, before meeting my eyes. "I'd like to request your formal permission to be amongst Leisel and Wesley's protectors during the battle. The young princess and your ward have both grown to be quite dear to my heart. I have thirty years of experience alongside many warriors of this pack. I was a captain before I retired from war to be closer to Cara and joined the castle staff. I also believe very strongly not only in our cause but in you, along with His Majesty, the king. It would be an honor if you allow me to protect your young."

I'm momentarily dumbstruck by her words, her valiant and insistent offer to help that I truly wasn't anticipating. I never knew Greta was a warrior; she seems to be a natural nurturer. Then again I've noticed she is very big on discipline and etiquette, which might've come from her time with the Rockwell Pack's military.

"Of course," I tell her. "I would be most relieved to know someone as fierce as yourself is looking out for the children dear to both of our hearts."

Greta inclines her head. "I shall protect them with my life, having every willingness to give it if it will save them."

I nod, thanking her again before dismissing her to go confer with Cara, while internally thinking, *as will we all.*

* * *

The next two days are a blur of activity. Nearly a hundred thousand troops are teleported to villages surrounding the battlefield, leaving Maddy just about comatose as she sleeps off her exhaustion. There's a flurry of movement at all times. The forest bordering the battlefield is rigged with traps of all sorts. A team of sorcerers heads to the coast, setting about working to affect the weather and ensure that the triads only have one place to land. Apparently, the king of sirens also agrees to help from afar—though he won't declare for us and send troops to fight, he's willing to manipulate the ocean's currents in our favor *and* sink as many ships as he can.

When I'm not spending time with Wesley and Leisel in the two-story home they share with Wyatt and Greta, a place that reminds me of a larger version of the cabin I used to live in, I'm training my fire with Claire, testing the bounds of it.

I see incredible sights over those days. A group of dragon shifters in their dragon forms fly over the field—at least one is always in the air. We set up fire-wielding catapults on our side of the field. Metallurgists and blacksmiths work around the clock on creating enough weapons for everyone to wield.

On the third evening, we receive word that the triads are about a day's march away. They'll arrive at our location the following evening. Amazing strides have been made. The stone tower on the battlefield has been warded and reinforced to the extent that even dragon fire can't harm it. Sorcerer and shifter warriors—not just wolves, but all sorts of breeds of canines and felines—are making excellent progress in fighting alongside each other under Reyna and Saunders' tutelage, and yet it still feels as though we're vastly underprepared. It feels like the war is happening too soon, and my heart hasn't dropped below a racing speed from the moment I found out the battle was impending days ago.

It's late into the evening when I choke down dinner in the one-story home I share with Camden. I've already put Leisel and Wes to bed in their house with murmured reassurances that I only half-believe. Camden's out finalizing preparations with commanders. I've done my work for the day, so I pace the small living room of the cabin, pausing every so often to warm my hands by the fire. We're deep into winter now, with snow dusting the ground, and the biting chill takes a toll.

When the front door creaks open and Camden steps in side, I barely have the mind to pay him any attention—I'm too caught up in my thoughts and fears. I only stop pacing when Camden sets something down on the brown leather sofa, a long object wrapped in cloth, and says, "I have something for you."

I pause, turning to him, still feeling jittery with excess energy.

Camden lifts the cloth onto his lap, then slowly starts unwrapping it, revealing a *gorgeous* gleaming short sword, looking to be a perfect length for me. "I had the metallurgist create it specifically for you. Then both Odelia and Kazimir imbued it with spells and magics to make it extraordinarily powerful. I want you to have every advantage tomorrow."

I walk up to him, taking the offered sword, and step back before swinging it in an arc to get a feel for it. Good balance, remarkably aerodynamic, with gorgeous sigils engraved both into the leather-bound comfortable handle and along the length of the blade. This sword is a true work of art.

"Thank you, Camden," I manage to choke out, fighting back tears. "It's...it's beautiful. Truly. I'll wield it with pride."

He nods. "I know you will, and you'll wield it with an expertise that I'll admit surprised me. When we sparred yesterday, I didn't think you'd *actually* manage to put me on my ass with a blade to my neck."

I feel a smile pull at my lips. "You got a good few hits in as well."

"I have decades of training. You have a few months," Camden comments dryly. "It was an embarrassment to my skill, but it also brought me great pride. You're remarkable, Sierra." He pats his lap and

I set the sword on the mantle above the fireplace before climbing onto him and wrapping my arms around his neck to hold him close.

"We'll prevail," he tells me. "We have to. Our army symbolizes light and hope; the triads are darkness, death, and decay. We'll beat them."

"I certainly hope so," I murmur. "They have a goddamn necromancer and shadow wielder, Cam, and while we have a great force, they can replenish their numbers at any time. Reports from scouts say that Rhaelar's been stopping at graveyards and reanimating the dead as his men march; he will be prepared. Ernesh can create an unlimited number of shadow beings. There will be inevitable losses on our own side."

Camden rubs his nose against mine, clasping my waist tightly. "Everyone knows that," he agrees. "Losses are inevitable during war. You have to stay alive, though, Sierra. I can't lose the woman I love when I've just gotten her back. I wouldn't survive it."

My breath catches as I go stiff, staring at him with wide eyes. His proclamation of love is coming at a choice time, when we're both facing the possibility of death, and it both stuns and humbles me. This man, this warrior, Alpha and *King*, loves me. I can see it in his eyes, and I've been feeling it through the bond, but to hear the words...it's startling.

His lips quirk at my reaction. "Don't look at me like that, like you didn't know or this is a surprise. You're immensely clever. You must know I've loved you for some time." He shakes his head, almost ruefully. "I've loved you since the moment I set eyes on you in your cabin in Aesara, wild eyes and flaming cheeks, telling me to go fuck myself in a dozen different ways. I didn't know it yet, but that was the beginning of the end for me. I was awed when you fought Aspen, awed by your love for your sister, to the point where I would've done anything to bind us together. Losing you only made me realize how much I loved you, and I loved you even more for your capacity for forgiveness. I'm crazy when it comes to you, Sierra. I'm crazy *for* you. I need you. You make me the best version of myself, even when you're set on irritating and fighting me."

Now I can't stop the tears from gathering in my eyes and brimming over as I stare at him. "I love you too," I hear myself say, as if in a daze, speaking the truth I've known for longer than I care to admit. "I can't say I loved you for as long as you've loved me, but it's been longer than I realized. I love your unshakable confidence and the soft center that lies beneath. I love how you toiled for my forgiveness and readily admitted your faults, doing what it took to win me back. I love you more than words can describe for how you are with my family—*our* family. Leisel's come to adore you in a short time, and Wes both trusts and respects you. You're such a powerful, *good* leader to your people, but you're willing to concede your faults and work on them with me. I fucking love you, Camden. I won't ever stop. As much as you need me to survive, I need *you* to survive. Without you, I'd only live half a life for the sake of my sister and ward. With you, I feel so whole, so complete."

Camden leans forward to brush a kiss across my lips, and I think his eyes glimmer with the barest bit of moisture. What starts as a soft touch quickly morphs into a consuming kiss filled with passion and so much love. In no time at all, we've both shed our clothes, and I'm impaling myself along Camden's length, all the while staring so deeply into his eyes that it makes me feel painfully raw and vulnerable, but also powerful and strong. He makes me the strongest version of myself, the best version of myself. I ride him slowly at first, until he takes over the movements, driving into me hard and fast, leaving us both quaking with powerful orgasms.

"When we've won and when you're ready, I'm going to put a baby here," he tells me in the aftermath, rubbing a hand over my belly as we lie on top of the furs beneath the couch, basking in the warmth of the fireplace.

Teasingly, I say, "As long as we talk about it first." Then more seriously, "I want a family with you. I want to make our family bigger, and give Leisel and Wes more brothers and sisters. I want to raise our children in a better, safer, more harmonious world that we'll build together.

"I want that too," Camden says. "Very much. So much I burn with it. But I'll wait. I'll never betray your trust again, never push you into something again."

"I know," I tell him. "Our falling out ended up bringing us together, stronger than ever. I trust you in a way I never would've had I never left. I love you even more for it. We have to live tomorrow, so that we can continue making the world a better place."

"We will," he vows.

We must.

Chapter Thirty-Eight

"At least we chose a good place to battle," Reyna says, looking around the long stretch of the grassy field, easily a mile wide, with a forest bordering on the far side. "Nice and even ground, with a good vantage point for your sister."

I look up at the stone tower not far behind me, one I've been warding to the maximum with the help of Odelia in the last days. That's where Leisel and Wes are and that is where they will stay throughout the battle, safe from anyone grabbing or hurting them. Wyatt's up in the tower with them, along with about a dozen other warriors of both sorcerers and shifters for protection. Claire will also join them in the tower before battle commences. I can't stand the fact that Leisel's power is needed for this fight; if I had it my way, she would be tucked away in Kinrith, far from all the chaos and bloodshed that is bound to ensue.

"Don't remind me that my sister and ward are here," I mutter, craning my neck to glance up at the single opening at the very top of the tower, where Leisel will have a direct line of sight to the enemy and be able to wield her golden light to chase away the shadow beings created by Ernesh.

Even the opening in the stone is warded with all the possible protection so that nothing can penetrate the tower and harm my sister.

She is my priority during this battle as much as killing Rhaelar and Ernesh; I could live with myself if I left this battlefield tonight knowing that I failed to kill the enemy, but I could not live with myself if any harm were to come to Leisel or Wes.

I look around the tens of thousands of gathered warriors, comprised of many different covens of witches, the clan of dark faye that declared for our side to kill their rogue brethren, and the army of shifters. Many of the shifters are already in their animal forms; wolves, lions, and panthers roam the open field, while the half dozen dragons fighting for our cause are stationed further back, where they won't accidentally kill our troops by stepping in the wrong direction.

Reyna swings her glowing white sword around in a circle before sheathing it at her side. She checks the three daggers strapped to her waist, the ones on her upper arms, and even pats her boot where there's presumably yet another hidden dagger before giving a satisfied nod.

"Your sister and the boy will be fine," she tells me offhandedly. "In fact, if there are any of us who're actually safe right now, it's Leisel and Wesley. They have Wyatt, three of his best pack warriors, and six of the best warrior witches in the tower protecting them. Not to mention the circle of people stationed below at the entrance, who are under orders to die before allowing anyone to breach the structure. Which, by the way, you and Odelia have ensured is unbreachable."

I shake my head irritably. "It's not enough. There's no guarantee of safety during battle."

I spot Odelia walking closer, weaving her way through dozens of people on her way to Reyna and me. She stops in front of me and puts her hand on my arm, her brows creased with worry. Her eyes drop to the golden cuff on my wrist before raising her gaze to meet my own.

"Are you ready?" she asks me.

I nod. "As I'll ever be."

She gives a half-hearted smile. "Good, because they're almost here. Claude said the army of vampires, darklings, and hybrids are on their way, marching about two miles south. It's only a matter of time before they arrive."

I blow out a long breath, trying to fortify and prepare myself as much as I can.

"You remember what we discussed?" I ask Odelia. "If things go badly, get Leisel and Wes away from here. Don't waste time saving me if I'm down; protect my kids. They're who really matter."

Odelia's lips thin. She's not happy about my request—no, *demand*—that my sister and ward's protection comes above my own, likely because it's not in the nature of a high priestess to leave any of her witches behind. I'm not giving her a choice though. The children come before me, no questions asked. End of story.

After a long moment of staring at me, Odelia inclines her head in reluctant agreement. Then she stalks off, probably to check on other witches before battle commences.

Bane cracks his neck loudly in the row of people in front of me, then turns around to shoot Reyna a bloodthirsty smile. "I'm about to even our score. By the end of tonight, I'll have killed more enemies than you."

A slow, diabolical smile spreads on Reyna's lips. "Is that so? Do you want to bet on it?"

"Now is not the fucking time to place bets, kids," Claire says loudly.

Reyna pouts. "You're no fun, Mom."

"And you never got past hormonal puberty, but you don't see me throwing judgement," Claire shoots back. "Fuck this noise, I'm going to the tower. I'll come down if it looks like you really need me, since Leisel and Wes are up to their ears with protectors. Try to stay alive, bitches."

Bane chuckles while Reyna throws her head back and roars with laughter, drawing several irate glances from the people surrounding us.

"Everyone assume positions and get ready to fight," Odelia calls out. "They're here."

I push through the people crowded in front of me, positioning myself so I can glimpse the far end of the field where the forest starts. I startle when someone behind me grabs my arm, only to relax when Camden's familiar scent envelopes me. He steps up beside me, releasing my arm in favor of cupping the back of my neck and pulling me towards him for a light gentle kiss.

"I wish I'd locked you up in Kinrith's dungeon," he says quietly, lips brushing against mine. "That way, you wouldn't be in danger right now."

I feel the exact same way about my sister. Unfortunately, we're both needed to end this war once and for all. Only my fire can fight the army of corpses Rhaelar has raised. Likewise, only Leisel's golden light can combat the darkness and danger of the shadows wielded by Ernesh. We have to be here, even though I'd much rather not put both myself and my sister at risk. I'd also rather not put Camden at risk, but that isn't an option as he's king of one of the fighting species.

"You should shift into your wolf," I reply, my voice soft. "I can feel the triads getting closer. It's time, Cam."

He exhales a long, shuddering breath, giving a nod. He gives me one last passionate kiss before releasing me. A moment later, he strips out of his clothes and shifts into his wolf, who gives a chuff before rubbing against my leg and butting his big head against my stomach, seeking a bit of affection from me as well before the battle commences. I only have time to give his furry ear a quick scratch before I see figures starting to emerge from the forest. The orbs of light that have been conjured over the field illuminate the enemy as a dozen people step out of the trees, followed by another dozen, and another. Slowly, hundreds, then *thousands* of figures make their way onto the field, all marching forward in step, the echoes of their boots hitting the frozen grass, traveling across the field, and reaching us.

I tense in preparation, flexing my fingers by my side and summoning my flames to the surface. The downside of the cuff I wear is I can only use so much of my black flame at once; the amount I can wield in a single blast is finite, which means I need to reserve it for living beings only when they're close enough, but conserve most of it for the dead. That's why I'm also armed with a sword, dagger, and a few smaller blades for throwing. Moreover, I'm fully prepared to utilize the battle magic I learned from Reyna and Cedrick, though I know battle magic is taxing, so I need to use it carefully. Most of my magical energy needs to be retained for the use of my fire to destroy the dead.

As if on cue, I hear the familiar groans and wails of corpses, a noise I've learned to associate with the bodies Rhaelar reanimates and directs with a mere thought. There are also the clacking sounds of the bodies so decomposed they're little more than skeletons. It's Rhaelar's power alone that drives the dead. Without him directing them, they'd return to their inanimate state instantly, which is why I know he'll be well protected. Getting to him would significantly deplete his forces. Likewise, killing Ernesh would rid any shadows that'll be aiding their army, so I have no doubt he'll stay at the very back of his troops, as well, giving him leave to conjure as many shadow beings as he pleases without risking his own neck.

Fucking cowards.

I crack my knuckles as the army marches closer, seeing that the dead are intermixing with the living, emerging onto the front lines and walking side-by-side with the triads, vampires, and darklings.

Reyna shoulders through our troops until she's beside me again. "You better stay alive, Sierra. Without you, we're fucked. You should be up in the tower with your sister."

I shake my head. "My blast radius is contained—I need to be on the field to reach as many enemies with my fire as I can."

She gives an annoyed glance at my cuff. "You should take that fucking thing off."

"Which would risk killing almost everyone on our side of the battle, so I'll pass," I tell her.

The warriors surrounding us shift into the formation we'd agreed upon earlier in the day, enveloping me with protection on all sides, while still giving me a clear line of sight to the enemy with a small gap in front of me that I can use to send out my fire safely. I tense up further as the men at the front of the enemy lines abandon their march and break out into runs; some of them are living, others are corpses and skeletons wielding weapons. I feel my heart pound in my chest as I focus in on the dead. The living should be taken care of by those around me—I can worry about them if they get close enough to harm me.

Once the first group of corpses is within reach of my fire, I extend my hand and let a blast of the black flame roll off of me, instantly incinerating four dead men grouped together, also clipping a few living men surrounding them, all of whom fall with cries of agony as my flames eat through their flesh.

At the same time, several dozen of my troops run forward to meet the enemy, keeping them away from the tower. The witches and warlocks throw spells that create a kaleidoscope of colors across the battlefield, instantly killing their enemies, and sending blood spraying across the grass. I spot three wolves tearing into their opponents with marked ease, growling and snapping and barking. Warriors in human form—both witches, darklings, and shifters alike—raise their swords and start hacking away at the enemy, also utilizing magic. The sound of steel meeting steel echoes in the air, and a mounting sense of trepidation raises the hairs on the back of my neck as the true fight begins.

It's gory, dismal, and terrifying. Body parts fly through the air, blood stains everyone in the thick of the battle, and the sounds of the wails of the reanimated dead combined with the cries of living beings dying create a cacophony of noises that feel like a cheese grater against my ear drums. I focus on sending out concentrated blasts of fire at the dead; the living are cut down before they can near me by the group of warriors surrounding me. My protectors are well trained and well instructed to keep the action away from me while giving me room to do what I must.

Overhead, half a dozen magnificent forms of dragons fly. They spit fire onto enemy troops, lighting up the night with brilliant flashes of orange and red, though they can only take out so many people at once. The roars of the beasts and the fire they breathe overshadows the shrieks from both the living and dead.

Wisps of shadows start pouring through the enemy lines—small tendrils at first that quickly come together and form shadow beings that can kill with a mere touch or swipe of their jaggedly sharp, amorphous limbs. A blast of light comes from the tower above me, and an inhuman wail sounds as the shadows at the forefront wither and die. Like everyone else here, Leisel's doing her part. Unlike everyone else, she's working from a somewhat safe distance, which is one of the few things keeping me sane.

I barely catch a glint of steel flying towards me as one of the enemy combatants, a vampire judging by his red eyes, manages to bash his way through the warriors surrounding me, aiming his sword for my throat. I duck down to avoid the blow, then wince as his warm blood splatters on my face and the scraggly vamp keels over.

I look up in time to see Reyna pull her sword from his back, mutters, "Spineless motherfucker." A moment later her sword slashes through his neck, severing his head to ensure he's dead before she's back to fighting full-force, not even giving me a chance to thank her.

The formation of battle-hardened warriors around me starts to splinter and split as more and more enemies make it through the front lines to us, though my protectors don't stray too far—just far enough to keep our opponents from getting to me. Several of them are taken down in the action, each of the fallen causes a pang through my chest, but that only hardens my resolve to stay alive to avenge them.

I spot a group of a dozen skeletons preying on a group of wolves and a lion not far away, through a cluster of fallen people to my left. They're too far away to hear if I tell them to duck, so I send out a burst of power that flattens them to the bloodstained ground, followed by a blast of fire that incinerates the skeletons.

Searing pain explodes across my waist as a shadow being manifests directly beside me, driving a jagged, knife-like arm along my flesh. A blast of light from above destroys it, but blood from my wound blooms to stain the side of my shirt. The injury isn't catastrophic and the battle adrenaline mostly does away with the pain, so I ignore it. If I survive tonight, I'll have one of the witches heal me after the fight's over. I won't impose on Leisel, who'll be using up a great deal of magic to subdue the shadows.

I unsheathe the sword hanging at my side as a battalion of armed vampires breaks through the line of people protecting me, running at me full pace. Reyna once again appears beside me, as if summoned.

"Let's see the skills I taught you put to good use," she says before swinging her sword in an arc to cut through two enemies at once, laughing like a maniac as their blood sprays onto her.

I raise my sword to block a strike of a man directly in front of me, then duck down and swipe my blade at his legs, cutting one of them clean off in a move Reyna taught me. I think I hear her call out, *nice,* but it's drowned out by the sound of shouts, screams, wails, and laughter from those who find battle more of an enjoyable sport than a last resort.

Two enemies fall upon me at the same time, just as an airborne assault comes at me; I leap to the side to avoid a dagger that flies directly at my head, then take one of my own throwing knives from my belt and return the favor, sending the blade sailing through the air and feeling a shot of pleasure as my blade sinks into the forehead of the darkling with pointed ears who tried to take me down with her dagger. *Turnabout's fair play.* I spin in a circle and strike out with my sword, cutting through the two men swinging at me before their strikes can make contact, and feel satisfaction as their bodies hit the ground. Spotting another man running at me, I take him out with a simple tactile spell that blows him to pieces.

A much larger unit of dead men, this one two dozen strong, close in on Reyna and Bane to the left of me, who are now fighting side by side, both laughing. I sheathe my sword, leap over half a dozen bodies, and shove both Reyna and Bane out of the way before sending out a crackling stream of my black fire that cuts the corpses and skeletons in half. It doesn't incinerate them, but it does incapacitate them, which is good enough for now.

I strain to look at the far end of the field, trying to catch a glimpse of Rhaelar. I might not be able to direct my fire to him this far away, but if I can find where he is, I can start fighting my way over to him and kill one of the two driving forces in this battle.

"Watch out!" Reyna's shout comes a moment too late as white-hot pain explodes on my thigh—I look down to see a crackling orb of red magic eating its way through my pants and flesh, sizzling and popping and blistering painfully like nothing I've felt before. I whip my head around to locate who sent the orb; my eyes lock onto a hybrid with violet eyes, who's baring his teeth with victory while staring at my thigh. I return the favor of his orb by sending one of my own careening through the air towards him; the difference between his orb and mine is that my orb, made of my fire, incinerates him the moment it touches his chest, burning through him and turning him into a pile of ash that flutters through the air to dust the ground.

Just then, I see a flash of silver hair and glowing silver-red eyes. My attention sharpens and hones in on Rhaelar, who isn't on the far end of the battlefield as I expected him to be; he's steadily making his way through his troops, moving closer to me and mine. The fucker probably wants to be the one to take me down. While I'd love to be the one to kill him, I promised Wesley that I'll do everything in my power to reserve the kill for him unless there's no other option. I narrow my eyes as he kneels on the grass amidst the chaos and presses his hands to the ground.

Beneath our feet, the ground starts to rumble and shake, like it would with an earthquake. It only takes me a moment to recognize the action for what it is; he's raising more dead men, right here, pulling from the bones and bodies buried beneath our feet. Piles of dirt and grass start to explode upward at too many points on the field to count as new corpses and skeletons are reanimated by his power, clawing their way from the ground. These ones are fresher, livelier, and more powerful. Even worse, many of the fallen who've died through the course of this battle are *also* reanimated, rising to their feet and instantly starting to attack the living people surrounding them. None of the dead on my side are reanimated due to a protective spell Odelia cast in the last days, but many slain enemies are once again back on their feet, fighting and killing with unparalleled vigor. A blast of blue, crackling magic flies out from someone on my side of the battle and hits Rhaelar squarely in the chest, sending him sailing backwards and crashing into the animated corpses of his own making. At the same time, more and more shadow beings start to form all over the place, reinforcing the fallen enemy troops and cutting through the people on my side of the battle with ridiculous ease.

A *blinding* flash of light comes from the tower, so bright and intense I have to squeeze my eyes shut for a moment. When I open them, I see that most of the shadow beings have dissipated, once again courtesy of my *incredibly* talented sister.

I look around the field, taking in those on my side of the fight, my heart dropping to my stomach when I see just how many of them are dead. Bodies of witches, warlocks, and shifters alike litter the ground in great numbers—I even spot a slain dragon lying on the far side of the field. Our losses are not as great as the number of dead enemies, but too godsdamned many nonetheless. I spot Claire not far behind me, having joined the battle; she's on the ground with a horrible wound in her chest seeping blood. Above her is *Kazimir*, and I catch a brief glimpse of him biting into his wrist before holding it to Claire's lips, feeding her his blood, which must have some sort of healing properties. *This needs to end now.*

Rhaelar's fifty feet away from me, having gotten back to his feet, and surrounded by his own men. He looks pale though, as if weakened by his trick of reanimating the dead from the very ground beneath our feet—a flash of hope bursts through me as I recall Kazimir telling me that Rhaelar could lose his necromancy if he draws on too much of it at once.

Before I can start forging a path towards Rhaelar though, he turns around and disappears into his troops, clearly valuing his own life far more than that of his men. I don't bother chasing after him because the dead start to override the living, surrounding me and mine from all sides. I send out stream after stream, blast after blast, orb after orb of my fire, feeling the cuff on my wrist start to burn with the amount of power I'm expending. I'm pushing against the limits of what I can safely do, which the pain radiating from my cuff tells me.

I look around, trying to catch sight of Camden's wolf to ensure he's okay. He's about thirty feet to the right of me, his dark fur stained even darker with blood, which also drips from his gleaming white fangs as he tears through every enemy in his path with impressive skill and vigor.

The ground starts to tremble again, and I tense in preparation for more dead men rising, only that's not what happens. Instead, a thick black fog rolls across enemy lines—not the tendrils or wisps that usually precede shadow beings forming, but a single continuous fog that spreads to cover nearly the entire field. Golden light once again comes from the tower, but this time, it's not enough to dissipate the shadows entirely; there are simply too many of them. Those shadows quickly start forming into amorphous creatures in all different shapes and sizes that make easy work of cutting through my men and women. Three additional blasts of light from the tower manage to clear most of the beings within a thirty-foot radius of the tower, but not nearly all of them. More and more keep coming, just as the dead keep rising, killing more and more of my people. I wince as I look at the fallen, feeling my heart pang.

I unsheathe my sword, using a combination of blade, magic, and flame to start cutting my way through enemy lines, trying to get within reach of either Rhaelar or Ernesh. If I can kill at least one of them, I can even the odds. Without prompting, Reyna and Bane both join behind me, covering my back and sides, swords clashing and magic flying to protect me. I don't get more than ten feet forward before a sharp pain stabs through my back, cutting through muscles and tendons and coming out the front of me. That blow feels like it takes most of the strength from me, and I look down at myself, expecting to see a knife, only to see a wispy, smoky shadow that disappears as quickly as it cut through me.

Chapter Thirty-Nine

I drop to one knee, the noises around me becoming muted as blood starts to pour from the wound. A glimpse of black fur precedes Camden's wolf tearing through people on his way to me, getting to my side, just as I fall forward onto my hands. A gurgled cough escapes me, and blood sprays from my mouth and onto my hands, staining my skin with red splatters. *Oh, fuck.*

Camden's wolf whines loudly, butting its head gently against my shoulder. I can feel the anxiety and fear radiating off of him as he stares at my wound, his agony at seeing me like this pulsing through our bond, looking entirely lost. His distraction costs him greatly; an enemy manages to make it past Reyna and Bane, and a blood-coated sword cuts into Camden's flank. That gesture infuriates me, which gives me *just* enough strength to send out a wave of fire that levels all of the enemies on Camden's side, leaving a ten-foot span of ashes and dust littered over bloodstained grass and trampled ground. That saps what little strength is left in me, and I watch with blurry vision as a dark puddle of my own blood starts to form beneath me. My vision dims, my body sways, and I understand with a dark certainty that the wound in my torso is very much a deadly one. The wound on Camden's wolf isn't though—the wolf turns his head to the sky, howls with despair, and then runs to my right to tear through the people cutting a path toward me.

Another blast of light, the brightest one yet, briefly robs me of what little vision I have left. This one feels like it lasts much longer than the others, and for the briefest moment, I have to wonder if I'm dead, being transported to whatever afterlife awaits me. Then, a small, warm, all-too-familiar hand clutches my arm, telling me that I'm still very much alive. I manage to crack my eyes open, seeing my worst fears confirmed when my sister kneels in front of me, placing her free hand on my stomach. Golden light blasts from her, doing away with many of the shadows closing in on us from all sides. Only a small bit of healing warmth trickles from her to me though, meaning she's focusing most of her energy on holding the shadows at bay, as she should.

I don't have the time or energy to ask how the fuck she got down here or yell at her to go away; instead, I push her behind me and shield her with my body just as a sword comes swinging toward me, burying into my shoulder instead of slicing through her, sending yet another round of explosive pain through me. The man wielding it abruptly drops to his knees, a blade protruding from the center of his chest, revealing Reyna, wearing a sneer as she pulls her own sword from his back in a classic *her* move.

"What the hell is the little healer doing here?" she hisses.

"*Protect her*," I croak. With the gurgled words, blood pours from my mouth, rushing down to join the blood spilling from my shoulder and chest.

I feel Leisel's hand clutch my wrist, right over my cuff, and a small warmth precedes the cuff snapping off, falling to the frosty ground with a clatter. Anxiety fills me to the brim, along with the sheer exhilaration stemming from the sort of power I haven't felt since first putting the cuff on; volatile, uncontrollable, *dangerous* power—stronger than it was even before the cuff.

"What the fuck?" I gasp, shifting behind me to look at my sister. Bane stands at her back, fighting off people, while Reyna protects us from the front. I groan as my fire starts to rile within me, trying to break through, and I use everything I can to keep it down because if it comes out, it will vaporize Reyna, Bane, *and Leisel* along with every living and dead being on this battlefield. Only I'll be left alive.

"Do you trust me?" Leisel asks, staring directly at me with wide golden eyes that are brimming with a strange conviction.

"You shouldn't *be here*," I hiss back, at once wanting to throttle her and do whatever it takes to protect her. More blood sputters from my lips and drips down my chin with the words.

Her voice rising, she repeats, *"Do you trust me?"*

"Of course!" I snap. Before I can tell her to get the fuck out of here, save herself, and get away from the single most dangerous spot on the battlefield, she shifts so she's kneeling right beside me and takes my hand in hers. The power steadily unfurling within me, driven by the unchecked power of my black flame, takes on a quality I've never felt before. The innately violent and bloodthirsty nature of my flames shifts, turning into something I can't quite comprehend but know is entirely foreign, and not all coming from me. When I glance down at our connected hands, I see a golden glow moving from Leisel's hand and traveling through my body, spreading up my arm and into my chest. It's not her healing power though; it's something entirely different.

"Let your fire out," Leisel says. "Trust me."

I don't think I could stop the flames from coming out even if I tried, but I let go of the tenuous hold I'm trying to keep on them and release them. A mixture of flames that are as much gold as they are black burst out from me *and Leisel* at the same time, forming an explosion that travels outward from us in a frightening storm of intensity and vigor, spreading and expanding until they're covering the entirety of the field, encompassing all of my people along with every single enemy.

I look to Leisel in shock as fire that doesn't just belong to me but to her as well reigns, barely able to comprehend what's happening. Warmth expands within me and I look down, feeling sheer amazement as the wound in my chest, as well as that on my shoulder, thigh, and side start to tingle and seal over, healing.

"What are you doing?" I whisper to Leisel.

Though she shouldn't be able to hear me over the racket of flames emanating from both of us and the screams and shouts of people dying all across the field, she responds, "What we're meant to."

The flames recede, disappearing, just as Leisel goes limp, eyes rolling into the back of her head. I shift beneath her to catch her body as she falls, feeling panic overwhelm me until I see the steady rise and fall of her chest that tells me she's alive, just rendered unconscious by the cosmic level of power we both just let out.

Warily, I look up and around, tensing in preparation to see the inevitable; everyone dead, my people and the enemies, only to gasp when I see that's not the case *whatsoever.* Reyna and Bane are still on their feet, looking as shocked as I expect I do. It's not just them; every witch, warlock, darkling, and shifter on my side of the battle who hadn't already fallen to the enemy is still somehow alive. Camden is still in wolf form far to the left of me, side by side with Wyatt who must've come down from the tower at the same time Leisel did. Everyone alive exchanges puzzled, dazed glances with each other, blinking blearily. I turn my eyes to the opposite side of the field, only to feel my breath catch to see that there *is* no enemy left, only piles of ashes, black threaded through with glowing gold, covering the field almost like a blanket of snow might. There are no shadows left, meaning Ernesh perished along with every single one of his comrades. There is only one figure left alive, wading through piles of ashes, bleeding profusely, his silver hair stained red with blood, as well as black and gold from ashes. He appears dumbfounded and stunned as he stumbles around, unsteady on his feet, looking in every direction, probably seeking aid that no longer exists.

"Reyna," I say, my voice calmer than I might've expected. "Take Leisel."

For once, Reyna doesn't snark or ask questions; she sheathes her sword at her side, closes the distance between us, and kneels on the ground beside me, taking Leisel from my arms and cradling my sister in her own, brushing Leisel's hair from her forehead.

"Silly little witch," she mutters. "Could've gotten yourself killed."

I spot Wyatt's wolf running across the field, making his way to Leisel. He gets to us in a matter of seconds, then drops to the ground right beside Leisel, resting his head on his paws right next to her and letting out a low whine.

I push my way to my feet, still feeling somewhat unsteady. Whatever magic-melding just took place with Leisel and I might've mostly healed my wounds, but blood loss and expending untold amounts of power have both taken their toll on me. I'm pretty sure the sole reason I didn't pass out, like Leisel, is my protective instinct towards her.

I slowly start walking across the field, my steps somewhat fumbled as I make my way towards Rhaelar, feeling the anger at all he's cost the population of witches and shifters fuel me. Rhaelar must hear me coming because he spins to face me, his expression aghast as he takes me in, eyes flicking between the ashes, all the living people on my side, and me. Something tells me there's a reason the fire didn't kill him; I still have my vow to keep. I promised him not long ago that I would destroy him.

Rhaelar stumbles back at my approach, tripping over a particularly tall pile of ash and falling flat on his back. He looks surprisingly weak and even pathetic without armies of dead and the evil living surrounding him for protection. He already raised all the corpses nearby; there's nothing left for him to reanimate, and by the looks of it, he tapped all the reserves of his borrowed necromancy power, leaving him power*less*. On his own, without his magic, he's useless. That thought gives me more satisfaction than it should.

Just as he manages to push to his knees, I stop beside him and grab a fistful of his dirty silver hair, using it to yank him upright. "Remember what I told you the last time we met?" I ask him, my tone strangely calm.

He stares up at me with wide, terrified eyes, attempting and failing to shake his head under my grip. "No. No, no, no, no, *no!*"

"You really are just another spoiled king without your men and your power, aren't you?" I ask him, tutting faintly. "Just as well. It makes keeping my word all the easier."

I hold up my free hand, watching as a crackling orb of black fire forms in my palm. My power is no longer rogue—the magical melding I did with my sister has somehow altered it. Rhaelar opens his mouth again to protest but before he can speak or I can shove the orb down his throat, I hear Wesley call out, "Sierra."

I pause, letting the orb dissipate in my hand, looking across the field to Wesley. He's meant to be up in the tower with Leisel, but since the battle's over, he must've come down. He's staring at Rhaelar with so much hatred and anger in his eyes that it prickles at my chest and reminds me that Rhaelar isn't my kill. He's Wesley's; I promised Wes as much. I also vowed to Rhaelar that I'd destroy him, which I have; his army's dead, his followers are dead, and he's tapped of all power. Letting Wesley kill him won't break my word to either of them. Instead, it'll fulfill my promises—Rhaelar will still be dying at my hands, but the killing blow doesn't belong to me.

Wesley quietly walks across the field towards me and Rhaelar, who's trembling more and more in my grip, shaking with fear of his impending doom. Wesley stops in front of us and I use my free hand to take the long dagger still strapped to my waistband, my last remaining weapon, and hand it to Wes.

"Don't do this, *please*," Rhaelar begs, looking between me and Wesley with wide, terrified eyes. "I can teach you both things you'd have never fathomed. I'll give you power you can't imagine."

I tighten my grip on Rhaelar's hair, pulling his head back further, arching his back. "We have all the power we need, vampire. It might be my village you destroyed, but I've already settled that score by killing your last living brother. It's Wesley's parents you decapitated. Your life is his to take, as promised."

Rhaelar opens his mouth, probably to bargain or plead more, but Wesley slices my dagger across Rhaelar's neck in a lightning-fast move, cutting off any last words and severing the vampire king's head. I release Rhaelar's head, which falls to the ground, a moment before his body follows.

Wes hands my dagger back to me, and stares down at Rhaelar's body for a long moment, tears filling his eyes. Then he promptly leaps over Rhaelar's corpse and throws his arms around me in a tight hug. I hug him back, stroking my hand through his hair, feeling my heart pang as his tears soak through my shirt.

"Mari and Parker will be able to rest in peace now, knowing their son has grown into a strong warrior who avenged them," I murmur to him. "You did your duty, to them and to yourself. You're finally done, Wes. Now your life's purpose is yours alone."

Camden walks across the field towards us, back in human form, wounded in several places, partially limping as he makes for me. Keeping an arm wrapped around Wesley, I steer us away from Rhaelar's corpse and to Camden, meeting him halfway.

He sweeps me into his arms in a bone-crushing hug, then releases me to look down at Wes who swallows and holds out a hand for Camden to shake. Cam's lips curl up into a smile, and he takes Wes into his arms in a strong embrace, surprising both me and Wesley at the paternal gesture.

"You did very well," he murmurs to Wesley, as Wes's arms slowly come around him, hugging him back. "I've no doubt your parents would be very, *very* proud."

They would indeed. When Camden releases Wes, he musses the young boy's hair. "Now go join the others fussing over Leisel—you've earned yourself a break." Wes nods and walks off.

Once again, Camden grabs me and holds me close. "Never, *ever* scare me like that again," he growls in my ear, though there's a hoarseness and lingering fear in his voice. "I thought you were done. You were dying in front of my eyes. Then Leisel appeared, and I thought I'd fail to protect you *both*. I would've followed you to the grave, Sierra. Where you go, I follow."

I give a watery laugh. "Good thing we're both okay then. Let's get you healed up—you've got a lot of wounds."

"Once I'm healed and the kids are settled, I hope you know I'll be fucking you until you know not to scare me like that ever again."

I bite my lip, feeling my heart burst with joy and love. "I look forward to it."

Epilogue

It takes weeks for the army of warriors to disperse, each heading back to their respective packs on whichever continent they came from. Rain washes the carnage away from the battlefield. Leisel sleeps for two entire days and nights before waking as strong as ever; only once she does do I finally fall asleep, also staying nearly comatose for close to two days. The witches start looking for a new home in the northern lands and the darklings also search for a place to settle, though I suspect they intend to stay close to the witches, as they're both species born from magic.

I grow closer to Camden each day, and our bond continues to stay strong. Greta enjoys a heartwarming reunion with Cara and receives a medal from Camden for her service in protecting the royal children. Samuel comes to visit with Lana, Korbin, and little Galantia, who Leisel delights in playing with. For the first time in distant memory, harmony takes hold. It's not a total harmony; there are still some stray factions of vampires and darklings who might pose problems, but it's greater harmony than what's been experienced in quite some time. There truly is nothing to make peace more desirable than a horrifying, realm-wide-threatening war.

The news of the war ending, and the unbelievable power Leisel and I are capable of when we work together, spreads across the continent.

The king of Sirens sends a letter to me, Camden, Rune, and Odelia, informing us that he was happy to help drown some of Rhaelar's ships in a whirlpool, reminding us of the aid he offered, and inviting us to meet him during a festival he's throwing in our honor in a month's time.

After the witches saved so many wolves during the Battle of Triads, as the battle that ended the war is now being called, Aspen slinks away from Kinrith, deciding to roam for a while in hopes of finding her mate. The dissent she attempted to sew amongst shifters and sorcerers is put to rest by the indisputable way the sorcerers fought side by side with shifters, protecting one another fiercely. Before returning to their homes in warmer lands, the leader of the dragon shifters formally introduces himself to Odelia, thanking her for her valor in battle.

Camden and I spend every night together, along with most days, loathe to be apart. Leisel, Wesley, and Wyatt join us in the mornings for breakfast and evenings for dinner, and our nights are often concluded with trips to the library. I revel in the time spent with the family, revel in the time I get with Camden, especially late at night when we spend long, passionate hours together. As I find out three weeks after the battle, the nights might be a little *too* passionate, when Odelia confirms a suspicion I've been having, coinciding with cycles of unpleasant nausea in the morning and bouts of unusual sentimentality.

Late into the evening after my startling conversation with Odelia, I lie with Camden, entwined together in our bed sheets. My head rests on his chest and our legs are tangled. One of his arms is slung under me, cupping my bare hip, while the other hand runs up and down my shoulder. We both alternate in staring at the ceiling and staring at each other. I feel connected to him at my very core, with the knowledge that our connection is about to strengthen even more.

"You seem lost in thought," Camden murmurs, the pillow rustling beneath his head as he shifts to look down at me. "Everything alright?"

"Mhm," I hum with a nod. "Very much so. I do have a bit of news for you, though."

His eyebrows lift. "Oh?"

I crane my neck up to look at him, feeling my heartbeat speed up. "We're...we're going to be parents."

His brows furrow. "Is that your way of telling me you want me to officially adopt Wesley into the royal family? I can certainly do that, but I think he's a bit old for us to be considered his *parents*—"

"No, Cam," I say, taking his hand on my shoulder and sliding it down to rest on the flat of my stomach. "I mean we're going to be *parents*."

He blinks several times before going entirely still, eyes widening. Then, with a shake of his head, he says, "No, I would've scented that, and you're taking drafts to prevent it—"

"The drafts are exactly what prevent you from scenting it—you should be able to in a day or so. Apparently, they're only effective if the witch consuming them actually wishes for them to work, which is a loophole I didn't know. Their potency can be subverted by a witch's will." When Camden continues staring at me in frozen shock, I grow nervous. "I didn't *mean* to get pregnant—I know we decided to wait, but I guess some part of me wanted the full package. A baby, a bigger family...all of it." When he still doesn't talk or move or even *breathe*, I finally murmur, "Are you...not happy?" After all, the last time he got me pregnant it was intentional and he *hid* it from me, but I guess he might've realized that he's not ready to have children—

"Are you sure?" His words are barely audible, though his grip on me turns steel-like, and I can feel his heart hammering away in his chest.

"Positive," I tell him. "Odelia confirmed it earlier." After a pause, I ask hesitantly, "Are you...okay with that?"

My words seem to snap him out of his stupor. He sits up, then lifts me into his arms, making me squeal, and sits me squarely on his lap, chest to chest.

"I'm fucking *thrilled*, Sierra," he says, with such jubilance in his voice I can't doubt it. One of his hands splays on my belly, and the look in his eyes as he stares at me is a mixture of reverence and awe. "You're carrying my baby."

"Our baby," I murmur with a nod. "Yes. It's very early—two or three weeks at most—but...it's happening. Odelia's going to mix me up some drafts that should help everything move along smoothly—"

Camden cuts me off by crashing his lips to mine in a heated kiss that takes my breath away, before pulling his lips away, breathing harshly, and resting his forehead against mine. "We're going to have a child. That *we* made."

"We are," I say, feeling my heart practically burst with love for this man, and the baby slowly growing inside me.

"I hope it's a girl," he says. "With her mother's hair and eyes and incredible powers. I want more little versions of you running around the castle, driving the staff up the wall."

I laugh. "Girl or boy, they'll most likely be hybrids. The powers of a witch and shifter—incredibly heightened senses and powerful magic. They'll truly bring our kinds together in a way nothing else ever could."

"Fuck our kinds," Camden mutters. "They'll bring *us* together. They'll bring the whole world together if they're half the diplomat that their mother is."

I brush my lips over his again. "As long as they're strong and healthy, that's all I care about. The rest will come."

"The rest will come," Camden agrees, staring at me with glittering eyes. "We're really in for an adventure now, aren't we?"

"Undoubtedly," I assure, feeling my lips quirk.

Despite the twisting, winding path that's taken us to this moment in space and time, a path filled with thorns and traps and so much pain, I couldn't be more pleased with the outcome. I'd take all the heartache a million times over knowing it'd lead me here, into the arms of the man I love, carrying our child. This truly is a fate worth fighting for.

Afterword

Thank you so much for reading A Court of Mythics and Magic. If you enjoyed it, please leave a review. Your support will help me grow as an author, reach new readers, and will mean the world to me.

If you'd like to connect with other readers and me, please join my Facebook group, Rose Gravestone's Readers: https://www.faceboo k.com/groups/397068176443890/

In my reader group, I take reader's opinions into account when deciding which characters/ stories I'll write next. Come tell me what you'd like to see!

About the author

Rose likes to write about complex, oftentimes twisted main characters who grow stronger together on whichever journey they take. Watch out for sexy morally grey heroes and sharp, intelligent heroines within settings ranging from fantasy to academia to the underworld of organized crime.

Find Rose Below:

Website: https://rosegravestone.com

Facebook Group: https://www.facebook.com/groups/39706817 6443890/

www.ingramcontent.com/pod-product-compliance
Lightning Source LLC
Chambersburg PA
CBHW031831310726

48972CB00005B/1238